THE BILLIONAIRE'S FAKE WIFE

L. STEELE

1

"You must forgive my lips… they find pleasure in the most unusual places."
— *A Good Year*. Director: Ridley Scott

Summer

"Slap, slap, kiss, kiss."

"Huh?" I stare up at the bartender.

"Aka, there's a thin line between love and hate." He shakes out the crimson liquid into my glass.

"Nah." I snort. "Why would she allow him to control her, and after he insulted her?"

"It's the chemistry between them." He lowers his head, "You have to admit that when the man is arrogant and the woman resists, it's a challenge to both of them, to see who blinks first, huh?"

"Why?" I wave my hand in the air, "Because they hate each other?"

"Because," he chuckles, "the girl in school whose braids I pulled and teased mercilessly, is the one who I—"

"Proposed to?" I huff.

His face lights up. "You get it now?"

Yeah. No. A headache begins to pound at my temples. This crash course in pop psychology is not why I came to my favorite bar in Islington, to meet my best friend, who is—I glance at the face of my phone—thirty minutes late.

I inhale the drink, and his eyebrows rise.

"What?" I glower up at the bartender. "I can barely taste the alcohol. Besides, it's free drinks at happy hour for women, right?"

"Which ends in precisely" he holds up five fingers, "minutes."

"Oh! Yay!" I mock fist pump. "Time enough for one more, at least."

A hiccough swells my throat and I swallow it back, nod.

One has to do what one has to do… when everything else in the world is going to shit.

A hot sensation stabs behind my eyes; my chest tightens. Is this what people call growing up?

The bartender tips his mixing flask, strains out a fresh batch of the ruby red liquid onto the glass in front of me.

"Salut." I nod my thanks, then toss it back. It hits my stomach and tendrils of fire crawl up my spine, I cough.

My head spins. Warmth sears my chest, spreads to my extremities. I can't feel my fingers or toes. Good. Almost there. "Top me up."

"You sure?"

"Yes." I square my shoulders and reach for the drink.

"No. She's had enough."

"What the — ?" I pivot on the bar stool.

Indigo eyes bore into me.

Fathomless. Black at the bottom, the intensity in their depths grips me. He swoops out his arm, grabs the glass and holds it up. Thick fingers dwarf the glass. Tapered at the edges. The nails short and buff. *All the better to grab you with.* I gulp.

"Like what you see?"

I flush, peer up into his face.

Hard cheekbones, hollows under them, and a tiny scar that slashes at his left eyebrow. *How did he get that?* Not that I care. My gaze slides to his mouth. Thin upper lip, a lower lip that is full and cushioned. Pouty with a hint of bad boy. *Oh!* My toes curl. My thighs clench.

The corner of his mouth kicks up. *Asshole.*

Bet he thinks life is one big smug-fest. I glower, reach for my glass, and he holds it up and out of my reach.

I scowl, "Gimme that."

He shakes his head.

"That's my drink."

"Not anymore." He shoves my glass at the bartender. "Water for her. Get me a whiskey, neat."

I splutter, then reach for my drink again. The barstool tips, in his direction. This is when I fall against him, and my breasts slam into his hard chest, sculpted planes with layers upon layers of muscle that ripple and writhe as he turns aside, flattens himself against the bar. The floor rises up to meet me.

What the actual hell?

I twist my torso at the last second and my butt connects with the surface. *Ow!*

The breath rushes out of me. My hair swirls around my face. I scrabble for purchase, and my knee connects with his leg.

"Watch it." He steps around, stands in front of me.

"You stepped aside?" I splutter. "You let me fall?"

"Hmph."

I tilt my chin back, all the way back, look up the expanse of muscled thigh that stretches the silken material of his suit. *What is he wearing? Could any suit fit a man with such precision?* Hand crafted on Saville Row, no doubt. I glance at the bulge that tents the fabric between his legs. *Oh!* I blink.

Look away, look away. I hold out my arm. He'll help me up at least, won't he?

He glances at my palm, then turns away. *No, he didn't do that, no way.*

A glass of amber liquid appears in front of him. He lifts the tumbler to his sculpted mouth.

His throat moves, strong tendons flexing. He tilts his head back, and the column of his neck moves as he swallows. Dark hair covers his chin—it's a discordant chord in that clean-cut profile, I shiver. He would scrape that rough skin down my core. He'd mark my inner thigh, lick my core, thrust his tongue inside my melting channel and drink from my pussy. *Oh! God.* Goosebumps rise on my skin.

No one has the right to look this beautiful, this achingly gorgeous. Too magnificent for his own good. Anger coils in my chest.

"Arrogant wanker."

"I'll take that under advisement."

"You're a jerk, you know that?"

He presses his lips together. The grooves on either side of his mouth deepen. Jesus, clearly the man has never laughed a single day in his life. Bet that stick up his arse is uncomfortable. I chuckle.

He runs his gaze down my features, my chest, down to my toes, then yawns.

The hell! I will not let him provoke me. Will not. "Like what you see?" I jut out my chin.

"Sorry, you're not my type." He slides a hand into the pocket of those perfectly cut pants, stretching it across that heavy bulge.

Heat curls low in my belly.

Not fair, that he could afford a wardrobe that clearly shouts his status and what amounts to the economy of a small third-world country. A hot feeling stabs in my chest.

He reeks of privilege, of taking his status in life for granted.

While I've had to fight every inch of the way. Hell, I am still battling to hold onto the last of my equilibrium.

"Last chance—" I wiggle my fingers, from where I am sprawled out on the floor at his feet, "—to redeem yourself…"

"You have me there." He places the glass on the counter, then bends and holds out his hand. The hint of discolored steel at his wrist catches my attention. Huh?

He wears a cheap-ass watch?

That's got to bring down the net worth of his presence by more than 1000% percent. Weird.

I reach up and he straightens.

I lurch back.

"Oops, I changed my mind." His lips curl.

A hot burning sensation claws at my stomach. I am not a violent person, honestly. But Smirky Pants here, he needs to be taught a lesson.

I swipe out my legs, kicking his out from under him.

2

***

Sinclair

My knees give way, and I hurtle toward the ground.

What the—? I twist around, thrust out my arms. My palms hit the floor. The impact jostles up my elbows. I firm my biceps and come to a halt planked above her.

A huffing sound fills my ear.

I turn to find my whippet, Max, panting with his mouth open. I scowl and he flattens his ears.

All of my businesses are dog-friendly. Before you draw conclusions about me being the caring sort or some such shit—it attracts footfall.

Max scrutinizes the girl, then glances at me. *Huh?* He hates women, but not her, apparently.

I straighten and my nose grazes hers.

My arms are on either side of her head. Her chest heaves. The fabric of her dress stretches across her gorgeous breasts. My fingers tingle; my palms ache to cup those tits, squeeze those hard nipples outlined against the—hold on, what is she wearing? A tunic shirt in a sparkly pink... and are those shoulder pads she has on?

I glance up, and a squeak escapes her lips.

Pink hair surrounds her face. *Pink? Who dyes their hair that color past the age of eighteen?*

I stare at her face. *How old is she?* Un-furrowed forehead, dark eyelashes that flutter against pale cheeks. Tiny nose, and that mouth—luscious, tempting. A whiff of her scent, cherries and caramel, assails my senses. My mouth waters. *What the hell?*

She opens her eyes and our eyelashes brush. Her gaze widens. Green, like the leaves of the evergreens, flickers of gold sparkling in their depths. "What?" She glowers. "You're demonstrating the plank position?"

"Actually," I lower my weight onto her, the ridge of my hardness thrusting into the softness between her legs, "I was thinking of something else, altogether."

She gulps and her pupils dilate. *Ah, so she feels it, too?*

I drop my head toward her, closer, closer.

Color floods the creamy expanse of her neck. Her eyelids flutter down. She tilts her chin up.

I push up and off of her.

"That… Sweetheart, is an emphatic 'no thank you' to whatever you are offering."

Her eyelids spring open and pink stains her cheeks. Adorable. Such a range of emotions across those gorgeous features in a few seconds? What else is hidden under that exquisite exterior of hers?

She scrambles up, eyes blazing.

Ah! The little bird is trying to spread her wings? My dick twitches. My groin hardens, *Why does her anger turn me on so, huh?*

She steps forward, thrusts a finger in my chest.

My heart begins to thud.

She peers up from under those hooded eyelashes. "Wake up and taste the wasabi, asshole."

"What does that even mean?"

She makes a sound deep in her throat. My dick twitches. My pulse speeds up.

She pivots, grabs a half-full beer mug sitting on the bar counter.

I growl, "Oh, no, you don't."

She turns, swings it at me. The smell of hops envelops the space.

I stare down at the beer-splattered shirt, the lapels of my camel colored jacket deepening to a dull brown. Anger squeezes my guts.

I fist my fingers at my side, broaden my stance.

She snickers.

I tip my chin up. "You're going to regret that."

The smile fades from her face. "Umm." She places the now empty mug on the bar.

I take a step forward and she skitters back. "It's only clothes." She gulps, "They'll wash."

I glare at her and she swallows, wiggles her fingers in the air, "I should have known that you wouldn't have a sense of humor."

I thrust out my jaw, "That's a ten-thousand-pound suit you destroyed."

She blanches, then straightens her shoulders, "Must have been some hot date you were trying to impress, huh?"

"Actually," I flick some of the offending liquid from my lapels, "it's you I was after."

"Me?" She frowns.

"We need to speak."

She glances toward the bartender who's on the other side of the bar. "I don't know you." She chews on her lower lip, biting off some of the hot pink. How would she look, with that pouty mouth fastened on my cock?

The blood rushes to my groin so quickly that my head spins. My pulse rate ratchets up. Focus, focus on the task you came here for.

"This will take only a few seconds." I take a step forward.

She moves aside.

I frown, "You want to hear this, I promise."

"Go to hell." She pivots and darts forward.

I let her go, a step, another, because... I can? Besides it's fun to create the illusion of freedom first; makes the hunt so much more entertaining, huh?

I swoop forward, loop an arm around her waist, and yank her toward me.

She yelps. "Release me."

Good thing the bar is not yet full. It's too early for the usual officegoers to stop by. And the staff...? Well they are well aware of who cuts their paychecks.

I spin her around and against the bar, then release her. "You will listen to me."

She swallows; she glances left to right.

Not letting you go yet, little Bird. I move into her space, crowd her.

She tips her chin up. "Whatever you're selling, I'm not interested."

I allow my lips to curl, "You don't fool me."

A flush steals up her throat, sears her cheeks. So tiny, so innocent. Such a good little liar. I narrow my gaze, "Every action has its consequences."

"Are you daft?" She blinks.

"This pretense of yours?" I thrust my face into hers, "It's not working."

She blinks, then color suffuses her cheeks, "You're certifiably mad—"

"Getting tired of your insults."

"It's true, everything I said." She scrapes back the hair from her face.

Her fingernails are painted... You guessed it, pink.

"And here's something else. You are a selfish, egotistical jackass."

I smirk. "You're beginning to repeat your insults and I haven't even kissed you yet."

"Don't you dare." She gulps.

I tilt my head, "Is that a challenge?"

"It's a..." she scans the crowded space, then turns to me. Her lips firm, "...a warning. You're delusional, you jackass." She inhales a deep breath, "Your ego is bigger than the size of a black hole." She snickers, "Bet it's to compensate for your lack of balls."

A-n-d, that's it. I've had enough of her mouth that threatens to never stop spewing words. How many insults can one tiny woman hurl my way? Answer: too many to count.

"You—"

I lower my chin, touch my lips to hers.

Heat, sweetness, the honey of her essence explodes on my palate. My dick twitches. I tilt my head, deepen the kiss, reaching for that something more... more... of whatever scent she's wearing on her skin, infused with that breath of hers that crowds my senses, rushes down my spine. My groin hardens; my cock lengthens. I thrust my tongue between those infuriating lips.

She makes a sound deep in her throat and my heart begins to pound.

So innocent, yet so crafty. Beautiful and feisty. The kind of complication I don't need in my life.

I prefer the straight and narrow. Gray and black, that's how I choose to define my world. She, with her flashes of color—pink hair and lips that threaten to drive me to the edge of distraction—is exactly what I hate.

Give me a female who has her priorities set in life. To pleasure me, get me off, then walk away before her emotions engage. Yeah. That's what I prefer.

Not this... this bundle of craziness who flings her arms around my shoulders, thrusts her breasts up and into my chest, tips up her chin, opens her mouth, and invites me to take and take.

Does she have no self-preservation? Does she think I am going to fall for her wide-eyed appeal? She has another thing coming.

I tear my mouth away and she protests.

She twines her leg with mine, pushes up her hips, so that melting softness between her thighs cradles my aching hardness.

I glare into her face and she holds my gaze.

Trains her green eyes on me. Her cheeks flush a bright red. Her lips fall open and a moan bleeds into the air. The blood rushes to my dick, which instantly thickens. *Fuck.*

Time to put distance between myself and the situation.

It's how I prefer to manage things. Stay in control, always. Cut out anything that threatens to impinge on my equilibrium. Shut it down or buy them off. Reduce it to a transaction. That I understand.

The power of money, to be able to buy and sell—numbers, logic. That's what's worked for me so far.

"How much?"

Her forehead furrows.

"Whatever it is, I can afford it."

Her jaw slackens. "You think... you—"

"A million?"

"What?"

"Pounds, dollars... You name the currency, and it will be in your account."

Her jaw slackens, "You're offering me money?"

"For your time, and for you to fall in line with my plan."

She reddens, "You think I am for sale?"

"Everyone is."

"Not me."

Here we go again. "Is that a challenge?"

Color fades from her face, "Get away from me."

"Are you shy, is that what this is?" I frown. "You can write your price down on a piece of paper if you prefer," I glance up, notice the bartender watching us. I jerk my chin toward the napkins. He grabs one, then offers it to her.

She glowers at him, "Did you buy him too?"

"What do you think?"

She glances around, "I think everyone here is ignoring us."

"It's what I'd expect."

"Why is that?"

I wave the tissue in front of her face, "Why do you think?"

"You own the place?"

"As I am going to own you."

She sets her jaw, "Let me leave and you won't regret this."

A chuckle bubbles up. I swallow it away. This is no laughing matter. I never smile during a transaction. Especially not when I am negotiating a new acquisition. And that's all she is. The final piece in the puzzle I am building.

"No one threatens me."

"You're right."

"Huh?"

"I'd rather act on my instinct."

Her lips twist, her gaze narrows. All of my senses scream a warning.

No, she wouldn't, no way—pain slices through my middle and sparks explode behind my eyes.

3

Summer

"You kneed me?"

He growls, actually growls. A shiver of heat ladders up my spine. My heart begins to thud.

Oh, hell I've done it now. Men and their delicate egos. Bet he won't take this lying down.

I shove at his shoulders and he lurches to the side. I spring up, glance down to where he glares up at me, hunched over. My nerve endings tingle.

Why do I have such visceral reaction to him? Pompous prick.

He straightens, then shoves himself up to standing.

What the—? How could he have recovered from that knee to his balls so fast? I blink. No one has that much endurance, not unless he's trained for it… *Nah!* I shove the thought aside.

He is a spoiled, pampered brat, no doubt. Typical. One of those who likes to flaunt what he has. Why do those with money think that is the solution to everything, huh? *Because it is?*

A hot sensation stabs at my chest. I've screwed it up. I've messed up my future and a chance for my sister to live a normal life.

The jackass in front of me swipes out his hand. I duck.

His features harden. He leans forward on the balls of his feet. Hell no, not going to let him catch me this time. I grab my bag from where it hangs on the hook below the bar counter, and head for the exit.

Shoving open the heavy glass door, I burst onto the sidewalk.

"You! Stop, right there." Something brushes my collar. I scream, lunge ahead. Adrenaline laces my veins. The blood slams so hard at my temples, I am sure I am going to faint.

Two cops approach me. *Oh, my God!* I wave at them. "Help!"

One of them catches sight of me; his forehead pinches.

The heat at my back turns up to a furnace. *Shit, he's close.* He's really, really, close. The hair on the nape of my neck rises. "Help me, please."

There's a low exclamation behind me.

My stomach flip flops. Damn the man, how did he get here so quickly?

The first cop reaches us, "Everything okay here?"

"This chap," I stab my thumb in Mr. Grouchy Pants' direction, "he's harassing me."

The second officer glances between us, then straightens, "Sinclair."

"Hello Josephine, Will." He nods at them.

What the — ! He's on a first name basis with the cops? Does he have them on his payroll?

Of course he does. Asshole here would do everything to ensure circumstances are always within his control.

I dart forward.

"We're not done." His low growl follows me.

I sprint past the cops, up the street, veer right, then a left onto crowded Oxford Street. Safety in numbers. Okay, I go this! The breath rushes out of me.

When I reach the entrance to Tottenham Court Road tube station, I peek a glance behind me. There's no sign of him. Whew!

I swipe my card at the barriers, run down another flight of steps onto the platform as my train pulls into the station. I jump into the first open doors and collapse into a seat. Sweat beads my forehead; my hair is plastered to my cheek. I bend over, gasping. Close call. The woman opposite stares at me, wide-eyed. I meet her gaze and she promptly looks down at her Kindle.

Yep. One good thing about the tube in London, most people avoid eye contact. The anonymity that this city affords is precisely why I love it… and hate it. I slump against the barrier on my right.

It means no-one cares how I dress, or what I eat, or do for a living. It is why no one gives a shit about my sister lurching closer to her grave every day.

Nope, not gonna happen, not on my watch. I am going to find a way out of this mess. I am. At the next station, I check my phone. There's a new email in my inbox.

From: Meredith Vincent
　　To: Summer West

Dear Ms. West,

Your appointment to pitch for the innovative marketing strategy for 7A Investments is confirmed.

Mr. Sterling, our CEO, will see you at 9am, tomorrow.

Address is below.

Pls confirm your acceptance of the meeting by reply.

Yours sincerely,

. . .

Meredith Vincent
    Executive Assistant

Wow! Okay. Did I write to 7A investments asking to pitch for their account? I don't remember it. I frown, toss my head. Doesn't matter.

This is my chance. It is an opportunity to salvage my future and I am not going to turn it down. I type out my acceptance, hit reply, then drop my phone into my shoulder bag.

I am going to get this account, if it is the last thing I do.

The train pulls into Mill Hill East tube station, and I step off.

The phone dings again with a text message.

Isla: Soooo sorry, had a work emergency. You know how it is with us wedding planners...

Me: *Now* you tell me! You got me into so much trouble you *biatch*!

Isla: What... what? Did you meet someone at the bar?

Me: No, I didn't. Is that all you can think of and... hold on... you wouldn't do that to me, eh?

I huff.

Me: Would you?

Isla: What are you talking about?

Me: You stood me up on purpose?

Isla: Moi? What are you talking about?

Me: So help me Isla, if I find out you did this to me...

Isla: Is he that hot?

Me: No.

Isla: A dominant stranger with a take charge attitude that melts your panties and makes you want to lick him up?

Me: What is it with your hang up with obstinate mules... I mean males?

Isla: Ha, ha. *snort* Don't mock it until you've tried it.

Me: I have no idea what you're talking about.

Isla: Sometimes you need a hug you know...?

Me: Exactly.

Isla:.... on your backside... with a paddle.

Me: What the...

Isla: Administered by an obnoxious know-it-all who doesn't take no for an answer.

Me: Sweet baby goats, are you getting off on this text message, Isla? I swear if you are...

Isla: Sorry... sorry... *not*, you're waaay too uptight my girl. Give in, live a little.

Me: If by that you mean fantasizing about some alpha male making rough love...

Isla: Don't bring that four letter emotion into the mix.

Me: Yeah, not all of us want to be controlled.

Isla: Famous last words.

Me: Thanks for shoving your kink in my face.

Isla: Hey, how did you guess that I love doing that?

Me: TMI, bye.

Isla: Are you blushing, West? I bet you are. Seriously I'm sorry for standing you up.

Last minute change, a bride called off her wedding and uh, it wasn't pretty.

Me: Wow, good luck handling the pieces of that.

Isla: I'm gonna need it for this one. PS, the bridegroom walked into the office and he's not happy.

Me: Can't your boss handle him?

Isla: She's not around. And gah! This man is completely unreasonable! But wow! Is he smokin' hot. *gulp* Wish me luck.

Me: Luck! Go get him GF.

Isla: Laters xxx

Typical Isla, always taken in by a pretty face. *And I'm not?*

I suck my cheeks in, drop my phone into my tote bag.

Walking out of the tube station, I race home, then up the short flight of steps leading into the one-bed apartment I share with my sister.

For how much longer, though? If I can't keep up the rental payments on it…? I'll find a way, I will.

"Karma?" I cross the living room into the tiny bedroom.

"Summer?" My sister glances up from her embroidery machine.

Her dark hair flows around her face. Her skin seems paler than usual.

I sink down on the bed across from her, "You okay?."

Her amber eyes flare. "Why wouldn't I be?"

"No reason." I shuffle my feet.

"No breathlessness, no numb fingers or toes. The hole in my heart hasn't eaten me up completely." Her lips thin. "Yet."

"Why do you get so defensive about your condition?"

"Umm, let's see." She holds up a finger tipped with black nail-polish, "Because I'm trying to live and you keep thrusting my disease in my line of sight every time you bring it up?"

I draw in a sharp breath. "That's being uncharitable. Just because I worry about you and do my best to take care of you—"

"—doesn't make you my mother."

All the blood drains from my face. Bet I'm as pale as her, though on Karma, her dark goth get-up enhances her luminous beauty.

On me... bet I am as chalky as the paint on the wall behind her.

"Hell, sorry, Summer." She blows out a breath. "I'm more on edge than usual. Tomorrow's market day, so I need to get my clothes done in time. I need to be at Camden Market before 5 am so..." She raises her shoulders.

"Right, I'll leave you to it then."

I jump up, head for the door.

"Summer, stop."

I cross the floor to the small counter on the far side that doubles as our kitchen. Fill a glass with water from the tap and drink from it.

"I'm sorry for what I said earlier." Karma pauses at the doorway to the bedroom.

"You know how to get to me, don't you?" I firm my lips.

"My specialty, Sis. Chalk it up to my teenage hormones."

I snort, then turn and lean a hip against the counter, "You're almost as clever with words as you are with your clothing designs."

She holds up a hand, "Uh, oh, I sense a Summer sermon, coming on."

"Don't be ridiculous." I redden. "It's just, I don't understand why you'd give up a paid fashion scholarship at Central Saint Martins..."

"They were too mainstream." She sets her jaw.

"What's wrong with that?" I throw up my hands.

"Do you see what you're wearing?"

I glance down at myself, "You made it." I raise my shoulders. "It's offbeat but... it mirrors my personality."

"Exactly." She tosses her head, "My ideas are too... off-beat for their sensibilities."

"So?" I tilt my chin up, "You could have... adjusted..."

She stares, "Says the woman who is a walking talking encyclopedia of trivia that's largely useless."

"That..." I rub my forehead, "That's different."

"Right." She snorts. "How many other twenty-one year-old women can give trivia nerds a run for their money?"

I wrap my arms around my waist. "I'm not sure that's something to be proud of," I mumble.

"You made enough money winning pub quizzes and TV game shows."

"It was one show—"

"That earned you £100,000." She raps her knuckles against the door frame. "It's kept us going this far."

That's how we've survived since I left the homeless hostel at nineteen.

It was because of the money that I'd been able to take on responsibility for Karma and pull her out of the care system. I'd also used a portion of it to launch my marketing consultancy.

I'd expanded the scope to supply quizzes to pubs, bars, parties and to my growing list of online subscribers who love to receive a daily trivia quiz from me... For a fee.

My dream job.

I thrust out my chest. I had defined it, created it, pursued it. I bite the inside of my cheek. What had I been thinking? Following my intuition? Thought I could earn a living from my passion for movies?

Why did I have to turn down the job of marketing manager for the—*ugh!* — accounting firm? I hunch my shoulders.

It would have paid well, allowed for specialist medical consultations for my sister. I'd been bloody selfish, that's what.

I'd held onto some stupid notion that I could have whatever I wanted without compromising on my dreams. Except, I'd lost the client who contributed to 80% of my business.

I twirl a lock of my hair, bring it to my mouth and chew on it.

"Horrible habit." She frowns.

"It helps me think." I push off from the counter, begin to pace. "I have a big meeting tomorrow. If I get the account..."

"You will."

My phone dings. I stare at my bag.

"You going to see who it is?"

I shake my head.

"Want me to?"

I raise my shoulders, and let them drop, "How much worse could it get, huh?"

She reaches for my bag, pulls out my phone, reads the message.
"Who is it?"
She drops the phone into my bag.
"It's nothing."
"Karma!" I scowl, then flounce over to her and check the screen. There's a new text message.

SmellyGuy: You have one week to pay the rent or else...

Right! I drop the phone into the bag, then for good measure zip my bag shut.
"Vanilla or chocolate?" I cross the floor to the tiny refrigerator, pull open the door of the freezer.
"Is that a trick question?"
"Yeah. No."
"Do I have a choice?" She returns to the settee.
"Nope." I chuckle, pull out the carton of vanilla ice-cream. "I did the shopping so..."
Karma sinks into the sofa, "Your tastes are boringly predictable."
"Yeah, well, I coulda been somebody, instead of a bum, which is what I am." I grab the carton of ice cream, straighten.
She blinks. "Is that from *On the Waterfront*?"
I chuckle. "You've been paying attention to my trivia quiz emails, huh?"
"Bet you can't guess which movie *this* is from? She flips her hair over her shoulder. "Don't let anyone ever make you feel like you don't deserve what you want."
I pull out two plastic spoons, then join her.
"Too easy." I scoop up some ice cream, *"10 things I Hate About You."*
Her face breaks into a smile.
Strange word games the two of us have. Spouting dialogues and having the other person guess the film it originated from is one. Words don't cost, and they comfort. We can use them to weave a world in which we are safe, away from the nightmares that haunt our lives.
"My turn." I pass the carton to her. "Gotta celebrate the Now. Live in the moment."
She licks the ice-cream from her spoon, scoops up more. Her forehead scrunches.
"Give up?" I snatch the ice cream carton from her.
She frowns, "Okay, which is that from?"
I snicker. "None, that was all moi." I lick the remaining ice cream from my spoon.
She grabs at the carton, then peers into it. "Gah! Not fair, you finished it."
I chortle, "See, you shouldn't underestimate me." I hand the empty carton to her.
"Now shoo, I need to work on the deck for tomorrow's meeting."
"Brilliant!" She brightens, "I have the right set of clothes for you."

4

—————

"Y'know, I could eat a peach for hours."
— *Face/Off.* Director: John Woo

Sin

"Have a good day, Mr. Sterling."

Peter my chauffeur pulls my *Aston Martin* up to the curb in front of my offices. The heritage building on the South Bank is prime London property that I acquired after a bitter bidding war. It does the job, I suppose. I swing open the door and Max bounds ahead. He pauses in front of the homeless man next to the entrance.

His sign today reads: *The Devil returned to Hell by two.*

I approach the homeless guy, drop a wad of bills into the upturned cap in front of him. "Byron, again, huh?"

As always, his face doesn't change expression. The two of us are similar that way.

The degree of separation between the man in the palace and the one on the street is less than seven, son.

My father's words echo in my head. He hated the homeless. Perhaps it struck something primal in him. This dread of losing everything, finding himself out on his luck, had intensified after the incident. He'd lost his job soon after, hadn't been able to afford the money for my mother's cancer treatment, if it had not been for my friends. Yeah, I have a few... Six, to be precise. The kind who'd stab me if I turned my back on them.

Figuratively speaking... In business, I mean.

Best if you never trust anyone, not even your friends. There is no way you can be hurt then, right?

I walk toward the heavy glass door where Max waits for me. I push it and he bounds ahead of me. The receptionist glances up; her face flushes.

"Good morning, Mr. Sterling."

I frown. "How long you been here?"

She blinks.

"You deaf, girl?"

"N... no." Color fades from her cheeks, and her color matches the wall behind her.

"Answer the question."

She gulps. "A week."

"You're fired."

"But..."

"You're on probation so no need to go to HR; you can leave right now."

She splutters, "My fault, Sir?"

"Don't like your face."

That is true. Also, because I am getting a little tired of her loss of composure every time I walk by. Reminds me of what my position in this city is all about. Something I hate.

I walk up to the elevator, the doors swish open, and I step inside. Seems the elevator maintenance company can keep their contract... For now.

"Stop." A hand appears in between the doors, halting their progress. A woman steps in. "Sorry... I can't afford to be late, I —" She looks up.

Green eyes stare at me, pink hair tied up into a knot that is already coming undone. The pale creamy skin of her neck colors. It reminds me of someone. I snap my gaze to her face and her jaw drops open. "You?"

The door slides closed. "About time," I glare.

She frowns, "You're acting as if you were expecting me."

"I was." Wisps of candy-fluff colored hair cling to her flushed cheeks. My fingers tingle to whisper it off of her face. *The fuck —?* I slide my palm into the pocket of my pants.

"Are you stalking me?" She chews on her lower lip and my dick twitches.

I widen my stance, "And what if I was?"

"If... if this is your idea of a joke —" Her shoulders go rigid; she glances up and around the corners of the steel cage.

"No cameras."

Her gaze pops back to my face.

"It's a private elevator." I punch the stop button and she draws in a sharp breath. The elevator jolts, then halts. "Oh, hell." She pivots, slaps her hand on the door.

"Too late." I lean a shoulder against the steel wall.

She swallows, "Why... why did you do that?"

I fold my arms, "Not for the reason you are thinking."

She sidles away. Her shoulder brushes the wall opposite me, and she jerks upright. "Wha... what reason would that be?"

I scan her features, down the arch of that neck — it's quite stunning, actually — down to the thrust of her breasts. Today, she's wearing a jacket that pulls in her shoulders. Clearly, it's a size too small for her. It's buttoned in the front. The material strains at her chest, showing off her curves.

Annoying little thing that she is, she's used to flaunting her assets to get her way, no doubt. I stare at her breasts, and she folds her arms around her waist.

"Not that either, as I clarified earlier."

Her cheeks flush. Hmm, interesting color. She's a natural redhead obviously, given how the color on her face highlights every single freckle on her beautiful skin. I stiffen. Why is my mind headed that way? I am used to controlling it, ensuring that my will is obedient to me. Every time I see her, though, my brain seems to drop to my groin. My dick twitches. I widen my stance and her gaze drops down to my crotch.

"You could have me fooled. From where I am, it seems you'd very much like 'that.' " She makes inverted commas with her fingers.

I stiffen. *Sod this.* I will not be insulted by the likes of her. "So that's your game, huh?"

"Now, what has that asshole mind of yours conjured up?"

"You don't want to know." I flex my fingers and she pales.

"Try me." Her chin wobbles.

"You wouldn't be able to stand it, Sweetheart."

"Stop calling me that."

"Oh?" I take a step forward and she blinks, scans the small enclosed space.

You're trapped, little Bird. Can't get away from the big bad bully now.

Her breath hitches; she retreats against the wall. "St… stop."

I take a step forward. "No one tells me what to do." I glare down at her.

"You think waaaay too much of yourself." She juts out her chin.

"You don't think enough about yourself, clearly." Which is why she turned up for the meeting today without checking for any ulterior motives. Anger ladders up my spine. I don't get it. *Why am I concerned about her well-being?* She's here, in my space, exactly where I want her to be.

She's here insinuating herself into my life. Doesn't she understand how bad this can turn out for her?

Doesn't she care that I could do things to her that she'd never recover from?

My groin hardens. One part of me, at least, relishes the hunt. Adrenaline laces my blood. This could turn out to be interesting. Imagine that? Something to work toward. Someone who challenges me, who doesn't grovel before me.

She dares go toe to toe with me? Interesting. I glare at her and she gulps. Fear radiates off of her.

"You uncomfortable, little girl?"

She shakes her head.

"Such a pretty little liar."

She jerks her chin. A bead of sweat runs down her temple.

I swipe out an arm and she flinches. I scoop up the drop of perspiration, then bring it to my lips and suck on my digit.

She makes a strangled sound deep in her throat. Watches me with unabashed curiosity… Or is that anticipation?

"I could take you right here and you couldn't stop me."

She freezes. Her pupils dilate. Her chest rises and falls; the jacket stretches further. The button squeezes out of the eyehole. *Bloody hell.* I reach for her and she opens her mouth; her features contort.

"Don't," she whispers.

She pauses. Eyes wide, mouth opened in an 'O.' Pink lips parted, lip gloss gleaming. My mouth waters. My balls pulse. Is she trying to taunt me? I reach for her lapels and every muscle in her body snaps to attention.

I drag her up to her tip toes, drop my chin, until my face is directly above hers. Her eyelids flutter shut, her thick eyelashes fringing those soulful eyes. Eyes that consume me with their vulnerability. That hint at the innocence beneath the surface. An awed hopeful-ness through which she surveys the world. With bated breath. Waiting for her future to unfurl. An optimism that I want to tear apart with my bare hands.

Rip into her and teach her never to trust anyone.

Not so easy. My breath raises the hair on her forehead and her lips tremble. Her chin wobbles and she tips her head back, showing me the curve of that gorgeous neck. Too fucking vulnerable. I am going to have to teach her a lesson.

"Little Bird?"

"Summer." She swallows, "My name is Summer."

"Are you a virgin, Summer?"

5

Summer

"Seriously?" I snap my eyes open.

This man has the ability to reduce me to surprised silence and that's not complimentary, though it does take a lot to rob me of my ability to speak, honestly. It's more a testament to his sheer audacity. "You didn't ask me that."

"Why not?"

"Because… it's incredibly rude, for one."

"Is it?"

"Are you kidding me?"

"I never 'kid.' " He says the last word as if it's a bad smell.

"Figures." I can't stop the chuckle that spills from my lips. "If you could stop long enough to actually notice your surroundings, you'd see that we don't live in the dark ages anymore. Perhaps you'd see how everything is wrong about this picture."

"You actually believe there is free will in this world, hmm?"

His voice tugs at my nerve endings; goosebumps dot my skin.

It's being enclosed in this tiny space that's making me faint. I am not claustrophobic, but being stuck in an elevator with a larger-than-life male who has a completely warped sense of his own importance is… is enough to sap the will of any strong-willed woman… and I am… but one desperate to get to her meeting, and wrap up this account. "I am going to be late."

"It can wait."

Anger flares low in my belly, "There you go again, presuming to know what I can and can't do."

"Why should I pretend?"

"Because…" I fidget, "Because… it's polite?"

"Which I am not. We've established that already. So why don't you cooperate?"

"That'll be the day." I huff out a breath.

"The faster you answer my question, the sooner we can both be on our way."

"So, if I tell you if I am a… a…"

"Virgin." His lips curl.

Bastard's having so much fun at my expense. I can't wait to wipe that look of satisfaction from his face. Honestly, I really, truly, want to see him on his knees and groveling. For mercy. And I'd never show him an iota of it, I won't.

"Yeah." I square my shoulders, "That. If I tell you… which by the way, I am not going to because, newsflash, this isn't the dark ages anymore. Women are allowed to live as they want, date whom they desire, sleep with…"

His eyes glitter.

"—not you." I gulp, "I definitely don't want that with you."

He glares at me, "So you're thinking about it, huh?"

Nope.

"Admit it."

Never.

"Since you saw me, you've wanted to find out how it would be to have sex with me?" He drops his nose to the hollow of my throat and nuzzles me there.

I shiver.

"Give me what I want."

I will not.

"Say it." His voice drops to a hush.

A thrill of anticipation heats my blood. Would he be as demanding in bed? Position me as he wants, push me until I give him what he needs, allow him to possess me, dominate me… The elevator lurches. His body bumps mine. Chest to hip to thigh. All of my senses focus in on him. My nerve endings pop. "Yes."

"Yes, what?"

The elevator moves up, "Let me go, the doors will be opening soon."

"Not until you complete your sentence."

"But."

"You have less than thirty seconds."

"Wait…"

"Twenty-eight"

"Fuck."

"Told ya already, that's not on the table."

"Asshole."

"Fifteen seconds."

My heart rate ratchets up, heat flares between my thighs. *OMG, I can't be turned on.* Surely not. The thought of the elevator doors opening and my being discovered, has a sick kind of appeal. The hell is wrong with me? Apparently, I enjoy being the object of his single-minded attention, something I haven't been at the receiving end of with anyone else.

"Five…"

"No, of course not, you asshole."

"See, that wasn't so difficult, huh?"

The elevator doors slide open. He peels himself off of me, steps back.

I break away, step out of the doors, which begin to close. I angle my body toward him, "Aren't you coming?"

He yawns, leans a shoulder against the elevator walls, "This floor is for plebs."

I open and shut my mouth. Did he actually say that? The doors close.

I watch the floors scroll up on the elevator's panel. It stops at the floor marked 'A.' Does that mean only assholes are allowed there? I snicker, then turn and march toward the reception desk.

"I am here for-"

"The pitch?" The sleekly coiffured woman behind the reception desk looks me up and down. *What? Do you have to audition with your superiority complex to be hired here?*

"No, the fork."

She blinks.

I stab my tongue into my cheek, "It was a joke."

"Oh!" She purses her lips. Hell, she'd be the perfect companion for the man I left behind in the elevator. Speaking of, "Why are there two receptions in this building?"

"I am the administrator to the upper echelons."

Did she say echelons? Does anyone use that word in daily speech?

Her phone buzzes. She straightens and touches her earpiece, "Yes, Mr. Sterling." Her breath hitches. "Of course, Mr. Sterling, I'll send her up."

She glances at me.

"I heard."

I pivot, then stop. Holdonabloodysecond. I swivel around. "How many offices did you say are up there?"

"I didn't." She huffs.

"How many?" I frown. Alphahole had gone up; he'd hinted he is the boss. Is he the person I came to meet? No, it's not possible. My heart begins to race. "Tell me."

She frowns, scans her nails, "I can't give out private information—"

I grit my teeth, force my lips to curve in the semblance of a smile, "Please, this could change the outcome of the meeting I am about to go into. I really need to be better prepared for whatever is coming."

She frowns, then jerks her chin, "One, just one, Mr. Sterling's."

6

Summer

I walk out of the elevator. This time, the trip had been accomplished mercifully alone, thank you very much. I get off on the 'Asshole' floor then move forward to the conference room at the very end, as directed by the second receptionist.

She'd cautioned me that Mr. Sterling hates to be kept waiting.

What a surprise, huh?

I glance past the doors that open off the corridor. The entire floor is hushed. The faint scent of leather and cigar smoke clings to the walls. The place smells like the inside of an old boy's club.

Figures. Of course, alpha asshole is a chauvinist.

Probably went to boarding school with other rich toffs, all of whom are now top politicians and captains of industry. Bet he could call up anyone to get a favor done for his company. That's how he'd established his company so quickly. Okay, maybe that was uncharitable. By all accounts, 7A had been set up by him and his partners and they'd built it up from scratch.

Though Sterling is in charge of the marketing, which is why I am meeting him. Just my luck. My shoulders droop as I approach the massive double doors of the conference room. Ornate woodwork laces the frame. There's a knocker with a lion's head on it in place of the handle. I blink. My fingers twitch. Before I can stop myself, I've grabbed the knocker. *Slam it down, do it.* Not as if you're going to get the account so why keep the pretense up, eh?

For Karma, yeah. Okay. Do it for Karma. She deserves you giving this your best shot. I push open the door and enter.

A rectangular glass table stretches the length of the room. There are at least ten chairs clustered around it. One wall is taken up by a white projection screen.

I walk around, until I am facing the table. I have a PowerPoint on my laptop. Which means I have to plug in my computer, or plug in my usb fob with the deck. Should have taken a print-out, but there hadn't been enough time. *Okay, don't panic. Deep breath. You can do this.*

I drop my tote bag onto the table, pull out my fob, and pivot to face the screen. I spot the console to the side, and walk up to it... *How the hell does it open?* I press down on the surface. Nothing. To the right... left... *What the—?* The hair on the nape of my neck rises.

"You won't need that."

A shiver runs down my back. I'd known it was him seconds before he had spoken.

"Of course, I will." I continue to flutter my fingers over the console, and it slides back. *Whew!*

I shove my fob into position, then straighten. His scent envelops me. Bergamot and fresh cut grass, saturated with testosterone. I gulp, walk toward the table.

He clicks his tongue. "You're going in the wrong direction."

I whip around, and he drums his fingers on his massive chest.

"I don't have much time."

I swallow. Of course. He is the client; this is his office. He knows where everything is.

"Fine." I round the table, drop into a chair.

"Didn't give you permission to sit."

I stiffen. "Controlling much?"

He drums his fingers on his chest, "I can't tolerate childish tantrums. Clearly, you don't have what it takes to manage our account." He pivots on his heels, heads for the door.

In that moment, I have never hated anyone more. Superior jackass with a God complex. If I didn't need his business desperately, I'd have told him that to his face, too.

"Wait."

He keeps going.

"Hold on, please."

He opens the door.

"Look, I'm sorry. I apologize. I shouldn't have said that."

"Too little, too late." He glares at me, "You should have thought of that before you directly contradicted me."

The blood fades from my cheeks. What am I doing here trying to negotiate with a man who has clearly lost touch with reality so much that he doesn't see anything except the tip of his own nose? His strong patrician nose that hooks above a square jaw and hints at the strength of his obstinacy. A strong will that could crush me if I let it.

If you give in now, you are going to regret it.

I need his business, and if I show my desperation, I can kiss any hope of gaining his account goodbye. No, it is time to change course. To hold my own, to fight him at his own game, with his own tactics. Say something, anything, to keep him here. I gulp, then toss my head, "Fine, leave then."

He frowns.

"But you'll never hear about how I was going to put myself at your disposal twenty-four-seven."

7

Sin

That was supposed to have been my proposition. *The hell did she come up with that?*

I glare at her.

She shuffles her feet.

Are you uncomfortable, little Bird?

My fingers tingle and I shove them into my pocket.

She tips up her chin, "Well?"

"Well, what?"

She twists her fingers in front of her, "Don't you want to hear about the rest of my proposal?"

Interesting. I am the one normally laying down the conditions. I am the one in charge, who likes to demand, and is never turned down. Not only has she stood up to me since we met; now, she actually wants to lead? I bare my teeth, "Clearly, you are delusional, or plain stupid."

"Clearly." She bites on her lower lip, "But you have to admit you are curious…"

Hmm.

"A teeny tiny bit?" She holds up her forefinger and thumb. Slender fingers tipped with pink nail polish. The woman loves that color.

Bet she also adores candies, flowers and teddy bears. The kind she'd love to receive on Valentine's Day, right after she'd belted out Karaoke on a drunken night out with her girlfriends. Then shagged the man she took home.

My gut tightens. Most females I associate with come well coiffured, long limbed, blonde hair, with designer outfits and high-heeled shoes that have never seen the inside of a tube station. This girl though—I take in her footwear. Chucks?

I blink. She is wearing chucks, with her slimline black skirt that comes to mid-thigh.

Why hadn't I noticed the ridiculous combination of her outfit? Probably because I was too busy staring at her breasts... or is it at her ridiculous pink hair, which really has no place in my boardroom?

Max huffs, then shuffles toward her with his ambling doggy gait.

She doesn't notice him... Or if she does, she gives no indication. He circles her, sniffs her ankles, then drops down at her feet. His tongue lolls out of his mouth.

I frown. Max can be stubborn, and when he sets his mind on something... Well, nothing, not even me, can dissuade him. I look at my watch, "You have five minutes."

Her gaze widens.

I stalk forward, drop into the seat in the middle of the conference table. "Starting now."

"B...but." Her mouth opens and closes.

"Do you often do that?"

"Wh... what?" She stutters.

"Sound like you are drowning?"

Her cheeks flame. Her blush is quite spectacular, actually. It sears the expanse of her throat, right up to the tips of her ears. Do the other parts of her turn pink too? Would her pert backside show off every single fingerprint of mine? I drum my fingers on my table.

"Well, you were here to pitch an idea, right?"

She nods.

"So give it your best shot." I kick out my legs.

She leans forward toward the panel that controls the console with the fob and, I shake my head.

"What?" She frowns.

"I don't have time for a long drawn-out presentation."

"Bu... but I pulled together a deck."

"Give me a summary." She chews on her lower lip.

Don't look there, don't. I peruse the glistening flesh. Pink, slightly swollen. Her mouth falls open slightly, and fuck, if I don't want it fastened on my cock right now. My groin hardens. I shove my legs further apart, "Ms. West."

"Mr. Sinclair?"

I tip my chin up, "You now have have four minutes and fifty seconds left."

She releases her death grip on her laptop, folds her fingers together on the table, "The brief was on how to humanize the face of the 7A Company, using innovative marketing communications, the kind in which my company specializes."

"Cut to the crux of the strategy."

Her eyebrows lower. "My idea is to go behind the scenes, tail the founders, share behind-the-scenes pictures of each of the Seven, your interactions with each other, how you come up with strategies, the chemistry, the banter, the fights, use the key individuals at the helm to bring out why your company is not as bad as the recent PR that surrounds it."

"Oh, so you think we have a bad reputation in the market?"

"Yes." She holds my gaze.

Took guts to own up to that. It is refreshing, I'll give her that. I place my elbows on the table, lean forward. "Go on."

"You and your fellow stakeholders are seen as cut-throat, mercenary, not caring about your employees, or anyone else, ready to take what you want, earn money for your stockholders."

I frown. "What's wrong with that?"

"Profiting by itself is not enough. Not if you were thinking of going for an IPO, which you are."

How did she find out about that? That is information privy to the seven of us... and our teams.

"If you're wondering how I knew about that," she raises her chin, "there was a piece in CITY A.M. last evening."

"There was?"

"Clearly, your PR team sucks if they didn't bring it to your notice."

"Hmm." I pull out my phone, search for the piece and find it. "We would have announced it in a week... No biggie."

I'm going to destroy whoever leaked the piece.

"It didn't necessarily come from within your company."

"Oh?" Did she second-guess my thoughts, hmm?

"The change in your messaging during the last few months is a clear indicator that you are planning something big. Besides, the brief was aimed at whitewashing your reputation, and companies do that when they are going to..."

"Raise capital?" I pocket my phone.

She nods.

Hmm. Okay, I'll grant her that.

"So you're not just another pretty face, huh?"

Her lips firm. She knits her fingers together in her lap, clearly trying to control herself from saying something she might regret.

Question is, why am I not able to control myself when it's about her?

I survey her features again. Taking in the bright look in her eyes, her enthusiasm writ in every angle of her body, the way her chest heaves, the tension that skitters off of her, for a second, I feel my age. Hell, I am only a decade older than her, if that, but the experience I have packed into that time has clearly made me into a cynic. Not that I'll admit to that. Ever.

"So, you think you can flounce in and tell us that our reputation sucks, that our confidential information has been leaked, and that you know better than us how we should be planning forward?"

She blinks, shuffles her feet. "Umm." The pulse flutters at her throat and I can't look away. It hints at her vulnerability, how tense she is... how nervous she's been throughout, really.

Guess not everyone has been fortunate to be blessed with a fighting spirit such as mine, huh?

"How desperate are you to win this account?"

She stiffens.

"It's clear that you're not the best agency in the market. I mean, your ideas are hardly original."

She curls her fingers at her sides. "It's as original as... as your beard."

"Is that a joke?" I lower my brows.

"What do you think?"

"I think..." I stroke my chin, "that you like how I wear it."

"I hate it."

"Good." I knock my knuckles on the table. "I'll keep it."

She shoots me a look that is so hate-filled, that I chuckle.

"It's not funny." She makes that sound—the one between anger and frustration, that I heard yesterday—deep in her throat.

My dick twitches.

How would she sound under me? When I am balls deep inside her melting pussy, while squeezing her beautiful tits? My groin hardens. *Fuck. Get your head in the game.*

I thrust out my chest, "It is from where I am."

"Have you always been such an arrogant prick?"

"Watch it, now." I glare at her. "Your idle prattle has ceased to amuse me."

"You know what's really not amusing?" She moves forward to stand in front of the table, then slaps her hand on the table, "That I let myself be subjected to the toxicity of your presence. "

Our height difference is such that even with my being seated, she has to tilt her head back to peer into my face. She really is petite, and exquisite. Made to be broken, to be put on a shelf and taken care of, then taken down on occasion, to be admired.

It's a compulsion of mine. To collect objects that elicit extreme emotions, which I admit is something that doesn't happen often with me.

That's no explanation for what I do next.

I tap my fingertips together, "So how are you going to put up with shadowing me for a week?"

8

Summer

"A... week?" I squawk. I didn't hear that correctly. "You mean seven days?"

He raises his eyes skyward, "She can count."

Jerk. I swallow, press my knees together, "I won't do it."

"Why not?" He drums his fingers on the table. "Don't you need this gig?"

"I do."

"Then?"

"My uh — my," I twist my fingers together. How do I put this without giving away more about myself? *How...?* "My personal circumstances don't allow me to —"

"Ditch him."

"What?" I stare.

The ego of this guy. I mean, it's not possible he's managed to get through life with this attitude, is it? Does everyone he encounter bend to him? Do they?

He rotates his foot, clad in Italian leather shoes.

"Time you got rid of whichever lover boy you're seeing."

My eyes bug out, "You're joking."

"There you go again, presuming to know what I mean."

I throw up my hands, "You're speaking in riddles."

"Good, one way for you to put that ol' brain matter to good use."

Anger thrums at my temples. My pulse pounds. Adrenaline laces my blood. "I've never met anyone quite like... like... you." I raise my palm, bring it down.

There's a blur of motion, and the next moment, he looms above me. His fingers lock on my wrist.

"Let me go."

"Your answer first, Pink."

"Don't call me that."

"I'll call you what I want, when I want to, and you'll answer to it."

"No."

"Yes."

Obnoxious ass. I stare at his face, searching for something... anything that would give me a clue to why he is acting so unreasonably. "Were you born this way or did you become such a repugnant beast along the way?"

"You don't get to ask the questions."

He tugs me forward and I squeak. My nose bumps his. That dark edgy scent of him envelops me. Moisture pools between my thighs. Hell. How could someone so horrible smell so delicious?

"Your boyfriend—"

"What about him?"

"Drop him."

Not that I have anyone currently. And if I did, would I do as he's commanded? Yes.

Yes.

"No." I jerk my head.

He lets go of my wrist only to wrap his fingers around my nape. I flinch.

"You will do as I say."

My nerve endings crackle. That hushed tone of his voice... the angle of his head, the intensity with which he peruses my features, holds my gaze, ripping me to shreds, cutting straight to the core of me, that frightened little girl who's inside of me. Bet he knows how much of a loser I am inside. One who has never managed to get her own way. I'm not going to give in now. If I do, the alphahole will win and I'll never... never give him that satisfaction; not unless it is on my own terms.

"Oh yeah?" I tilt my head, "And if I don't?"

"Hmm." His eyes gleam, "You sure you want to know?"

The hair on my forearms stands on end. This is a trap. Every single action of his since he walked into this room has been carefully calculated to put me on edge, to unbalance me, to ensure that I am so angry that I'll lose my composure. *Don't say the obvious, don't.* I toss my head. "Bite me, motherfucker."

He peels back his lips. His white teeth flash. Wow. The sheer enjoyment on his face? It changes his features, transforms him into what he might have been as a boy. Full of life, excitement, ready for the next challenge... which in this case, is me. I pull back. "No, don't —"

He lunges forward. The next moment I am splayed across the length of the table, my breasts crushed against the hard surface. "What the —?" I struggle and he leans his heavy arm on the small of my back. I jerk my hips, push up on my toes. A weight behind my knees pins me in place.

"Let me go, bastard."

"Nice of you to have spotted my true lineage, and on our first meeting."

I huff. *Don't say, it , don't.* "Technically, it's our second meeting."

"Don't correct me." He yanks up my skirt.

Cool air assails my skin. I freeze. No way, he isn't going to... "Unhand me."

He pauses, "Did you say 'unhand'?"

Is there a glimmer of laughter in his voice. I angle my head and he increases the pressure on my back, holding me immobile.

"You wouldn't dare..." My chin trembles.

"You should realize that I don't take kindly to dares." He cups my butt and my thighs squeeze together. I clench my fists at my sides. When I get out of here, I am going to file a sexual harassment lawsuit. I am going to sue the living daylights out of him.

"Won't work," he growls.

"What?"

"Whatever you are plotting."

I freeze.

"Everyone in this office will support me. It's your word against mine, and yours doesn't count for much."

My guts clench. The sheer audacity of this man! Does he really think he can get away with what he is doing? "The cameras."

"None in this room."

"From the entrance to the building?"

"I've ordered them wiped already."

"The bar yesterday..." I bite on my lower lip. Of course, he owns it and everyone there, as well. "Fuck you."

Pain explodes across my backside.

I scream. "You spanked me, what the bloody hell—?"

"Language, Bird." He smacks my butt again.

I howl. No one has ever smacked me before.

I haven't let anyone get this close to me. Certainly, no one in the revolving door of foster homes had cared enough to admonish me. So, how had I put myself in this position with this intolerable asshole?

I strain against his hold and he leans more of his weight on my back. I kick out with my leg as he spanks me again, and again. Five, six... ten. "Stop." I wheeze.

"Learned your lesson yet?"

"Get off me, you brute." I yell, and he slaps my arse so hard that my entire body jerks up the table.

"Sinclair."

"What?" My breath stutters; the pain sinks into my blood, coils in that empty space between my thighs.

"My name, little Bird." He cups my butt, "My name's Sinclair."

Moisture pools in my core. Why the hell is my body reacting this way?

"Say it." His voice lowers to a hush.

I tremble, open my mouth, wanting to oblige him. *Do it. Give him what he wants.*

"No."

Whack.

"Now." He growls.

My skin stretches; my nerve-endings pop.

"Sinclair." I huff.

His large hand palms my butt. "See, we get along so well when you obey me."

Right. I swallow, firm my shoulders. "This is not about a boyfriend."

He stills, but his body is braced for action. Dense clouds of energy vibrate off of him.

I turn my head so my cheek is flat against the table. "My sister." I peer up at him. "She's unwell, I can't leave her."

"Not my problem."

Anger threads my veins, "She's not well you... nincompoop. I can't leave her."

"Too bad."

The blood pounds at my temples. Until now, I hadn't' realized how protective I feel about her. Me? I can deal with shit. But Karma? No way am I going to let her suffer because of this. I twist my torso. His grip loosens. Enough for me to pull free. I scramble up on the table, raise my hand,

"Do it and you lose this account, and your home. You and your sister will be on the streets."

I pause, "You wouldn't."

He raises an eyebrow. Of course, the asshole would go all out to destroy me.

Then another thought strikes me, "You already knew?"

He leans back, straightens the cuff of his jacket. "You don't think I'd let you walk in here without running preliminary checks on you?"

"You had me investigated?" My gut churns. The thought of this man searching out the nooks and crannies of my life? My butt throbs. Every fingerprint of his seems to be etched into my arse.

I clamber off the table, glad to put the width of the barrier between us.

"Didn't take too long, by the way." He straightens, his tone already preoccupied. No doubt he's moved on to other things already. He's dismissed me in his mind. Me and my petty little life. I am inconsequential, not even a blip on the expanse of his beautiful life. I hate him... No, loathe him.

I am going to find a way to avenge this humiliation.

Ensure that he feels as helpless as I do in this moment. I smooth my skirt down my hips, then square my shoulders.

"Good-bye, little Bird." He pivots, struts to the door.

His large body cuts out the sight of the doors. That's how massive he is. Slim waist, jacket stretched across a firm butt. Powerful thighs that ripple with each step he takes away from me. More wetness pools between my thighs. It's not fair that the devil has such an irresistible body.

If he leaves, I can forget about my fledgling business, or paying next month's rent... And if Karma's condition were to flare up..? No, she is stable. That's what her last examination showed, but I have to be prepared for the worst. I can't afford to be selfish anymore..

"Wait."

He continues walking.

"I'll do it."

He reaches the door, "Tonight. 8 pm. I'll send my chauffeur to pick you up"

"I can't drop everything..."

"Don't tempt me to change my mind."

Hate him. Hate him. Hate him. I press my lips together, hold up my middle finger, then for good measure stick out my tongue at his back. Childish, but what he's done to me, how he's coerced me into this situation, is nothing short of crazy; like, completely out of this world, unbelievable.

"Why are you doing this? This entire set up... It's too elaborate, smacks of desperation."

He pauses at the threshold.

"What is it you really want from me, Sinclair?"

He draws himself up to his full height, "I'll tell you when the time is right."

My heart begins to thud. OMG... that... didn't sound ominous. Not at all. The hell is he hiding from me? I bite down on my lower lip. Not yet. Now is not the time to throw more questions at him. I can play his game. If he can bide his time, so can I.

"Oh, and Bird? That spanking today, was nothing." He pushes open the door, holds it open for a beat, "Next time, your rudeness won't go unpunished."

9

Sin

The door shuts behind me. Something hits against the barrier; I ignore it.

She's angry. Good. I flex my fingers.

So far, things are going smoothly. In fact, it has been too easy. I frown.

I can't believe she allowed me to spank her. I'd expected her to run out of there screaming, maybe reach for her phone and dial for help... which, of course, I'd have stopped her from doing. It hadn't taken much coercion to bait her, actually.

I stab my finger on the elevator button. Max butts my leg. I glance down and he darts toward the stairs. Why not? My office is a floor above.

And after that run in with that little spit fire... My cock hardens. The shape of that gorgeous arse is burned into my palm. For someone I've spent most of my life hating... Too bad her physical attributes are so enticing.

I clench my fingers into fists. All a ruse to tempt me. Bet she'd dabbed on that infuriating perfume—jasmine and something more complex lurking below. Notes of pepper that had twisted my guts and had tested my patience.

I hadn't meant to lose control, honestly... but what's done is done. I square my shoulders. Next time I won't veer from my plan. I will not give in to my hate... It hadn't been hate. Far from it. There had been something in the air between us. Something that had annoyed me, had squeezed my chest and hardened my balls until I couldn't stop myself.

Not again. One slip up... one more than I have allowed myself in any other project. Nope. I have to look past that enticing face, to the darkness that taints her. The darkness, so like mine. *The fuck?*

I shake my head, prowl toward the stairs, hold the door open for Max. He darts ahead and I follow him up the stairs to the floor above.

I shove the door open and he breaks out in a flurry of barks. No one in the foyer looks up. My staff is too well-trained to show any signs of recognition. I shove my office door open and he darts in, jumps onto the rug in the corner. When I'd brought him here the first time, he had headed for it and claimed it as his. I'd been mildly amused, enough to allow him to own it.

"Stay," I stab a finger at him. He pants, tongue lolling, then places his head on his paws.

I swerve right, walk into the adjoining room, as Damian throws his ball at a basket strung up in the corner. The ball bounces once, then rolls toward me. I pick it up, pitch it at him.

"Wassup?" His long blonde hair haloes his face.

"Isn't it time you got that cut, Goldilocks?"

He grins, "Jealous?"

I frown, "Why would I envy your lifestyle?"

"Oh? Let's see." He holds up his fingers, "The women throwing themselves at me, the ability to hold a crowd with my magnanimous presence, the chance to travel the world while following my passion…?" He cocks his head, "Not to mention the fact that I have more than enough to invest in our new venture, and fly down at the least pretext."

"It isn't a pretext, douche-canoe."

"Speak for yourself." Weston turns from the window, jerks his chin. "I need to return in half an hour to prep for a very important procedure."

Fucker's the quietest of us, the most serious, the most accomplished.

I lean forward on the balls of my feet, "Is that a surgery you're talking about or your latest sub?"

His lip curls. "What do you think?"

"Not going there. What you do with your personal time is your own thing. We all have a dark side, but you, Weston, you scare me."

Yeah, did I mention he's the meanest? Still waters run deep and all that.

"High praise, coming from the master sadist." He smirks.

"That's a back-handed compliment. I'll go with the positive meaning of it… For now."

I crack my neck. "I wouldn't have called this meeting if it wasn't important. I realize all of you can't wait to bugger off to whatever depraved pursuits I pulled you away from."

A chorus of snickers greets that.

Like I said, assholes, each and every one of them.

I stalk to the bar, pour myself two fingers of the whiskey and toss it back.

"You gonna share?" Saint prowls over.

"Get your own."

"Why should I, when…" He snatches the glass from me, "…it's so much more satisfying to take what's yours?" He sets the empty glass on the bar counter with a thump.

A slow burn builds inside of me. Saint has always managed to rile me up the wrong way. Bastard enjoys it, probably because we've been competing with each other since the day we met. On the first day of kindergarten, when he'd been knocking a ball around the yard in front of our school, I'd taken the ball from him and run. He'd pursued me.

He hadn't stopped since. Neither had I. No wonder he'd ended up a lawyer, and me a banker. Neither of us had much going for us in the good will department.

"Sore loser, huh?"

"I am not the one holding an empty glass."

"Because I won the last bet?" He smirks.

"I won the three before that."

"You were on a lucky streak."

I drum my fingers on my chest, "You're hurting my feelings."

"Not since you decided to pursue Mary Jane Nokes in sixth grade."

"You barely noticed her." I crack my neck.

"I didn't... until—"

"She succumbed to my charms," I widen my stance. "which, you have to admit, was a bloody given."

He stabs his finger in my chest. "Don't provoke me, you *chutiya*."

"Settle down children." A new voice sounds. "Would have thought you'd have found a more mature way to fight out your differences by now, huh?"

I turn to the entrance of the room. A tall, broad shouldered man, stands inside the doorway. He has dark, closely-cropped hair, a scar down one cheek, and a tattoo peeking up his neck, enclosed in a priest's collar.

"Edward." I step toward him, Saint at my heels, "Didn't think you'd make it."

"And miss the chance to redeem the souls of the most debauched men on this planet?" He clicks his tongue..

My grin widens, "Life treating you well, Father?" I grip his shoulder.

"Not as good as it's treating you sinners, apparently." He surveys the room, taking in the furniture. The conference table that had been converted to a pool table, the deep-set leather sofa, the fireplace, the wet bar, the floor to ceiling bookcase.

"You like?"

He angles his head. "Nice one, Sin. Almost as beautiful as the woman I ran into who was in such a hurry to get away that she took the stairs going down."

Edward hates elevators because... reasons.

I knit my eyebrows, "Tiny, curvy, pink hair and a face so cute you take an instant dislike to it?"

"Dislike is not quite the word I'd use, but if that's what you want us to believe." He raises his shoulders.

"Huh?" I tilt my chin up, "You're a priest, not a mind reader."

"You're a cut-throat entrepreneur, not someone who's the best judge of character."

"Present company proves your point accurately." I lower my brows.

Edward chuckles, pats my shoulder, "Good to see you too, Brother."

"Now that you pussies have the touchy-feely stuff out of the way, can we get down to business?"

A massive monster of a man prowls through the entrance.

His blonde beard catches the sunlight, the sparkle rivaled by the golden brown of his hair, and his tan that seems to clothe him in a perpetual amber glow.

I groan, "Don't recall inviting you here, Arpad."

"Which is why this is the place I need to be."

"Right, are we starting or what?" Weston asks from his perch by the window.

"Is this a reunion?" Damian drawls, then bounces his ball on the floor of the office.

"If all of our meetings are going to be such a waste of time, count me out." Saint swerves past me and heads for the door.

The fuck? Asshole needs special treatment, apparently. He's not getting any from me.

"You walk out of here, Saint, and I promise I'll cut you out of future deals."

He takes another step.

"You're going to regret it."

He twists his head and shoots me a look, "I regret being here already."

"Get your arse in gear, you tosser."

Saint turns on Arpad, who merely stabs his thumb in the direction of the room. "Surely, you want to find out what he's up to? If you miss this, your curiosity is going to haunt you unless you commit industrial espionage and break down his plan of action."

"Hmm." Saint leans his hip against the door frame.

"Right." I pivot, then walk into the room, "Sit down everyone. Didn't call you here to mess with your time."

"Yeah, it'd better be worth it." Saint growls.

I glare at him.

He smirks. "Go on then."

"How long has it been since you had a decent night's sleep, huh?"

His features close. "What's it to you?"

I glance at the doc, "And you Weston, have you spent a single day not wondering about what happened to the disaster we left behind that day?"

Silence descends on the room. I toss my head. Figures. They are like me — larger than life, big egos, razor sharp minds, the best in their fields... Yet here we were, in search of that one thing that has eluded us since the incident that changed us all.

I fix my gaze on Edward, "How many times a day do you ask the Lord to forgive you for your sins?"

Edward's jaw firms. "Rhetorical questions, Sinner?"

"Takes one to recognize one, Father."

Color bleeds from Edward's face.

"Shit, I didn't mean that."

"Sure, you did." Edward sucks in his cheeks. "That why you called us here? To rehash the mistakes of our past?"

"What's your plan?" Saint stalks into the room, drops into the nearest armchair. "You are too smart, Sin, It's the one thing I hate about you... Possibly the one thing I admire about you too. You've managed to emerge relatively unscathed from the incident, put your life back together, the first of us to earn a million."

And a billion... many times since, but who's counting, huh? I widen my stance, "What do you want in return?"

"50% of whatever profit you are proposing," Saint growls.

"Hold on a second." Weston strides forward, "I am a surgeon, that doesn't mean I'm going to settle for less than my proportionate share of the profits."

"And I am the most in demand Angel Investor in Silicon Valley." Arpad drums his chest.

"That's because Jace decided to turn his attentions to philanthropy," Damian smirks.

He's referring to our mutual acquaintance JK aka Jace. He is part of a select circle of people that Arpad and Damian have become close to in LA.

"Tosser got married and decided to retire." Damian bounces on the balls of his feet.

"More power to him." I snort.

Losers, all those who follow their hearts and get involved in that emo shit. The result: they lose their killer edge, become soft at their edges. Not something that I'll ever fall for. Especially since there is one goal on my horizon — to bring down the man responsible for my ruin.

Arpad tilts his head, "Jace and I were never in competition. Besides," he cracks his neck, "I hold the record for maximum ROI in a quarter amongst all of us. So," he flexes his fingers, "I stake the claim to the biggest share of the profits."

"Don't you want to hear what Sin's proposing?" Damian aims the ball in my direction. I snatch it up, bounce it once, then balance my foot on it.

"I'll tell you, on one condition."

Saint scowls, "Baron?"

I widen my stance, "Fucking Baron."

Arpad's jaw hardens, "Bastard always manages to insert himself into our conversations without being present."

"He *is* annoying that way." Edward concedes.

Saint jerks his chin. "The seventh wheel, but clearly, whatever we are planning, he needs to buy into it too."

I tilt my chin up. "He's in."

"You spoke to him?"

"In a manner of speaking." I'd had to follow the security protocol he'd laid down, which involved old fashioned snail mail, and an unsigned typewritten note, to a PO Box. Apparently, physical mail leaves less of a trail than communicating in a clandestine electronic method. "He's happy with whatever we decide."

"Fucking Baron." Arpad snaps his fingers, "Always knows how to use his time most efficiently, while the rest of us are working our asses off."

"Not you" Saint snickers. "You're too busy sailing around the world in that dinghy of yours."

"It's a sailboat." Arpad curls an eyebrow. "And PS, it's called generating passive income, baby." He spreads his hands, "What can I say? I have a knack for investing in exactly the right start ups... Speaking of which..." he stabs his finger at me, "...you going to tell us what it is?"

"FOK Media."

"FOK Media?" Edward blinks.

"What's that short for?" Arpad smirks, "Full of Kink?"

"Funny Ornery Kangaroos, maybe?" Damian rolls his shoulders.

I shake my head.

"Oh, wait, let me guess." Saint snaps his fingers, "Fill or Kill?"

"An obvious guess," I make a mock gun with my fingers, point it at him. "But no, it's Full of Kindness."

Silence descends.

Saint snickers, "You're joking?"

"No." Not completely. I begin to pace, "After our last unmitigated PR disaster," I turn to Weston, "because of which we had to sell off our shares, divest our portfolio—"

"Hold on." Weston raises his palms, "I made you a profit. We dumped the shares before the stock market tanked."

"Maybe..."

Weston frowns.

"Your sins turned out to be damn profitable for us, this time." I lower my chin.

"As long as you don't repeat them." Edward tilts his head.

Weston raises his hands, "I never should have been caught on that sex tape... Besides, everyone who is anyone has one of those. And it hasn't affected business, has it?" Weston steeples his fingers, "On the contrary, it's brought in a flurry of new patients. Seems the sight of my arse inspires confidence, as much as my success rate in surgeries."

"Win-win situation..." I prop my fingers on my hips. "So we are ploughing in the profits, forming a charity that will invest in a cause—"

"—that gives us legit write offs." Saint drums his fingers on his chest.

"But what's the real business?" Arpad widens his stance.

I scan the room, "We invest in start-ups, in upcoming artists, in musical talent, medical scholarships, we cast our net wide."

"And the returns?" Saint widens his stance.

"Twenty-five percent of their income streams for the rest of their lives."

Weston hums, "It's steep."

"It's fair." I set my jaw.

"It does good." Edward's tone is considering. "I concede that much."

Not that it matters to me. My soul is going to rot in hell, but it's not a bad idea to have side benefits.

I'll also say whatever it is these assholes want to hear to get them to agree.

"If it weren't for the incident, the Seven of us wouldn't have kept in touch. This..." I jerk my chin, "shared venture would be a more positive reason to keep us together."

"All the more reason to walk away from it," Saint grimaces. "If I see any more of you guys, I'll end up resembling one of your ugly faces and that's not on my wish list, no offense."

"None taken." I bare my teeth.

"But." He pauses.

"But?"

He drums his fingers on his chest. "You have my interest, I'll give you that."

Fucking cunt.

Damian scratches his jaw, "And we do this meeting... What? Yearly?"

"Monthly." I firm my lips.

"Monthly?" Damian scowls. "You are aware of my schedule."

"You have a private jet, bitch."

He glowers.

"This way, we meet each month, in person, to evaluate the risks."

Saint smirks, "You'd think you want the strength of the group behind you or something."

I do, but not in the way he thinks.

Makes it easier to keep track of what they are up to. Sure, I have eyes on them, but there's only so much you can trust what the hired help gets you. Best to meet them face to face, read their expressions, study their body language. Deciphering the unsaid, yeah, that's my specialty.

"And the meetings will be in London." I thrust out my chin.

"No fucking way. Why London?" Arpad growls, " I hate this bloody city."

"I proposed this plan. I get to dictate where the meetings happen." I curl my lips, "And it will be on my home turf. Anyone who doesn't agree can sod off."

I scan the space. "No? It's settled then." I thrust my chin forward, "Besides, London is the center of the universe."

The moody, overcast weather the city wears for most of the year suits my temperament fine too.

"Bloody anglophile." Arpad grumbles.

"Filthy Frenchman." I snicker.

"Children, please." Edward walks up to me, grips my shoulder. "For the first time, you've had an idea that I am comfortable putting my weight behind. I'll put half of my investments behind it."

I frown, "In return for?"

"50% of profits."

My jaw drops, "What the — ?"

"Kidding." Edward chuckles. "One seventh works for me. Though I won't say no to more, since my share of profits will be donated to the good of my flock."

"You're in a good mood, Father."

"I feel in fine form." His lips twitch.

"Who have you been taking lessons from?"

The smile switches off. He blinks, "No one."

"So, there is… someone?"

He shakes his finger under my nose, "Now, now. You can't trip me up. I take my vows seriously."

That much is true. The guilt in his eyes though, had I imagined it? Nah, not likely.

I survey the room, "Don't go getting your knickers in a twist people. I can assure you that, unlike Father here, I don't have an altruistic bone in my body. This way, we own these people until the day they die, not to mention ongoing revenue streams."

"Self-perpetuating assets? Works for me." Arpad stretches, yawns. "We done now?"

"Hold on." Saint prowls over, "How do we choose what to invest in?"

"Prospective applicants present their projects, and — "

"We get them to pitch to us." Arpad lowers his chin.

"That's good."

"You bet it is." He walks up to us. "It's a good idea, Sin, for once."

Right.

"The next meeting is in my offices." Saint growls.

Of course, he'd want the last word.

"Sure." I tilt my head.

His eyebrows knit. "If there isn't anything else…" he stalks to the door.

"I am not done yet."

"FOK Media is taking on an agency to help with the marketing."

"Oh?" Saint swings around. "Who heads the agency? Someone you're shagging?"

I glower at him.

"Interviewed her earlier. She'll manage our social media presence, and start seeding PR stories, get the ball rolling."

"Definitely shagging her." Damian scratches his chin.

"Did you think she'd have merits of her own?"

"Does she?" Weston's mouth quirks.

Not only.

"At least she's not an employee. That's something." Arpad drags his fingers through his hair.

"You have something to say to me, dipshit?"

He holds up his hands, "Hey, I am not the one with a hard on for her."

I frown. How dare he talk about her in that fashion?

He drums his fingers on his chest, "If she's not an employee, at least it doesn't open us up to further legal issues, when you pursue her."

"That is not going to happen." I grind my teeth so hard that pain slices up my jaw.

"So you're not interested in her?" Saint scratches his chin.

"No."

His eyes gleam. "I can pursue her?"

A growl rips from me. Anger twists my guts. Only when my hands knit in his collar, do I realize I've crossed the floor to him.

He smirks. "Someone's edgy."

I draw my fist back, "Shut the fuck up."

"Wanna try to hit me, Sin?" His tone is pleasant.

It wouldn't be the first time. Fucker knows how to get under my skin good. I smooth my palm down his collar.

"Nope, old chap." I pat his shoulder. "Actually, I do need your help."

"Hmm?" He frowns.

"Summer will be shadowing me for the next seven days to get in-depth information for the social media strategy."

"Oh, yeah?" He snickers. "Is that a euphemism for what you have in mind?"

I ignore it, "She also has a sister."

Saint straightens, "Oh?"

"Who's unwell, asswipe."

He tilts his head. "And you want me to what? Play nanny?"

Damian pipes up. "Technically that would make him a Manny."

"What?" I shoot him a sideways glance.

He shakes his head. "You should keep up with the trends. Not that this is something new or anything. Oh, wait." He snaps his fingers, "Not that you would be aware of that either, huh?"

"I leave those pursuits up to you, Pretty Boy." I turn to Saint, "Can you send your chauffeur to pick her up and move her to my Hampstead Heath apartment?"

His eyebrows knit, "You're taking care of her family? What next? Pay off her debts."

I narrow my gaze.

"And what will you be doing during this time?" Saint curves his hand, makes a pumping motion.

"None of your goddamn business."

I turn to the man on my right, "Doc?"

Weston straightens.

"The sister also has a heart condition, and considering that's your specialization, will you check her out, find out how bad it is?"

10

Summer

I drag my suitcase toward the imposing door to what has to be the most beautiful three-story house I have ever seen.

The street is off Primrose Hill. Celebrities live here… And of course, the Jerkenstein.

His chauffeur had dropped me off in front of the beautiful wisteria-covered town-house and I had almost been sorry to see Peter leave.

Not that we had spoken much. I'd been too taken in by the Aston Martin the alpha-hole had sent to pick me up.

It had smelled of Sinclair. I bring my sleeve up to my nose and sniff. Bergamot and pepper. Correction, *I* still smell of him.

My stomach flip flops. A hot sensation coils in my chest. I haven't seen the man and already my palms are damp. From hate. That's all it is, right? I raise my fist and knock on the door. It swings open. Huh?

I push open the barrier and walk through, into the large foyer. Ahead, a stairway winds its way up.

To my right is an elevator. Huh? Guess when you're rich you can't be bothered with climbing the stairs?

How much had it cost him to buy the place? Take a number and add at least another seven figures to it. My head whirls. Guess all the money in the world can't buy politeness though, huh?

He is the richest, the snobbiest, the most infuriating man I've come across. And I am going to spend the next seven days with him. Hell.

I bypass the elevator and head for the stairs. He could have been here to welcome me, guide me around. Of course, not. Why had I expected that, huh?

At the foot of the stairs, I pause. I have no idea where I am going, and no way am I dragging my wheelie up the steps.

Hence, elevator...

Hell, does he have to be right even when he isn't physically present to rub it in? I pull my bag to the side, and deposit my tote on it. Then clomp past the foyer, taking a left, through the living room that opens out onto a massive garden.

I pause at the decking that leads out onto a green lawn, flanked by cherry blossom trees in full bloom in the spring sun. Rows of flower beds grace a garden path that leads down to a pond whose water glistens in the distance. I lean forward on the balls of my feet, wanting so much to walk out and explore... I take a step forward when a sound interrupts me. Huh? Was that a moan? I hesitate.

A rustle reaches me from somewhere behind. I pivot, move forward. Another soft sigh. No, I am not imagining things. My heart begins to race. He wouldn't dare. He wouldn't have called me here to humiliate me.

No, actually, that would be exactly his style. Embarrass me further. I stiffen. Why should I hesitate? I haven't done anything wrong, have I? I head past the bay windows on the opposite side of the room, into the adjoining kitchen. And pause. There on the side of the island, he stands, shirt unbuttoned, the lapels parted to show off that sculpted eight pack.

Whoever has an eight pack outside of models and film stars, eh? This alphahole, that's who.

His stomach is concave, and the pants at his waist are unzipped. My mouth goes dry. The blonde hair of a woman covers the most important part of his anatomy. Damn it. Not that I'd wanted to catch a glimpse of his dick. Of course, not.

His fingers dig into her hair, he tugs on it, and she makes a humming sound deep in her throat.

Bet her cheeks are hollowed as she takes him down her throat.

He drags her hair back, then presses her close. Her shoulders tremble and a sucking sound reaches me. My cheeks redden. My thighs clench. The hair on my nape rises and I jerk my gaze up.

Indigo eyes burn into me. His features are hard, his jaw set. His gaze is hot, lust-filled, yet shuttered at the same time. As if he were watching me watching him. I take a step forward, not able to stop myself. If I were closer, would I see myself reflected in his eyes? Would I see how much he wants me? Would he sense how much the entire tableau is turning me on?

I gulp. My scalp tingles. My toes curl. Every part of me seems to be alight with a strange fire. I shouldn't find this erotic. I shouldn't.

A nerve throbs at his temple. He jerks his chin. When my foot slaps the ground, I realize I have taken a step forward. *The hell?* I blink. One side of his mouth curls.

His biceps flex and he pulls her head back, then forward again. And again. I was wrong. She isn't giving him a blow job. He is taking it from her. He is using her mouth for his pleasure. And yet it is as if he is completely dissociated from the entire proceedings. He set this up for my benefit. He wanted me to find him in this position, of course, he orchestrated this entire scene.

I stiffen, angle my body. I should leave, should get away from him.

His grin broadens. His chest rises and falls. He yanks her away with such force that she falls on her arse.

"Hey," she protests.

"Leave." He says it without taking his gaze off of me.

She glances up, "But, I'm not done."

"I am."

He lowers his hands to the front of his pants. The harsh rasp of the zipper being pulled up, grates on my nerves. All of my pores seem to pop at once. Damn him and his account.

Turning, I race to the door

"Summer, stop."

His hard voice crashes into me. I shudder. My steps seem to slow of their own accord. *The hell is he doing to me?* I'd been wrong to indulge him this far.

Been wrong to think that I'd survive a week with him... Hell, a few seconds in his presence and I am unravelling. Pinpricks of heat slice my skin and my thigh muscles spasm. I hate the man... No, I loathe him.

No way am I going to allow him to see how much he's gotten under my skin. That I'd wished I had been the woman on her knees in front of him. That he'd been using me to pleasure him. This is sick.

I don't want him. I don't want be part of this charade. Reaching the front door, I wrench it open and race out.

11

Sin

It wasn't meant to be like this; it wasn't. Let her go; you don't care; you don't.
"Sin?"
Ava glances up at me, her features pinched.
"Get out of the way."
I walk past her and she grabs at the hem my pants. "What's wrong?"
"Nothing." *Everything.* "Leave, now."
"I thought you wanted me."
"Not anymore." As I say the words, I realize that it's true. Fuck that and fuck her and fuck the woman who distracted me enough for me to stop a blowjob half-way.
I stalk to the living room.
"Who was she?"
"None of your business." And she isn't. Not mine either. My Bird is an irritant to be dealt with. With her messy pink hair, the jeans and plaid shirt that she'd tucked in, teamed with a pair of chucks... pink, of course. Does the girl own any other color? If she'd intended to highlight how young she is, she succeeded. Every time I see her, her freshness takes me by surprise. No one was meant to look this chaste, this squeaky clean —enough to highlight the differences in our life paths and experiences, right there. I want to taint that wholesomeness, want to mark that pristine air that accompanies her. Mark her, defile her... *Fuck.* I curl my fingers at my sides. What I feel for her goes beyond hate. I want to destroy her. Then build her up again, a finer, sophisticated version of what she was. *Fuck me.* When had I thought of this? Breaking her down was part of the plan. Anything else? Unacceptable.
I've come this far, haven't I? I've inched forward toward my goal.

I'd had her on my turf... Then I'd lost her.

I stalk toward the open door, buttoning my shirt up. "I want you gone when I return."

I prowl out the door, down the steps.

Peter straightens. "She went toward the hill." His eyebrows knit.

I ignore him.

Don't need my hired help telling me that I was wrong in what I did.

Max darts out of the house; his collar shines in the last rays of the setting sun.

I head toward Primrose hill, start up the slope, Max at my heels.

By the time I reach the top of the hill, the shadows have lengthened. I pass a group of people huddled on the grass, then a couple sprawled on the bench. His head is in her lap and she bends down to kiss him. *Romantics.* I snort under my breath.

Life is not about love and hearts and all that stupid shit that Hallmark dreams up in a bid to keep people buying its products. Suckers fall for that crap; good thing I am not one of them.

A squirrel darts past. Max barks and gives chase. That's his weakness. He sees one of those little critters and loses his shit. Like I seem to do with her.

I reach the top, turn to take in the view.

The vista of the London skyline stretches out before me. Lights twinkle, reflecting the setting sun. I survey the space. Where the hell could she be?

I stalk to the edge, past the signs that highlight the landmarks of the skyline. Can't see anyone. I angle my body to turn, when... There! A shock of pink catches my attention.

I head toward it.

Find her hunched into herself, seated on the ground, facing away from the crowd. Her shoulders are bent. She's drawn up her legs and her chin rests on her bent knees. I hesitate. She seems alone, lost in her thoughts... so fragile. Hurt radiates off of her... Nah, must be my imagination. Since when am I so sensitive to the feelings of others?

Besides, she doesn't mean anything to me. She is merely a pawn in the larger game I have going on.

Which means I need her to survive and get through what has taken place... and everything that is going to be hurled her way.

Why does it matter to me that she survives as unscathed as possible? That she come out stronger, able to take on the world.

Why do I want to go to her and draw her into my arms? Soothe her hurt until she smiles again? Why, when she means nothing?

I close in on her. A gust of wind blows toward me. The scent of her—cherries and caramel laced with cut grass—envelops me. My dick twitches. *What the bloody hell?* So, some part of me finds her interesting. Sure, given half a chance, I'd shag her. I'd do the same to half the willing females that come my way. Except I haven't.

I had had a woman on her knees, in front of me, face in my crotch, in the process of sucking me off and I had walked away. *In search of her?* Only because I need her to return. I can't lose her, not after having come this far. She plays an important role in my plan for revenge, except she isn't aware of it. Something I plan to rectify at the right time... just not yet. I pause next to her. She stiffens; her fingers tug at the grass, pulling away handfuls.

"Done sulking?"

She doesn't give any sign of having heard me.

"Didn't take you for the jealous kind."

Her shoulders draw back.

"Did you want to be in her place, taking my dick into your mouth, hmm?"

Her head comes up.

"If you ask me nicely, I might fuck your mouth."

She springs up to her feet. Her cheeks are pale, her eyes like glowing emerald orbs. *Whoa, stop right there. You don't find her beautiful, remember?* She closes the distance between us, and my groin tightens.

She stabs a finger in my direction, and I have this insane need to bend my head and suck on that digit; though that would be a poor imitation of what I've wanted to do to her pussy since the second I'd laid eyes on her. *Screw that.*

I bare my teeth, angle my head, "Go on then, spit it out, Sweetheart."

"You have a nerve."

I scratch my chin.

"You staged that entire thing for me."

"Oh?" I pretend to yawn, pat my mouth with four fingers.

"You knew I was on my way, and you set it up, including keeping the door unlocked so I could walk in and find you."

"Why?"

She frowns. "What do you mean?"

"Why would I do that, Bird? Why would I go to such elaborate lengths to stage that entire little charade?"

"Because you are some kind of kinky flasher? You enjoy showing off your cock?"

"Wanna touch it?"

Her cheeks flush. "Ego much?"

"I might let you blow me off, if you ask nicely."

"OMG!" She throws her hands up, "you are... are..."

"Irresistible?"

"Obnoxious." She chokes.

"You mean, virile? Admit it, that you are attracted me."

"No." She sets her jaw, "No way am I feeding your already inflated sense of self-worth."

"If the shoe fits." I allow my lips to curl.

"You're such a cliché." She huffs.

I tilt my head, "Every stereotype has its roots in a spark of truth."

"Didn't take you for the philosophizing kind."

"Didn't take you for a sore loser."

"You're right." She juts out her chin. A tear winds down her cheek, trembles at the edge of her jaw. I lean forward, lick it up.

She flinches.

"Why did you do that?"

"Because..." *I wanted to taste you? Find out if your essence is as prickly as your demeanor? Because I have this insane desire to break you down and find out what makes you tick, little Bird.* "Because I can."

Her jaw hardens and she takes a step back. "You're the most arrogant, most dominating, most selfish man I've ever met."

"You noticed, huh?"

She makes a sound deep in her throat, "It will be my pleasure to take you down a notch before we are done."

"Is that any way to talk to the man who's gonna be paying your bills?" I rock back on my heels, "Don't forget I hold yours and your sister's future in my hands."

She pales, "Not fair." Her breath hitches. "If you keep throwing that at me at every turn, then the deal is off."

12

Summer

"Oh?" All expression fades from his face. He schools his features into that emotionless mask I am coming to recognize and hate. "You sure about that?"

I nod.

"Okay."

Huh?

He pivots on his heels and stalks away.

Hold on a second. He's leaving? I chew on my lower lip. Why isn't he stopping me? I'd thought he'd laugh at me, perhaps force me to stay... Instead I watch that tight butt of his recede.

My mouth waters. My thighs clench. *Stop it.* Ogling his gorgeous frame is not going to get your job back. *Damn him.* Damn him for calling me on my bluff. He is aware of exactly how much I want this position... and how I'd do anything to have it back. *Will you grovel to him though?* No... No. Do I have a choice?

He takes the path leading down the grassy slope of the hill.

"Wait."

He speeds up.

Asshole. I break into a run. By the time I catch up, I am panting. My hair sticks to my cheeks. Oh, great. Add being shiny with sweat to my already bruised ego. Whatever. "Stop."

He keeps walking.

"Hold on, Sinclair." He pauses.

I draw abreast with him, then brush past him to plant myself in front of him. His big body blocks the sight of the rest of the space. I tilt my face back, all the way back. His face is in shadows. In the lengthening darkness of twilight, he seems formidable.

He folds his arms and his biceps stretch his shirt. I gulp. The heat of his body spools off of his chest, envelops me, reels me in closer, closer.

I squeeze my fingers together in front of my body, as if that will be enough of a barrier. He could haul me up and march away, and there wouldn't be a thing I could do about it. Moisture pools between my legs. Damn him, for the way my body responds to his every move. His presence, his scent, his every action has me attending to him. All of my senses zoom in on his face. I peer up, trying to discern the sharpness of his cheekbones, the hooked nose, the thin upper lip, that pouty lower lip that makes me want to reach up, draw his face down until it's parallel to mine, then sink my teeth into that sensuous, fleshy part of him. And that's not the only part that calls to me either. A chuckle ripples up my throat.

His glare deepens. His mouth firms. "Are you going to apologize or what?"

"What the —?" I dig my heels in my chucks into the muddy path. To be honest that's exactly what I'd been hoping to do, or at least I thought that's what I'd intended, when I'd set off after him. Now, with him watching me with that superior smirk — okay, I concede that look of disdain is hot on him; it makes him unapproachable, yet so sexy... my nerve endings jangle — and that is the last straw.

No way am I going to give him the satisfaction of winning this round. *It's not a game, oh stupid one, it's your life.* Yah. And it's my prerogative to screw it up, so long as I ensure that Karma is taken care of.

I jut out my chin, "No."

His mouth opens, closes. He blinks once. Ha, guess Mr. Smirky Pants is at a loss for words. Stroke. In my book, that counts as a win.

He closes the distance between us, until his big body brackets me in.

I gulp.

He lowers his chin, and our eyelashes almost kiss. "Say that again."

My body trembles. I fight the urge to step away. Anger scrolls off of him. Nervousness thrums my skin. "No." I tilt my head further back, "No way am I apologizing for that."

"I would have let you walk away, if you hadn't stopped me. You made a mistake by coming after me."

My throat closes.

"What... what do you mean?"

"You had your chance, and lost it." A nerve throbs at his temple.

Oh, no, that... that's not good, is it?

I scuttle away from him and he doesn't stop me. That's not reassuring.

His eyes gleam; his nostrils flare.

Whatever that evil mind of his has conjured up, I am so not going to like it.

"Run, little Bird."

"Eh?"

"You have until I count to five."

The hairs on my nape rise. I angle my body away, ready to take off, anything to get away from this blackhole of a man, who attracts every part of me, even as his temperament repels every cell in my body. Every action has an equal and opposite reaction... Who said that? Einstein? Strike that. Not the time for stupid trivia, not.

"Explain." I clear my throat.

"If I catch you, you do as I command for the next seven days."

"And that's different from now, how?"

He raises an eyebrow, "Want me to spell it out for you?"

"You mean..." I blanche, "you mean the deal—"

"Extends from the meeting room to the bedroom."

"Go fuck yourself."

He smirks. "If I were egotistical, I'd say that you would enjoy that, but it's not your physical surrender that I want."

"Th... then?"

"It's your emotional submission, your mental breakdown."

"You're raving mad."

He raises his shoulder and then lets it fall. "My choice.'

"And if I don't agree."

"I don't remember this being a negotiation."

"Jerk."

"You need a new vocabulary."

"And you..." I drag my fingers through my hair. "...you need a new attitude."

"I suppose you're the one who's going to change me?"

No, what's he talking about?

"Many have tried and failed, Sweetheart. I am not the bad boy you can tame. Not the hero of a romance novel come to save you."

"Th... then?"

"Take your worst nightmare and multiply it by 1000... Then add another few zeroes."

"Your wanker instincts are showing."

He bares his teeth, "Your... fight or flight senses need sharpening."

My heart begins to race. Adrenaline fills my blood.

"I meant every word I said." He thrusts out his chest.

The pulse thunders at my temples.

His nostrils flare. Bastard senses my fear. Sweat beads the inside of my palms and I hold up a finger. "Hang on."

His shoulders bunch, every part of him on edge, ready for the start of whatever insane race he has in mind. Darkness bleeds off of him. He's excited. Damn him. This entire thing is a joke for him... and I stupidly came along for the ride. I have to take control, have to. "So, let me get this right."

He angles his head.

"If I evade you now, I can leave?"

"I don't repeat myself."

Icicles crawl up my back.

"If... if you catch me?"

"Then you're mine to do with as I want."

"For the next seven days, right?"

He raises an eyebrow.

"And you'll pay off my debts and arrange for my sister to be treated by a specialist?"

He nods, "I'll deposit another million in your account, in good faith, so both of you are taken care of for the immediate future."

I swallow. Why is he doing this? Something is not right. What is he not telling me? What choice do I have?

I had upped the stakes. He's made this deal impossible to resist... All the more reason to cut and run. I have to get away from him, before he ruins me completely.

"Deal." I hold out a hand.

He ignores it. He peels back his lips and his pearly white teeth shine in the first rays of the moonlight.

My legs quiver; my thighs spasm. *Get away, get away from him now.* My body leans away from him, ready to bolt. Something primal inside of me insists that I stay, meet his gaze. Not look away as he bends in closer.

His breath sears my cheek.

"Run now. You have until I complete my countdown."

"Five."

I tense. *Go, go.* The hard edge of his glare bores into me. He can see my heart, my soul, my every desire lies unleashed in front of him.

"Four."

I take a trembling step back. *What am I trying to prove? Why am I not taking the small advantage he's offering me?* Because it's a trap, it's a—

"Two."

"You cheated." I gasp, "You missed a count."

He bares his teeth, "One."

I turn and bolt.

13

Sin

I watch her run down the slope

She picks up her pace, her butt cheeks stretching and pulling against the seat of her jeans. My dick twitches; my groin hardens. My entire body begs me to follow her.

The hell?

I hadn't meant to initiate this little game, but when she'd held her own and dared me, something inside of me had snapped — the hunter inside that loves to play, to race after his prey, toy with it, before he claims it. *Claim her? No.*

I never meant for this to go this far.

It was supposed to have been easy — crowd her into a corner until she is helpless and alone, then throw her a lifeline, and watch her entangle herself in the snare. Instead, the fine threads of the net tighten around me.

Sweat trickles down my spine.

Bloody long-sleeve shirts; I prefer to be casually dressed... but the front. It always comes down to the face I show the world.

The importance of keeping up this façade until I find those responsible for turning the lives of the Seven upside down.

I can't fail them; not now.

I break into a run, covering the ground in half the time it took her.

Heart pounding, pulse thudding at my temples, adrenaline laces my blood. The hunt, it always comes down to the hunt. The ability to track down my victims and entrap them. It's why I had been chosen to lead this foray against our enemy. Coming from the rest of the Seven, I assure you it's a compliment that I don't take lightly either. Nor my responsibility to them. *Catch her, coerce her, make her bend willingly to your maneuvers.*

All of the pores on my skin seem to pop. I stalk her as she runs out of the park, up the street that leads to my home. Is she aware of the route she's taken? A pigeon to a homing device. Fly away, little birdie, lead me on the chase.

She rushes up the sidewalk, careening to the very edge where it meets the road, then over to the other side where the walls of the houses skirt the hillside. The hell is she doing? I frown, increase my pace. She continues her hap-hazard retreat. Her shoulders shudder; her speed slows. She must be tired, winded from the descent.

At least she's made it this far without falling arse over tit. The woman needs a keeper.

Max races up from behind to join me. He keeps abreast, his mouth open, tongue lolling.

I prefer to give him his freedom. He has full run of the house and the grounds.

In fact, I have faith in his capacity to look after himself. Unlike her. She needs a goddamn leash to be kept in check. I can't allow her to hurt herself. Not until she's played her role in this charade, of course.

That's all it is. My fingers twitch. How would it be to encircle the expanse of her neck, as I bend her over my desk and take her from behind? My dick lengthens, instantly excited by the thought. I growl low in my throat. This primal reaction I keep having to her is unacceptable. I must maintain my distance from her, or it will complicate things further.

I click my tongue and Max lunges forward. He circles her and her speed slows. She staggers to the gate leading up to my home. Max brushes past her, darting past the open gate, up the garden path. She follows him. Good girl. I'll go easier on her when I catch her. A surge of something fierce unrolls in my chest. Anticipation? Lust...? Admiration that she's lasted this far? Yeah okay. I am not a sore loser. I'll give her her due where it is due to her.

The fuck—? I can't string together a sentence with words, apparently. I slow to a walk, stalk up the garden path. Reach her where she's sitting on the steps. She stares ahead, her legs bent at the knees, her features pinched. I lower myself next to her.

We sit there in silence. The wind rustles the trees that skirt my property. Ahead on the front road, a cyclist races past.

"What were you doing earlier?" My voice emerges huskier than I intended. I clear my throat and she stiffens.

"What do you mean?"

"You careened back and forth as if—"

"As if there were people shooting at me." She brings a strand of that pink hair to her mouth and chews on it.

"There wasn't anyone aiming at you."

"Wasn't there?" She shoots me a sideways glance. "I could feel your gaze drilling holes into me."

I frown. "You are not making any sense at all."

She flings her arms up, "Says the man who is the epitome of all things sane, huh?"

I rub the back of my neck. *Well, damn,* "You have me there." I drop my arm to my side. "There's a method to my madness, while you are—"

"Spontaneous? Interesting?"

"A little confusing is what I'd go for."

She presses her lips together, "Hmm."

"I have to admit that it piques my curiosity though."

Her head whips around, "Oh, my God. You realize what you did?"

"What?"

"You gave me a compliment." She shoots out a hand and places a palm against my temple, "Are you feeling okay? Not dizzy or anything?"

Blood rushes to my face, the rest of it to my groin. If she looks down, she'll see exactly what her touch is doing to me. How engorged I am. How her nearness crawls under my skin and coils in my gut, urging me to lean in closer... closer.

"Admit it, that you needed an excuse to touch me."

Her lips purse, "You and your ego —"

"Are made for each other."

"Which is unlike what I can say about the two of us." She withdraws her hand.

"Oh, no, you don't." I shoot my arm out and catch her wrist.

"Let me go."

"You should have thought of that before you came back to my lair, little Bird."

"It's not as if I had a choice."

"You always have a choice."

"Easy for you to say that, from your position of power."

"Everything you see here? I fought for it. I created my future and now I am giving you a chance to do the same."

"Right." She tosses her head and her scent deepens. A pulse beats to life at my wrists, my temples, even at the backs of my eyelids.

"Why did you come back?"

"Not to be insulted by you, that's for sure."

"That's for me to decide."

She glances away, her breathing harsh in the still night.

I rub circles over her delicate wrist, "Tell me."

Her pulse rate ratchets up, mirroring mine. Bloody hell. It's the hottest thing I've ever experienced, and I haven't kissed her yet. Something hot coils in my chest. My mouth waters. "Say it."

Her chest rises and falls. Her features twist. Then she squares her shoulders, peers up into my face, "Your money. I need the money, of course."

14

"Well, maybe I don't need your money. Wait, wait, I said maybe!"
— *Friends*. Episode, directed by James Burrows

Summer

Something buzzes next to my ear, and I crack my eyes open. Where am I? The large windows let in sunlight. The sun beams light on the wooden floors. My fingers catch on the soft fabric of the futon. I take in my surroundings. Oh! I'm stretched out on a bed. And it's not a normal sized one. The massive bed seems to stretch from one side of the room to the other.

Of course, I'm in Sinclair Sterling's house, in his guest bedroom.

The buzzing sounds again. I spring up to sitting position, and reach for my phone that's plugged in on the side-table next to the bed.

"Hello?" I clear my throat.

"Ms. West?"

"Who is this?" I frown.

"It's Alia from 7A Investments, this is your wake-up call."

"Wake up call?" I blink.

"Yes. Ms. West. Mr. Sterling wanted me to call you to make sure you make it to the office on time for the meeting at nine."

"Meeting?" Was I supposed to meet him? Bet he set it up without giving me notice. Would be just like the alphahole to pull a stunt like this on me.

"Wha.... what time is it?"

"It's 8.15 am."

"8.15?" I scramble towards the edge of the bed.

"Good day Ms. West." The line goes dead.

I glance around the room trying to get my bearings. After that conversation with Sinclair when I'd told him that I had returned to him because I needed his money... He had shown me to my bedroom and I'd crawled into bed and fallen asleep. A-n-d, I hadn't charged my phone.

Which means.... he must have done it.

How the hell had he managed to access my password protected phone. Like that isn't stalkerish at all? I hunch my shoulders.

And he was here in my room while I was asleep? Did he watch me sleep? Goose-bumps pop on my skin.

I should be creeped out by it... except... hmm... what had he thought of as he watched me? Had it aroused him? Had that beautiful bulge between the corded muscles of his thighs engorged further?

My thighs clench; my nipples pebble. *The hell is wrong with me? I hate the man, remember?* I don't find him attractive, I don't. Except I do. The meaner he is to me... the more I want to slap him and simultaneously snog him. Lick him all over his sculpted pecs too, while I am at it. *Jeez!*

And he's not impervious to me either. Not the way he'd eaten me up with his eyes last night, gah!

There's something between us, some strange unspoken chemistry, that hums and flows and seems to take up all of the air in the room when we are together.

It's the reason I should have run from him when I'd had the chance. But I hadn't. I couldn't.

I need what he is offering too much. It isn't only my life at stake, and he is aware of how desperate I am. It's why he lured me in, trapped me... The worst thing is, every step of the way he's pretended to give me a choice.

Choice, hah! The kind where you point a gun at a girl when she is poised at the edge of the cliff and say, choose now. Lean back and fall to your death, or come forward and I'll decide when that death will come for you. That's what he is going to be, my untimely fall from grace. And I am going along with it willingly. For now.

I survey the room and spot folded clothes on the chair next to the bed. There's a note on top of them.

Yep, he'd definitely been in the room while I'd been sleeping. The hairs on my fore-arms rise.

I scoot across the bed and snatch up the note.

Office. 9 am. Same conference room.
Wear this.
You're welcome!

That's it? The note isn't signed, typical.

He'd been angry last night. Oh, there had been no outward sign of his fury... except for the flared nostrils. Oh yeah, and the vein throbbing at his temple.

What had he expected, eh?

That I'd throw myself at his feet and tell him how much I wanted him to kiss me, make love—no fuck—me? For that's all it would be with this man. A complete, one-sided power struggle, which would end only one way. With my submission. He'd take me with no compromise, tear into me, and imprint himself in every one of my cells.

He'd possess me absolutely, mark me and change me forever; and there wouldn't be a damn thing I could do about it.

Just as I'd been unable to beat him at his own game. I may have started that little contest yesterday, had thought I could hold my own against him, but he had turned the tables again.

Like a good little soldier, I'd marched right back to his house, to my prison—a gilded cage where he can keep his bird captive.

My toes curl. My scalp tingles. His little bird. Why does the thought of bending to his will seem so tempting?

It has to be because I hate him, loathe the sight of him and everything he stands for. There's a thin line between love and hate, after all, and surely, I am mistaking the signs of whatever it is that stretches between us. I have to get through the next few days, survive them as best as I can, and then I can walk away. Assuming he'll let me go. Assuming there is something left of me that I can call my own.

I glance at the face of my phone, "8:20 am."

"Fuck, fuckity, fuck." I scoot out of bed so fast that I fall on my arse. "Damn."

I spring up and race for the shower. Only Sin-fucking-Sterling, douche-canoe of the first degree would pull a cheap shot like this.

Leaving me to make my way through rush hour traffic. How the hell am I going to get there by 9 am? No way could a car make it through the traffic, not that I have the money for a taxi. Public transport is my best bet. Hell.

Five minutes later, I'm out. I pick up the clothes, put them on, then survey myself in the mirror.

A pencil skirt that clings to my thighs and comes to below my knees. It is a respectable length, actually, but the cut…? Wow.

It enhances my curves, makes my voluptuous body seem almost… Sexy? The blouse has long sleeves that cover me all the way to the wrists, but it is made of lace. I prop my arm on my hip and my flesh peeks through the pattern.

It's coquettish and erotic at the same time.

And the shoes… Okay, they are stilettos; but not very high, they're the right length needed to enhance the turn of my ankles. I look way too well put together. I seem different. Like someone who belongs here in this house, with him, under him. *Stop it.* I straighten my shoulders, grab my phone.

I've begun to recognize his little glances, the crease that appears between his eyebrows when he is pondering something, the tight curve of his arse, the tented stretch between his legs. Hell, if that was permanent resting position, then how would it look when he was aroused, huh? I gulp, smash my knees together. *Don't go there.* Not now. I hum to myself under my breath.

An old trick, to try and keep my mind occupied and out of the gutter… More precisely, out of Sinclair Sterling's pants, which is where it would happily dwell given half a choice. The screen on my phone shows 8:35 am.

Oh, hell. I pull off the stilettos, shove them in my bag and put on my chucks. No way am I running to the tube in those things. I grab my phone and bag, race down the steps, and out of the door.

I race up the quiet street, my skirt hampering my progress. Bet he planned all of this, to test my resolve. What had he said? He wants to break me down mentally and emotion-ally, huh? Well, we'll see Mr. Sterling.

Once I'm in the elevator, I change shoes. He doesn't need to know. The doors open on the floor of the 7A offices.

I walk down the corridor, to the conference room I'd been to the last time I'd been here.

I pull out my phone. I'm five minutes late.

At least he'd set the alarm for 8.15 am... which had given me enough time to make it here despite the rush hour jam on the tube.

Speaking of, why had he thrown me that little carrot?

The hairs on the back of my neck rise.

I shove open the double doors, step inside, come to a pause.

At the head of the table is Sinclair, "You're late." He glares at me.

"As you planned." I step inside; the door snicks shut behind me.

"Explain?"

"This entire sabotage operation of yours is not going to work."

"Oh?"

My knees wobble. I grip my tote bad, and lurch forward.

"Ms. West?"

I stutter. "Wh... what?"

"Lock the door, will you?"

15

Summer

His voice slinks down my back. Every hair on the nape of my neck rises.

I pivot, shove open the door and place one foot over the threshold.

"With you on the inside, Ms. West."

My mouth goes dry. I pause mid-step. I should get the hell away. Run out of here, take the steps, never look back—

"Don't think about it."

I angle my body forward.

"You leave now, and the deal's off. I'll ensure the doctor never sees your sister again, that she is back in your little hovel of an apartment. Oh, wait, that's not possible because your landlord has already rented it out so—"

I whip around. "How dare you bring my sister into this."

He raises his shoulders and lets them drop, "Because I—"

"—can?" I toss my head, "Tell me something new."

"This entire exchange is getting tedious." He pulls out his sleek phone—latest model, of course, privileged schmuck— presses a number, then holds it to his ear, "Ah, Saint, that girl I told you about yesterday... Would you cancel her next appointment with Doc because—"

"Stop." I fold my arms in front of me.

"Yeah, the deal is off." He says into the mouthpiece.

"Please, I'll do anything you want." Damn him, I am groveling now, but I can't let Karma end up on the streets, I can't.

"Definitely over, you can take her back and—"

I stalk up to him, grab the phone from his hand and raise it above my head.

He tilts his head, holds out his palm. I stare at the phone.

"You'll regret it." There's an edge to his tone that assures me he means the threat.

I stare at the screen. There's no evidence of a call in progress. *Bastard.* I snap my head up.

"You pretended to get on a call. Why would you do that?"

His features resolve into a mask.

"You know what your problem is?"

He pretends to yawn.

"You think you are the sole adult when you walk into a room, and that you are superior to everyone else."

"That's because, I am." He props a hand on his hip.

"Newsflash, asshole, your confidence is going to be your downfall."

"Oh?" He pulls back his lips and his eyes glitter. He doesn't seem angry. Far from it. He's excited. Intrigued even? He leans forward on the balls of his feet, "And of course, you are the one who's going to bring down the king?"

"You are the leader of this company because your team is too scared of you. They need you to pay their bills, so what do they care? They'll never question you, they'll dance to your tune—"

"But you won't?" He flicks off an imaginary piece of lint from his shoulder.

"No." I take a step forward until we are almost toe to toe.

The heat of his big body pounds into me, weighs me down. The dark edge of anger vibrates off of him, forming a tension-filled bubble that encloses us, not that I care.

I've come this far, haven't I?

May as well get it all off of my chest, huh?

"Those people out there?" I stab a thumb in the direction of the door, "They have no idea what darkness lurks under that polished demeanor. That at heart you are insecure about your wealth, your position. You think you could lose it all in a flash, so you hold onto it with your greedy hands."

His left eyelid twitches. He clenches his jaw so hard, I can literally hear him gnash his teeth together. Oh, good. I hope some of those pearly whites crack on the edges.

"Go on." His voice is so soft, so low; yet the threat in his tone, sinks into my blood, rolls down my stomach to pool between my thighs. I gulp. Resist the urge to curl my fingers into fists, to blink and look away. *Pivot, run away, now, before everything goes beyond the point of no return.* Ha, likely story. I passed that point a while ago. No turning back now.

I square my shoulders, hold that burning indigo gaze.

"You'll use your power to get anything, to solidify your fake space in the world. Perhaps launder the profits from your business into some bullshit non-profit, so you can build up a fake reputation. Because that's what you are—a fake. Someone who has no idea what it is to do real good, to use your money to actually make a difference. You have no idea what it means to have no money, to live in fear of where your next meal is coming from, stressing about the roof over your head, about the health of your loved ones.

"When you are convinced that you are a failure because all of your dreams have gone up in smoke and every passing day brings you closer to your grave as you fight to hold onto the present and try to make a living of your wretched life because time is running out. It's running out right in front of you and all you see is yourself, in the mirror... a failure."

My chest heaves. Adrenaline laces my blood and I feel tears threatening to spill over. When had I gone from talking about his faults to laying bare my soul? Every single thing

I said about him is true... and about me, too. This has become a strange war of sorts, in which there will be no winner. Correction. The person who'll lose everything is me.

He has his money, his position. And his reputation...? He can always rebuild it. While me? I set myself back by zillions of years. I am going to lose everything that matters to me, be left with nothing, not even tattered dreams to hold onto. I called him a fake, when really, the pretender in the room is me. My shoulders slump. A dark feeling of despondency courses through my veins. Every millimeter of my body suffuses with so much cringeworthy shame that I am sure he can spot exactly how much I already regret this outburst. Some fighter I am.

I pivot, drag myself toward the door.

"Oh, Bird?"

"What?" I don't turn. I don't want to see his face, take in the smug triumph that, no doubt, crowns the alphahole's features. Someone, kill me now. Oh, wait, never mind. I am doing a really good job of burying myself alive all by myself.

"My phone."

"Eh?" I glance sideways at the sleek device I clutch in my fingers. Damn it, could have at least done my nails, huh? Maybe not a salon manicure, but I could have allowed Karma to buff them up as she'd often offered to do. Stupid, stupid thought.

I turn once more, shuffle toward him.

Each step brings me closer to his heat; that edgy masculine scent of his deepens. The dominance of his presence creates an invisible circumference in the vicinity. If I step into his field of influence I am gone, caged, trapped forever in the layers of huskiness that would subsume me, draw me in and consume me until I forget about myself, about everything that was of significance to me... Like the world, which has brought me only disappointment so far.

I pause a few steps away from him and hold out the phone.

A beat. Another.

There's no movement from him. I peer up at him and gasp. Those eyes... The darkness of his irises seems to have gone impossibly deeper. His features are so hard that they could have been carved out of some yet to be invented alloy—like "Spider Steel."

What are you blabbing about? Now is not the time to show your preoccupation with useless pieces of trivia.

"Excuse me?" He glares at me.

"Uh... It's the strongest bio-material—stronger than steel and its biodegradable."

"So?"

"Your face could be carved from it, it's so..."

"Breathtaking?"

He says it with a straight face. He actually believes in his own invincibility.

"Ugly." I tilt my chin up, wave his phone in front of him, "Like your stupid phone, which, since you don't seem to want it, I am going to—"

He clicks his tongue. "Temper, Bird. And after that beautiful dialogue that you spewed, too?"

"Guess what, asshole?"

"I'm waiting." He holds out his hand, palm face up.

"Too late." I pitch the phone over his shoulder.

16

Sin

She pivots and runs for the exit.

It's sheer luck, pure instinct, that I flick up my arm and snatch the phone from out of the air.

"Why, you little hellion!"

I lunge forward and grab her around the waist with my free arm. She yells and strains against my hold. I haul her back against me, her back flattened to my stomach, the curve of that sweet arse pressed up against my groin. Of course, I am instantly hard. The column of steel between my legs tents my pants and stabs into the valley between her butt cheeks. She shudders, then her shoulders stiffen. Every part of her goes rigid.

"Let me go." She huffs.

"After that stunt?" I dip my head until my lips graze her ears. She winces. Her scent deepens in the air. Oh, yeah, the little tease is as turned on as I am. "Which, by the way, failed."

"Huh?"

I thrust the phone in front of her face.

"Damn it." Her body slumps, "Can't do one thing properly, huh?"

Her self-loathing is evident in her tone. Something hot stabs at my chest. Why should it bother me that all the confidence seems to have drained out of her? This is what I wanted right? Her at my mercy? And after that spectacular tantrum that she pulled, which had lodged somewhere deep inside of me. Nothing she'd said about me was accurate. Of course, not.

I am not insecure, not the one who is holding onto my position in the world as if it is all that matters. Which it does, of course. Not that I am admitting to that.

Everything I've done so far was to a plan. It is a means to an end. As is she. So why am I hesitating now that I have her where I want her? Powerless. Because I prefer her fighting me, challenging me, standing up to me... So much more entertaining than the rest of my employees, who scuttle away at the mere sight of me. Maybe I'm bored, and wanted someone other than the rest of the Seven to banter with me, huh? And I admit it, she is far easier on the eye than any of them, of course.

"You going to apologize, Bird?"

She strains against me again and I tighten my hold on her.

"You going to admit you were wrong in what you said earlier?"

Her spine stiffens, "No."

My left eyelid twitches. "What did you say?"

"I didn't do anything wrong... If anything, I was spot on in my opinion of you. It's the one thing I am good at, sizing up a person."

"Oh?" I grind my groin against her arse. My cock thickens. "And what do you say about the size of that?"

Her entire body jerks, "I could sue you for sexual harassment."

"Don't be crude."

"I'm being crude?" She makes a gurgling sound.

"And untruthful."

"Seriously, you need to get your head examined."

"I'd rather examine... you."

"Aargh." She pulls up her bent arm and I sidestep. Good thing I am so agile, huh? Her elbow grazes the side of my abs and she huffs.

"Stay still or you'll hurt yourself."

"Stop telling me what to do."

"I haven't begun."

She makes a hissing sound.

How cute. I bite the inside of my cheek. "You're beginning to sound like a scratchy vinyl."

"And you're seriously pissing me off." She snaps her head back and connects with my chest. The vibrations ricochet down to the inevitable destination... my groin. My shaft engorges further. *Fuck.*

I widen my stance. She links her fingers, snaps back her arms and buries her elbows in my solar plexus.

Stars flash behind my eyes. My vision narrows.

"That's enough."

I push her against the conference table, and she squeaks.

I bend her over, so her cheek is flat on the surface. Her arse sticks out in the air, and slots in very nicely against my front, thank you very much. I drop the phone face up on the table, then flex my fingers. "If you continue this way, it's going to make things worse."

"Buzz off." She kicks out, catches me in the shin.

My thighs flex, my balls throb in reaction.

"I can't let that go unpunished." I step back, putting a smidgen of space between us, then spank her arse, once.

Her entire body jerks, "Jesus," she yells.

"You called, Babe?"

"OMG, that was beyond corny. Did you read the book on Ten Ways to Seduce a woman? Newsflash asshole, this is not one of them, by the way."

"It's a million ways actually. I wrote it."

There's silence for another beat, then a chuckle wheezes out of her. Something lifts from my shoulders. Guilt at how I am behaving with her? How being with her pushes me to indulge myself; actions I always regret later, me second-guessing my own actions? What the hell is happening here?

"We're too bloody combustible together," I whisper my knuckles over her delectable jawline, "and therein lies the problem."

"Oh, no... no, no, no." She shakes her head, "Don't try to put this down to some weird chemistry that riles us both up, and that I hate you because secretly, I am attracted to you, because I am not. I am not."

"Let's find out, shall we?"

I grab that pencil skirt and yank it up and over her butt.

17

Summer

The cool air hits my exposed arse.

What does he see? My backside covered in slinky red panties. The underwear that he bought for me. I gulp. Is this why he laid out that silk and lace concoction of lingerie for me? And I hadn't been able to resist it, huh? Had he been planning this scene all along? I push up, try to turn, and he clicks his tongue. The blood pounds at my temples. *How dare he treat me so?* I use my elbows for leverage and twist my torso, or at least try to; he leans the weight of his arm around my waist, effectively pinning me down. "Hey what are you —?" He kicks my legs apart and I stutter.

He eases his fingers under the waistband of my panties. I gulp.

The heat of his body sears the back of my thighs. "So you were saying...?"

Was I? What had I been saying? What —

"What happened to all that sass, huh?"

Why is he still talking? Why can't he deliver whatever humiliation he had in mind, huh?

"Should I spank you again?"

Yes.

Yes.

I shake my head.

"You liked it that much, little Bird?"

I actually am growing attached to that name, not that I'll ever tell you that. If I did, I bet you'd insist on flinging it in my face all the time, and hey, didn't I shake my head earlier?

"That was a 'no,' Smirky Pants —"

He spanks my butt and I squeal.

Honestly, the slap wasn't all that hurtful. It's my ego that's taking a real kick to the rear right now... Rear... Haha, so not the time for word play.

He slaps my arse, harder this time; bastard probably read my mind. And his hand connects with my backside again. My entire body moves forward this time with the force of the hit. A moan bleeds from my lips. *The hell? I didn't enjoy that. I didn't.*

He brings his palm in contact with my arse again, and pain warms my blood. Moisture pools between my thighs.

"So, you were saying that you are not attracted to me?"

Crack. I yelp.

"You said I couldn't seduce you?"

"Hey that's not what I—"

Crack. My entire body jerks. My back tingles. My toes curl. I huff, squeeze my fingers together. I will not scream again. Will not.

"You said there's nothing between us—"

"You're twisting my words, jerkass."

He flips me around, "It's your knickers which are all twisted out of shape, Sweetheart."

He cups the space between my legs, and I stare up at him, my breath coming in pants. My back throbs, my scalp seems to be on fire.

He squeezes my fabric-covered pussy, and the dampness between my legs intensifies. Heat sears my cheeks.

"You're fucking soaked."

Thanks for stating the obvious.

He massages my core, and a groan trembles up my throat. He slips his fingers under the seam of my panties, and I pant. Goosebumps flare on my skin. Please. *Please do it.* Please slide your fingers into my underwear, thrust your massive fleshy fingers into my melting, aching pussy. *Hell, what does one have to do to get a finger fuck, huh?*

"Say it."

I frown.

"You know you want it."

"No."

He grinds the heel of his palm into my core, and the heaviness of his palm combined with the friction of the fabric against my clit... *Gah!* A trembling sensation sweeps up from the soles of my feet. *No, no, no.* I can't come. Not like this. I bite down on my lower lip and his nostrils flare. He lowers his head, until our eyelashes tangle.

"Ever climaxed in a boardroom before, Darlin'?"

I scowl at him and his mouth quirks.

"That's what I thought." He raises his hand and I blink. *What the—?* He brings down his palm on my already sensitized pussy.

A scream boils up.

My entire body tenses, my spine curves, the orgasm swoops up to envelop my thighs, my waist, it bursts up my spine and crashes behind my eyes. Sparks of red and black squeeze my vision. Moisture gushes out from between my thighs. My shoulders tremble, my breasts hurt, the hollowness in my womb intensifies.

I crack my eyelids to find him perusing my features. "You're beautiful when you orgasm, little Bird." Something burns deep in those eyes, "You're unique, you know that?"

Heat flushes my cheeks. "Did you just say what I think you did?"

All emotions fade from his face and his features shutter. *Oh, so it's like that, huh?* So, we are going to ignore that the alphahole showed me the first crack in his countenance?

He scrunches his forehead and a line appears between his beautifully arched eyebrows. "You enjoy trivia, Pink?"

Here we go again. I am beginning to get familiar with his manipulative nature. And PS, I like this nickname less. I jerk my chin.

"How many orgasms do you think a woman is capable of in the space of five minutes?"

Don't think that's a rhetorical question. Also, I have a feeling I am going to find that out. Btw, if he thinks I am going to answer that question, he has another think coming.

"I hope you are keeping count, hmm?"

His lips curl at the corners; intent glitters in his eyes.

Wait. What? Don't, don't.

He slides his finger inside my panties and eases it into my melting pussy. "Oh!" I stutter. My hips tremble.

"Did that turn you on, little Bird?" He adds a second finger, a third. I gasp. Pinpricks of pleasure radiate out from my core. He thrusts all three fingers deeper, then curves them. My breath catches; my thighs spasm. My eyes roll back in my head. OMG. What's he doing to me? A vibrating sensation buzzes up my spine and down again. My entire body seems to be humming with an out-of-body sensation. The vibrations intensify. I sense him lean toward me.

He's suspended above me for a second, enough for me to pick up the shift in the air. He pulls his fingers out of me, and I crack my eyes open to find him reaching for his phone which is buzzing in my line of sight. He picks up his phone, plonks it between his ear and his shoulder, "Hello?"

What the hell? Did he just answer his phone, and in the middle of getting me off? Anger explodes low in my belly. I tilt my chin, raise my shoulders off the table and he jams his fingers back inside of my thrumming core. Too much. Too full. I hit the table with a thump. His gaze locks with mine. Indigo eyes intensify to a color that is almost jet black. Dark, brooding, edgy like the rest of him. His features tighten with almost painful intensity; his jaw tics.

"Tell me." He speaks into the phone.

Is he actually holding a conversation while being knuckle deep in me?

I mean... honestly... this is... not happening. No way. Adrenaline laces my blood.

I rear up from the table, and he hooks his fingers inside of me again. Sensations shudder up my spine, my toes curl, and my fingers tingle. My scalp feels as if it's on fire. *Oh, no, no.*

I am not coming again for this jackass, not when he has no respect—like negative two hundred and fifty regard or feelings of any kind for me—and not when he's holding a conversation with someone else on the phone. The hair on my forearms prickles; my nipples pebble. No way, and I'm turned on? My sex clenches. *Jesus, I can't be turned on.* My bullshit barometer didn't spontaneously combust just now, did it?

He yanks out his fingers, leans in close enough for his breath to raise the hair on my forehead.

"Those projections are way off. No way am I paying 50% more for a brand that is clearly on the decline."

The voice on the phone squawks back something that I can't discern.

And he's mouthing off figures while jerking me off? Color flushes his cheeks; his nostrils flares. The bastard's enjoying himself immensely. It has to be the ultimate show of superiority, a fuck you to the world, that he can do whatever the hell he wants and will never be punished. I clench my fingers into fists. I will be his downfall. I swear it upon all that I hold dear, I will have my revenge for this utter compliance that he's wrought from me today—he thrusts his fingers inside of me again and the trembling zooms up my thighs—right after this unholiest of all orgasms that threatens to overwhelm me. A moan spills from my lips.

The voice on the other side of the phone falls silent. Then, "Sinclair, are you with someone?"

"Of course not, there's no one in the room with me."

No one?

Hey, I am more than the sum of all the people you've ever met, asshole. I open my mouth to tell him.

His gaze narrows, his chest heaves, he drops his head and closes his mouth over mine.

18

Sin

The taste of her seeps into my mouth.

Honey and cherries laced with something so intangible, so delicate, my head spins. I tilt my lips and her entire body goes rigid. I lick her mouth. Ripples of sensation tremble up her chest and her breasts heave. I nibble on her lower lip and her mouth opens. I ease my tongue in, dance it over hers. The taste of her intensifies.

Not innocent, not at all.

Something husky, sensuous, layers so complex that it would take me months, years to decipher her, to solve the puzzle that is her. My groin throbs; my balls harden. I swirl my thumb around her clit and a whine trembles up her throat. I absorb it.

I swipe my tongue past her sharp little teeth and goosebumps flare on my skin. A low growl rumbles up my chest, I lean forward, so my chest brushes the full ripeness of her breasts.

"—so you see we have to see this deal through."

I deepen the kiss, and the trembling of her body intensifies. Her spine curves. Her breasts thrust upwards. I grind the heel of my palm into the swollen bud of her clit, and she explodes.

Her body jerks, her head falls back, mewls of pleasure bleed from her mouth into mine. I swallow it all. Swallow down every last drop of her pleasure. My chest hurts. My dick lengthens. No way am I going to come in my pants. Her body goes limp under me.

"Sin, you there?"

I tear my mouth from hers. "I am not budging. They can accept my offer or they can go to hell."

There's silence at the other end. Then, "Got it."

I toss the phone aside, making sure to disconnect the call.

Her eyelids flutter and a husky moan spills from her lips. My balls harden and my legs tremble. And t-h-a-t's my cue. I should step back from her. Should pay every last penny I owe her and cut her loose. And put aside everything that I've fought for my entire life?

She opens her eyes, and those beautiful green irises stare up at me, pupils blown from the orgasm I wrenched from her. Her eyelids are hooded, yet deep inside, hurt flickers. I misused my position. Hell, I've broken every sodding rule in the book, from the first time I had encountered her. So what, huh?

What's another falsehood, in my every growing list of guilty pleasures? At the top of which is her.

I pull my fingers from inside of her and we both shudder. I raise my hand to her mouth and ease my fingers in between her lips. She curls her tongue and sucks on my digits.

I feel the suction all the way to the tip of my dick. My balls grow harder, if that were possible. *Got to get away from her. Now.*

I drag my fingers from her mouth, then bring them to mine and lick her combined juices. Her pupils dilate further, the scent of her arousal... and mine, intensifies. *Oh no,* not going to stay for the rest of this clusterfuck that my life is fast descending into. I draw back and her gaze widens. Her lips stutter. And I can't stop myself. I can't.

I drop my head and kiss her. So damn sweet. So irresistible. I nibble my way up her jawline to her temple. Press my lips to the soft skin there. "You okay?"

Silence. A beat. Another. Then she nods.

"Good."

I lean back, hold out a hand. She scowls up at me, glances from my face to my palm, then grips my fingers. I pull her up to a sitting position, then to her feet. She stumbles and I lean into her, then pull back, steady her with my grip on her shoulder. When she stays standing for another second, I release her. Then smooth her skirt down her hips. My fingertips brush her calves and she shudders. I step back, putting distance between us.

"You never did get to share your plans."

She stares at me, a dazed look in her eyes. "Plans?" she mutters.

"My office, ten minutes." I pivot, stride past the table, then pause. "You'll be safe there." Why did I have to give her that? It's unlike me to concede an inch, let alone give someone another chance. It has to be because she is crucial to the success of my plan, and I had almost screwed it all up. Almost. Well... I raise my shoulders and let them fall. Too bad. Time to move on. If there is one thing I am good at it, it is learning from my mistakes, and this little bird here is the biggest of them all.

"You expect me to believe that?" Her voice is unwavering. Good. A flush of pride fills my chest. She is stronger than she realizes.

I glare at her over my shoulder, "Your belief, or lack of, is immaterial."

She draws herself up to her full height, which still means she has to tilt her head back to meet my gaze. Damn, if the little spitfire isn't fearless. Or naive. Or possibly, both.

"I have many faults, lying isn't one of them."

And isn't that the biggest whopper of them all?

She wraps her arms around her waist. "As if I have a choice..." she mutters.

"You don't."

"No need to rub it in." She tosses her head, "Where's your office?"

"One floor down, the office at the very end. You can't miss it."

"Does it have whips and chains and little baby goats waiting to be sacrificed to the devil?"

I can't stop my lips from curling, "Only if you want it." I turn, stride to the door, then stop, "Oh, and Bird?"

"What?"

"Don't be late."

19

Summer

I hold my wrists under the running water from the tap. Goosebumps pop on my forearms. *Get a hold of yourself; it's okay.*

It will be okay.

I came all over my new work client's fingers while he negotiated some kind of deal on the phone. My thighs clench. I stare at myself in the mirror. *What the hell is wrong with me? I seriously don't think that what he did to me is hot, right?*

The complete control of his actions as he'd finger fucked me to not one, but two orgasms, right there on the conference table, was… hedonistic. It was a hundred ways screwed up. These things don't happen in real life. The audacity of the man. He seriously thought that he could get away with it, too. Has he tried this with anyone else previously? I shut off the tap, and my fingers clutch at the cold metal.

Of course, he must have.

Had he done it in that same conference room? The one where there are no cameras so there can be no incriminating evidence of his trysts. I tip up my chin. I am not going to be yet another in a long list of fuck buddies that he's gathered along the way. Someone he thinks his power and money can buy off. Isn't that what brought me here in the first place?

The fact that he holds all of the cards. He has the money I need so desperately. Hell, I could sell myself and not come up with the kind of cash he is offering, at least not as quickly as I need it. It is my life, my sister's life, my fledgling company.

How far would I go to secure my future? Would I sell my body to the fucked-up machinations of one man? A power drunk, obnoxious jerkface. Too bad he has a countenance that could floor a woman at twenty paces. And that body? I gulp. He could have stepped off the pages of a fashion magazine. Not to mention a razor-sharp mind, with the ability to stay fully in the present and navigate his way through a complex deal, while the rest of him is focused elsewhere. The man had literally split his attention with cold calculation to ensure all of the tasks at hand were fulfilled to his satisfaction.

And mine.

Moisture laces my already damp panties. I shift my weight from foot to foot. Damn it, I didn't have a choice. I shove my underwear down my legs, and stuff it into my bag.

The door opens and an older woman walks in. She's dressed in a fitted skirt, obligatory jacket, and stilettos. She pauses at the wash basin next to mine, and pats her already sleek bob. Not a hair out of place. I stare at my own flushed appearance, the strands of pink hair stuck to my forehead. Grabbing a paper towel, I dab at the shiny skin. Her gaze meets mine in the mirror.

"You have beautiful skin."

I bite the inside of my cheek. "Thank you."

"You're new, huh?"

"No prizes for guessing?" My voice comes out sharper than I intended.

"Don't let him get to you."

"Who?"

"Sinclair." She flips out her compact and dabs at her nose, "His bark is worse than his bite."

"Oh?"

"It's the difficult upbringing he had."

I tilt my head, "Difficult?"

"The kind of horrific things he and the rest of the Seven faced as children would have forced many others to have committed suicide or turned to the wrong side of the tracks... which," she snaps her compact shut, "I admit they dabble in the gray area, but they have each other's backs. And true loyalty among men... Well, there's something that marks out the character of a man, huh?"

The Seven? Who are the Seven? Is that what 7A is all about? How do I find out about them? I wad the tissue into a ball and drop it into the slit provided. "There's no honor among thieves. Doesn't mean their actions can be condoned."

"What if you weren't seeing the whole picture and your point of view was biasing you?"

I turn to her, "What are you not telling me?"

Her features soften. "That's for you to find out. You are a resourceful woman. Surely you can solve the rest of this puzzle on your own?"

She reaches out a hand and pats my shoulder. "Come dear, he hates to be kept waiting."

She turns and heads to the doorway.

"Wait."

She pauses, angles her body.

"Who are you?"

"I work with the Seven; I've been with them since the beginning."

"The beginning..."

"When they formed their first company."

Ah. I had searched for Mr. Alphahole's background, of course, but hadn't found much. He'd kept his tracks covered, until he'd come out of nowhere, or so it seemed, and bought the flailing Tenor Investments. He'd rebranded it as 7A Investments. He'd kept himself out of the limelight since. Bet he used his power/money to buy his privacy. And then there's FOK Media. The company I am working for, which just launched. That had been the latest news I had found, when I'd searched the internet last night before falling asleep. Hmm. I walk toward the woman, "That's all you are going to say?"

"For now." She dips into her pocket and pulls out a card, "Come find me when you get a chance."

I take the card. *Meredith Vincent.*

"You're the one who emailed me?"

She nods.

There is no designation, no phone number or email address. "And you're so high up in the company you don't need any introduction?"

She giggles, and the sound is so girlish, I can't stop my lips from quirking.

"Don't be silly." She searches my face, "My job is highly confidential. I work with the Seven, and I don't need to introduce myself to them, do I?"

Right. That doesn't quite make sense, but I'll take any support I can get in this place.

"So, you'll help me?"

She pushes open the door, "I have a feeling we are going to help each other."

20

Sin

She is exactly fifteen seconds late. I pace the floor in front of my desk. Glance at the watch on my wrist.

Twenty seconds now.

How dare she keep me waiting? I drag my fingers through my hair. And she threw my entire morning off course. I'd missed the second meeting of the day, because I'd been sidetracked. At 9 am in the morning, which was arguably the time of day I was at my sharpest, I hadn't been able to function because I had taken one look at her and all thoughts had drained from my head... leaving me with a part of me that throbbed and ached, and was very alive.

My dick twitches again. My fingertips tingle. I bring my digits to my face and sniff. The scent of her arousal clouds my senses. My cock lengthens immediately. Damn it, why didn't I wash her off of my skin?

I'd wanted to hold onto some evidence of how I had made her writhe and throb under me, had her begging for more, if that call hadn't interrupted me—fucking Saint.

Remind me to take him on the next time we meet— Yeah, if he hadn't phoned with some negotiation detail or the other... We won, by the way, and will be expanding our presence in South East Asia. Another market, another day.

World domination is what I live for, right? We had been negotiating this acquisition for the last six months, and things had gone our way. Another billion in the bank by the end of this financial quarter; we'll be richer. Have resources to go after the bastard who caused us so much grief. And I have the biggest pawn in this move right where I want. In my grasp. At my mercy. I roll my shoulders. So why am I not satisfied? I rub the faint sensations that stab at my chest.

There is nothing personal about what I am doing. She is a means to an end. It isn't her fault that she is the personification of my worst nightmares. I just need to use her to break my enemy. So why am I pacing back and forth, wearing a line in the wooden flooring? Everything in the space is muted—wooden paneling, plush leather sofas, floor to ceiling books.

This is one corner of my domain which I haven't hesitated to furnish to my taste, given the amount of time I spend in it. The armchair is made to order, and opposite it, a wide settee, big enough to double up as a bed on the occasions I've had to sleep here.

The dark leather would highlight her creamy skin beautifully; set off the freckles on her arms, lend a sheen to those glossy pink curls on her head... unlike her pussy where she is as bare as the day she was born.

My dick lengthens, stretching the crotch of my pants. Fuck the woman for worming her way into my thoughts. I pivot toward the door, walk toward it, just as there's a knock.

I pause, roll my shoulders. "Come in."

Silence stretches for a beat, another.

So, she is gathering herself too, huh? *Game on, little Bird.* I pivot toward the table... Nah, best to put a barrier between us. I round the expanse of the desk and drop into my chair.

She steps through, pauses inside the doorway.

I lower my eyes to the chair opposite, then back to her face.

Her lips tighten. Fire burns in those eyes. My dick instantly stretches my pants. *Damn, the spirit of this girl.* She is a fighter through and through. Good. She'll need every bit of that strength to hold up to what I have in store for her.

She stomps to the desk, plops her bag on the floor, then drops into the chair.

"Ms. West."

"Mr. Sterling." She pulls out a brick-like device from her bag and places it on the desk.

"What the fuck is that?"

She flips open the cover, presses down on a button. "It's a time machine." There's a grinding noise as the machine boots up. "What do you think?" She frowns down at the screen.

"It certainly seems to be something that's teleported forward from the eighteen-hundreds."

There's a whirring sound and she frowns.

"No, strike that." I rub my chin. "It's from way earlier."

"Ha, ha," she deadpans.

The laptop makes crackling noises; she rolls her shoulders, "Come on, come on," she mutters under her breath. There's a wheezing sound and she stiffens her spine. "Not now." She slaps down the cover, turns the brick over and proceeds to punch it.

"What are you doing?" A headache begins to pound at my temples.

This entire scenario isn't going as I'd planned. I am so close to getting my revenge... Not just mine, but a comeuppance for all the Seven, and this tiny thing is threatening to destroy every inch of my carefully orchestrated scenario.

I lean forward and grab her wrist; she freezes. Her shoulders go so rigid, I am sure she's having a seizure. "Relax." I place my fingers on the pulse that flutters against her skin.

She tugs at her hand and I release her. *What is this weird compulsion to touch her, huh?*

"You don't need that... that device for our discussion."

"But," she shuffles in her seat, "I had a presentation, all prepared for the social media plan."

"Bet you have all the highlights up here." I tap my temple, "Give me the key points."

"I don't do impromptu." She wrings her fingers together. "Mr. Sterling, I put a lot of thought into that deck."

"So you must be bloody familiar with the gist of it. Summarize it for me."

Her chin wobbles and a bead of sweat slides down her cheek, "I… my mind is a blank."

Stage fright? More likely, she's still riled up about what happened in the boardroom. I lean back in my very comfortable leather chair, place my elbows on the armrests.

"You are going to learn a few things in the time you are with me, Pink."

"You mean like how to misuse your power." She starts ticking items off on her fingers, "How to use your money to buy the silence of your team, manipulate people's lives as if they were mere playthings…" She draws in a breath.

"Is that how you speak to the man who holds your future in his hands?"

She blinks, looks down. "I'm sorry… I am not always this impolite; it's just, you can be annoying."

"Oh?" I tilt my head.

"I am also not used to losing." She juts out her chin.

I peruse her features, "Neither am I."

I hold her gaze for a beat, then steeple my fingers together. "Better?"

Yeah, so that little diversion had been to take her mind off of the task at hand; one way to get past nervousness. A little trick I've learned along the way, and apparently, it worked for her.

Her forehead furrows. She peruses my features, then nods. "As we've already agreed, I'll be shadowing you —"

"Living in my house"

"—for six days more."

"Six days and three hours"

"Right." She opens her mouth as if to tell me off, then squeezes her lips together.

I frown. Is she going to behave herself? I hope not. It was more interesting when she was fighting me, hmm?

She sits up straight, "The original strategy had been to humanize the face of FOK Media, in order to generate positive PR in the hope that it would rub off on the faces of the people involved i.e., the same people who are the promoters of the 7A company."

"Agencies are always good at this, huh?"

"Huh?"

"Summarizing the brief I give them and throwing my words back at me."

She balls her fingers into fists.

I raise an eyebrow.

She stuffs her hands in her lap, then seems to compose herself.

"As I was saying, that was the purpose behind FOK Media, except I don't think your idea will work."

21

Summer

Shut up, shut up. What are you saying? Couldn't you have found a way to share your opinions in a diplomatic fashion? This is when he loses his shit, and fixes his cold glare on me, and probably buzzes for security to throw me out. My stomach churns. I swallow down the bile that taints my throat.

All expression leaches from his face, leaving behind a cold hard mask. It's as if every single emotion inside of him has been flash-frozen. His jaw tics. *Ugh, that's not good, right?*

A vein throbs at his temple. I gulp. Here it comes. I grab the arms of my chair, brace myself.

A chuckle vibrates up that massive chest.

I freeze. No, no, he's having a complete breakdown. Wow. Did I cause that?

His eyes gleam. "Go on."

"Eh?"

"You've certainly gotten my attention, little Bird, don't waste it."

I draw in a deep breath. "There's only so far that you can pull the wool over people's eyes." *Unlike those in your inner circle, the general populace cannot be bought.* "Why do you want them to believe that you want to right your wrongs?"

"I don't."

"Right. So why are you embarking on this entire plan? Why FOK Media?"

He taps his forefingers together.

My hold on the chair tightens, "I signed the non-disclosure agreement, so whatever you say stays within these walls."

His eyebrows knit. "Very well. As you're already alluding to it, I estimate that you have guessed that FOK Media is a cover. We need to buy goodwill with the public. We also need a legitimate business that is a tax write off."

"Ergo, a nonprofit."

"Besides, the money channeled through the entity will be used for doing good."

"Finding the best talent in the world, from different fields, sponsoring them, providing seed investment in return for a percentage of their lifelong profits."

He drums his fingers together, "Get to the point."

"I suggest that you a) change the name to reflect your intention; b) that instead of a percentage of profits, you give the chosen talent a portion of the share capital, along with the immediate funding. That way you bind them to your company, while helping them grow their own nest eggs for the future. Everyone wins. And c).."

He doesn't move a muscle. Well, except for the bulging vein at his temple, he may as well be carved out of rock.

"You Seven not be involved at all with the company."

"Oh?"

I nod.

"Who do you recommend should lead this initiative?"

My guts churn; my heart beats so hard I am sure it's going to jump out of my ribcage. "You've come this far, Pink, don't stop now."

"Me."

"Eh?" He blinks. Yeah, the man actually seems surprised. I rendered the notorious gazzillionaire alphahole silent. Fist pump.

Adrenaline laces my blood. I tip my chin up, "Me. I suggest that I lead the initiative."

Color sears his cheeks. Okay, strike that. Maybe it is too early to celebrate. His biceps bulge; the tendons of his neck flex as he swallows. Guess he didn't like what I said, huh? I don't blame him. If I were in his shoes—though his pants are what I'd rather be in, actually— *Shut up, what are you thinking? Get the hell out, while he's too shocked to react.*

"Umm. I'll be going then." I slip out of my chair, grab my bag, slink toward the door.

"Ms. West."

I keep going.

"I didn't dismiss you yet."

The look on your face said it all, asshole. If you think I am going to wait for you to dole out any other punishment—my stomach flip flops—nervousness that's all it is. The faster I get out of here, the better. I reach the door and squeeze the handle.

"Okay."

I freeze. He didn't say that. No way. Nope. Nah. I open the door a crack.

"If you leave now—"

"Yes, I am aware." I raise a finger above my shoulder "You'll get my sister's appointment with the doctor cancelled. And you won't give me the account to FOK—which, by the way, the name sucks— I mean it's intriguing, but not exactly what you'd call a public relations success, considering all the connotations that go with it—"

A feminine groan fills the air.

I stiffen.

The sound of skin hitting flesh, a low moan bleeds into the space between us. All the hair on the nape of my neck rises. Bloody fish in boots, it couldn't be.

I spin around. His burning indigo gaze clashes with mine. I flinch. The force of his dominance seems to swell, until the air is thick with unspoken words... desires... lust. Anger coats my blood. At him. At myself. For hating him. And wanting him. Dense hatred for everything he stands for; the absolute power that he wields crashes home. "You didn't."

He doesn't move a muscle.

Another harsh gasp pulses from the phone on the table and the blood thuds at my temples. I race to the table. He doesn't react. I snatch up the phone. Don't look at the screen. *Don't.* My gaze drops to the expanse.

My face is front and center. Head thrown back; eyes closed. Color flushed cheeks, hair clings to my forehead. It's the visage of a woman in the throes of absolute ecstasy. Bile rises up my throat. The camera angle had caught me in all my pre-climactic glory; and him? There's only the hard muscle of his bicep from the arm he'd thrown around me —it could have been anyone. Of course, he'd ensured that his reputation wouldn't be touched by this.

The on-screen me grips the muscle of his forearm, arches her neck, her mouth rounded in an O. It's filthy, dirty… and completely arousing. My stomach clenches. I can't tear my eyes off of the screen.

An arm fills my line of vision. He takes the phone from me, shuts off the video.

Silence descends on the space.

He stands not a few inches away from me. The heat from his body envelops me. I shiver. My palms and feet are so cold. "I thought you said there were no cameras—"

"I lied."

Of course. "Hangonabloodysecond," I force the words out through lips gone numb. "You answered your phone, so you couldn't have been recording on it…"

He curls an eyebrow. I stiffen. "So there was another camera in the room…?"

He circles the air with his finger.

"More than one camera?"

He tilts his head. My knees buckle, I dig my heels in for purchase.

Honor among thieves? Meredith has no idea she is working with the devil in disguise. As am I.

The world spins, my knees seem to buckle, and darkness closes in.

When I open my eyes, all I see is blue and turquoise and shades of cerulean. Eyes, his eyes. They aren't cold and empty. There is an ocean of hidden emotions, tucked away deep inside. So deep, so intense. Angry waves crashing on a stony shore. Pulling at me, tugging on me. My skin feels too tight. My hands and legs tremble.

"Don't you dare faint again."

Fury vibrates off of him, and all of my nerve endings seem to flare at once. The world comes into focus again. I swallow, and my throat hurts.

"Drink this." He holds a glass to my lips.

No way! If he thinks I am going to accept a drop of water from him, he's—

He glares at me; I purse my lips.

"Don't be stubborn." He growls.

I turn my face to the side. My heart begins to race and my vision wavers again. "Fine."

I hear him step back, then hear the thunk of a glass hitting a surface.

"I didn't poison the water. Honestly." He shakes his head as if he can't believe I'd suspect him of such a thing.

My tongue feels swollen in my mouth. A bead of sweat slides down my back. There's silence a beat, then another.

"Please, Summer."

Goosebumps flare on my skin. Maybe it's the fact that he spoke my name, or he used the 'P' word. I chuckle to myself. Why do I care about that, huh? But I'm too thirsty; an itchiness crawls down my throat. I turn on my back, then sit up and swing my legs over. The world tilts then straightens. I reach for the water. My fingers are shaking. How strange. I mean, nothing much has happened, except... My entire world has come completely undone. All the moorings gone, everything I thought I was, had worked toward, all my hopes and dreams and ambitions. My company, my sister... Karma. Focus on Karma. I need to get through this for her. I drain the glass, place it on the table. Then wipe the back of my palm across my lips.

"Why?" I raise my head, take in those features that I've come to hate. "Why do it?"

"Because I need revenge against your father."

22

———

Sin

"My father?" She pales further. The pink strands of her hair seem too bright against her gaunt features. She's too damn skinny.

"When was the last time you ate?"

She blinks, presses her knuckles to her eyes, "Answer me first, why do you want revenge against a dead man?"

"Because—" I take a step forward, stop. I'd meant to tell her all of this, of course, just hadn't thought it would come so early in the game. Too bad. She'd thrown me a bouncer and I'd flung the ball right back at her.

I hadn't meant for it to lay her so low that she'd faint.

Bloody fucking hell. When she'd collapsed… my heart had stuttered. Everything inside of me had come to a halt. Only when I caught her before she hit the floor, did I realize that I had raced to her.

Ha! The cold-hearted gazillionaire who's swallowed companies for breakfast, laid low by the sight of a woman fainting. If the business media had seen me then, eh? Thank fuck I'd caught her before she'd hurt herself. If she had, I'd never have been able to forgive myself. I shake my head. *The fuck am I thinking?*

I square my shoulders, thrust out my chin.

"Because?" She lowers her hands. Her gaze is a little wild, her pupils dilated from the shock.

"Because he destroyed my life and those of my friends, and because…" Why do I care that I'd wanted to break the next piece of news to her gently? Why does it matter that it would hurt her? This is what I wanted, right? To sway her to our side, no matter what it takes.

To lure her father into my trap. I need to see the bastard pay, and this is the most fool-proof way, so damn the collateral damage, right?

I set my jaw.

"Because he's alive."

She blinks. "No."

"Yes."

"No, you don't. My father was killed in a plane crash. They never found his body…he—" Her chin wobbles, "He didn't die, did he?"

I shake my head.

"So… where… where is he?"

"In the States."

"How did you track him down?" She frowns, "Or for that matter, me and my sister?"

I click my tongue. "Do you really have to ask me that question?"

"How many people did you have to pay? How long did you search before you found us?" She squeezes her elbows into her sides.

"Does it matter?"

She draws in a breath. "Guess not." She wraps her arms around her waist, and I notice the goosebumps on her forearms.

"He never reached out to me in all these years." Her shoulders slump, "He let me and my sister think he was gone. He left us alone."

Emotions spike her features. Her hands clench at her sides. My heart lurches. I shouldn't have sprung this on her without warning. Eh? What am I thinking?

I ball my fists.

I did exactly the right thing. The faster she realizes the real reason for this charade, the better it will work.

She shuffles her feet, "So all this... this drama of meeting me in the pub, then calling me in to pitch for your company's account... It was all a farce?"

"Not completely. 7A and FOK Media need marketing help, though you wouldn't have been my first choice to take it on."

"I'm bloody good at my job." She growls.

"You lost your biggest client."

"Through no fault of mine. Hell, the last out-of-the-box marketing campaign I delivered, had their brand retention increasing by 75% year on year... If that isn't a good result, tell me what—" Her gaze narrows. "You?" she breathes.

Oh, this is getting interesting.

"You did it?"

"You have to be clearer than that." I tilt my head.

She stabs a finger in my direction, "You made sure that they dropped me."

"Maybe." I drum my fingers on my chest.

"You ensured I'd be so desperate that I'd jumped at the opportunity to pitch."

"I may have... ah, had a hand in them moving on, yes." I fold my fingers, glance at my fingernails. "But the events that followed?" I click my tongue. "It's entirely your fault."

"Mine?" Her eyebrows knit.

"If you had listened to me at the bar—"

"You were a complete jerkface." She juts out her chin. "What did you expect? That I'd throw myself at your feet and agree to do your bidding because you commanded me to?"

I tilt my head.

"Oh, for heaven's sake!" She makes that noise deep in her throat again, and fuck, if my dick doesn't twitch. I frown. Who is this woman who thinks she can hijack every single conversation we have?

"Time's running out." I pull down the cuff of my shirt sleeve. "Fall in line with my plan... or... Well, you don't have a choice, do you?"

Her lips tighten, "You are as callous as my parent who kept away all these years. One who clearly wants nothing to do with us... So why would he care what you do to me?"

"Oh, I think he'd care very much if he found his daughter was marrying one of the richest men this side of the planet."

She stares at me, then chuckles, then throws her head back and laughs. She leans into the settee, rocks from side to side. Tears run down her cheeks.

I stalk to the other side of the room, pour out a generous finger of whiskey, then stalk toward her. When I pause in front of her, she flinches, and my gut lurches.

Of course, she hates me as much as I had despised her — or rather the concept of her — all this time.

She had been merely a pawn in a much larger game and now... Now I can't give up. I am too close. So things haven't proceeded exactly how they should have, thanks to her. She's resourceful, I'll give her that. Nevertheless, nothing will come in the way of this last mile. Not after a decade of planning and plotting every last move. So close, I am so close.

I place the glass on the table, move away. "Drink it."

"I don't need it."

"You look like you are about to pop it, and believe me, while I don't care one way or the other, I need you to be alive for the time it takes to see this through."

She shoots me a stare. Her green eyes burn into me, color flushes her cheeks, and her breasts heave. *Damn, she is magnificent.* My fingers tingle. My groin hardens. Oh, that fire, that fury inside of her. It had all been locked away, behind that scatterbrained façade. She is a little volcano, waiting to erupt, and guess who will be at the end, receiving all of that goodness? *Not me. Nope. N-a-h. Don't fall for her. Don't try to rescue her.* Just because she didn't turn out to be exactly what you'd thought she would be.

"Drink it... or not. Your call."

I saunter away, toward my desk. Behind me, I sense her move. By the time I reach the desk and prop a hip against it, she's drained the glass. She coughs, splutters, then stares at the glass, "I fucking hate you." She throws the glass against the wall. It bounces off, hits the ground, rolls to a standstill not half a foot away from her. She springs to her feet, picks it up, and pitches it at the wall again. It shatters, pieces raining down on the floor. She stays there, shoulders heaving.

"Did that help?"

"No." She pivots around, "You were joking, right, about what you said earlier?"

I allow myself a half-smile, "Do I seem as if I am joking?"

Her shoulders sag, "No." She raises a hand to her hair. "But marry you?" Her fingers tremble as she tugs on a strand. "It's preposterous."

"You woman. Me man." I shrug. "What's wrong with it?"

"Everything."

"Who cares? It will be an event your remaining parent will not want to miss."

"One who's been absent all of my life, who preferred not to tell us about his existence. Why would he care?"

I twirl a finger in the air. "Ring a bell, Sweetheart?"

"What? He wants to see the decor of this room?"

I motion with my palm.

"He wants to sit behind your desk?" She squeezes her eyebrows together.

"Go on."

"He wants a liaison with your company?"

"Not bad." I drum my fingers on my chest.

"He's in debt, I assume?" She grabs a strand of her pink hair and brings it to her mouth.

Interesting habit, if a little weird for my tastes. *The fuck do I care?* I need her for as long as it takes to bring the old man to my doorstep.

"After the massive losses that his business suffered, he had to sell off his assets. He moved to the US."

Her forehead crinkles, "If you are aware of his whereabouts, why don't you take revenge on him?"

"What's the fun in that?" I widen my stance. "I want him to pay for his sins in the city where he instigated his crimes, in front of those who once knew him."

"You want to destroy him completely?" She locks her fingers together in front of her.

"Guilty as charged."

Her lips firm, "Why would he return?"

"A chance to redeem himself in front of his peers in his home country, courtesy of the contacts I'd introduce him to." I spread my arms wide, "It would be a wedding gift to my bride-to-be, to ensure her father is taken care of."

She flinches. "So, you'll bring him here with the lure of money?"

"And a fresh start, not to mention the chance to be reunited with his daughters."

"What if he refuses to come?" She brings her arms down and tucks her elbows into her sides

"Oh, he'll come all right."

Her chest heaves, "Why is that?"

"Because I'll be personally inviting him, to attend his daughter's wedding which takes place in..." I glance at my watch.

"In?"

"Three days."

She throws up her hands, "What world are you living in where the paperwork can be completed in such little time?"

I flick some imaginary lint off my lapel.

"No." Her chest heaves and she clenches her fists. "You... You..."

"It's amazing how money can buy you anything, anywhere... especially when you can call in favors to those in power." I bounce a little on my heels. This is fun.

"You... You can get the registrations and such done by then?" She blinks rapidly.

"With time to spare." I angle my head. "You don't have to do anything."

"I have to show up." She pinches her lips together, glances toward the exit.

I hold up the phone. "Don't even think about it."

She pales further.

I stiffen. "If you're going to faint again, make sure that you're sitting down."

Her shoulders draw back, spots of color burn her cheeks, sparks of gold flare in her eyes. *There you are, my little Bird*.

She juts out her chin. "Name the place and time and I'll be there."

"Not so fast." I lean forward, and the scent of her body intensifies.

My dick twitches and sweat slicks my palm. Fuck her for the response she always elicits from me. I scowl, "Move in with me for the next 30 days."

"What the—" She opens and shuts her mouth. "The original deal was for a week!"

"I changed my mind."

"I agreed to 7 days." She trembles.

"It's not enough time to see this plan through." Why am I bothering to argue with her? It's not as if she has a choice.

"Bu... but... 30 days?" She swallows. "That's too long."

I raise my shoulders, "Gotta convince the world it's real, huh?"

Fuck that.

I don't care how it seems on the outside. Truthfully, I hadn't thought about the time span as such, except... Okay, I *did* need time... Just enough to figure out what the hell I am going to do about this little—okay, big—problem I have, for when it comes to her, I am not myself.

Not in control... and that... I can't stand. I have to get to the bottom of what it is about this woman that constantly claws at me. An itch. An irritation. She is a rash that clings to me, refusing to fade from my skin, my blood and I... must find a way to resolve it.

I allow my lips to smirk, "So?"

She squeezes her fingers together, "So?"

"That wasn't a request."

"Will you keep me here against my will."

I glance at the phone.

"Yeah, yeah." She drags her fingers through her hair, "So you have incriminating evidence on me... but... 30 days?"

I narrow my gaze.

"It's a much longer period of time than I had anticipated."

My heart begins to race. So, the Bird has claws after all, huh? My gut clenches. What had I thought? That she is different from the rest? That it isn't about the money? That she is actually attracted to me? I'd coerced her into this arrangement, after all, pushed her to the edge, hoping... Hoping what? That she'd emerge from it like some bloody phoenix? *Fuck.* I straighten my spine.

"How much?"

She blinks.

"Think of a figure."

"Right." She bites her lower lip, and I squeeze my fingers at my sides.

"Say it before I change my—"

"Five."

I lower my eyebrows.

"Five million." Her chin wobbles.

Not bad. She has the presence of mind to pull a larger figure than I expected.

"Two." I wipe all expression from my face.

She straightens, "Four."

My pulse thuds at my temples. And she negotiates too, huh? At least, she is a survivor. I have to give her that.

"Two point five." I keep my arms loose at my side.

She opens her mouth. I hold up a hand. "Final offer and we both know it's more money than you'll ever see in your lifetime."

"Asshole."

I yawn, raise my phone. "Fine, guess I'll upload this to—"

"I'll take it."

"And sex."

She pales; her breathing grows shallow. "Not part of the deal."

"Hmm." I touch my finger to her cheek.

She winces.

"I'll never force you." I draw back, "But by the time we are done with this arrangement, you'll be begging me to own you, possess you, to have me balls deep inside of you, as you come on my dick."

She shudders, then straightens her shoulders, "Never."

I slide the phone into my pants, "You will give in to me, little Bird, this I promise, and it will be of your own volition." I brush past her, toward the exit.

"One day..."

Her voice follows me.

"One day I'll make you regret what you're doing to me."

I bare my teeth, and the blood pounds in my ears, at my temples, my wrists. Fuck, if that's not the hottest thing I've ever heard from anyone.

I glare at her over my shoulder, "Oh, I'm counting on it."

23

"These damn things are as hot as a stiff cock!"
—*Julie & Julia*, Director: Nora Ephron

Summer

"Cruel." Stab. "Sadistic." Stab. "Twat." Stab, stab. "Alpha-fucking-hole." I bring the knitting needle down toward the cushion again, only for Karma to pull it away from me.

"That bad, huh?" She pats the pillow and places it behind her neck.

"Swine. Pig. Horseshit." I fume.

"Manure." She holds out her palm and I place the knitting needle in it.

I spring up and begin to pace, "Bastardo."

"Is that Italian?" She loops the wool around the needle, drags it out in that rhythmic fashion that makes my head boggle.

"Does it matter?" I walk toward the other end of the room, turn, head toward the other side.

"Guess not. He's certainly helping you expand your vocabulary."

"It was already quite extensive, thank you very much."

"You talkin' to me?" Her needles clack.

"*Taxi Driver*." I toss my head.

"Keep your friends close and your enemies closer." She tugs wool from the yarn.

"*Godfather*." I smirk. "Is that the best you can do?"

Her eyes gleam, "You know how to whistle, don't you, Steve? You just put your lips together and blow."

"What are you trying to tell me, huh?" I throw up my hands. "I always know when you are trying to manipulate me."

"Moi?" She coils wool between the needles. "As if I'd ever try to get you to do anything you didn't want."

"Yes, you. You're every bit as scheming as that nasty jerkface."

"Thought you liked his features." She frowns at the wool.

"What's that got to do with anything?" A headache begins to drum against my temples.

"You can't handle the truth."

There's silence, broken by the clack-clack of the needles.

I turn, flounce to the front of the settee where she's sprawled out.

"What are you trying to say?" I frown. "And that line is from A *Few Good Men*."

She doesn't answer. Her fingers flex, the wool is eaten up in the space between her needles to be spat out on the other side, woven into a perfect design. Unlike my life, which is as messy as a knotted, all-over-the-place, dirty, cast aside, bag of unwanted thread. This must be a new low for me, comparing myself to fabric... Not even—the raw material that goes into making cloth. Ugh.

"How do you enjoy knitting?"

"It's calming, helps me focus on something other than what's going on in my mind."

"Right."

"You should try it."

She glances at me over the needles.

I sidle away to the far side of the settee.

"No, thank you, I have better ways of getting rid of my frustrations."

"Oh yeah? How? By destroying cushions?"

"I barely touched it. The surface is all smooth... Look." I pull the pillow from behind her neck and fondle the fabric.

Silky cotton, soft, yet packed with textures. Like the skin on his chest, the sheath that envelops that turgid muscle between his legs. *Concentrate on the topic at hand. Ugh!* I bury my head in my palms. "What am I going to do, Karma?"

"Nothing."

"Huh?" I survey her through the gaps between my fingers. Yesterday morning—after that stunt that he'd pulled on me, the asshole had stayed away from me for the rest of the day; or vice versa. I'd done my best to avoid him completely.

Which was easy, considering he'd been away from the office, or so Meredith had informed me.

She'd shown me to my cubicle, which is nowhere near his office—thank God. It is on the floor below his, with the rest of the marketing team.

Should I be thankful that he isn't showing me favoritism, or be upset that minutes after proposing to me he was casting me aside as if I was some... piece of disposable machinery? Or a stain on his carpet that he could walk over.

Hang on a second. I am not seriously considering his stupid proposal, right? I mean, this entire scheme is insane. I slide down to the floor, then tilt my chin up. "What do you mean, nothing?"

My sister knits another stitch, "Exactly that. It's not as if he gave you a choice, right?"

"Eh?"

"Whether you like it or not, he's going to put you through the scheme. He's not going to take 'no' for an answer."

My heart begins to thud. "So what? I play dead?"

"Oh, no." She weaves the yarn between her needles, taking her time. I follow her action, trying to focus, focus—*ah, hell.* "Gimme that." I tear the knitting out of her hands and fling it aside.

"Fifteen minutes." She chuckles.

"Huh?"

"That's how long you lasted this time, before yanking away my piece of art."

I snort, "It's a scarf… Or whatever…" I frown, "What were you making anyway?"

"It's a stole… for you."

"Oh!" Something hot coils in my chest. My sister can be a bitch, but she does love me. She has my best interests at heart, like I have for her… Right?

She snickers.

Blood thuds at my temples. "You idiot."

"You believed me, didn't you?" Her shoulders shake, chortling sounds issuing from her.

"Gah! Can't believe I fell for that." I spring up and onto the sofa, then dig my fingers into her side.

She laughs harder.

I drag my fingers down her sides, tickling her, squeezing her. Her laughter rises in volume. "Stop." She gasps.

"Swear you'll never do that to me again."

She slaps the arm of the sofa; tears run down her cheeks. "Swear. You win. Peace."

"Too late," I crow, tickling her under her armpits. She snorts, gasps, pushes at me. I duck, lose my seat on the sofa, and pitch over, onto the carpet. I lay there gasping, glance up at the ceiling. The skylight is open and light pours in.

She follows me down, throws herself next to me. "You are horrible."

"Says the Wicked Witch." I smirk, referring to our childhood nicknames for each other.

"All the better to eat you with." She makes a growling voice.

"Bet, that's what Mr. Big Bad is saying about me, right now." The chuckle catches in my throat. It isn't funny, not at all. I'd run out of the office yesterday at six pm on the dot, the official closing time for 7A Investments. I hadn't spoken to anyone, just messaged Karma, and when she'd replied with the address she was at, I'd come here.

"Is he?" She tilts her head.

"Bad?" I trace the pink lighting up the edges of the clouds far above. "Yes.'

"And the other." She turns onto her front. "Is he?"

My cheeks redden. "None of your business."

"Aww. You're blushing. So cute." She pats my cheek.

I shove it away. "Oh, get a life."

She coughs—on cue. Come on, don't be uncharitable okay? She's unwell. But her sharp thinking and general bitchiness makes up for what she lacks in the stamina department. Enough that sometimes I forget that she's technically unwell. Then, of course, she pulls up her condition, and hell. I curl my fingers at my sides.

She coughs again, and her entire body shakes. "Jeez, thanks girlfriend, so blame me for living vicariously."

"Hardly, vicarious." I sniff. "Nothing happened."

"Something did."

"You mean other than what I already told you—?"

"About him proposing that you marry him, then invite our father who we'd presumed to be dead to attend the wedding, and plot his downfall — ?" She counts it off on her fingers.

"Exactly." I drag my fingers though the carpet again. "By the way, this place is nice."

"Don't change the topic." She surveys the sunny three-bedroom apartment. "It is, isn't it? The car that brought me here was as nice."

"Oh?"

"The chauffeur helped me pack what I needed too. He drove me here, then told me I have an appointment with a specialist for tomorrow."

I wave my hand in the air. "And you agreed to... to all of this?"

"He had an official letter, all signed by Sinclair Sterling of 7A Investments, which is where you were going for an interview. He told me part of the deal is that you get company quarters."

Something he had neglected to tell me.

"And you believed him?"

"What's not to believe?" She wrinkles her nose. "He seemed trustworthy, the signature on the note was legit. Besides, when I peeked out of the window and saw the Aston Martin..."

"You saw the car, and that was it, you forgot everything else."

"Not only, it was the 7A connection."

"Wait until I get my hands on them." I flex my fingers.

"You have actually, on precisely one of them, to be accurate."

"A-n-d, finally we tackle the issue at hand." I grab a strand of hair, chew on the tip, "What should I do?"

"Go along with it." She straightens, walks past me to retrieve her yarn.

"Easy for you to say. You don't want to lose this pad."

"No one says pad anymore." She surveys the remnants of her knitting.

"I do."

"It's a beautiful apartment in Regent's Park." She sniffs.

"Aren't you worried about what happens if all this goes pear-shaped?" I drag my fingers through my hair. "What if our father refuses to come, or hell — " I shoot up to sitting position. "What if he agrees?

"He definitely will." She twists her fingers together in front of her.

I spring up to my feet, begin to pace again. "Which means I have to go through with this wedding — assuming I don't kill the alphahole first, that is. And then, what if... what if...?"

"He demands sex?"

I shoot her a glance, "Not funny."

"Has he asked you?"

Yes.

"No." I shake my head.

"You two discussed it?"

Boy, have we!

"Of course, not."

"Is he as highly sexed as the tabloids claim him to be?"

"What have you read about him?"

She curls a lip, "See, I knew you were interested in him."

"Of course, I am." I drag my fingers through my hair, "I am supposed to fake an entire relationship with him and then walk away unscathed."

My shoulders slump. Therein lies the problem. If I spend more time in his vicinity, I am going to throttle him... Or worse, throw myself at his feet and beg him to lick me all over... After I've kissed him, and sucked on that Adams apple of his, and dragged my tongue down his chest, to—no don't go there, not yet. Not ever.

"You're attracted to him, huh?"

"No."

"You wish this was real?"

I pause, glance at her. "What?"

"The marriage, the life of privilege, father returning to our lives, and attending your wedding, with you wearing my wedding dress that would be showcased for all the paparazzi, and me, of course, as your bridesmaid..."

"There you go, inserting yourself in the tableau. Not that I mind." I don't. Truly. But the rest of it? Yeah, she is right. I mean, no. I mean, yes, I'd wanted all of that, but not with a man I love to hate. And hate to lust after. And want to throttle to within an inch of his life... After he's given me enough orgasms to keep me high on endorphins, of course.

"Oh," I push my knuckles into my eyes, "What am I going to do, Karma?"

She pulls at the patchwork of her knitting, and the entire thing comes undone. She flings it aside, then crosses the floor to me, "You know what I'm going to say, right?"

I blow out a breath. "What?"

"Show me the money!"

And ain't that the goddamn truth?

When it comes down to it, that's all that really seems to matter.

It sure does make the world go round; it's what brings grown men to their knees, what buys you the best treatment from the foremost specialist in town, what ensures that you can pursue your dreams, your goals, your ambitions, ensure that you never go to bed hungry, or feel helpless... Okay, maybe not the last.

But nine out of ten times, it is the money that wins out.

And it is why I am going through with this crazy scheme, of marrying this billionaire-bully. I link my fingers together. Damn it, why are my palms sweating?

I pivot to face my sister. "Really? You're scraping the bottom of the barrel if you're referencing *Jerry McGuire*. It's... waaay too iconic. A child would have guessed it."

"So?" She raises her shoulder and lets it drop.

"Guess what my response is going to be?"

She tilts her head, "Try me."

"Money's something you need in case you don't die tomorrow."

There's a lesson somewhere in those words, about my life, but damned if I can decipher it.

She purses her lips, "Wall Street? You stooped low enough to quote Wall Street?"

Desperate times and all that... What can I say, huh?

She grips my shoulder. "You'll be okay, Summer."

"Famous last words."

24

Sin

"You did what?" Saint looks up from pouring the hundred—or was it two-hundred-year-old?—whiskey from the bottle. Some of the amber liquid splashes onto his tie.

It's a red color today. For fuck's sake, you'd think the man was all dressed up for his wedding. Oh, wait, that's what we were discussing. Only it isn't his nuptials, it's mine.

"Yeah." I drag my fingers through my hair. The strands are long enough to brush my collar, the longest I've worn them. I need to cut it, but when she'd run her fingers through it, the sensations had been pleasant—okay, more than pleasant.

I'd loved that she'd dug her fingers in and held on as I'd brought her to orgasm... *Wait. What?* Now I am changing my look, and because it reminds me of how she came all over my fingers, as the sugary scent of her arousal teased my nostrils and I plunged my tongue between her lips and tasted of her, from her, drawn on that honeyed essence of hers—fuck. My dick is instantly erect. Clearly, it didn't get the memo this is all a pretense. I march to the phone on my desk, scoop it up.

"Meredith? Can you fix an appointment with my barber? Yeah, tonight after work is good." I pause. "No wait, have him come to my residence." One of the perks of being a gazillionaire? You can get the service to come to you, whenever you want. What? It's true.

"Your mind is wandering, asshole."

Saint places the bottle on the counter with a thump.

"Your aim is off the mark, you knobhead."

"Huh?"

I jerk my chin at his tie.

He glances down, shrugs. Then pulls off the tie, and drops it into the wastepaper basket.

"Why do you bother with those things?"

"It has its uses." He picks up the glass. "And that particular brand, withstands a lot of wear and tear."

"Spare me the details of your kinky tastes." Not that I am not aware of them. My PI keeps me informed about the proclivities of the others in our little 'happy family.' Which is how I am aware of the particular club that he likes to frequent. So do I, on occasion, except I ensure never to cross paths with him. Some things need to be kept hidden, capisce? "Your personal life is none of my concern."

"But you went and made yours of interest to all of us."

I glare at him. He's right though; dipshit states the obvious every fucking time.

"Marriage?" He brings the glass to his lips and drinks from it. "Really? What were you thinking?"

With my dick, obviously.

He takes another healthy swig, then gestures at me, "You are attracted to her, I get it. She's hot… in a certain fashion." He lowers his chin, "So shag her, you twat, get it out of your system, but, marriage?"

Anger curls in my guts.

"Don't talk about her that way."

"Oh?" His shoulders go solid. "Do I detect a trace of sentimentally in your rather boring facade?"

"Bugger off."

"Very original." He raises the glass at me, then knocks it back. "So, tell me then, what were you thinking?"

Yeah, I will, as soon as I sort things out in my head. I clench my fists at my side, then stalk to the window and stare at the square outside. A couple kissing in one corner of the space. A little girl runs after a dog, her mother calling out to her. That's the thing about London.

Every damn building faces a green space, a park, a patch of woods. Enough for families to thrive and prosper. Well boo-fucking-hoo. That was never part of my plan. No family… or any of that emo shit for me. So then… *Why did I do it?*

I had reacted on instinct when I had made that statement, had been thinking on my feet. Although, if I'm being honest—Ha! Why start now?—I'd known I might need to escalate things to ensure the bastard takes the bait. Plus, I kind of like the idea… *The fuck am I thinking?*

"Sleeping with her wouldn't have been enough." Not that I hadn't come close to that. And for the life of me, I don't know why I didn't just do it.

I could have taken advantage of her that day in the conference room, when she had been spread out, legs wide apart for me. My mouth waters. My groin hardens. A pulse flares to life in my balls.

Of course, my body is right on track to win the Olympic gold medal for being ever-ready to find a way to get aroused at the merest hint of thoughts of her.

"You saying what I think you are, old chap?" Saint drawls.

"Which is?"

"That you are attracted to her? Maybe you've developed a soft spot where the poor, defenseless, little bird is concerned."

I stiffen. *How does he know that I call her Bird?*

"Yeah, you're not the only one to have eyes on the ground, old chap."

My vision narrows; anger thuds at my temples. "You had me followed."

He clicks his tongue. "Tit for tat… Although the tit I prefer to be thinking about comes fixed to the female anatomy."

"This isn't about sex."

He raises his eyes skyward, "And that is exactly what I've been trying to get through your thick skull, you *chutiya.*"

"What?"

"Fuck her—"

I glare at him.

"Sayin' it as I see it." He raises his hands. "Since when have you started pussyfooting around the four-letter word, by the way?"

"Not pussyfooting."

"Just pussywhipped."

"Ah, fuck you, dickhead."

"Real creative with your insults too." He shakes his head. "I fear you are crossing over to the dark side, my man. Better get your dick in hand and point it in the right direction."

I flex my jaw so hard, pain slices up my face. "Told you, don't talk shit about her, not when I am around, and especially when I am not in the room, you feel me?"

His jaw drops open. He scans the space, then walks to the table, grabs an antique letter opener, and slices it across his other palm.

Blood gushes out.

"The fuck you doing?"

"Relax, I don't have a death wish. Besides, if I wanted to off myself, there are other ways which would ensure I go down in a blaze of glory."

"You really should stop listening to classic rock."

"A much-overrated Bon Jovi song, by the way, but if the shoe fits." He pulls out a handkerchief, wraps it around his hand.

"The point of this entire exercise being—?"

"To prove to myself that I wasn't dreaming.

"Man, and I thought I was the cold-blooded of the lot?"

"You?" He tilts his head, "You, Sinner, have a conscience. Me, on the other hand, I never hesitate."

As I have witnessed first-hand. I drum my fingers on my chest, "You saved my life that day in the basement."

"My hand was just as steady, when I buried the bastard's pen in his neck. His blood sprayed across my face." He holds up his fist, now clenched around the ruined hand-kerchief.

"And I'll never forget that." It's why I tolerate his general fuckedupedness, not that I trust him or anything. I crack my neck, "Don't underestimate me or the rest of the Seven."

"I can assure you that I don't spend any time thinking of the rest of you. Speaking of, to complete the point of this tedious exercise, all I can say is, do whatever the fuck you must to get her out of your system. Don't get entangled with her."

Too late.

"You feel me, Sin?"

Fucker's right. Again. That's what I should have done. That's what I had been planning to do. That's where it had been headed. Me taking advantage of her, bending her to my will, forcing her to particpate in my plan to bring her old man out of hiding, and making him pay for everything. No, we are not going to leave it up to the law. The thing about money? When you have enough of it, you can use it to mask all of your sins. Except me, of course. I use my wealth to amplify my reach, to ensure I am never forgotten. To imprint my mark on the revenge that we have been planning all of these years. And then I had to go and mess it all up.

Okay, so maybe that's not entirely true. Maybe I'm not giving myself enough credit for my strategy, or my instincts, for that matter. "Don't get your knickers in a twist, *ol' chap*," I spread my arms, "This is all part of a plan."

"It is?"

I nod, "I needed to find a way to tie her to me in a way that would convince Adam it's serious."

He rubs his jaw. "Hmm."

"What?"

"Don't believe you."

"What-fucking-ever."

"You should never have embarked on this slippery slope. You could have just had her move in with you, pretend to be in a relationship."

"Like you know so much about relationships, huh?"

"Hey, I know how to avoid them, and have been far more successful at it than you, or the rest of the Seven, for that matter."

He's right, of course.

All of us—with the exception of Edward—have played the field, and well, you don't dip your dick in pussy without occasionally something sticking to it, if you get my drift. What? So, I am an uncouth bugger. I may wear £10,000 suits, get chauffeured around in an Aston Martin, and never fly commercial, doesn't mean I can't tell it like it is, huh?

"I wouldn't count preferring to pay for liaisons as experience."

He stares at me, then chuckles. His shoulders shake so hard that he has to hold onto the edge of the bar counter.

I frown. "What's so funny?"

"You, douchebag. You, who's gonna pay for the biggest fuckin' mistake of your life."

"You're getting on my nerves." I stalk toward the phone on the conference table, reach for it, and depress the speaker phone.

"Sin?" Meredith comes on the line.

"Call Security," I growl.

There's a pause, then, "Is this about Saint?"

"How did you guess?"

"Because whenever you two speak, one or the other threatens to call Security on the other. Don't waste my time, I have a lot to do."

The dial tone rings out.

"What the—?" I release the switch and the annoying buzz cuts out. "She hung up on me?"

"She saved your life, and that of the rest us. She anchored us lost boys by giving us a home away from home to hang out in. It's thanks to her that we are here and didn't end up as crackheads or criminals—present company excluded."

"Of course." A headache begins to squeeze my temples.

He straightens, "She's entitled to ignore you if she thinks that's the right thing to do."

"You had to bring that up, huh?"

"Someone needs to keep their feet on the ground, and stick to the plan." He ambles toward the exit, "Especially since you seem hellbent on screwing it up."

My stomach churns. I'd hoped talking to Saint would help me come up with a solution. *As if.*

The twat has a way of flagging my mistakes. He is the devil's fucking advocate. The only one of the Seven who can stand up to me. Which means, I hate his guts and yeah, also rely on his particular brand of meanness to call me out at my own game. Which he had successfully done. And that leaves me where? Holding my fucking balls in my hand.

"Stop."

He reaches the door, keeps going.

"Fuck you, Saint. What do you want me to do? Beg?"

"Words are overrated." He twists his shoulder, and throws me an amused glance, "We've always dealt in a different currency from the rest."

I stiffen, fold my fingers into a fist. Of course, it has to come down to a bargain with this wanker. He is way too similar to me. A fact I loathe. And which is also why we are the ones who can go toe to toe with each other. Hell, I'd call him a worthy opponent if I was feeling charitable. Which I'm not now, not when a sinking feeling pervades my stomach. I square my shoulders.

"Name your price."

25

Buttercup the Princess Bride: We'll never survive.
Westley: Nonsense. You only say that because no one ever has.

— *The Princess Bride*. Director: Rob Reiner

Summer

"I'll get it." My voice echoes in the wake of the doorbell.

I am alone, again, in the mansion on Primrose Hill.

It is the start of the weekend and I haven't seen him...or anyone else for that matter. He seems to subscribe to the philosophy that servants shouldn't be noticed, except for the results of their efforts.

He definitely has a staff... for food seems to appear magically in the refrigerator and the entire place is spotless, so someone does clean the space. Besides, I'd returned home last night to find my bed made up. It is disconcerting, like living in a hotel... which isn't quite one. I shiver, scrutinize the massive library. I've adopted the space as my own. The floor to ceiling bookshelves, framing the window that looks out on the garden, is my happy space. So why do I keep glancing toward the door, hoping to see him, huh?

Not that I missed him. Nope. N-a-h.

It is a relief not to be on tenterhooks, or peeking around corners before daring to go to my destination within the house. I'd come home from the office—on the tube—again, not complaining. If anything, I am envious of folks who go about their everyday life with scarce in the world to worry about except which bar to go out to on Friday night. Which dress to wear to work in the morning. Which job to hop to next. Which date to shag and take home for the weekend… Oh, on the last… Okay, I've always really admired those who could do that.

Not that I hadn't tried, mind you, but apparently, I have a weird set of morals; imbued, no doubt, from the nuns in the convent school that Karma and I had last attended.

While I had held onto those beliefs—perhaps desperately, for they had grounded me — Karma had gone the other way.

Maybe that's because she had been such a sickly child.

When she should have been laughing and playing with the other kids, she had been confined to peering at us from behind the windows. So, when she'd finally come of age, and had joined me in the real world, she couldn't wait to explore her fledgling sexuality. On the days that her health permitted, of course.

I race down the steps and fling open the door.

Karma swaggers in.

She's wearing dark skinny jeans, torn at the knees. Boots that have massive platforms, a blouse that slipped down one shoulder and is held together by safety pins; another of which is pierced through her lip. Her lip? I blink.

"Didn't the Gwen Stefani look fade with the Nineties?"

"Shows how little you are in touch with current trends, Sis."

Huh? I frown and she chuckles. She tugs on my hair, "So easy to pull a fast one over you, huh?"

She saunters past.

"You could, at least, pretend to be a responsible adult."

"Hey, I knit… That's my two-pence contribution to *The World According to Garp*."

"What are you talking about?" I knot my hair around my fingers.

"It means, adulting is overrated. Besides, you do enough of that for the two of us."

Her boots leave muddy footprints on the polished floor. Should I say something? Why do I care? This isn't my home. I am borrowing it for the duration of... what? A fake marriage to a cold-hearted, obnoxious alphahole, who is trying his best to forget about my existence, apparently.

"Why are you here?"

She does a turn, blows out a low whistle "Damn, you hit the jackpot, woman."

"Or the end of my patience." I tighten my hold around the half-open door.

"Being able to recognize a good thing when it hits you in the face has never been your strong point."

"What do you mean?"

She pivots, waves her hands in the air. "All this, honey. All of this can be yours. Correction, is yours, already—"

"It's all pretense." I huff.

"Haven't you heard?" She leans forward on the balls of her feet. "You gotta fake it till you make it."

I grimace, "You mean like, *Legally Blonde*?"

"I was thinking more, *Pretty Woman*."

What the—! "So, I should prostitute myself?"

"You said it." She smirks.

"Honestly, Karma, you sure can be a bitch sometimes."

She drops her hands to her side, "OMG, that was a low, low hit even for you."

"And your stupidity in telling me that I need to accept my fate, and go along with whatever this weird-ass plan spun by a psychopath—"

"He's not a psychopath—" She scowls.

"Full of himself, vicious billionaire-"

"Gazillionaire, actually—"

"—has concocted, and actually be happy about it, is sheer and utter nonsense."
My chest heaves.

Her features tense. She moves toward me. "Hey, Summer, I'm sorry that I upset you."
I snort. "No, you're not."

"I really, truly am. You're right, I can be a bitch sometimes. I think it's some self-fulfilling prophecy. After all, with a name like Karma I didn't stand a chance, huh?"

"It's better than Summer."

"You're not the one having to pronounce your name to people, when you introduce yourself."

"Better than people instantly assuming I am some kind of a hippie."

"Of course, your get-up doesn't inspire that at all, huh?"

I glance down at my long skirt, teamed with a peasant blouse, and pink Chucks. "What's wrong with what I am wearing?"

"Nothing."

"Not my fault if people go by appearances." I snort.

"Woman, you are an optimist. The world is ruled by how you appear. Haven't you gotten that through your head yet?"

"What I reflect to the world is not what I am on the inside."

"It's true." She nods and her lips quirk.

"Don't go laughing at me. As you are aware, I am more rebellious than I seem."

She looks me up and down. "Let's agree to disagree on that, Sis. You're more of a quirky misfit."

Huh? Is that good or bad?

"You're someone who wants to soothe things over, make the world a better place, someone who yearns for male approval."

I glower, "You think I have daddy issues?"

"Don't we all?" She raises her shoulders, then lets them drop.

"That is the most honest thing you've ever said. I mean, given how we were abandoned by our own father, of course, we'd be looking for approval from the men in our lives, huh?"

"Difference is you fear loss of control. You'll do anything to tame your circumstances, while I…" She looks past my shoulder.

"You?" I jerk my chin.

"I leverage the cards I've been dealt, rather than upset the entire table, looking for that one Ace that'll probably never land in my lap."

"If are implying that I'll never settle for anything other than the *one*, you're right." I tip my face up, and peer into her eyes.

Damn, I could do with some heels about now. Except this isn't a power play. It isn't. This is me and my sister having a conversation about priorities, huh? And it's time she understands where I stand on this.

"I won't stop searching for the person who is compatible with me in every way."

She shakes her head, blinks, and I frown. Did something go into her eyes? Doesn't matter. This once, I am going to have the last word.

"This marriage is as fake as Posh Spice."

The hair on the nape of my neck prickles; a frisson of electricity ladders up my spine. Too late, I realize what she'd been trying to tell me. *Don't turn. Don't.* A blast of heat at my back makes me wince.

"Care to repeat yourself?"

26

Sin

Her shoulders stiffen and every part of her goes rigid. "You heard me." She pivots around.

I glare at her.

Her cheeks redden, but she holds my gaze. Impressive.

My little bird is trying to flex her fledgling wings, huh? Why should it matter to me that she's dismissing this relationship as a pretense? It is, isn't it? I was the one who'd initiated it, so why am I so angry that she's insisting that it is all a fake, huh? Because that's all this is ever going to be. Another lie in a long string of deceptions, which is what I excel at, after all.

I prowl over to her. Closer, closer. Her chest heaves; her breathing grows shallow. I pause when I am right in front of her. She tilts her head back, all the way back, to look at me.

"Actually, I don't think I did." I raise my hand and she flinches. She's afraid. Good. I drag my finger down the side of her cheek. "Say it again."

"You mean play it again, Sam?"

"Huh?"

"*Casablanca.*" She gulps. "That scene where Ilsa—"

"Asks Sam to play 'As Time Goes By'?"

She nods

"You have it wrong."

"No, I don't." Her eyebrows knit.

I smooth the crease between her eyebrows, and she turns her head away.

"Listen," she huffs, "you may be the boss in the office but when it comes to movie trivia—"

"—I am always right." I curl my lips.

"You can't be perfect about everything." She huffs.

"Oh?"

This should be good. "What will you give me if I prove you wrong?"

She sets her jaw.

"Well?"

"What do you want?"

"You."

"Excuse me?" She whisper-screams.

"You heard me."

"You already have me right under your thumb, agreeing to every sneaky plan you've no doubt spent the last many years—"

"A decade, actually."

Color smears her cheeks. "—thinking about. You made me agree to this pretend marriage—"

"That's where you are wrong." I lean forward until my chest almost grazes her chest. Almost.

I don't need to glance down to find out that her nipples have puckered. (Expected.) Or that my pants are suddenly too tight at my crotch. (An unfortunate byproduct of our proximity, one that I'm going to alleviate as soon as I have called her out on her mistake.)

"That's twice in as many minutes, by the way."

Her gaze widens. "You are such an arrogant know-it-all. It's not possible to have a single straight conversation with you."

"Right?" I allow my grin to broaden.

A pulse beats to life at the hollow of her neck. I want to drop my head, nuzzle that space where her scent would be the most concentrated. *Fuck, why would you want to do that, huh?*

I start to raise my arm, then lower it; my fingers tingle. *How can I ache to touch her again?* Feel that silky smooth softness of her skin under my palm, cupping her, palming her arse, thrusting knuckle-deep inside the soft core between her legs—

"Hey." She claps her hands.

I tip my chin, up. "Don't raise your voice."

"I'll do whatever the fuck I want."

"Summer!" A new voice sounds within the space.

I glance past her, spot the woman Summer was talking to when I entered. "Who're you?"

"Hi." She moves forward, "I'm Karma."

"Karma?"

She blows out a breath. "Excuse my parentage, and hers." She jerks her head toward Summer. "We are what happens when you cross a flower-chewing hippie with a loser ex-millionaire with a penchant for gambling."

No kidding! And isn't that the root of this entire fucking problem.

"Good to meet you by the way," she holds out her hand.

I glance at it, then at her face. "The jury is out on that."

She blinks, her features taking on a stunned countenance, then she chuckles, her shoulders shaking. She bursts out laughing, a full-throated giggle that's oddly infectious.

I find my lips twitching. "You must be the sister."

"You must be the alphahole." She grins.

I frown, "Alpha—?"

"Shut up, Karma." Summer pivots, and I pull her against my side. She struggles and her hip grazes my side.

I wind my arm around her tiny waist, dig my fingers into the curve of her butt. She shudders, then falls still.

"So, that's my nickname, huh?" I smirk.

Summer snorts, "Only you would take it as a compliment."

"I'll let that pass."

"Why do I find that so difficult to believe?"

"You're right to be suspicious."

She huffs, "Why don't you say what's on your mind?"

"Where's the fun in that?"

Karma Chameleon's gaze darts between us. "Guess you two get along quite well, eh?"

"What are you talking about?" Summer throws her arms in the air, "We hate each other."

"Right." Karma's eyes gleam. "My sister is rather good at believing her own lies."

"It's the first thing I noticed about her, though in this case, I hate to admit she is right."

Summer turns on me, "OMG, are you feeling feverish or something?"

"Eh?"

"You agreed with me. That's a first? Is it raining outside?"

"It always rains in London, haven't you noticed?"

She makes a noise deep in her throat.

I chuckle. "By the way," I tug on a strand of that pink hair, "completing what I started earlier—"

"Do you always have to have the last word?"

"Definitely getting to know me better." I tilt my head, "Be careful, you may end up liking me."

"Never." She wrinkles her nose.

"I'll hold you to that, and as I was saying earlier, I was right."

"About what?"

"What you quoted was a misquotation of the line "Play it, Sam"."

"No." She blinks.

"Look it up." I smirk.

She scans the room, pats the pockets of her skirt.

"You searching for this?" I produce her phone and she snatches it up, stares at the screen.

"You called me—?"

"What's the point of a phone if you never keep it with you?"

"Twenty times?"

"I expect you to be at my beck and call at all times. Have you forgotten?" I shoot up an eyebrow.

"It's the weekend."

"You work for me, twenty-four-seven."

"How can I forget!" She sets her jaw.

"Well?"

"What?"

"Are you going to look it up?"

"I'll save you the bother." Karma steps forward, "He's right."

"So, what else is new?" I can't keep the slightly victorious tone from my voice. Cheap shots.

For some reason, when I am around her my control seems to slip, and hell, if I am not going to take every single opportunity to come out on top. Literally.

Summer glances between us, then pulls up her phone. Her fingers tap on the screen, then she stiffens. Tucks her elbows into her side.

"Told ya."

"Yeah, yeah." She blows out a breath and the hair on her forehead flies up. "That's a first. I'll give you this one."

I lower my voice, "You'll give me every one of your firsts."

Her chin comes up, and she whips her head around to look at me. "Happy?"

I shake my head.

"What more do you want?"

"We made a deal at the start of this conversation, have you forgotten?"

"I am losing count, asshole."

I lower my head, nuzzle her cheek, then whisper, "Much prefer alphahole."

"I think I'm going to call you pain in the ass."

"At least wait until I've stuffed my cock into that hole too," I murmur.

Her breathing hitches.

I pull back, survey her features. Pupils dilated; creamy skin of her neck flushed with color. My dick instantly lengthens.

Her mouth opens, and that's when, cunt that I am, I move in. I close the distance between us, drop my head and close my mouth over hers.

She stiffens; every muscle in her body solidifies. I swipe my tongue between her lips and a small sigh escapes her. I nibble on her mouth, suck on her tongue, and her spine curves. I bring her firmly against my side. She literally seems to melt into me.

My cock hardens, my balls throb, an answering pulse flares at my temples. *Fuck.*

The sound of a throat being cleared reaches me. I lessen the intensity of the kiss, move back, and she follows me. I can't stop the rumble of pleasure that vibrates up my chest. She must have heard it too, for she stiffens. Then pulls away. I let her put some distance between us. Not too much, for I keep my arm about her waist.

"So." I turn to Karma. "Glad you could make it."

"Wouldn't miss helping my sister plan her wedding."

"Wait." Summer shuffles her feet, "You're the one who invited her?"

"He did," Karma confirms.

Summer shoots me a dirty glance, "Did you hack the password to my phone?"

"Didn't need to. I used your favorite number."

"How did you know...?" She purses her lips. "You had my laptop rigged so you could figure out my patterns?"

"You give me too much credit. Turns out, you are predictable."

She snarls low in her throat. Damn it, those little sounds she makes? I'll ensure it's an all-out cry when I have her spread out on my desk and—

"It's an invasion of privacy." She hisses.

"That's not the only thing I'm going to invade."

She reddens, and her chest heaves in the way that implies that she's seriously turned on. Bet her panties are soaking wet, not that I am complaining. I wish we were alone so I could shove my fingers between her legs and confirm my theory. My fingers twinge and I fold them into a fist at my side.

"Are you going to use every word I say against me?" Summer mutters

I arch an eyebrow.

She swipes her hair back, "Forget I asked."

"Mr. Sterling," Karma interrupts. "That sure is a generous offer, by the way."

"What is?" Summer frowns.

"He didn't tell you?" She blinks, "How many men would give carte blanche to their bride to organize the wedding their way."

"Only the cunning, conniving, obnoxious ones." Summer mumbles.

So fucking feisty. This woman, she hasn't a hope in hell of keeping up with me. Still, I have to give her full points for trying, which is more than what I'd acknowledge with any other opponent. She is turning out to be nothing like what I had expected. Surprises, I hate them. Challenges... Yeah, I can definitely credit her as a puzzle to be solved, a game to be played, safe in the knowledge that there will be one winner—me.

"That all you've got?" I allow my lips to curl.

"And you..." Summer glowers at Karma, "I can't believe you are ganging up on me with him."

There's a loud bang on the front door, which flies open. "Are we too late?"

Summer blinks. "Isla, Amelie?"

"I took the liberty of inviting your closest friends too."

27

Summer

"He gave you his credit card, right?" Karma hops up and down on her heels. My sister is excited. And she's also right.

I hold up the black piece of plastic he'd slipped into my palm. Yeah, hadn't expected that. Not sure what I am going to do about it either.

"I vote we put it to good use." Amelie snatches the card from my hand.

I reach for it and she holds it out of reach. "Oh, no, Ms. Goody-Two-Shoes, I am not going to allow you to spoil this fun."

I tuck my elbows into my sides, "Christ, Amelie, this is seriously not on. I am not going to spend time being indebted to him."

"You already are," Karma drawls from the comfortable leather armchair in the corner, a glass of wine held between her fingertips. She looks at home in the living room, which overlooks the beautiful garden behind the house. The doors are thrown open to allow the warm summer breeze to waft into the house. Large pink and yellow roses bloom to the side; a meadow of wildflowers stretches out on the other side. A path stretches out, leading to the pond in the center of the garden, and beyond that, tall trees overlook a waterfall that gushes down from the wall that brackets the property on three sides. Idyllic. Beautiful. And so wrong.

I don't deserve to be here, soaking in the rightness of the moment, when everything else about this picture is wrong. Wrong place. Wrong time. Wrong groom. What had I been thinking, agreeing with him? Oh! Wait, I didn't have a choice. If I had refused, I'd have been on the streets, scrambling to save my life and that of my sister's. The very sister who, right now, pours out wine from the, no-doubt, obscenely expensive bottle, and raises it in my direction. "Salut."

I frown. "You're not supposed to be drinking. It neutralizes the impact of the medications you are taking."

"Not what the doctor said," she mutters.

"Oh, yeah?" I march up to her. "Why didn't you call me when you went to see him, huh?"

"Does it matter?" She chugs down the wine. "They're all the same—not able to diagnose what's wrong with me, only to start me on a different medication, then tell me to be careful about my diet, exercise... As if I were eighty instead of eighteen."

"It's a good thing drinking in this country is, at least, legal at your age."

"Which really takes the edge off this rebelliousness." She takes another mouthful of wine, then hiccoughs.

"You've had enough."

"And you haven't had any yet." She offers me her glass.

I stare at it, then purse my lips.

"Aww, come on, Sis, indulge me. It's a time for happiness. Time to celebrate."

"You sound strange."

"I know, right?" She stares into the glass, "Must be the alcohol, or the rather pleasant surroundings we find ourselves in. It's certainly not your temperament, which as usual, leaves much to be desired."

She raises the glass to her lips and I snatch it from her.

"Hey!" She protests.

I drain the glass. Then blink.

"Yummy, huh?" She smacks her lips.

"So that's how wine's supposed to taste?"

"It's certainly a step up from my last drink, which came out of a cardboard box." Amelie walks up to us, a freshly-opened bottle in hand, and tops me off. Then reaches for a new glass, fills it up and hands it to Karma.

"I think she's had enough," I mutter weakly.

Amelie grins. "Come on, we need the liquor to brainstorm."

"Besides the wine is sooo good," Karma giggles.

Isla rushes in from the garden, hair tousled, her cheeks flushed. "Guys, the flowers, OMG, there's a hot house with orchids. Those blooms must be worth thousands."

"Try millions." Nothing I have encountered in this house gives me the confidence that their value is anywhere in the area of the numbers I have in my head. Best to add many zeros after any of our guesses.

"This man, he's beyond loaded." Isla flings out her arms so wide, she almost decks me.

I retreat to a safe distance.

"He's a gazillionaire, many times over." She walks over to the massive mirror that takes up almost one corner of the entire wall. "And this is one helluva space." Our reflections greet us, with the garden stretching out in the background.

It is overwhelming, dominating, yet brutally sensuous, with a tinge of sophistication—very much like the man who owns it.

"It's... ah... something." I swallow.

Karma laughs. "Damn, she's already mastered the art of understating stuff, huh?"

"Yep, have you noticed?" Amelie snickers. "The more money you have, the less you talk about it."

"Now, that's not fair." I turn on them. "I'm a little overwhelmed with the speed of everything that's happened, that's all."

"Hey." Amelie walks to me, "Didn't mean it the way that came out. And for the record, I think you're doing the right thing."

"What?" I scoff. "Mock marriage to an obnoxious Mr. Moneybags who's using me to further his empire?"

"Is that what he told you?" She narrows her gaze. "That it's a pretend wedding?"

I nod.

"I think he's lying."

Karma and Isla move in closer.

I wrap my arms around my waist. "What makes you say that?"

"Calling your sister and your best friends to come out and help you plan your wedding." Amelie waves her hand in the air. "Do those seem like the actions of a man who feels nothing for you?"

"Oh, he has feelings all right." I snicker.

"Aha!" Her eyes gleam. "You fucked him, huh?"

"No... uh..." I shift my weight from foot to foot. "Not quite."

"Either you slept with him or you didn't." Amelie tilts her head.

My neck heats. "It's kind of complicated."

"It always is." Isla nods.

"As if you'd know. Miss I'm-saving-myself-for-marriage." I quirk my lips.

Karma props her palm on her hip, "And you're not?"

"Nope." I jut out my chin. "I've been too busy earning a living, to consider wanting to sleep with anyone. Besides, I haven't meet anyone I wanted to have sex with, okay?"

"Summer, no." Amelie rounds on me. "Tell me that's not true."

I lean back, "Hold on, what's going on in that head of yours now?"

"Are you a virgin?" Amelie frowns.

"Now you sound like him."

"I knew it." She snaps her fingers.

"What are you talking about?"

"Bet, that's part of the attraction. You're probably the first halfway decent looking woman he's encountered —"

I cough into my hand, "Gee, thanks."

"—who's also never been with another man. Bet it brought out all of his possessive instincts and he decided he was going to claim you."

I snort, "Asshole whisperer, that's me." I swipe my hair over my shoulder, "He could have slept with me without wanting to marry me, you know. Besides," I jut out my chin, "I told him I wasn't a virgin."

Amelie stares, "Bet he subconsciously knew that you were lying."

"Like, we have some secret connection, so he can read my mind?" I scoff.

"Do you?" She lowers her chin.

I stare, "Of course not."

"But, you haven't fucked him yet?"

"Jeez what is this, the Spanish Inquisition?" I throw up my hands. "And no, I haven't. Besides, all of you are forgetting one thing. This entire thing is a pretense."

"I don't know, the oncoming wedding seems all too real." Isla squeezes my shoulder. *Tell me about it.*

"Karma did mention that there's a deal involved."

"She did?" I growl.

"It's perfectly okay." Amelie pats my cheek. "You're finally wising up, leveraging your best assets to earn a living."

"Jeez, thanks, with friends like you who needs—"

"Enemas?" Karma smirks.

"Ugh." I make a gagging sound in my throat. "Hate it when you come up with gross jokes."

"Which this wedding isn't." Amelie frowns at Karma who makes a gesture as if she's zipping her lips.

I sober. "How am I going to plan a wedding in 2 days? I mean, I never thought I'd be walking down the aisle." The entire scenario is fake, but you know what I mean.

I wring my fingers together in front of me. Swallow down the tears that prick at my eyes. *Why does everything seem so overwhelming all of a sudden?* I sniffle.

"Hey." Amelie rubs my back, "We're here for you. I, for one, think you should do exactly what your heart dictates."

Which is what? Throw myself at him and beg him to fuck me? No, not that. Rewind. Throw myself at him and demand that he release me from this stupid charade? Better. Which he is not going to do. He is hellbent on taking revenge for whatever my father did to him, which he hasn't revealed yet. I mean, how bad could it be? Some corporate war gone wrong, no doubt. I'm sure that's all it was. He's probably blown it all out of proportion too.

"My skills as a wedding planner were clearly honed for this day, huh?" Isla brackets me in from the other side. "Besides, you have one thing going for you."

"I do?"

"Yep." She grins. "You have his credit card so..." She raises her shoulder.

Yeah. My shoulders slump further. Money really can buy anything, even the arrangements for an unplanned wedding, huh?

"Listen, Babe, we are all on your side, even if we are constantly taking the piss." Karma folds her arms behind her back.

"Hmm. You sure about that?"

"Completely." Her features resolve into an expression of determination. "I promise not to say anything bitchy—"

"Hallelujah."

"At least for the next half an hour."

I laugh, "Thank you for your kindness."

"Oh, and leave your wedding dress to me."

"I... I'm not so sure Karma." I twist my fingers together.

Her eyes gleam. "You do want to catch his attention?"

I bite on my lower lip.

"You want to ensure he never underestimates you again? You want to surprise him, huh?"

"Yes... but, can you create it in 2 days?"

"It's difficult, but not... impossible." She taps her finger to her cheek. "Not if I take the barebones of the dress I had been working on... and...." She brightens, snaps her fingers. "Oh, I think I know just the thing." She squeezes my shoulders. "Trust me."

Famous last words.

"You won't regret it." She winks.

Oh, hell. My stomach plummets.

"That's settled then." She grins. "Let's get this show on the road."

Amelie waves the black credit card, "Right, what should we order first?"

28

Sin

"Is it too warm in here?" I run my finger around the collar of my shirt. I opted for a straightforward long-sleeved shirt, tapered pants and a jacket. No tie for this occasion. My way of showing it doesn't mean anything. A pointless gesture. *Who am I trying to convince?* My stomach rolls and I tug at the sleeves of my shirt. My fingers tremble. *The fuck?*

"You nervous, ol' chap?"

"The fuck you dithering on about?" I pull out my handkerchief, rub at the bead of sweat that trickles down my temple.

"Should I turn up the air-conditioning?"

"Fucking hate that artificial atmosphere." Truth is, being stuck in any enclosed space makes my head spin. Unless I have something to distract me. I play with the clasp of my watch. Some of the nervous tension drains from my shoulders.

"Yeah." He sobers. All seven of us have that specific phobia in common. All of us have different ways of coping with it.

"Here." He snaps open a wooden box.

"If you were thinking of proposing, it's little too late. Besides, I am not into you that way."

"Har, har." He smirks politely. "Knowing how much you abhor jewelry, I figured I'd get you the next best thing."

He holds out the box. Rolled tobacco leaf columns nestle in the humidor. "Aww, you remembered. I am so touched."

He chuckles.

I gently pull out one of the cigars. It is one of my bloody weaknesses, along with rare whiskeys. Turns out money grows on you, sensitizes your tastes so you began to appreciate the finer things in life.

He takes one for himself, then places the box on the table. Producing a cigar cutter, he snaps off the ends, then holds a lighter to my smoke, then his.

The pungent scent of crushed leather and toasted almonds, woven with something sweet—cherries?— almost as fine as the taste of her, fills my senses.

I tilt my head back, puff out a smoke circle. My muscles unwind a little.

"I hate to tell you, this was a good idea."

"Feel that?" He tilts his head.

"What?"

I raise the cigar to my mouth, take in a puff.

"That stillness inside, that calm before the storm, that sense of everything about to hit a shitstorm, your last few minutes as a single man, when the fragrance of a 100-year-old cigar loosens your tensed-up tissues?"

I cough, "Only 100 years? You disappoint me."

His eyes glint, "You're welcome."

I draw in another reverential puff, "I'm touched you remembered my weakness for these."

"At half a million dollars per smoke stick, well, you'd better be."

"Now who's counting their pennies, huh?" I grin.

He smirks, takes a puff of his own. "I see what you did there, by the way."

"Oh?"

"You're not fooling me any, Sin."

"Not trying, you pretend toff."

"If you wanted to marry her, you didn't need to pull this elaborate shenanigan. I mean, you could have told the rest of us that you were in love."

Love? I cough. "I barely know the woman."

The collar at my throat digs into my skin. I resist the urge to loosen another button.

"It's a pretense, 30 days and we are done."

He taps his fingers together, "Did you sign a contract with her?"

I freeze. I didn't. I was confident that the incriminating video would ensure that she'd do whatever I wanted. Besides, I was planning on letting her go as soon as I sign my deal with her father, which should be happening very, very soon.

"I don't need one."

He opens and closes his mouth, then chokes. His shoulders shake, he chortles, and tears fills his cheeks.

"Don't die on me yet." I thump his back, hard enough for him to stumble forward.

He staggers away, leans his hip against the window. "Is it a magic pussy? Is that what this is? Is she so damn succulent that your dick overpowers your brain now?"

"Told you already, don't—"

"Yeah, yeah." He straightens, "Don't talk about her that way. I know. And honestly, no disrespect to whatever there is between the two of you..."

"Which is nothing—"

He cups a hand behind his ear, "Are you listening to yourself? No contract, asshole.

You've left yourself open to some crazy-arse shit here. Possible sexual harassment in the workplace. No pre-nup either. If she doesn't take you to the cleaners by the end of this..."

I set my jaw, "She won't."

Fact is, it honestly hadn't crossed my mind to draw up a contract with her. Why is that? Do I trust her that much? Am I so sure about my ability to control her? Did I really think that I would be able to manipulate her into doing exactly what I want? An interesting conundrum. One I haven't found myself in ever before. I survey the ash building up on the cigar.

He scans my features. "You have something on her?"

I tilt my head.

"Something incriminating enough that it'll make her bow to your every whim?"

I allow my mouth to curl with a smirk.

His muscles unwind. "Well then." He puffs out the fragrant smoke. "I want to believe you..."

So do I.

"—and for your sake, I hope you come out of this unscathed. Considering...."

I slip a hand into my pocket, "Do pray tell."

"Clearly, you are slipping."

I frown. "What do you mean?"

"This may be a fake ceremony, but it *is* legally binding. It has to be for it to work. So clearly, that's what's making you nervous."

"Not." I raise my cigar to my mouth. My fingers are rock steady. "I know what I am doing, but do you? Considering the £150,000 you spent on this cigar—"

"Its £500,000..." His cheeks hollow as he takes a puff, "per smoke stick."

"Hmm." I narrow my gaze, watch him through the fragrant cloud. Bastard outdid himself on this one. He never did know when to stop.

"Consider it my gift." He raises his cigar in a mock toast. "After all, it's not every day that my worst enemy gets married."

I snarl.

"Sorry, I mean," he air quotes, " 'mock married.' " He speaks out of the corner of his mouth, "Without any kind of paperwork to cushion the fall."

Luckily for him, I ignore that last part. "It's not going to distract me from my ambitions, nor take away my instinct for business."

He chuckles, "I think thou doth protest too much."

I bare my lips, "We'll see, shall we?"

29

Summer

Alphahole: Ms. West, have you forgotten that you are getting married in precisely 3 hours?
    Me: I am trying my best.
    Alphahole: Stop being obstinate.
    Me: Stop being so dominating.
    Alphahole: I was born this way.
    Me: You know what they say about people who try too hard to project themselves?
Silence
    Me: It's that old saying about how those with small balls try to overcompensate in all other fields of life.
    Alphahole: I can assure you my balls are bigger than normal size, as is my dick. As you must have guessed from the way you thrust your pelvis wantonly against my groin.
    Me: Anyone ever told you that you're crude? And does anyone use the word 'wanton' anymore?
    Alphahole: I do.
    Bet the jerk has his lips curled in that smirk. My thighs clench. Damn it, can't I have a single normal interaction with this man without getting hot and bothered? I wipe my clammy palms on my shirt.
    Alphahole: Are you there, Ms. West?
    Me: Does it make a difference?
    Alphahole: No.
    Jerk.
    Alphahole: As long as you turn up for the wedding, I don't care what you wear.
    It'd serve him right if I turned up naked.

Alphahole: Don't do that.

Me: You have no idea what I was thinking.

Alphahole: Don't I? You're too predictable, Pink.

Bite me. I am going to spring a surprise on him, and he won't see it coming.

Alphahole: You won't have the courage to do that after our time together, either.

Me: Stop putting words in my mouth.

Alphahole: That was too easy.

Me: What? Being able to predict that your ego has no bounds? You think you can manipulate anyone and get away with it.

Alphahole: Can't I? I've gotten you to toe the line thus far, haven't I?

I toss the phone aside. Begin to pace. Think of the money in the bank. The million that was already deposited. Another million on the day of the wedding—today—then for every day after until we reach the thirty days, or my father agrees to join forces with him, whatever comes first. If he wasn't holding that video recording over me, I'd have walked out by now.

If he hadn't been holding it over me, I wouldn't have agreed to this in the first place, either. Damn, poverty sucks. Except, I am no longer poor. I just have to get through the next twenty-five days. That's all.

The phone vibrates again and I ignore it. And again. After the third buzz, I swoop down and pick it up.

Alphahole: That was uncalled for, I'm sorry.

Wait, what, he apologized?

Alphahole: Don't expect me to do so again.

Just as I was thinking he had no heart he had to go and break the illusion. That's not good. I don't want to see him as human, for he isn't. He's a freakin' heartless monster and I am best served thinking of him as one.

Alphahole: You there?

No.

Me: Yes.

Alphahole: The doc gave you a clean bill of health.

Right. He'd arranged for his personal doctor to check me out in the privacy of my bedroom yesterday. Of course, he could have warned me about it, but no, why would he? The doctor had shown up and I'd been livid.

I'd wanted to refuse... until common sense had won out.

When he'd recommended I use the contraceptive injection, I'd agreed. Best to be protected. The last thing I want is to become pregnant. I swallow.

Alphahole: I'm clean too.

Riiight... I chew on my lips. *What does that mean?*

Are we going to have sex on the first night of our marriage? My cheeks flush. God, I sound so archaic. Besides, no way do I want to have to sleep with him... Do I?

Silence. A beat. Another, then the dots jump on the screen.

Alphahole: I know what you're thinking.

Me: So you can read my mind now?

Alphahole: Very easily. Right now, you're stressing out that I plan to seduce you on our first night. You're wrong.

Eh?

Alphahole: I'm going to take what is already mine.

Me: I'm not yours.

Alphahole: We'll see.
Me: Fuck you.
Alphahole: I am counting on it. Oh… and Pink
What?
Alphahole: Don't embarrass me.

30

Summer

Embarrass him, huh? If he hadn't goaded me, I wouldn't have fallen in with Karma's plan.

I survey myself in the mirror.

What had I been thinking when I'd agreed to wear the dress that she had created? I'd gone along with the idea, because... yeah, I did want to shock him. Show him that he shouldn't underestimate me. I toss my head.

This entire pretend wedding is a car crash waiting to happen. It's inevitable that everything is going to go wrong. I am nudging it along.

It is his fault, for treating me like... like worse than dirt. Like I don't exist.

Hell, he treats that damn old school watch of his with more affection. At least he massages it, touches it, tinkers with it. He gives it attention.

Me? He dismisses as if I am an errant child, or a dimwit who has no idea what I am doing. Which I don't, I admit. Else why would I have landed in this situation? Faking a wedding that I very much want to be real.

I tighten my fingers around the bouquet of flowers.

There, I've acknowledged it to myself, huh? Although logic dictates that I abhor him, my body cannot deny the effect he has on me.

It isn't that he's good-looking. *Not only.*

It's that complete confidence that clings to his every move, the way he seems to walk into a space and own it, how everyone else in the vicinity acknowledges he is the most lethal of them, how he wears his arrogance with absolute single-mindedness. A cockiness that the world owes him—a mindset that is so alien, so different from everything that I am used to—a sureness I wish I possessed.

Is that what this is? Am I envious of everything he represents? What I lost out on, thanks to the error of my parents? Except, that isn't me. I've always been proud of being my own person and making my way through this world on my own steam. I don't need anyone to rescue me. I don't.

So, what am I doing here? I glance down at my posy.

Wildflowers. White, pink, and violet blooms mixed with green. Thankfully, it isn't the expensive bouquet that Amelie had wanted me to order.

It isn't that I was averse to spending his money... More that every single option that Amelie had shown me in the catering, the decorations, the entire idea of how I'd wanted a wedding to be, well, it had all felt strange.

I'll be honest. I've never spent time imagining my dream wedding.

When you grow up trying to figure out how to survive and where your next meal is going to come from—especially after you had all of it one day and it had been taken from you the next—well, you learn not to think too far out in the future. You really do try and focus on the now and what you have. Maybe it also had to do with my mother's slight obsession with seizing the moment.

Perhaps she had an intuition for things to come, that her life would be brutally cut short one day when she'd contracted blood poisoning. I mean, for hell's sake, what were the odds, huh? The dye from the hand painted fabrics she'd loved wearing had bled into her skin and prolonged exposure to it had killed her. Hell. The mind boggles.

It had wrecked my father enough for him to throw himself into his work.

He'd neglected me and Karma, progressively, and one day had not returned home. Apparently, he hadn't been the above-board businessman he'd made himself out to be. He'd made a series of bad business decisions, then borrowed from the Mafia—*bad idea, Dad*—and when he hadn't been able to pay them back, he'd abandoned us to the system and left the country. The coward.

We'd been lucky to be able to escape with our lives. At least our foster homes hadn't been too bad—I'd heard some of the horror stories of the other kids. I'd thanked our stars that we'd ended up with people who, while they weren't too loving, hadn't been monsters either. And they hadn't separated me and Karma. We'd stayed together until I'd turned sixteen and found myself at a homeless hostel. I had tried to protect her, but my sister's illness had made her far older than her years, too soon.

I raise the blooms to my nose and inhale. The scent of the open countryside envelops me. Whoever had plucked this had known exactly which blooms to fold into the mix.

There's a knock on the door.

"Come in." I face the mirror and survey myself.

Footsteps sound, then Karma's face appears next to mine. "Wow," she breathes.

"Is that good or bad?"

"Umm." She tilts her head. "You look..."

"Go on." I grip my bouquet until my knuckles whiten.

"Nice flowers. Your favorites?"

I glance down at the burst of colors. "Aren't they beautiful? Wonder who got them for me?"

"Maybe Amelie or Isla?" She leans forward, brushes a piece of lint from one of the panels of my dress.

"Maybe." I shift my weight between my feet. "And you haven't answered the question."

Her lips quirk, "Which one?"

"You know," I huff out a breath. "How do I look, Karma?"

She puts distance between us, looks me up and down. Her eyebrows knit. "You look..." She bites her cheek.

"That bad, huh?" I swallow.

"You look... Not as I expected." Her face breaks into a grin. "You're going to make such an impression."

Oh. The breath rushes out of me. "Not too much?"

"Yes, much." She brushes away a strand of hair from my temple. "Isn't that what you were going for? To shock him?"

"Kind of." My heart begins to hammer. "Maybe I should forget about—"

"No."

She grips my hand. "You are strong, gorgeous, one hell of a woman. No one can show you up. No one. You are the queen of all you survey, who can have anything you want. You were born to live an epic life, on your terms. You are going to fulfill your destiny and no alphahole can take that away from you, for you own your power. You are you."

I blink, "Wow."

Her eyebrows furrow, then she straightens herself, pulls away. I swoop down and grab her arm. "Did you mean everything you said?"

She hesitates, then glances away.

"Do you believe in me, Karma?"

She draws in a breath, then tilts her head up. "I do."

Something in my chest lightens. Tears prick the backs of my eyes, and I blink them away. "Thank you."

She nods, shuffles her feet, then peers up at me from under her eyelids, "I also believe in this dress that I created for you."

"Ha." I toss my head. "I can't believe you turned it around so quickly." I grip her shoulder. "Thank you, Sis."

Her chin wobbles.

For a second, I am sure she's going to hug me. I move forward, but she ducks, drops down, straightens the skirt of my dress.

"Your little speech earlier," I wrinkle my brow. "It wasn't from a movie, was it?"

"No."

"Then?"

"Something I read in a self-help book."

"You read self-help books?"

"Naah." She hesitates, "Happened to find it on the tube. I read a few pages, and the sentiment of it stuck with me."

"Hmm."

She rises to her feet, "I really do love the dress. It's audacious, outrageous. It's so not you, that it is you."

I straighten, survey myself, one last time. It made sense in a funny Karma-esque way. "You're right. This time."

She meets my gaze in the mirror. Her eyes are too bright.

"Do you have something in your eyes, Karma?"

"Of course not." She turns her head aside to wipe her cheek. "Come on, you want to be on time."

"On the contrary." I grin. "Let's not."

31

Sin

"She's late."

I crack my neck, shift my weight from foot to foot.

"Where the fuck is she?" I rub the back of my neck, "I hate being kept waiting."

"Better get used to it, old chap." Saint smirks from his position by the window.

"The fuck is that supposed to mean?"

"Simmer down."

"Don't tell me what to do," I grumble, begin to pace.

It's not that I am uncomfortable... Okay, maybe a little. Not because I am the cynosure of all eyes. I thrive on the attention. But the fact that I am here, cooling my heels, in front of the people who know me for always being in charge, the one who calls the shots and ensures everything always runs to plan—that she is making me wait? Unacceptable.

This woman is taking advantage of the fact that I can't do much about it. Not yet, not right now in front of the group of people assembled in the back garden of my house.

Summer loves this space—I'd caught her walking among the flower beds, her head raised to the sun to catch the sun rays—and no that's not why I chose it as the venue for the nuptials. It was practical. That was the only reason... right? I rub the back of my neck.

"Good thing it's not raining, huh?" Saint stares up at the clear blue skies.

"So that's what we've been reduced to talking about, the weather, huh?"

"I'm being considerate of your pride." He shoots me a sideways glance. "Better unlearn that attitude of yours. It's downhill all the way from here."

"Shut your trap, you fuck."

His grin widens, "This is only the beginning, her making you wait at the altar. When you're enjoying marital bliss, don't forget about the reason why you embarked on this trip."

"You have it all wrong."

"Do I?" He arches an eyebrow.

I drag my finger around the collar of my shirt.

A trickle of sweat runs between my shoulder blades. Could do with some cloud cover about now. But, of course, on the one day that I'd counted on the weather behaving per norm, everything has to turn out to be as surprise. I glance at the watch on my wrist. *She's fucking late.*

"Fifteen minutes." Edward's voice interrupts my thoughts.

I peer up at him. "Sixteen minutes now."

"She's the bride."

"It's a fucking pretend wedding." I lower my chin.

"Not from where I am." One side of his lip arches up. The Father is enjoying himself.

"Don't get too used to it." I growl.

"I don't know, from where I am, it's a wonderful sight, seeing you all uncomfortable, Sin."

"Won't last forever. And I demand a 25% share of the profits of FOK Media."

"No way." Edward shakes his head.

"*There* you are." Saint snickers. "Wondered how long it would take for the asshole part of you to show up."

"It was never gone. I had it temporarily shielded out of deference to the rest of you."

Edward frowns. "Here I thought your bride was finally beginning to round off your edges."

"Never." I crack my neck from side to side, trying to loosen the muscles that have somehow knotted themselves up. Where the fuck is she, anyway?

I glance at my watch again. "Seventeen minutes." I breathe. "No one... No one has kept me waiting this long."

"There's always a first time." Saint rocks back on his heels.

"Wait until you stand in this position, dipshit."

He chuckles, "Never gonna happen."

"Never fucking say never." I grumble.

"Think you can refrain from swearing for another few minutes?" Edward stares past me, then stiffens.

An electric tingle runs down my back. *She's here.* Silence descends. A complete and utter stillness. My skin tightens. My throat closes. I should turn, I should. I stare straight ahead. There's no music—my choice. This wasn't supposed to be a fucking happy occasion. It is a formality. I needed enough gravitas to convince her old man, who is about five minutes away from the house, so Peter has informed me. I'd timed this down to the last detail. Good thing they'd been stuck in traffic and had taken a little longer than expected to arrive. That's how much to the last detail I had orchestrated this little circus; the only thing I hadn't expected was for my bride to screw it all up—back up a second. Not my bride—my business partner. No, hostage, in this little arrangement that will ensure I can finally put the ghosts of my past behind me and... Her scent envelops me. Cherries and caramel laced with that mysterious note of anticipation. A uniquely feminine scent that could belong to only one woman. Her.

Don't turn, don't.

I pivot, and every muscle in my body tenses. All of my senses hone in on her. My vision narrows; the blood drums at my temple. *She didn't. No way.*

A long line breaks through the slit on the skirt that runs to mid-thigh. The lace and chiffon clings to the curves of her waist, nipped in to show off that impossibly tiny circumference, that begs me to wrap my hands around her body and haul her close; before I place her across my lap and spank that luscious butt for what she's done. That dress... She doesn't wear it, she owns it. It is her.

The fact that it is a neon pink sets off the color of her hair that pours in glorious waves around her face. Bold. Daring. It personifies that streak of sassiness that she tries so hard to hide, and which slips through the cracks in her facade anyway, especially when I push her. She can't control it. No more than I can rein in the desire that rushes to the fore. My groin hardens. My dick twitches. I take in the proud thrust of her breasts, ensconced in the delicate lace that runs up her chest, and over one shoulder.

I bet if she turns around, I'll see the plunging dip of the dress at the back. My fingers tingle. *How dare she exhibit herself so?*

Next to me, Saint draws in a sharp breath.

I don't need to turn to find out that he's turned on. All of my friends—no, strike that—none of them deserve to be called anything except my most hated acquaintances because they've seen her in that dress.

I want to tear the fabric off of her, bury my nose in the cloth and drag her essence into my lungs. Right before I spin her around, bend her at the waist and claimed her for myself. Imprint myself in every orifice of her body, until every pore on her skin oozes with my sperm. *Fuck.*

"Who is she?"

"What do you mean?" I growl. "She's my bride."

"Not her." Saint jerks his chin. "The other woman, in the golden-brown sheath who just walked in."

The hell is he talking about?

There is no other woman here except the siren wrapped in that delectable dress that I am going to ensure will be burned. Only so that she'll never tease me again with the hint of flesh that peeks from between that slit as she takes a step forward. Another.

Summer's gaze locks with mine, holds.

Her hips sway under the silky soft fabric. Her cheeks are pale, despite the blusher. Good. I narrow my gaze and her throat moves as she swallows. She is within a foot of me when I glare at her. Her pupils dilate. Her chin trembles. She pauses.

Don't give up now, little Bird. Come closer. Closer.

She inches toward me. Her scent deepens. The pulse at the base of her throat flutters with such speed that I am sure she is not only afraid but also aroused. As turned on as I am in this instant, my cock jumps forward, and I widen my stance to accommodate my arousal. Bet it's clear to the rest how aroused I am, but what-bloody-ever.

She takes the final step that brings her within a few inches of me. Nervousness vibrates off of her. She blinks and the chemistry between us seems to ratchet up. Takes another step, then pitches forward.

32

Summer

Fuck, fuckity, fuck.

The floor comes up to meet me. This is it; I am going to fall and ruin every bit of impact I've created so far. Gonna make a fool of myself after all that effort I went to, to appear sexy and alluring. So damn clumsy. *How could you do this, Summer?* I squeeze my eyes shut, wait for the inevitable collision with the floor. A hard band fastens around my waist and I am tugged against a very hard, broad expanse of what seems to be pure, unforgiving, muscle. *No, no, no.* I hold onto the bouquet of flowers. Then scent of bergamot and expensive leather fills my senses.

"You need to look where you are going." His warm breath sears my cheek.

The hair on my forearms stands on end.

"Open your eyes, Bird."

I shake my head.

"You can't postpone it forever. You may as well accept your fate."

Never. I'll fight this... this thing between us, no matter that the attraction thrums at the edges of my nerves. All of my brain cells seem to have turned into mush. My knees tremble. His hold on my waist tightens.

I peer up and my gaze collides with his.

Silver flecks flare deep in those indigo eyes.

"You need to be careful about what you decide to take on."

I tremble and he straightens me. I try to pull away. His grip on my chin tightens. He peers into my eyes, the intensity almost a physical caress. My thighs clench. Damn him and this overwhelming physical response I always have to him. I straighten my spine, hold his attention. Will not look away. Will not. One side of his lips curls. He tilts his head. In acknowledgement? An acceptance of the battle lines that I have drawn?

Why am I intent on making this difficult for the two of us? Why can't I fall in line with whatever he has in his mind, toe the line, and then walk away unharmed? Because that is never going to happen. If I give in to him, he'll only want more. The only way to come out of this in one piece is to hold my own. To dig in my heels and show him that he can't take me for granted. If that means I have to resort to grandstanding, then so be it.

"I know exactly what I am taking on." I jut out my chin.

"Oh?"

I tilt my head back, not breaking our connection. "Question is, do you?"

His nostrils flare; the skin around his eyes tightens. A cloud of heat spools off of his body and slams into my chest. I gasp.

The weight of his dominance seems to intensify, pinning me in place. I can't move. Can't breathe. Can't turn away from the heavy weight of his presence which seems to coil around me, squeezing my hips, my thighs. I gulp. A bead of sweat slides down between my breasts and his gaze darts down, then swivels up to my face. His lips curl in that infernal smirk. All of my nerve-endings seem to flare at once. Damn the man.

"Typically, you'd kiss the bride after the wedding, but perhaps you want to do the honors now?"

A voice cuts through the tension between us. I stiffen.

He leans in closer, drops his head until our eyelashes tangle. I part my lips. *Do it. Please.* My breath catches.

Sinclair lets go of me so suddenly that I stumble, then right myself. *Jerk.*

I clutch the stems of my flowers with such force that my nails bite through the tender stems and into the palms of my hands. Why did I think this day would be any different from the other times we've spent together, eh?

He turns to face the minister. "I can wait."

A hot feeling stabs inside my chest. I didn't want him to kiss me anyway. So why is there a heaviness behind my eyes? I raise my head, stare forward.

The minister's lips move. I don't hear what he's saying. I stare past him at the wall at the far side of the property—the water rippling down the surface, the birds that fly off a tree to the side, taking with them, the last of my composure. My lips tremble. Damn the man.

"Sinclair Amadeus Sterling, do you take Summer Cora West as your lawfully wedded wife?"

"I do."

I hear the words as if from far away. Above me, the wind picks up. A gust blows past me and I stagger. *I can't do this. I can't.* The world swims around me. The minister's face fades in and out in front of my eyes. *I. Can't.*

A wide palm grips my fingers, coaxes me to loosen my grip. I watch as the bouquet slips from my fingers. He catches it midair, hands it to someone next to me.

Sinclair tugs at my arm and I turn to face him.

Indigo eyes fill my vision. Turquoise and cerulean and so many shades of cyan that they seem to reflect the skies overhead.

"Summer Cora West, do you take Sinclair Amadeus Sterling as your lawfully wedded husband to love, respect and to obey?"

I blink. *Obey?* Of course, he'd highlight that, huh?

His gaze intensifies. Those dark pupils seem to sweep away all barriers and tear right into my soul. He can see me naked. All of my fears and hopes and aspirations—he owns all of them. I've been his from the moment I set eyes on him. When he'd commanded me, the bartender, that I'd had enough. When he'd swept into my life with the force of a hurricane sweeping aside all protests. I never stood a chance. I'd added my yes to his every command. And yet I am here, standing in front of him, trying to make a last stand. A ball of emotion plugs my throat. I try to draw in a breath and my lungs burn. I shake my head. Open my mouth.

His glare deepens. Then he drops his head and closes his mouth over mine. He thrusts his tongue between my lips, draws on any remaining air I had left. He sucks from me, drinks from me, buries his teeth into my lower lip with such force that I taste blood. Pain sweeps down my spine. My thighs spasm. All thoughts drain from my mind. A silence replaces the screaming echoes in my head. He softens the kiss, swipes his tongue across my lower lip. Once, twice. A trembling springs to life, low in my womb. A moan bleeds from my mouth and he swallows it up. His entire body seems to shudder. Nah, must be my imagination. The next second he pulls away. Searches my features. He must have found what he was looking for, for he nods.

"Ask her again." He addresses the priest without taking his eyes off of me.

"Sin…" the priest's voice has an edge of something hard to it.

"Do it." He growls.

Silence for another beat, then the priest asks the question.

Sinclair doesn't break the connection between us. He rubs his thumb over my wrist, a gentle circle that leaves a trail of sparks in his wake. I gulp.

"Summer?" The priest's voice coaxes me.

Sweat beads my palms.

"I do."

My heartbeat ratchets up. My guts churn. A gust of wind blows my hair about my face and I shiver.

He pushes the strands of hair away from my temples. "You did well, Bird." His lips quirk.

Something warm coils in my chest. I can't tear my gaze from his features. Those high cheekbones, that hooked nose, and the pouty thrust of his lower lip.

"Do you have the rings, Sinclair?"

His features harden.

"Sin?"

His jaw tics. "No rings."

Oh! I blink. What had I expected? That he'd have rings for the both of us? I mean, I hadn't consciously thought of it, to be honest. I'd assumed, though, that he'd surprise me. And he had, just not in the way I'd expected.

His features harden and he scans my features again. If he wants a reaction, he'll be disappointed. It's better this way. No physical signs that there is anything between us… Nothing except that piece of footage which he holds over me, which ensures that I'll comply with his every demand. I firm my lips.

"… I now proclaim you man and wife. You may now kiss the bride."

He lowers his head, I turn my face, and his lips brush my cheek.

He whispers, "Enjoy your last few seconds of freedom, for soon you'll be caged."

I draw in a sharp breath, peer up to find his lips curved in a smirk. He tilts his head, and the fire in those eyes switches off. How does he do it? Blow hot one second and cold the next. Why can't I be that heartless, that single-minded in my quest? Because I am too human, too emotional. Too good for him. I am no match for his iron will, the sheer strength of determination that resides in every pore of his body. And I am wedded to him… At least, for the next twenty-five days. Anger floods my chest and my guts heave. I raise my palm.

He shakes his head. "You'll regret it."

He's right.

The realization sinks into me, at the same time a trembling grips my body. The pulse thuds at my temples; adrenaline laces my blood. I need to get away from him before I have a complete breakdown. I pivot and rush down the path I had taken earlier, when a man steps in front of me.

Tall, broad shoulders, gray streaks his temples. His green eyes with specks of gray similar to mine brighten with recognition.

"Summer, look at you, my little girl, all grown up."

33

Sin

"Father?" Her spine tenses.

The older man walks toward her.

"I'm sorry I wasn't here to walk you down the aisle."

I'd made sure of that. One of the many wedding gifts I'd had in store for my new bride.

Her father extends his hand, and she flinches. He folds his arm around her and draws her in for an embrace.

She stands stiffly in the circle of his arms as he pats her back.

She cringes and I clench my fists. Of course, I hadn't expected the meeting between them to be effusive. After all, the man had abandoned his daughters and left them to their own fate. But hey, I'm not completely heartless. I had given her enough warning that he would be here… She hadn't known exactly when and I'd made sure it would be at her weakest. I'd wanted to see her fall apart in front of her father. Wanted to see how he'd react to seeing her after all this time. Well, I have my answer. The bastard is gloating at the chance to use her to further his own interests, while Summer is in complete shock.

If she'd been close to falling apart earlier, clearly, she's reached the end of her tether.

Adam's features twist. He glances past her and his gaze locks with mine. I tilt my head.

What will he do next? How will he orchestrate the rest of the meeting on which depends the rest of his future? This is what I excel at, right? Putting the pawns together, watching their interaction, enjoying their discomfort, and waiting for something to give. It's how I've won my business successes. Constantly on the move, looking for my next victim, which in this case, happens to be him.

I should be happy, celebrating how I am so very close to getting revenge for everything I had lost. So, why is my heart heavy? Why is there a burning sensation in my gut?

Adam's lips twist in a half smile. He grips her arm; she pulls away.

He wraps his arm around her shoulders and every muscle in her body goes rigid. *Fuck this.* I cross the distance to them.

"Aren't you going to introduce us, Summer?"

She doesn't react.

I slide my arm around her waist, tug her close.

Adam steps back, a gleam in his dark eyes.

Bastard had been trying to get a response out of me. He'd been trying to gauge how far my feelings for his daughter actually go. Have I underestimated him? I frown. Did I make a mistake by calling him to be witness to this wedding?

Does Adam actually care about his daughter or is he trying to figure out how much I do, then use it against me?

It doesn't matter. I'll find a way to get what I want from him. I always do. Right now, I need to get my wife away from the cause of her discomfort.

Her body trembles and I tuck her into my side.

"Adam Rhodes." The older man thrusts out his hand. "Pleasure to meet you."

I glare at his palm, then tip my chin up, "Can't say the same."

Summer shifts her weight from foot to foot.

I rub the curve of her hip, and she draws in a breath. Some of the tension seems to drain out of her. Good.

"Well, at least you're straight talking. We have that in common."

"Do we?" I thrust out my chin.

He raises his hands, "You invited me, Sinclair. When do we talk about the business proposition?"

My gut clenches and I tighten my hold on Summer. "You came this far for your daughter's wedding, the least you could do is pretend to be happy on her behalf."

"Hmm." He taps his chin. "Oh, I think my daughter understands how happy I am on her behalf." He peers sideways. "Don't you, Summer?"

She drops her head and her features fold into a hardened mask. I've never seen Summer this... cold, this defeated. She's been sassy, full of life, angry and upset... but always, always she's worn her emotions on her sleeve. It's one of the things I've come to expect of her, that she can't hide from me. That is also her appeal. It gives me the security that she'll speak her mind, challenge me, always get a rise from me. It is a fucking turn on. It's also what I miss the most right now. I don't relish seeing her this defeated, this on the verge of being broken... Only I get to do that.

"My wife is tired."

Summer doesn't react to my using that term aloud. *Damn it, that isn't good. Why isn't she saying something?*

"I think she needs to get some rest."

"Of course," he angles his body, "but first I want her to meet someone."

"Victoria," he beckons to the woman behind him. "Come dear, meet your stepdaughter."

A woman steps forward. She's wearing an exquisite golden-brown dress that falls to below her knees. The cut clings to her curves and highlights her pale skin. Her dark hair is a lustrous cloud about her shoulders. She's at least two decades younger than Adam, about Summer's age. Broad forehead, sharp features, her ethereal beauty is enhanced by the haunted look in her eyes.

Behind me, I hear a sharp inhalation of breath. Saint draws abreast with me. I glance sideways and find him staring at Victoria.

Victoria frowns then inches away from Adam. Her movement also takes her closer to Saint, who stares between the two of them.

"Summer, it's lovely to meet you." Victoria stretches out a hand.

Summer swallows. "I didn't realize…"

"That you had a stepmother?"

"…that I had a father." She spits out the words, then straightens.

Adam's jaw firms. "I was hoping you two could get acquainted."

Saint shuffles his feet; his hands are clenched at his sides. Huh? It's as if the man is upset about something.

Victoria's lips twist, "I didn't mean for this to come as such a surprise. I wish there had been a way I could have warned you of our coming… but…"

Summer nods, "You don't need to apologize." Her gaze travels to her father, her eyes narrowing, "I understand how it could have been."

No doubt, the bastard planned this out, springing his new wife on his daughter. I clench my fists at my sides.

Victoria glances from Summer to me, "Perhaps, we can catch up once you are recovered from your wedding and the honeymoon —"

"There is no honeymoon." I interject.

Summer's body tenses again.

Damn it, I hadn't meant for it to come out quite that way… Okay, so I *had* planned to drop that little piece of knowledge at the most opportune time, which is clearly now, seeing the way Summer's breath caught in her chest. She tries to pull away and I grip her to me tighter.

"Not until we've sorted out the little business between us." I nod toward Adam. "Tomorrow."

Why am I postponing this meeting, one for which I've waited for so long?

I step around the couple. Summer follows my lead without protest. That's so not like her. Clearly, her father's presence has completely taken the spirit out of her. It's not exactly what I'd intended. And I don't like it, not one bit. I increase my pace, dragging her along.

I hear Saint strike up a conversation with Adam's wife, "So, Victoria, is it?"

"Mrs. Rhodes to you." Victoria cuts him off. "Are you the hired help?"

34

Summer

"Did she actually ask him that?"

I turn to Sinclair in time to see his lips twitch.

"I do believe the chemistry between Saint and your stepmother is interesting, to say the least."

"He's not the kind who'd seduce a married woman—"

Sinclair shakes his head. "Not that he has many ethics... But *that's* something he steers clear of. Which is one reason I find that scene intriguing."

"You could have warned me that he remarried." I tug my arm free from his and he lets me go. His warmth recedes and chills pepper my arm.

"So could you." He jerks his chin to my dress.

"It's not the same thing."

"Oh?" He tilts his head, "My wife parading herself in almost next to nothing—"

"This is a completely decent dress—"

"Not." He growls, taking the steps two at a time.

I increase my pace to keep up with him. "Aaannd... I'm only your pretend wife," I pant.

His jaw tics and a vein bulges at his temple.

"So, you can't really tell me what to do or wear, considering I don't even have your ring on my finger."

Reaching the landing leading to his room, he stops, turns to peruse my features. "Is that why you're pouting?"

I force all emotions from my features. "This is my normal resting face."

"And it's a beautiful one, too."

"Did you pay me a compliment?"

He frowns.

"Yes. No." He drags his fingers through his hair. "Maybe."

I go to brush past him and he stops me. "I had your belongings moved."

"Huh?"

He jerks his chin toward the closed double doors. "My suite."

"Bu… but."

"We need to put up enough of a front for people to buy into the pretense."

"No one's gonna pry into your living quarters, are they?"

"They wouldn't dare." He widens his stance, "Consider it a precaution. As much as I trust my staff—I wouldn't have them employed if I didn't—still, I am not taking any chances until the deal is done."

"But—"

He blows out a breath. "Look, Summer, you look beat and I could do with a rest, before we have to join the guests for dinner."

I pale.

"I don't think I can survive having to put up this pretense again today."

"Tell me about it," he mutters. The lines around his mouth seem pronounced. His hair is mussed—from standing outside and because he'd run his hands through the thick strands. Not that I had been watching him closely or anything.

"Can we have this conversation inside my suite?" He runs a finger around his collar as if he finds it particularly constricting. He isn't wearing a tie. Come to think of it, I've never seen him in one, in the little time I've known him.

He shoves open the double doors.

I hesitate.

He raises his shoulders, "Suit yourself." He disappears inside.

I shift my weight from foot to foot, grab a strand of hair and begin to chew on it. Better stop that. Don't want him to realize how nervous I am feeling right now. I walk toward the suite. Then step inside. The doors shut behind me with a snick.

The living space is massive. Three times the size of the room I had occupied. Right. Lifestyles of the rich and famous, huh? I walk to the massive window and peek outside.

A balcony wraps around the entire floor. On one side of the house the rolling slope of Primrose Hill extends down. I turn the other way and the skyline of London stretches in the distance. It's rare to get a panoramic view of the city, considering government regulations dictate that you can't build above a certain height. To see it here at will is a treat.

The sound of water running in a bath reaches me. I turn, walk toward the door that leads into the bedroom. The room sprawls out about the same size as the one I'd left behind. The pride of place is the massive king size bed that takes up almost one wall. It's draped in a royal blue, the sheets flowing down the sides.

Large pillows are thrown against the headboard, which is made of unembellished wood. At the foot of the bed is a bench, on which he's discarded his jacket.

The sound of running water grows louder. He stalks out of the bath, his shirt sleeves rolled up. I take in the veins that run up the sides of his powerful forearms. Does the man work out? He has to, considering the shape he is in. The light from the bath highlights the gap between his narrow waist and his forearms. His pants cling to his powerful thigh muscles, showing off the bulge between his legs. Is that his normal resting condition? The man's packing all right, as I discovered from my brush with that particular muscle of his anatomy.

"If you keep staring at me, I'll think you want me to exercise my husbandly duties."

My cheeks burn. I glance up at his face, to find his lips curled in that smirk that I am coming to associate with him. Why does he have to be so overpoweringly handsome, so completely sure of himself? It's part of his appeal and yet—it also makes me want to say something to show him I am not affected by him. *Liar.*

"Where do I sleep?"

He glances past me.

"But there's only one bed—"

"Which is wide enough for the two of us to sleep without touching each other all night.

I chew on my lower lip.

"Trust me." He looks me up and down, "I am acquainted with what you have under that dress, and while I'd love to shag you, I promise you I am not that hard up."

"That's not what it looked like when you finger fucked me in the conference room."

"There was a reason for doing that."

The video.

He prowls past me, walks toward another door at the far end and shoves it open. He glances back, "I ran a bath for you."

The hell? I walk to the bathroom door and peek inside. It's a beautiful bright space, wide enough to run the length of the bedroom and the living room, a sunken tub takes up a large portion of one entire wall. Beyond that, huge windows open out to let the sunlight inside. To the other side are twin sinks. Piles of folded towels, soap bottles, other bottles of various sizes and colors grace one of the sinks.

I pivot around and he drawls, "You're welcome, by the way."

"You had to go and spoil it by saying that?"

He leans his hip against doorway to the walk-in closet. "Ah, but that's the point. You're still trying to find something nice about me, when really, every single move of mine is calculated to ensure that I get closer to my goal."

"Your revenge, your empire, that's all that matters."

He folds his arms across that broad chest, "Is there anything else?"

"Obviously, *The Wolf of Wall Street*, took lessons from you."

"Actually, it was Gordon fucking Gekko." He smirks.

"This entire thing is a freakin' joke for you, huh?"

"On the contrary." His smile switches off, "I've never been more serious about anything else in my life."

A nerve throbs at his temple. His gaze intensifies.

My breath hitches, my pulse pounds, and liquid heat curls between my legs. I don't realize I've taken a step forward, until he straightens.

He nods toward the bath, "Rest up, Bird, you're going to need it."

35

Sin

"Surprised you went through with the reception, bro." Damian, the self-designated bartender for the evening, hands me a tumbler of whiskey. I grip the glass, toss back its contents.

He raises an eyebrow, but tops me up.

"You okay?"

"Peachy." I suck down the 200-year-old whiskey like it's going out of fashion.

"How's the bridegroom?"

I glance up to find Jace walk in, flanked by Arpad and Weston.

I scowl, "What are you doing here?"

"Wouldn't have missed seeing you hitched for the world, bro. Besides, your friends made sure I knew the date and time."

"Sinclair." A woman shoves herself between Jace and Arpad. The men move apart, and she stalks through. "How could you?"

Bloody hell! "Sienna?" I hold out my glass, Damian shakes his head. "You're drinking this way too fast. You need to be sober."

"Bollocks." I grab the bottle from Damian and top myself up. I'm halfway through emptying the contents of the glass before Sienna reaches me.

"Really, Sin. You thought you could get away with keeping this a secret?"

"I prefer to keep things low-key."

"Huh?" She props a hand on her hip, "You expect me to believe that?"

"Umm." Damn it, I don't want to lie to her.

Sienna and Jace are the only two outside of the circle of the Seven that I'd count as friends. I survey the room. The fuck do I do with this bottle anyway? Damian takes it from me. I shoot him a grateful glance, as he shakes his head and walks off. "You tell him, Sienna. He hasn't introduced his bride to us yet."

Her gaze widens. "Why, Sinclair, how could you?"

"It's not like that." I glance past the comfortable chairs arranged on the decking. Everyone who means something to me—not necessarily in the friend space, but you know what I mean—is there. They look at me with varying expressions of curiosity. There's a hum of anticipation in the air. They're waiting for the bride to arrive. Well, technically so am I, though I don't want to admit it.

A laugh breaks out from a corner, and I turn to find Amelie, engaged in animated discussion with Isla and Karma.

Weston follows my gaze. "Who's that?"

Like I care.

"Why don't you go ahead and introduce yourself? You can find out for yourself that way."

"Maybe I'll do just that, but first..." He turns to the bar and pours out two flutes of champagne. "Can't believe you trusted this wanker to man the bar." He jerks his chin at Damian.

"Hello to you, too." Damian raises his whiskey tumbler and takes a sip. "I do think I am livening up the environment quite nicely."

"Surely you mean bringing down the collective IQ of the place by a hundred, old chap?" Weston chuckles.

Sienna looks between them. "You guys are so delightfully British."

Jace saunters up, pulls her close. "It's the only time I am thankful to my old man for insisting that I go to boarding school in the UK. That accent always does it." He palms her stomach.

"As long as our son or daughter speaks like you, I'm good." She peers up at him.

Damian straightens, "When are you due?"

"*We* are due in less than four weeks." Jace's chest seems to expand.

Well fuck, the man's done for. Hook, line and sinker.

"I am right chuffed for the both of you." Weston straightens. "However, I see something that needs my attention." He excuses himself and walks over to Amelie.

The three women fall silent as Amelie eyes him suspiciously.

Good for her. She has street smarts written all over her, unlike my wife who is clearly trusting. She has to be for having allowed herself to be ensnared by me. And why do I keep insisting on calling her mine? When she isn't. I haven't touched her, not since that day in my conference room, when I had almost come in my pants, as I had fingered her to orgasm. The taste of her lips, the feel of that soft wet core as she had climaxed on my fingers. The hair on the nape of my neck rises.

I pivot and see her.

She stands at the doorway, the simple pale pink-colored sheath covering her from the high collar to below her knees.

I'd chosen it for her from the wardrobe I'd had delivered for her. It is the most conservative of all the dresses I'd personally picked out for her. What I hadn't counted on was that the sheer simplicity of the cut brings out her curves. It enhances her luscious figure rather than hide it. And the color... The soft pink deepens the flush of her cheeks and compliments the highlights in her hair. My mouth waters. My groin tightens.

I want to lick up the creaminess of her skin, bury my nose in her scented hair, grab the upright perkiness of her breasts and squeeze until her nipples bead, her thighs clench, and the soft flesh between her legs melts with anticipation for me. My cock. My essence inside of her, filling her up and overflowing from her every orifice. *Fuck*. I squeeze my eyes shut, shake my head. When I crack my eyelids open, she's still there. She surveys the room and her gaze homes in on me.

She swallows and I swear I can hear the sound from across the space of the room. She tips her chin up. My dick instantly mirrors the move. This woman... I'd sense her in a packed stadium. Blindfold me and I'll home in on her in a crowded room.

Every pore in my being snaps to attention, every muscle in my body coils with tension. If you cut me open now, my flesh would hum with the need for her. To be inside of her. To pin her to the ground with my cock and thrust into her.

Shag her, mark her, claim her.

The bloody hell—?

One make-believe almost-ceremony and I want to show the world who she truly belongs to. Why is that? Why does it matter that every damn male gaze in the room is drawn to her? And yes, they are people whom I trust, as much as I can trust anyone, and who'd never breach their loyalty for me—well, all except Saint. That twat, I don't trust. He throws me a smirk. Then crosses the floor toward her. *The fuck—?* What does he think he's doing?

Only when my feet eat up the ground in front of me, do I realize I am moving.

I stalk toward my newly-wedded wife—apparently being at the ceremony did not get the message home to my soon-to-be-murdered ex-friend and business partner—when a man steps in front of me.

36

Summer

What's wrong with him?

Sinclair pauses to speak to my father, his gaze never wavering from me. His nostrils flare; his eyebrows knit. Those indigo eyes blaze as if he's got murder on his mind. Why the hell is he so angry?

Was it something I did?

He fists his fingers at his sides; the skin stretches white at his knuckles. Huh? There's a fierceness to the set of his features that hasn't been there before.

"Jealousy suits him, don't you think?"

His friend steps in front, cutting off Sinclair from my line of sight. That is, if you could call this six-foot six-inch giant of a man—with the elegant gait and the £10,000 pound suits to rival—a friend.

He holds out his hand. "I'm Saint."

"No, you're mistaken." I tilt my head back, all the way back, to peer into his eyes. What is it with these guys? Did they put something in their water growing up, that all of them seem larger than life?

"Trust me when I say this. I've known Sin for a long time, and I've never seen him so riled up about a woman before."

"Maybe it has something to do with—" I hesitate. How much is this guy aware of Sinclair's agenda, huh?

"Revenge?" His lips quirk, "Your father?"

I nod.

"That's primary on all our minds right now. Why do you think all of us—well most of us—are here today?"

"Not for the wedding—" I mumble.

"—As much as to pin your father into a corner and make him, and the men he worked for, pay."

He holds out his arm and I take it. He leads me to the side.

I glance behind to see that the rest of the men have closed in on where Sinclair and Adam are speaking.

"What did my father do to make all of you so hellbent on revenge?" I chew on my lower lip.

Saint stiffens, "How much has Sinclair told you about what happened to us?"

"Nothing." I huff out a breath. Why would he? He doesn't have to. He doesn't owe me anything, except I am now his lawfully wedded wife. No, not even that. "He didn't have to, right? After all he—"

"—Coerced you into this wedding, huh?"

I shoot him a sideways glance, "You don't think I would have done this willingly, do you?"

"Well, he has a way with women."

"Not this one." I pull away from him and he holds on.

"It's in your interest to play along."

"Huh?"

"You want something out of this entire arrangement."

"I'm already getting—"

"Other than a monetary pay off."

"Are all of you as egotistical as him?"

"The jury is out on that. We each have our strengths." He looks up, and I follow his line of sight to the woman standing on her own, staring into the fireplace.

"And weaknesses, apparently," I mutter under my breath.

He shoots me a quick glance. "How well do you know Victoria?"

So, he doesn't want to refer to her as my stepmother, huh?

"First time I've met her."

"Ask her to meet me before she leaves for the States."

"Why?"

"I have a proposition for her."

"Why would she be interested?"

He rakes her figure from head to toe, "Trust me, women like her always are."

I stiffen. I owe nothing to Victoria, but she... is family... sort of. It isn't that I want to look out for her, or my dad... A little bit maybe. Besides, what is Saint's motivation here?

I frown. "We've only just met."

"So?" He pats my hand. "You help me, and I promise, I'll help you find a way to get even with Sterling there."

"I thought you were friends."

"Of the competitive kind.'

"Why do you want to meet her?"

"My intentions, I promise you, are..." He hesitates. "I want to get to know her better."

"You want to get in her pants."

He chuckles. "That too. I won't hurt her." He peruses my features. "Not unless she wants me to."

Does he have the same proclivities that Sinclair has hinted at? "Did whatever happened to all of you... result in the same warped tastes tainting each of you?"

He frowns, then drops my hand, "You'll have to ask Sterling that."

"I thought you were going to help me with him?"

"What do you want to know?"

"What's his weakness?"

His lip curls; he surveys me from toe to head.

"No, you're wrong."

"Yes."

"I don't understand.'

"You, Summer West, have singularly ruffled him. You've gotten under his skin to an extent you don't realize."

"What do you mean?"

"This marriage, it wasn't part of the plan."

"Oh."

"We tried to dissuade him."

"We?"

"The Seven." He makes a circular motion with his fingers.

Ah! I scan the faces of the men in the room.

"Jace isn't one of us," he adds. "The Seventh, Baron, is not here currently." Saint slides his hand into his pocket, every inch the picture of a self-assured, domineering, upper-class twat. "Sinclair feels something for you. He's so far gone in his emotions that he doesn't realize how much he is vested in this sham."

My heart begins to thud. "What are you trying to say?" I can guess, but I want him to tell me. Want to hear it in his own words.

"You, my dear, are his weakness."

A hand descends on his shoulder. I glance past Saint to find Sinclair glaring at me. "Get away from her."

"Just a conversation, old chap."

"Anything you want to say to her, goes through me."

"Hold on a second." I huff, "I am still here."

Saint steps away, "Whatever you say." He turns to me, "Ask her, will you?"

Sinclair plants his body between us, "Here, asshole," he indicates his face, "you direct your questions here."

Saint's eyebrows fly up. "Possessive much?"

"Bugger off."

"You can take the man out of the gutter, but not the upbringing that clings to every part of your core, eh?"

Every muscle in Sinclair's body goes solid. His shoulders seem to bulge, stretching the already tight fit of his shirt. He withdraws his arm and I grab it. "Don't."

The tension radiates off of him, under his skin. The warmth of his body sinks into my fingertips, travels straight to its logical destination. My core.

I dig my fingertips into his forearm. He's so big that I have to use both of my hands to circle the circumference of his muscle. "Please."

He leans forward on the balls of his feet; his jaw tics. "I am going to kill you for touching her."

I stare. *What's gotten into him?*

Saint glowers, "Getting tired of your empty threats, Sterling."

Oh, for heaven's sake!

I shove my body between the two of them.

Sinclair glares at Saint.

I stand on my tiptoes and grab Sin's collar.

"What the—?" He glances down.

I tug him toward me, rise up on my tiptoes and kiss him.

His lips are softer than I remembered them to be. Which must be my imagination because there's nothing soft about this man. I nibble on his lower lip, and his entire body goes solid. He stays there, unmoving. I'm trying to distract him from getting into a fight? *Why?*

Why does it matter to me, that I don't want him to embarrass himself in front of his friends? They know him better than I do, for much longer than I have. They are probably used to him creating a scene. But instinct had taken over, and a surge of possessiveness, maybe. My heart stutters. For that second, I'd felt a kernel of ownership over him, concern about his reputation. Or a thrill at the fact that he'd been jealous because another man had touched me? Either way, I had been stupid to act on impulse. I disentangle my arms and step back.

"Sorry." I mumble. "That was not warranted."

I angle my body with the intent of leaving. The next second his arms loop around my waist. I squeak. He hauls me up and to him. His mouth crashes down on mine. I gasp aloud and the sound is lost, consumed by him.

His tongue thrusts between my open lips, tangles with mine.

The dark taste of him fills my palate. The heat of his body slams into me, surrounds me and ties me to him. His palm cups my cheek, cradling my head, tilts my face up, deepening the kiss further. He yanks me close, until my breasts are flattened against the unforgiving wall of his chest. My nipples bead and my sex clenches. Every pore in my body seems to open with anticipation, and still, he doesn't stop.

His teeth clash with mine, his tongue laps at mine, the scent of him fills my senses. His hard thighs cradle my hips and the turgid length of his cock jumps against my core. I swallow, try to pull away, but his large fingers wrap around my neck. I stutter. He holds me in place, every millimeter of my body pressed against his, branding me, owning me, a clear signal that I am his.

I won't be able to escape him. Will not be able to leave this relationship unhurt. He's possessed my soul since the second he'd laid eyes on me, had claimed my body from the moment he'd met me. I'd been so wrong to think that I could find my way out of this, because I can't. I am caught, going to burn up in the flames that are Sinclair Sterling, for he gives no quarter. Cares for no one. Looks out for no one, except himself... and perhaps, the Seven?

A trembling sweeps up my body. My hands shake and my knees knock together. The utter rightness of my thoughts sinks into my bones. My heart begins to thud. He is every bit the untamable alpha male that his reputation paints him to be. Is that why I am so drawn to him, unable to pull away from him, as he ravages my mouth, brands me with his touch? Is that why I can't stop the moan that bleeds from my mouth? He bites down on my lower lip. I gasp. Goosebumps dot my skin. He tears his mouth from mine, and I sway.

"Look at me."

I crack open my eyelids, meet that indigo gaze. The silver flecks in them flare.

"You're mine, Bird."

I swallow. Can't look away. Can't refute the heated possessiveness in his eyes.

The sound of clapping reaches me. I wince. My shoulders shake. He wraps his arm around me, turns me around and tucks me into his side.

My hands and feet are so numb. A cold sensation slides down my back, and I shiver.

He tugs me closer, searing my side with the heat of his intention. My throat goes dry. He wants me, that much is clear. That doesn't change anything. Yet something has shifted in the last few seconds. The balance has tilted further in his favor, if that is possible. I want him, want to feel his touch on my skin. Yet everything inside of me wants to turn him away. My head spins.

The blonde man from behind the bar, steps around the barrier. Comes toward us with two glasses of Champagne. "A toast."

Sinclair takes the two glasses and hands me one.

The voices in the room quieten. A beat, another.

He releases me, only to step around to face me.

I stare at the strong cords of his throat. If I leaned in, I could press my nose to the space between them, inhale that dark edgy scent of his. I shiver.

"The moment I saw you, I knew you were the one, Summer."

A hush descends on the room. I swallow hard, and in the silence, hear the blood pound in my ears.

"Then you walked into that elevator and I was sure." He pauses, unbuttons his jacket. His white shirt clings to the hard planes of his chest, the buttons opened enough to reveal a few strands of black hair. Heat pools between my legs and I squeeze my thighs together.

"The third time I saw you, you were talking to yourself."

What? I tilt my chin up and—mistake, *dammit*—his gaze locks with mine.

My throat closes and my pulse begins to race. His eyes gleam with sincerity; a warmth that draws me in and insists that he's telling the truth. Is he? The skin around his eyes creases.

"That's when I fell in love with you."

I blink. This man... he's such a consummate liar. If anyone could reflect their heart in their eyes, then it would be him, in this instant.

"I knew then, I had to make you mine. To tie you to me irrevocably, so you could never leave me."

A sigh sounds from behind me. A drawn breath. Can no one here see through his pretense?

He moves closer and the chemistry between us ratchets up. His broad shoulders shut out the sight of everyone else. He could be talking only to me, revealing his true self. I watch entranced, a part of me applauding at the show he's putting on.

"For, you complete me."

He did not just say that.

The most overrated movie dialogue of all time; and he's using it at this precise moment.

If he'd wanted to cut right through my heart, he couldn't have done it better. Oh, he's smart, this man. He knows me too well. Knows how to throttle every last one of my silly desires.

Someone claps, and another, and a third joins in.

Without anyone in the room realizing what he's done.

"I am the luckiest man alive to be able to call you my wife."

I turn away, tears pricking my eyes. My throat closes. Pressure builds at my temples.

"Summer Sterling."

The complete confidence in his tone lashes me about my shoulders. I strain against the pull he exerts on me, force myself to take another step forward. And another.

"Can I call you by my name?"

I pause. My feet refuse to move. Damn this man. How can he throw me down one moment, then lift me up high above the clouds, make me reach for the sun the next?

Doesn't he realize how cruel it is when he does that?

It will leave me floundering in the gutter, mired in the throes of the passion that laces his words; the one that compels me to turn around and swallow.

"Never."

37

Sin

She wasn't supposed to be this smart, this magnificent, this able to match me step for step.

After that rejoinder to my completely unplanned speech—yeah, that's how much she's managed to throw me off course—the entire room had gone silent. Anger had crawled down my spine, mixed with fierce pride.

Then the room had erupted in applause.

"Bravo." Arpad had come forward and kissed her on both cheeks. I hadn't stopped him, only because the tosser's heart is keen on someone else. Besides, it is a typical Gaelic affectation, one that I'd let him get away with, this once.

Her friends had surrounded her. Saint had held back. Good. Guess he'd gotten the message, finally. Don't hold your breath.

I'd stepped forward and the crowd had parted.

Had approached my new bride. "Touché, Darling." I'd raised my glass at her, and she'd shot me a look, one filled with so much anger that my dick had jumped to attention. *Fuck.*

She'd jutted out her chin, held my attention, refused to cave in as I'd glared at her; and that took a lot of courage. Not even the Seven—except Saint, maybe—would have taken up the gauntlet I'd thrown down. She had.

She'd known what I had been up to; that I'd used her love for movie trivia against her. I hadn't been kidding when I'd said that I was a master at it—an old love, that I had forgotten and which she'd rekindled in the past few days. I was using it to undermine her. It could have very much been code language that I was speaking. I had intended the underlying meaning for her, had no idea if she'd pick up on it. Especially the last movie title I had pulled on her? It wasn't a mainstream Hollywood film but an Indie flick based on a novel. *The fuck?* Those forgotten loves from my childhood... of reading, running in the countryside. Those had been idyllic days before her father had changed my life forever.

It's why I had tracked her down, ensured that she'd have to agree to my plans. Only she'd overthrown them completely. She'd turned out to be something completely different. She may be younger than me in years, except she makes up for it by her sheer determination. That hunger for survival which had kept me going all through the time that the Seven and I had almost lost our lives—? I sense that naked intent in her too. She's my perfect foil. I couldn't have chosen a better life-partner if I had set out to intentionally find one. I stiffen. The accuracy of my words sinks into my blood, confirming what I already knew. I need to stop this crazy one-track road to my destruction. Need to focus on the end goal. The big finish I have been setting up for so long.

The end of her father, destroying him so he no longer has the will to survive. Which, means one thing—taking away his money, his freedom, his new wife, and any remaining connection to his daughters.

And getting permanently tangled up in *her* life, with her relationship to him always at the forefront of my mind, is unacceptable. It is time I fuck her out of my system.

I glance up from the window of my bedroom, twist my neck to find her by the entrance. I'd made our excuses and hustled her here.

Not that anyone would have missed us.

Each of the Seven knew what was expected of them. All of the players were assembled on the lawn below. They'd do their bit. It was time I put my own plan in action.

"Shut the door."

She trembles, and I tilt my head.

She firms her lips, turns and slams the doors inward. They close with a soft snick.

"Look at me."

She hesitates.

I wait a beat, another.

"Don't keep me waiting, Bird."

She pivots to face me. Her fingers curl into fists at her sides. Guess I pissed her off, huh?

I jerk my chin and she takes a step forward. Another, until she reaches the bed.

"Stop."

She pauses.

"Undress."

She stiffens.

This is when she protests, yells at me, or better still, turns and rushes out to appeal to our guests, who are partying below.

Instead, she reaches behind.

I hear the hiss of a zipper and fuck me but I'm instantly hard.

She raises her hand to the neckline, tugs the material down one shoulder, then the other. Her movements are precise; her fingers tremble. The dress whispers down to pool at her hips.

My mouth waters; my chest hurts. "Take it off completely."

She shimmies out of the outfit. It pools at her ankles and she kicks it aside. She stands, chest thrust out, the perfect globes of her breasts bared. I rake my gaze down her chest and her nipples harden. Down the concave of her stomach to the satin triangle of her panties.

I glance at the scrap of cloth, then at her face.

Her cheeks pale.

I raise my eyebrow and she sets her jaw. Then shoves her underwear down and kicks it off. I drop my gaze to the flesh between her thighs, the completely bare flesh with the tiny slit at its base that glistens pink in the late evening sunlight.

My cock thickens. A pulse drums at my wrists, at my temples, even in my fucking balls. *The fuck is she doing to me?* I need to be inside of her before I explode right here in in my pants.

Her fingers clench at her sides, "Happy?"

Not even close.

"Get on the bed, on your hands and knees."

Her chest heaves. Her beautiful green pupils dilate. From anger? From lust? I am going to find out. "Do it."

She draws in a breath, then clambers onto the bed. On her elbows and knees, her sweet butt thrust out in the air. My dick lengthens. My throat closes. She has such a hold on me, and she doesn't realize it. I plan to keep it that way.

I stalk over to her, stand at the foot of the bed, "Open wider."

She wriggles her hips, then increases the 'V' between her thighs. The blush pink of her pussy glistens between her legs. The blood empties to my groin so fast that my head spins.

I lean forward, cup her arse. She whimpers.

Drag my thumb down the valley between her butt cheeks. She shudders. A moan bleeds from her lips. Her spine bends.

I pull back and let my palm connect with her arse. She hiccoughs.

"You defied me."

Crack. I slap her curved behind and her entire body jerks. She huffs.

"In front of everyone."

I spank her again, and she snarls.

"You like to challenge me, Bird?"

I slap her curved tush. She makes a noise somewhere between a growl and an assent.

"Tell me, you want to go toe to toe with me?"

She nods.

"Speak."

"Yes." The word comes out on a moan.

"Good, then you must pay the consequences for your actions. Let it not be said that I did not give you enough of a warning, sweet Summer."

I spank her beautiful, tight arse again. She howls. And again; she cries out. Six, seven, eight. I increase the intensity of my beating—faster, harder, more frequent. Her thighs quiver; her body sinks down into the mattress.

"Hold up your butt, or else I swear, little Bird, I won't stop until I've forced an orgasm out of you, without touching your cunt."

She growls something unintelligible. Lowers her head, until her cheek is smashed into the mattress. Glances over her shoulder. Her green eyes blaze at me; her lips tremble. Color flushes her cheeks. Ever curve of her body is defiant, every angle of her spine rigid. Her fingers dig into the fabric of the bedspread. Good. "Are you turned on?"

She stares.

"Speak now, or so help me Bird, I'll—"

"No."

I spank her butt and she shudders.

And again.

"Are you going to fight me again?"

She winces.

"Say it."

"Yes." She juts out her chin and I can't stop my lips from curling. "Good." *Then you won't mind if I punish you a little longer?*

Her lips part, "No, don't—"

Ten, eleven, twelve… I spank her heart-shaped behind again and again. With each slap, her entire body bows, trembles, her knuckles whiten, the scent of her arousal deepens, her feet, still in the satin custom-made stilettos, dig into the mattress.

Her chin quivers, her shoulders heave, a tear rolls down her cheek; she doesn't lower her eyes. Doesn't look away. Doesn't make a noise, until I raise my arm again.

"Stop." She wheezes.

"Why should I?"

"Because…" She swallows, "I'm sore."

I bring down my palm again on her butt and she moans.

"Because I want you to."

Wrong answer. I spank her again and her entire body shudders. Her chin wobbles; her shoulders pull back, "Because I am your wife?"

"That's right." I lower my arm, loosen the buckle of my belt, and her gaze drops to my crotch. "It's why I am going to fuck your cunt, so you'll never forget it."

I drag down the zipper of my pants and my dick swings free. She draws in a sharp breath.

"It's why I am going to imprint myself on every cell of your body." I lean forward until my dick is lined up with her pussy. "Until your every thought, every sentence, every last string of trivia in your mind will begin and end with me."

She shudders. "Fuck you, Sinclair Sterling."

"With pleasure."

I back up, then bring down my palm.

38

Summer

His palm connects with my pussy, and I explode.

Moisture pools between my legs. The trembling sweeps up my calves, my thighs, zings up my spine and shatters behind my eyes. My hands shake, my legs give way. I lurch forward and come to a stop.

Wha—?

His hands grip my waist, the width of his palms span me end to end. The warmth from the connection sinks into my blood, rolls toward its inevitable destination—my melting center.

"Sinclair—"

"Sin."

"Eh?"

"Call me Sin."

"Goddam you." I bite down on my lower lip, "Why don't you fuck me and be done with it?"

"Ask for it."

"No."

He palms my throbbing arse and sensations coil in my core. He drags the head of his cock between my melting lower lips and I moan. The thick length of him hints at how good it would be if I gave in to him. The emptiness inside of me claws, deepens. So hollow. So incomplete. I dig my fingers into the bedspread. No way am I giving him what he wants.

"So stubborn."

I sense him move. The heat of him envelops my back, sidles down the dip between my sensitized thighs. My throat closes.

"So responsive."

He nuzzles the skin at the point where my shoulder meets my neck, and my sex clenches. Goosebumps flare on my skin; my breath catches. He moves my hair aside, presses little kisses to the nape of my neck. I shiver. He sucks on the skin right there where I am the most sensitive and I moan.

He massages my hip, his blunt fingers long enough to graze the edge of my sensitive slit. The rough hair on his groin grazes my tingling backside and pinpricks of pain radiate out from his touch. A whine spills from my lips.

Is that me? Why do I sound so needy? Why is my body betraying everything that I am trying to communicate to him?

"So beautiful." He nibbles a path down the length of my spine and my heart begins to thud. Blood engorges my clit, my nipples pebble with such intensity that they hurt. I bite the inside of my cheek to stop myself from asking him to take me, to put an end to this craziness, whatever it is that stretches, connects me to him. My mind to his. My heart to the essence of his being that is surely the darkest, blackest soul to ever exist. So why am I aching for him?

He drags his chin down the length of my spine and goosebumps flare on my skin.

"Ask me to fuck you."

I shake my head.

"Please."

I shudder. My heart clenches. Something inside of me snaps. Oh, hell, I am so going to regret this. I draw in a breath, "Fuck me, Sin."

His entire body seems to freeze. Tension radiates off of him. The heat from his body intensifies, until I am sure I am melting inside and out. Sweat beads my forehead, my nerve endings pop, crackle, waiting, waiting.

His breath teases the shell of my ear, "Thank you, Bird."

My throat closes.

I sense him draw back, his hands grip my hips, then he plows into me. I scream. Pain slices through me and I try to pull away.

"The bloody fuck—?"

His grip tightens.

"You lied to me?"

"Nothing you didn't do first. I was returning the favor."

His fingertips dig into my side, "You were using me?"

"As were you."

"You wanted me to feel guilty about taking your virginity?"

"Do you?" I glance at him and wince.

His face is all hard planes and shadows. His cheekbones stand out so sharply that I could cut my skin on them.

"No." He sets his jaws with a snap, and I can literally hear the sound of his molars grinding. "You want to know how it makes me feel, Bird?"

A vein throbs at his temple.

"Answer me."

"H... how?"

A bead of sweat slides down his temple; a muscle jumps at his jaw line. The white lines that crease his mouth reveal how close he is to losing control. The force of his dominance leaps off of him, and crashes down on my shoulders. It pins me down. I stare unable to move. Unable to glance away.

His hand slides down my belly and grazes my clit. Sensations of heat spiral from his touch. He leans his upper body closer, until the hard planes of his chest seem to envelop me from all sides.

I gulp; my toes curl. What's he going to do next?

He drops his head and licks my lips, "It makes me want to fuck the defiance out of you, so you'll never lie to me again."

My throat closes. A ball of emotion fills my chest. All of my brain cells seem to ignite together. How can he sound so harsh, so uncompromising, yet so filthy at the same time? And why the hell do I find it so arousing? My pussy spasms and he groans.

"You like the thought of that, eh?"

Yes.

Yes.

I shake my head.

"Still lying, hmm?" He tilts his hips, and his dick twitches. "Time you learned not to lie." He pinches my clit.

More wetness pools between my legs. A moan bleeds from my lips.

His shoulders bulge, his biceps seem to grow larger. "Those tiny sounds you make fucking turn me on, you know that?" His eyelids half close, until only a sliver of indigo shines from between them. I shiver. His features close, his gaze intensifies.

"I don't want to hurt you."

I swallow.

"Though I am beginning to think you like it when I do."

I bite the inside of my cheek, to stop myself from agreeing.

He pulls out of me and the pain recedes; he stays poised at the entrance to my lower lips. His fingers strum my clit. I shiver. He releases my hip to bring his other hand up to cup my breast. His palm is so big, it dwarfs my flesh. My nipples grow turgid. He tugs at the sensitive peaks, and I shudder. Throw my head back, arching my neck. He drags his chin down the delicate column. My scalp tingles, my toes curl.

"I am going to fuck you now."

I swallow. He strums the swollen lips of my pussy and a trembling starts from deep inside.

He releases his hold on my breasts, only to wrap his fingers around my throat. Panic bubbles up from somewhere deep inside and my skin stretches until it feels too tight. He presses his thumb to the pulse at the hollow of my neck.

"Shh." His warm breath lifts the hair at my temples. "Let me do this right for you, Bird."

I shiver.

"Focus on my touch, my heat, my voice; forget everything else. Follow my lead. Can you do that, hmm?"

I nod.

"Good girl." His warmth cocoons me, his thighs cradle mine, his fingers play with my pussy. He nudges my wet entrance with his dick, "Do you trust me?"

No.

No.

I nod.

His chest expands behind me and his muscles seem to go solid. "Hold onto me." His shaft nudges my wet entrance; his grip on my neck tightens.

He thrusts forward and his dick fills me. I gasp; my thighs clench.

Tendrils of heat coil deep inside, as the pressure at the base of my spine grows.

He stays there, and I draw in a breath. His cock pulses inside of me and a moan wells up.

"You okay?"

"Y... yes."

His muscles tense; his arms vibrate with the stress of holding up his body weight.

He pulls back, then pumps his hips forward. Pain slices through me, the pleasure welling up on its heels.

The vibrations slam against the fingers that stroke my throat and I can sense every single separate intonation.

"Shh, let me make this good for you."

His lips touch my nape. Pinpricks of heat radiate out from the contact. He draws my hair aside, nibbles on the skin at the juncture of where my neck meets my shoulder. I shiver. He licks his way down the curve of my arm, then bites down.

My sex clenches; moisture pools between my legs.

A groan rumbles up his chest. "You're killing me."

He buries his nose against my skin, "And you smell so fucking good."

A pressure begins to build between my legs...

"I can't hold back, Bird. I have to move."

I jerk my chin, bite down on my lower lip. "Please." The word spills from my lips.

"Thank fuck." He tilts his hips and thrusts, sliding into me again. Too much, too full. Pain thrums up my spine. I huff, curve my spine.

"Shh." He kisses the side of my neck, then fastens his teeth on my earlobe. He tugs and a melting sensation unfurls somewhere deep inside.

"Oh." I tilt my head, giving him access and he obliges.

He strokes his tongue over my earlobe, then eases it inside the hollow of my ear. I shiver; goosebumps flare on my skin.

What the hell?

How had I not known that it could be so erotic to have him nibble on my ear lobe, suck on it, as he grips my hips, propels forward and buries himself inside me?

"Sin. Please."

I squeeze my eyes, throw my head back. His grasp on my hip holds me in place. He cups my breast, pinches the nipple. *Jesus*. Flashes of heat go off behind my eyes. I am flying, floating... somewhere in that space between pleasure and pain.

He releases my breasts, and I groan.

He slides his hand down to cup my pussy, strum my lower lips, pinch my clit, and I cry out.

The pressure intensifies, grows, radiates out to my extremities. My feet dig into the mattress, my fingers clench, and every pore in my skin seems to open.

He slams into me again with enough force that my entire body bucks. His lips brush my ear. "Come."

And I shatter. The sensations sweep up my chest; my heart pounds against my ribcage with such force that I am sure it's going to jump out. He loosens the grip on my throat and the climax engulfs me. The blood drums against my temples. Sparks of red and white fill my vision. Then, that too, fades away. Darkness pulls me under.

. . .

Something cold slides between my legs, and my eyelids flutter. I glance down to find that I am on my back, legs spread wide. A dark hand wipes a pristine white towel down my throbbing center. I wince.

"Shh! Let me take care of you."

He dabs the cold towel on either side of my thighs. The coolness permeates my skin, and the burning eases, somewhat. "Better?"

I nod.

He straightens, walks into the adjoining bath. The door is open, and light pours out. I hear the sound of a cabinet being opened and closed. Then he walks out again. The bed dips as he places a knee between my legs. He squeezes out something from a tube. "What's that?"

He spreads it out onto my thighs. A cold sensation sinks into my blood and all remaining aches instantly recede. "Is that — ?"

"Aloe."

"Do you do this often?"

"What?'

"Take care of virgins in your bed."

He straightens, caps the ointment, then walks past the bed to place it on the side table. "I've never slept with one before."

"Oh."

"And I am only taking care of you, so you are ready for another round."

"Wait... what?"

He slides onto the bed, "Scoot over."

"You don't mean that?" My pussy clenches. Moisture seeps from my core.

I shift to the other side, making sure there's the width of the bed between us.

He folds his arm behind his neck, "Don't I?"

He closes his eyes, and I peer at his features. That hard countenance, the hooked nose that caps the surprisingly pouty lower lip, and I am familiar with how that tastes.

"I suggest you get some sleep."

"And round two?"

He opens one eye, "I'm beginning to think you can't get enough of me."

Jerk. I scramble back, then pull the covers up to my chin.

Close my eyes, try to sleep. Turn on my side. Wriggle my feet, then turn over on my back. Dammit, now I have an itch on my back. I shift my hips, arch my spine, try to reach the spot which is below my nape.

"What are you doing?" He grumbles.

"Trying to scratch an itch, you mind?"

"I can do that for you — "

"Not that kind." I huff.

"Hmm."

I roll my shoulder blades against the bed.

There's a long inhalation of breath. Then the mattress, dips. He shifts toward me. "Turn over."

"But."

He grabs my shoulder and moves me on my side.

"Where is it?"

"Center of my back."

He places his palm unerringly on the right spot and drags his fingers down the length of my back.

"Oh," I can't stop the moan that bleeds from my lips. He repeats the action, this time in reverse.

"Ah."

I stretch into his touch, and he obliges. He digs his fingers into the space between my shoulder blades, and all the way down to the cleft of my butt. And again. Soo good. A sound of pleasure escapes my lips.

"You remind me of a kitten I had."

"You used to have a kitten?"

His actions stop for a second, then he continues his strokes.

"It doesn't matter."

"Of course, it would only humanize the bad-tempered alphahole if you were to share something of his personal life, huh?"

"Exactly."

Getting this man to talk about himself is like... trying to find a seat on the tube during rush hour. "Soo... Amadeus huh?"

He caresses his big palm up my spine and I arch into his touch.

"Is there a story there?"

His touch stills, then he massages his fingertips over the knotted muscles of my shoulders. *Oh!*

"My mother."

I still.

"She loved classical music. She was listening to Mozart when she went into labor, hence..." He digs his fingers into the back of my head and scratches my scalp.

Goosebumps tingle down my skin. I shiver, "Where did you learn to do that?"

"Experience."

Of course. My stomach lurches; something hot stabs at my chest. I am not jealous. *Why am I jealous?*

"That's enough." I pull away and he doesn't comment.

I peer into the darkness, then clear my throat.

"What?" He sounds half-resigned, half-aroused. "I can hear you thinking, so say it aloud."

"That... What happened?"

"What...?"

"You know, 'that,' when I almost blacked out —"

"You mean your second orgasm in as many minutes?" I can't see his face, but damn, I can sense the smug satisfaction in his voice.

"You're welcome."

Jeez.

"How can you be both considerate and an alphahole?"

"You do realize that's technically not an official word in the English language, hmm? Not that I'm protesting its usage." He smirks. "And it comes naturally to me."

Why did I ask? I groan aloud.

Silence for another beat. *Don't ask him, don't.*

"Is it... ah, always like that?" I mean, I know it can't be, but I have to ask. Not that I expect him to answer or anything.

The silence stretches. It's completely quiet. In the shitty apartment I'd shared with

Karma, there was always some noise at night. The ambulance screaming, late night party-goers returning home, the staff from the pub downstairs cleaning up before heading home. Here, I can hear my thoughts. Which I am not sure I appreciate. Not when all of them seem to lead back to him.

"It's never been that way for me." His voice is low.

Oh! "You mean —"

"Go to sleep, Bird."

He turns on his side.

His breathing deepens. Apparently, that stupid switch on-switch off mechanism he has that allows him to flip the switch on his emotions can also help him fall asleep in an instant. The man really doesn't have a soul.

Taking the virginity of the woman you blackmailed into helping you get revenge by destroying her father? Check.

Ensuring you make her life completely and utterly miserable during the process by crawling under her skin, and occupying her every waking thought and invading her dreams? Double check.

I close my eyes, and my limbs grow heavy. My breathing deepens, then catches.

One second, I'm empty. The next, he is there. His heat sears my back, envelops me from behind. I lean into it, rub my butt against the hardness that throbs between my legs. He slips inside of me, filling the emptiness, stretching me from end to end. I shiver and a whine tumbles from my throat. I stretch my spine, seeking that delicious presence, the complete comfort, that absolute awareness of what it is to be so in sync with another. *Wait, what?* I crack my eyes open and peer into the dark. "Sin?"

"Shh, I didn't intend to wake you."

He drags my hair away from my nape, whispers a kiss to my shoulder. Moisture pools between my legs. I turn my face toward him, and he takes the hint. He nibbles his way up the column of my throat to my ear lobe and bites down. "Ah!" I shudder, raise my arm and wrap it back and around him.

He's so massive, that I barely reach halfway around his broad back.

He brings his hand up and cups my breast. The warmth of his fingers sinks into my blood and I thrust myself into his grasp.

He plays with my erect nipple and heat ignites between my legs.

He drags his hand down my stomach to cup my pussy. The gesture so possessive, so completely confident, that my head spins. Or maybe that's because his hardness lengthens inside of me, bumps against my inner walls. Pinpricks of sensations shimmer up my spine.

"You're so gorgeous, Summer." He presses little kisses down my jawline.

I twist my upper body, crane toward him, and he closes his lips over mine. His tongue sweeps inside my mouth, sucking on mine, drinking from me. His possession is absolute, his strength incomparable. He's taking from me, marking me, re-forming me into a shadow of himself, and I can't stop him. Another whine tumbles up my throat, and he swallows it. He propels his hips, and his cock leaps forward. The hard ridge of his pelvis chafes the soft bump of my arse, every part of him rigid, unforgiving. A complete contrast to me. I've never felt this helpless, this vulnerable. This open and giving. This… unable to get ahold of the emotions that twist my stomach, coil in my guts. What is he doing to me? I open my mouth to ask and he deepens the kiss. His tongue scrapes across my teeth, his fingers pinch my clit, and his cock seems to expand further, pervading my pussy. A groan rumbles up his chest and the vibrations sink into me. My blood thuds at my temples; my heartbeat ratchets up. Sin, Sinclair. Mr. Sterling—the alphahole who swept in and turned my entire life upside down.

He tears his mouth from mine, then pumps his hips. His cock leaps forward and I gasp.

"Look at me, Bird."

I crack my eyes open, meet his deep indigo gaze.

A trembling urgency builds from somewhere deep inside. He thrusts again and again. Grinds the heel of his hand into my clit. Sensations coil at the base of my spine.

He wraps his other hand around my throat, shoves his thumb into my mouth. I suck on his digit, and his pupils grow darker.

He holds my gaze, pumps his hips, impaling me further on his dick. A bead of sweat runs down my spine and I shiver. He bends his head, until our noses bump.

"Come for me, Bird, come all over my cock."

His whisper sears through the silence in my head and I explode. The climax grips me, and my entire body bucks. My back stretches, my stomach rolls, and cum gushes out from between my legs.

"So fucking beautiful, my little Bird."

A groan rumbles up his chest. His cock lengthens, throbs, then liquid heat bathes my insides. He raises his palm from my pussy to his mouth and sucks on his fingers, then drags the liquid of our joint essences down my breasts.

"Sleep now."

My eyes flutter shut. I float in that space between sleep and wakefulness. He draws me closer, and his dick twitches inside of me. *He can't be hard again, can he?*

"I am, Bird. It seems where you are concerned, I have an insatiable appetite. Apparently, I like to punish myself." He draws in a breath and his entire body seems to expand. "Another first." The tone of his voice dips further.

Did he say that? Nah, must be my imagination. He can't read my mind. Nope. This was a really good dream, all of it. I snuggle into the warmth, begin to drift off, then it comes to me. "Timotheé Chalamet."

"Huh?" His grip on my waist tightens.

"I loved him in *Call Me by Your Name*."

"Hmm."

A whisper brushes my hair. *Did he kiss me?*

"How did you know that was my favorite movie ever?"

He hesitates. "I didn't." He cups my pussy, "But I wanted to taste your cum as badly."

Wow. "That's... ah..." I swallow. "The most romantic thing anyone has ever said to me."

"Good." He tucks me firmly into his chest. "Go to sleep."

I drift off with his cock inside of me.

When I awake, his side of the bed is empty.

39

"...I believe in the soul, the cock, the pussy, the small of a woman's back, the hanging curve ball, high fiber, good scotch... I believe in the sweet spot, soft-core pornography, opening your presents Christmas morning rather than Christmas Eve; I believe in long, slow, deep, soft, wet kisses that last three days."

—*Bull Durham*. Director: Ron Shelton

Sin

"Whiskey at 9 am? Isn't that a tad hard core?"

I down the rest of the liquor and it burns a trail down my throat. "The fuck do you want now, Saint?"

He walks to the bar at the corner of the office and the coffee machine kicks into action.

"What's the point of having this £5000 machine if you never use it?"

I shrug. I had it brought in only because the rest of the Seven prefer coffee. Me? I am a tea drinker. Blame it on growing up in the East End. Tea so strong and with enough sugar that you can float a spoon on it. That's the first drink I'd ever had, and its taste is something I have never been able to shake off.

He walks up to the window, peers outside. "Anything interesting?"

I snarl.

"Bad night huh?" He snickers.

"What do you care?"

"You're the one who's spearheading this entire scheme. I'm checking that my investment is in safe hands, bro."

"You're not the one who has anything to lose."

"And you do?" He turns to me. "Anything you want to 'fess up to, Sinner?"

"Bugger off. I am not looking for a priest." *What I need is a bloody surgeon to look inside my brain and tell me, what the hell had I been thinking last night?* I had taken her without an inch of empathy, smacked her butt, torn into her pussy.

Then, I had pretended to drift off on my side of the bed, hoping she'd take the hint.

She'd mumbled to herself, then her breathing had deepened.

I had turned to face away from her, yet every morsel of my attention had been focused on her. The way her scent had intensified as she'd slept. The soft inhalations, the twitch of her limbs which indicated that she had fallen deeper into slumber.

I'd had my eyes closed, yet I hadn't needed to see her to imagine her features. The flushed cheeks, parted lips, the rise and fall of those sugar plum breasts, the quiver of her flat belly, the melting triangle of her pussy. My dick had lengthened, and I had palmed myself.

I could have turned and helped myself to her and she wouldn't have resisted. She is no match for my deviousness; fucking innocent that she is. Okay, not completely. She's packed a lot into her years so far. She is a survivor. I have no doubt she'll get through everything I have planned. Question is, will I? I hadn't anticipated wearing a raging hard on while lying next to her. Me fisting myself, trying to jerk off, without disturbing her.

I'd taken her virginity. And that had been unexpected.

She'd denied it when I had asked her, and although that question had been to rile her, I had taken her answer at face value.

I had had no reason to suspect that she was one.

I had been her first. *Fuck! Her first!* I had assumed… *What?* That she was experienced enough to stand up to my inclinations? That I could take what was mine. *Is she mine? The fuck am I doing thinking along those lines, huh?*

And why am I in my office at the crack of dawn, leaving her warm willing body in my bed? It had been too fucking right, that's the problem. Her skin, her scent, the taste of her is in my mouth.

After I'd taken her that second time, I hadn't been able to sleep. I'd waited until she'd drifted off, then crawled between her legs, like a starving schmuck, and eaten out her pussy.

Even asleep, her thighs had tightened around my ears, and that had spurred me on. I'd cupped her arse, scooped her up and sunk my tongue inside of her.

I'd lapped at her cunt, sucked on her, pinched her clit, rubbed the engorged nub between her lower lips. I'd cupped her butt, brought her closer, sunk my thumb into that tight little back hole, and she'd come again. The sweetness of her cum had exploded on my palate as she'd moaned out her release.

Those little noises she makes when she is close to coming? Fuck. They are going to be my destruction. Her voice, husky with lust, is fast becoming the soundtrack of my life. One I can't do without.

I'd known then it was a bloody mistake. I am in too deep, trapped by the lure of that sexy little body… No, not only. It is her spirit I crave. Her thirst for life which I had once had but I've lost along the way. In her presence, every part of me stands to attention—my dick twitches—yeah, especially that particular appendage. *Fucking hell.*

She's imprinted herself in every part of me, and fuck, that's a scary thought. No one is allowed to get this close to me. No one.

I pull away from the window, walk to the bar and pour another, then toss it back. The liquor sparks a burn deep in my stomach. I can still feel my hands and legs though. Her taste still laces my tongue. Her scent lingers on my skin—I hadn't wanted to shower. Don't judge. Just another twat throwing himself off a literal cliff; all in the name of some stupid emo shit. *Jesus, have I lost my balls completely?*

I grab the bottle to pour another finger.

Footsteps approach. Saint snatches the bottle from me.

"Hey."

I reach for it and he clicks his tongue. "Get your head in the game."

I glare at him, and he holds my gaze. He's as tall as me, as broad, as able as me to lead any initiative for the Seven; he'd had as much at stake, but he'd withdrawn and given me enough rope... To hang myself, as it were.

"You knew."

He angles his head. "The fuck you talking about?"

I thrust out my chin. "You wanted me to fall for her?"

"Are you falling for her?"

"Stop answering one question with another."

He clicks his tongue. "You have it bad."

"Don't change the fucking topic." I grab his collar and yank him forward. "Tell me, you didn't set me up to take the fall in this."

"I didn't."

He lowers his eyebrows. "You're imagining things, old chap."

Am I?

"Why?" I growl, "Tell me Saint, or so help me I am going to punch in your pretty face."

"You couldn't." He smirks. "The last time we went a round, you know what happened."

Neither of us had won. It had been a fucking tie, again. He and I are too well matched. It's what makes us compete with each other for everything.

"What were you doing speaking to her yesterday?"

"What are you doing in the office the day after your wedding? Shouldn't you be busy taking your bride on a honeymoon?"

"A pretend honeymoon, and no, that was never on the cards, as you well know."

What the fuck is his problem anyway? How dare he talk about her?

"Let go of my collar, Sin." I glance down to find I am gripping his shirt. I let go, step back, and hold out my arm.

He thrusts the bottle at me. "Your funeral."

"Since when are you so concerned about my well-being?"

"Ah, let's see," He holds up a finger. "Since you decided to come up with a hare-brained scheme of doing good to salvage our reputation—which I could have told you for free was a bad idea. Then hired the one woman you should have kept your distance from, then married her. All in the name of revenge?"

I swig from the bottle. The liquor goes down smoothly, burning a trail in its wake. My toes feel numb... That's good.

"You don't fool me."

"Blah-fucking-blah." I mimic a mouth talking with the fingers of my left hand. "You done?"

His lips firm. "You need to get it through your head that not all of us are your enemies."

"Oh? And let you come in and rob me blind in front of my eyes?" I snicker. Then, toss back another swig of the alcohol. Yep, can barely feel my fingers. I lower the bottle to the bar counter with exaggerated care.

The conference call device in the room buzzes and I wince.

Saint struts to it and depresses the speaker. "Rich Prick's office."

Meredith's chuckle fills the space, "Hello, Saint."

"Hey, M."

"Is Sin there with you?"

"Barely."

She laughs.

"Loser." I can't feel my lips, or the tip of my nose either. Makes for a nice change. "Anyone ever tell you that you're an annoying motherfucker?"

"What's up, M?"

"Ask her why she didn't come to the wedding," I grumble.

"You're on speaker, Sin." Saint smirks.

"I knew that." I blink, stalk to the table. "You're not off the hook, M. You didn't turn up yesterday."

"I'll come when you decide to have a real wedding."

Huh? Don't know about the wedding, but the night sure felt like the first of a new life together. *Hold on, back up.* Emo central. "The woman's too smart." I peer up at Saint.

His face fades in and out in my line of sight.

"I may be old but I am not deaf... yet." Meredith's chuckle sounds from the phone. "I heard you, Sin."

"Oops." I curve my lips. "It was a compliment."

"I know." She laughs. "Called to remind you to eat your breakfast. It's on the desk in your office."

I glance through the adjoining doors, spot the tray laid out.

"Thanks, M."

"You're welcome, my boy."

The woman makes me feel like I am a kid again.

After the incident, I'd gotten into so many scraps on the street, it's a wonder I made it through that patch of my life alive. I probably wouldn't have if Meredith hadn't found me beaten up and rushed me to the hospital. She'd met the rest of the Seven... and had become a big part of our lives.

"Sin?" Meredith's soft voice breaks through my thoughts. "The books you ordered are here."

"Cool scene."

"I'm sending them up."

The line goes dead.

"Cool scene?" Saint frowns. "Books?"

"None of your business."

A knock sounds. I walk through to my main office and fling open the door. A girl—an intern? How many of them do we employ? — walks in.

She glances at me and her cheeks redden. She stands there, blinking. I point to the desk and she walks toward it. Drops the books on the wooden surface. She straightens and Saint enters the main office.

Her gulp is audible. Her chest heaves. Here we go again. My presence can be overwhelming on its own. Then add in Saint, and the entire area is a pheromone kill zone.

"You may leave now, Tanya."

"It's Alia."

"Bye, Stella."

She huffs out a breath, walks past me, stumbles, then rights herself and darts out the door.

Saint chuckles. "My effect on the opposite sex is not to be underestimated, huh?" *Wanker.*

He prowls to the table, stares at the books. *"Movie Trivia Unleashed. Advanced Movie Quizzes. Dialogues from Movies You Always Wanted to Know —* "

"Thanks for spelling out the titles." I stalk over, gather up the books.

"You feeling okay, Sin?"

"Eh?" I shuffle my weight from foot to foot.

"Something you want to tell me?"

"About what?"

He stares at the pile of books in front of me.

That? "It's a new hobby."

He tracks me as I stride to my desk.

"You don't do hobbies, Sin."

"Things... have changed." I pick up a book, relax into my swivel chair.

"You don't say?"

I plant my feet on the table, begin to read the book. I glance past the cover to the corner, where Max normally keeps me company. He'd refused to leave the house, had spent the night moping outside the bedroom door.

Yeah, I'd locked him out last night. Apparently, I couldn't share my bride with my own mutt. *Fuck!* When I'd opened the bedroom door this morning he'd shot inside, then curled up on the floor by her side.

I'd left both woman and dog sleeping peacefully.

"What are you doing?" Saint's voice cuts through my thoughts.

"You're still here?" I mutter.

He ambles over as if he owns the office — which he doesn't — okay, maybe 1/7th of it, but this is my domain, and I am getting a little tired of one or the other of the Seven constantly dropping in.

It's almost as if they are checking in on me... More likely, their investment is what keeps them returning. I smirk.

He reaches for the book I'm holding and I hold it out of his reach. "What the — ?" I glower.

"You're losing it, old chap." He rubs his chin.

"Piss off." I jerk my chin at the door.

"Fine." He holds up his hands. "But you should know that there is lot of talk already."

"Oh?" I pick up another book flip it open.

"The tabloids got wind of the wedding.

"Took them what, 24 hours? They're losing their touch."

"No, you are."

"You're seriously pissing me off." I crack my neck.

"You're pissing on everything we've worked on."

"Don't be so dramatic." I turn another page.

He grabs the book and tosses it on the table. "Get your head out of your arse for one second."

I tilt my chair back, yawn. "You're getting on my arse."

"I'll do more than that if you don't come clean with me on what's happening."

"I have it in hand." *Right.* My heart begins to thud. I fold my palms in my lap. "But since you've obviously got a bee in your bonnet about this…" I jerk my chin. "Say your piece or forever hold your piss."

He widens his stance. "This sham of a wedding didn't convince anyone. Not me, and certainly not her father."

"It was meant to bring her old man out of hiding and into our net, which it has."

He drags his fingers through his hair, then begins to pace. "It's not enough. You're the fourth richest man in the country. Your net worth ranks below mine—"

"Hold on a second." I slam my feet on the floor, lean forward. "Last I checked, our net worth was exactly the same."

"That was…" He taps a finger to his chin, pretends to think. "Twenty-four hours ago, before you took your name off 'the most eligible bachelors in the country' list."

"What does that have to do with anything?"

"Only everything?" He chuckles. "You have your head so far inside your arse that you didn't realize this would have been the perfect occasion to drum up some PR, paint the picture. 'Most sought after playboy of the decade, settles down, finds his happily ever after.' Blah, fucking blah."

I press my lips together. "Your point being?"

"Not too late. You wanted a simple, romantic, wedding under wraps. You got it. Now throw the press a bone, do a quick briefing, introduce your lovely wife, and launch—"

"FOK."

"FOK, indeed." He widens his stance, props his palms on his hips. "It may work in your favor. The pretense of wanting to keep things private. When they can't have something, you know how crazy the press gets trying to sniff up a story."

I shuffle around in my seat, trying to find a comfortable position. "What's in it for you?"

"Launch FOK properly, get all attention on that and your nuptials. It'll ensure her father has no reason to doubt the relationship. Then when he's at ease, we lower the trap."

I chuckle.

Saint nods, "Strip him of all his assets, and then you divorce his daughter."

I can do that much. As long as I don't get any closer to her. I rub my clammy palms on my pants, "You any closer to breaking up his marriage?"

He rubs his chin, glances at the watch on his wrist. "3, 2—"

His phone buzzes. He flashes me a glance and picks it up. "Hello." He nods, then bares his teeth. "You bet. I'll meet you at Claridge's for tea, in an hour." He shoots me a thumbs up sign. "Looking forward."

He slides his phone into his pocket. "See? You can count on me, old sport."

"Stop shittin' me."

"You're welcome." He raises his hands. "I only had to intervene to salvage every last tactic in your very sorry plan… Which sucked from the beginning, by the way."

A headache begins to drum at my temples. "Get off my balls, man."

He half bows, "Avec pleasure." He pivots, heads to the door as it's flung open.

My wife barrels into the room, "Sinclair Amadeus Sterling, you have a bloody nerve."

40

Summer

"Hi Summer."

I glower past Saint at the obnoxious, douche-canoe, conceited waffle, rat's arse of a man, aka my husband, and all the breath promptly leaves me.

"You okay, there?" Saint frowns.

"Of course." I make a sound deep in my throat. "Why wouldn't I be?"

"You were muttering to yourself."

"He has that effect." I growl.

Saint glances from me to Sinclair, who gives no sign that he's surprised by my appearance. Asshole hadn't waited for me this morning. He'd left, after laying out a dress for me to wear—he hadn't forgotten that, of course.

He'd ensured that one of the interns in the office had helpfully woken me up at a quarter to nine.

Giving me enough time to drag my sorry arse out of bed, and into the shower. I'd raced to the tube and managed to reach the office by half past nine. "You could have waited and offered me a lift to the office."

"Oh?" Sinclair folds his arms behind his neck, his legs up on the £5000 custom-made desk which, no doubt, he could replace in an instant. Like he could switch me out for another. Which he will do. The question is, when, and it is something I intend to find out.

I take a step inside the room, and Sinclair smirks.

My pussy instantly salivates. *Hell.* Something in that meanness of his glance, the way he rakes my body from top to bottom, undressing me…Just as he had made me take off my clothes less than nine hours ago. It already seems far in the past, in the cold light of the gray London morning.

"And why, pray tell me, Bird, should I have delayed my very important meeting, while

I waited for you to stop snoring?"

"That was you, asshole." I pull out my phone, "I have proof. I recorded it."

"What?" He frowns.

I wave the device at him, "Guess none of your girlfriends dared tell you about your condition, huh?"

"Are you fucking kidding me?"

Saint chuckles, "Damn, this should be interesting."

"Get the hell out of here." I snarl at the same time as Sinclair.

"If this is what marriage does to people—"

"Fake marriage."

Sinclair echoes my indignation.

"Right." He looks between us. "Bye, Summer." He lowers his voice, "I'd wish you luck, but I think that tosser needs it more than you."

He heads for the exit; the door snicks shut.

"Missed me, Darlin'?" Sinclair drawls.

His rough tone tugs on my sensitive nipples, then slithers down to the valley between my legs. I shiver.

Damn the man. He's unshaven, his hair mussed up as if he's been running his fingers through it, or like he rolled out of bed and came here, which he had, considering I had his dick buried balls deep inside of me less than 3 hours ago. My sex clenches. Hell. I fold my fingers at my sides.

Why the hell does his potency only seem to magnify every time I see him? Considering the number of times he fucked me last night… Were the last two times my imagination? Had he actually gone down on me? He'd made me come, then kissed me, making sure I'd tasted our joined-up fluids. I flick out my tongue and his nostrils flare. Even across the room, I swear I can see his biceps expand. His shoulders stretch the width of the custom-made shirt. No tie, of course.

The first two buttons of his shirt are undone, revealing the sculpted chest underneath. The planes of which I had drummed my fingers over, had tugged on those dark hairs that arrow down to the part of him that is currently hidden.

My fingers tingle. I'd felt him inside of me… Clearly, he is massive—my pussy throbs —okay, bigger, much bigger than I had expected, but I hadn't had a chance to touch him, circle that thick muscle and find out for myself how big he really is.

What? I may have been brought up by nuns, but my education is far from lacking when it comes—*haha! No, don't go there*—to the opposite sex. Blame it on Karma. My sister has her faults, but some of her curiosity has rubbed off on me, enough to read her romance novels… None of which had prepared me for the sheer dominance of the man who stalks me as I saunter into the room.

Keep it casual, don't blow this. Don't show him how pissed you are at him. I walk up to the desk, keeping my arms at my sides. "We had a meeting this morning."

"I'm aware."

"We could have spoken at home before you left."

"You forget, I prefer to keep work things strictly in the—" he air quotes, "—official space."

Jerk. What does that say about us? "I thought this, whatever-it-is-between-us, was work. You don't seem to have a problem bringing this," I wave my finger, indicating the space between us, "home."

He ignores me. "Speaking of, you are officially—" He checks the cheap-ass watch on his wrist — *What's the story there, huh?* " —five minutes late."

"I don't fucking care."

"Language, Mrs. Sterling."

"Fuck you very much, Mr. Sterling."

He chuckles, "You're welcome." He swings his legs to the floor, leans forward, then pours tea into a cup. He reaches for the sugar, adds a spoonful, another. He reaches for the third and I huff.

"What?" He shoots me a glance from under those beautiful thick eyelashes.

"If you keep poisoning yourself with that stuff, you're gonna be diabetic before you know it."

"Oh?" He pauses, with the third spoonful of sugar poised above his tea. "You worried about me, hmm?"

"Hardly," I swat away an errant strand of hair, "I'd have said the same to... any stranger I'd meet in the street."

"Really?"

"You bet."

"So you wouldn't mind if I..." he lowers his spoon toward the cup and I dart forward, grip his hand with enough force that the sugar spills in an arc on the table.

"Oopsie." I lurch back. "Sorry, didn't mean to get so..."

"Possessive?" He smirks, then stirs his tea with the now empty spoon.

"Aggressive." I shuffle my feet.

"I am beginning to see the appeal of both versions, in fact —" He brings the cup of tea to his lips, sips. The beautiful tendons of his throat flex as he swallows. "I enjoy all of your emotions, revel in every single insult that you throw in my direction." He licks his lips, and hell, I am instantly wet.

I chafe my thighs together, shuffle my feet, then squeeze my bag in front of my chest, as if that will diminish the impact of his ridiculously sexy presence on me.

He returns his cup to the breakfast tray.

"Why don't you take a seat?" He pushes the platter aside.

"I'm fine here."

He frowns. "Even standing up, you are barely at eye-level with me —"

Thank you for pointing out my lack of height, you reprobate.

"So, if you think this gives you an edge —"

"God forbid," I look skywards, "anyone try to show up Mr. Big Bad himself."

"Cute."

"What?"

"Your nickname for me."

"Not a nickname, you perv."

"But you enjoy that part of me so much."

The blood rushes to my face. He peruses my features and his eyes gleam. "Why I do believe, my darling, that was a blush."

"So, sue me." I blow out a breath, then drop into the chair. A burn sears my bottom and I jump up. "Ow!"

"What's wrong?" His brow clears. "I see."

"You know nothing, Jon Snow."

"Even I know that's from *Game of Thrones*... That was too easy. You're slipping, Bird. Unless —" he frowns, then straightens, "Guess, your butt must really hurt, huh?"

"Thanks for figuring that out, genius."

I grip the edge of the desk, look to the right, the left, where there's a rug, the kind used for pets, in the corner. Strange, had it been there the last time I came in here? Of course, I'd been distracted then.

He stalks to the door, locks it.

"What are you doing?"

"Making sure you're okay."

"Of course, I am. I came here, didn't I?"

"Hmm." He prowls closer. His big body blocks out the sight of the room, draws in all the oxygen in the space. I try to breathe and my lungs seize.

He pauses in front of me. "Turn around."

"What?"

"So I can check your behind."

"You did it already last night." My cheeks flame.

Damn it, why does his proximity reduce me to a spineless blushing female? I am better than this. I don't need him. I don't need a knight to ride in on his white horse and save me — which, by the way, he's not. Though he probably has many Arabians in his stables —

"Thirteen."

"What?"

"Arabians, and they are all white."

My jaw drops. "What the — did you read my mind? You can't read thoughts, can you?" I frown. "Is that how you win in business, you have a secret ESP-ish instinc —"

"Stop. Bird. Your expressions are way too easy to read." He laughs. His entire face lights up. His indigo eyes lighten until they are almost sky blue. Something hot stabs in my chest.

He's a 100% obnoxious-as-hell, pompous prick... but damn, he's a magnificent, utterly irresistible one, who somehow, somewhere, perhaps, has a flicker of humanness hidden deep inside. Of course, you have to look for it with a blow torch... But hey, I've never backed down from a challenge, huh?

He cups my cheek, "Go on, let me assess the damage I inflicted."

"It's nothing... really —"

"Let me be the judge of that, hmm?"

I twist my fingers in front of me, scan the space.

"No cameras."

"Yeah, that's what you said last time."

"You weren't my wife then."

I stiffen. Does he mean what I think he means? Can his alphaholiciousness actually acknowledge that the ceremony yesterday meant something to him? I grab a strand of my hair and bring it to my mouth, chew on it. He reaches out and gently tugs on the strand until I release it.

"I promise I won't take advantage." He holds up his hand, "Besides, it's nothing I haven't seen."

Thanks for reminding me about exactly how you reduced me to a melting blob of jelly. I bite the inside of my cheek, glower at him.

He merely smiles. He seems almost harmless... Almost. Yeah, and I am the Queen of England. I snort, pivot to face the table.

He presses his big palm into the small of my back and I shiver.

He applies pressure. I follow his lead.

I bend over the polished surface of his antique executive desk.

41

Sin

I have her where I want her. Bent across my desk.

I've imagined this scene a hundred, no a thousand times, since the day I saw her at the bar. She'd reached across the bar for her drink. One glimpse of the creamy column of her neck and I'd been a goner.

Her dress had clung to her impossibly tiny waist, then swooped down to cup that gorgeous heart-shaped arse, and fuck me, but I'd known she was trouble. My fingers had tingled to touch her, caress her, palm the eggshell shape of her butt, and fondle her. I do just that. Cup that sensuous curve, the parabola of my desire, the shape that has haunted me, called to me, the one that has competed for attention with the circle of her breasts. I palm her butt and she trembles. A moan spills from her mouth. "Does that hurt, Bird?"

She shakes her head.

"You okay, if I drag up your skirt, Sweetheart?"

The fuck? Was that another endearment? They come so easily, like rain falling from the leaden London skies. Something inside of me burst open, at some point in the last twenty-four hours. Something shifted, and I cannot, for fuck's sake, put my finger on it. A corner was turned, a line crossed. I slipped into the gap between the platform and the tube train, crushed by thousands of metric tons of steel. *Ha!*

There is no going back, after this. *What does that mean?* I am going to find out.

"Summer?"

"Hmm."

"Can I check out your butt?"

She giggles. "Umm, a bit late to be asking that question, huh?"

"Never say never."

"Sean Connery, James Bond. Hated that film, actually," she murmurs.

I knew that.

I am beginning to echo her love for movie trivia. It is addictive. *She* is addictive. The water vapor to my clouds; the sunshine to my rainy weather. We are opposite, and yet we fit. *Fuck. Get your mind off the poetic license wagon.*

"And it's *Never Say Never Again*." She turns her head, so her cheek is flat on the table, then peers up at me.

"I must be doing something wrong."

She frowns. "What do you mean?"

"You're still talking, still thinking." I curl my lips. "I am going to take that as a personal challenge."

"What?"

"I am going to distract you, Bird. Gonna take care of your poor hurt arse, then shred your asshole, and make you come so hard there will be no other thought in your head, no other word, no other name, except mine."

Her pupils dilate; her cheeks redden.

She opens her mouth to speak and I draw up her skirt.

"Sinclair—"

"Sin."

She chews on that damn lower lip of hers and the crease deepens, that beautiful dip which makes me want to rest my cock on it, as I thrust my heavy length inside of her mouth.

"Say my name."

She shakes her head.

Hmm.

I reach down, tear off her panties, and she squeaks. Her gaze widens. I bring the piece of silk to my face, bury my nose in it. A whine wheezes out of her.

"You enjoy that, hmm?"

She rubs her cheek against the wooden surface. "I shouldn't."

"But you do." I drop the scrap of fabric into the pocket of my pants, then bend and kiss the reddened surface of her behind.

Her hips wriggle. I slide my thigh between her legs, spread them apart, and she stiffens.

"Relax." I press tiny kisses up the curve of her spine, making sure to keep space between me and her reddened butt cheeks.

I swipe the heavy fall of her hair to one side, then kiss her nape.

"Why are you doing this?" She shivers.

"What?"

"Being so nice to me?"

"You don't like it?"

She blinks, "I am not sure."

"How about this." I nuzzle her cheek, then press another kiss to the corner of her lips.

"You've been drinking?"

"I tried, Bird."

"Tried?" The skin at the corners of her eyes creases.

I nod. "Tried to forget the memories we made last night. How you felt under me, your pussy clamping on my shaft, the slickness of your cunt as I moved inside of you, the trembling flesh of your breasts as I squeezed you, the firm indentation between your arse cheeks as I spanked you."

She swallows, the sound loud enough to echo in that tiny, infinitesimal, hair's breadth of space that separates us. "You sound like... like—"

"A man who's losing his mind?" I allow my lips to curl.

"A man who's falling for me."

My shoulders go solid.

"It's too late for that."

Her lips turn down. "Ah."

"I'm more than halfway in love with you." I peruse her beautiful features. "You are all that keeps me from sliding into some dark place."

"*Cold Mountain.*" Her features light up.

"Directed by Anthony Minghella." I tilt my head.

"You've been reading up?" She reaches for one of the books scattered on the table.

"I've been trying to keep up."

"So, what's next?

I snatch the book from her, put it aside.

"We fuck like minks." I smirk.

"I hate minks." She whispers.

"That's from *Basic Instinct.*" I snicker, "And you got that wrong."

"*You're* going about this all wrong." She reaches up and strokes my lower lip.

My dick is instantly hard... Okay, harder.

I've been throbbing since the moment she flounced into my office spewing fire. I knew then, I can't let her go, not until I've satisfied a particular fantasy of mine.

"You're right."

"Wow!" She draws in an exaggerated breath. "That's twice in two seconds that you've ceded to me."

"Don't get used to it. The truth is—"

I stare into those ocean green eyes. I get distracted, and not just by her sexy-as-fuck mouth, or those wide eyelashes that stand to point when she cries, or that pert little nose, turned up at the end, which doesn't begin to do justice to her. It is the entire damn package. It is her, all of her.

She clears her throat, "Truth is?"

"—I haven't started." I straighten, reach for the food tray, pull it close.

"What are you doing?"

"Shh." I grab the tiny silver crucible and place it next to her face.

"No." She quivers.

"Are you saying *No*? Or are you, *saying* No?"

"I'm not *saying*, No."

She draws her hand back, and I reach for her wrist.

"Then?"

"I'm scared."

"So am I." I lower her palm to the tent between my legs, turning her arm enough for her fingers to cup my hardness. "See what you do to me? Whenever I am near you, all I see is you. Especially when I am not in the same space as you."

Her forehead furrows.

"What are you saying?"

That I want you, I need you. "I need to be inside of you. I want to write my intentions onto every part of you, saturate your cells with my essence, pour myself into the fabric of your being until all you can do is think of me, hear my voice in your dreams, scent me first thing in the morning, melt into me when you fall asleep."

"Oh."

"I am saying," I squeeze her palm, press her fingers against my cock. She has me by my fucking balls, literally and physically. "I am going to fuck you."

"I thought you were going to make the pain better."

"That too."

"How?"

I can't stop the smirk that tugs at my mouth, "I admit my methods are a little unorthodox, Bird, but I believe they'll prove to be effective."

"Tell me." She tips her chin down.

"With my ministrations I will distract you." I squeeze her hand, then release it. She keeps her fingers wrapped around my dick. Good.

I reach for the rest of the butter, scoop it up.

"With my mind I will ensnare you." She licks her lips.

"With my cock, I will—" I drag the butter down the valley between her arse cheeks. She shudders.

"Sin."

"That too." I curl my finger into her back hole.

42

Summer

His finger prods at that forbidden part of me and every muscle in me curls with tension.

"Relax, Bird."

I squeeze down on the rigid length of his dick. My Sin. He is that, and so much more. Forbidden. Out of reach. Yet so much everything I need. Am I going to allow him to do this to me? *Yes.*

There, that is the answer. I'd gotten on the fast train to hell from the moment I'd heard that rough voice of his. No turning back now.

His dick seems to lengthen, thicken, in his pants. The scent of him is overwhelming. The air saturated with his dominance, his intentions, the heat of him that burns me, invites me to cross the line.

"Sin."

"Summer." He reaches for the remaining butter on the silver dish and scoops it all up.

I gulp, lower my gaze.

My distorted reflection on the polished wood surface gapes at me. Eyes wide, nostrils flared. My mouth quivers; my nipples harden. Damn him for making me want every single thing that is wrong. This is wrong. *We* are wrong. This goddamn venue is a mistake. A never-ending movie on a loop, repeated, again and again. I raise my gaze to his face.

He's watching me from under hooded eyes.

"Do you want me, Bird?"

I nod.

"How much?"

"Take me to bed, Sinner, or lose me forever."

"That's from *Top Gun*." His brows draw down. "Did I say that? Jesus, I can't believe I am playing this your way."

He glares at me. My nerve endings stretch.

My skin crawls, my toes curl, and I wriggle my hips. I can't... cannot contain this craving, this yearning, this sheer carnal hunger to have him buried inside of me.

"No more games, Summer. Tell me you want what I have in mind."

I swallow.

"Say it. Tell me 'no.' "

"Yes."

His cock leaps in my grasp. I squeeze it and a pulse beats to life at his jawline. *Wow.*

He dips his fingers into the crease between my butt cheeks, unerringly finding my back hole. He slides one finger in.

I gasp. Too full. Too much. It's tight, but not really. It's beyond my comfort level. Enough that I want... I need...

"More?"

I jerk my chin.

He eases the finger inside and I swallow. He curls the finger inside and a trembling grips me. "Sin."

"I'm here."

He inserts another finger and my body bucks.

"My God." Color sears his cheeks. "You're so..." the tendons of his throat flex. "Beautiful, my Bird." He licks his lips and goddamn him, I sense that swipe deep inside in the most intimate part of me.

"You're unique, exotic, one-of-a-kind, my Summer. Your every response is my salvation."

His words envelop me, sink into my blood, curl in my chest, satisfying something deep inside. Something I hadn't acknowledged in all these years. That I'd wanted more than the physical. I'd hoped to meet someone who'd match me word for word. Who'd teach me, push my boundaries, understand why the trivia is more than sentences. More than emotions. They are images of my unsaid desires, that I can hold in the palm of my hand, relish in real life, in front of my eyes, just as he worships me. Here. Now. In this very moment, there is nothing else. Just me, him, and the pleasure he's going to wring from my body.

"Sin."

"Tell me."

"I want you inside me."

His indigo eyes blaze. "Anything you need." He slips a third finger inside and my pussy spasms. Liquid heat drips from my core. I drag my fingers up the length of his dick, constrained by my position. I strain toward him "I want—"

"I know."

He pulls out his fingers and I am empty. Hollow. A shell of my former self. Ready to embrace—

He pushes away the food tray, then drags my fingers down, and onto the table in front of my face.

His eyes never lose their steady calmness. He's a man close to reaching his goal. The one thing he's sought since he'd stated his intent. My complete and utter destruction. My submission. And I'm giving it to him, willingly. "Take it."

"You possess me." His voice chafes my already sensitized nerve endings.

He loosens the buckle of his belt, drags down his zipper, and his cock springs free. There's Sin… A whole lotta Sin there. And it's all for me… At least for this instant. And after… After? *Don't go there.*

"What's wrong?"

He pauses, dick in hand. His fingers grasp the base of his thick length. It's massive, veins run up its length, a drop of precum glints at the tip. Of course, I'd felt it inside me. But seeing him, naked, wanting, greedy for what I can give him… *Is that right?*

Is it only me that he wants to claim? The others? Why am I thinking of that? Do I have a claim on him? This entire marriage thing is getting to me. I was beginning to believe my own lies. Fake it till you make it has never sounded truer.

"Summer." His jaw flexes.

"I.."

"What do you need?"

"Thought you could read my mind."

He hesitates. "I don't want to get it wrong."

"You won't."

A vein throbs at his temple; his shaft pulses. So much emotion, so many secrets all coiled up under the surface. He's not in control. It's all a sham. A face he shows the world. A mask he wears, and I ripped it away from him. Sensations crawl inside my chest. I am getting to know this man too well. Too quickly. Everything is happening at breakneck speed and I am powerless to stop it.

He reaches down with his free hand and grips my nape. The strength of his intensity drips into my skin, and I swallow. I've never felt closer to anyone else, as much as I have in this instant.

He draws in a deep breath. "I can't give you that."

I bite the inside of my cheek.

"I've always been up front about what I wanted."

Have you?

"I should have stopped before things got so out of hand, and for that I take the blame."

Blame? What does he mean?

"I'll tell you this much. I've never wanted anyone as much as you. Never felt this… close to anyone else before. Never allowed anyone to see the parts of me you have."

But it's not enough. Can't you see that?

"I don't know if I can give you my heart. Hell, I doubt that exists after everything I have done so far, but my body, it's yours for the taking."

My throat closes.

This man, he could talk forever, and I could listen to him. Hell, I could orgasm, multiple times, one after the other to the timbre of his voice. *I want more.*

What? What do I need?

"How about a deal?'

"Oh?" He tilts his head.

"You've gotta admit, you're not exactly in any position for negotiating."

He smirks. "Clever girl."

"I'm learning from the master."

"Damn right." He squeezes his dick from base to tip and my gaze drops to his crotch. Droplets of cum drip from the tip of his cock, which has definitely engorged further in the last few seconds.

"Why, Mr. Sterling, I do believe, that you love it when I sass you."

"Never denied that." He growls. "Stop dicking around, Bird, what's your game?"

"Not a game." I bite down on my lower lip and he inhales.

See? He's definitely not as much in control as he pretends. He's as much at a loss as I am. I draw up my shoulders, cross my fingers, "I get to take the lead in bed."

43

Sin

"No." My voice sounds almost as hard as my dick. I wince. She could have asked for my money, my empire, my fucking heart, at that moment and I'd have given it... Okay, maybe not the last one. Dominance in bed is the one thing I will not compromise on.

She tilts her head, the expression on her face a mirror to the one I've pulled on her so often. The back of my neck heats. My cock leaps against my palm. How is it that I can possibly find her attempt to take control so... so arousing?

I glare at her, and she sets her jaw.

"You said you'd give me your body."

I jerk my chin.

"Then this..." she stares at my crotch, "all of this is mine."

This woman. *Fuck.* How can she surprise me so much? Blood rushes to my groin. My balls grow so hard that I am sure I'm going to jizz myself right there, right now.

"You'll let me take your ass."

She nods.

"Your pussy."

She hesitates, then tosses her head.

"Your mouth."

The pulse beats so fast at her throat that I am sure it's going to tear through her skin.

"At the same time?"

I tilt my head and she juts out her chin. "Okay."

"Anytime I want?"

She squeezes her eyes together, "Why do I get a feeling I am going to regret this?"

You have no idea, little Bird.

She cracks her eyelids open. "What else?"

Smart woman, she knows I am not done yet, hmm? A surge of pride fills my chest. She's come far, my wife, in a few days.

"I will allow you to lead…" Her breath catches.

"Once."

"You…" She swallows. "You'd do that?"

Yeah, what I said earlier? Clearly, I am bloody good at lying to myself, for when it comes to her… Turns out, I am unable to disappoint her. All for a reason, of course. It's the long game that matters. That's me. I bide my time. Never retreat. Keep my focus on the target. Revenge. What a hollow word. It's second nature now. It's what's driven me so far. I can't let down the Seven either. Giving up the thing that defines me? A price I hadn't thought I'd ever have to pay.

Doing it for her? Yeah, only her. Only for her.

"Don't celebrate yet." I splay my fingers on the back of her waist. She flattens her shoulders, her arse juts out. Perfectly heart-shaped. *My beautiful responsive, Bird.*

I line up my dick with the crease between her butt cheeks. She squirms. I apply enough pressure, so she turns her head toward me. I drop my head and brush my mouth over hers. She stiffens. I swipe my tongue between her lips and she whimpers. I tilt my head, deepen the kiss and she opens for me. I draw from her, suck on her tongue, bite down on the infuriating crease in her lower lip. She cries out and I swallow down the sound, at the same time that I slide my hips forward.

My cock nudges against her back hole and she murmurs deep in her throat.

I slip my fingers in between her legs and play with her pussy. She shudders, parts her legs, and I slide two fingers into her melting pussy. Her spine arches, she thrusts out her butt, and I slip in. I rub my heel on her clit, kiss her with even more intensity.

Her arm comes up and she holds onto my neck as she bows into me.

My sweet Bird. I slide my finger inside her pussy and her knees buckle. I tighten my grip on her nape. A trembling sweeps up her body. She digs her fingers into my skin. I tear my lips from hers and she swallows. Pupils blown, lips parted and swollen from my kisses. I drag my palm down her spine.

When I apply pressure, she bends.

Lowers her head to the desk, her cheek, once more, flush with the antique surface. A thing of beauty, a perfect composition. A merger that clicks into place effortlessly. She's all that. *She's mine.* I grip her hips and thrust forward; her entire body jerks. And again. My balls harden and pressure builds in my groin. I need more. Much more. I pull out of her, then flip her over. The front of her dress falls open.

She blinks, wide-eyed. Her lips part.

I don't hesitate. I bend with her, over her, touch my lips to hers and kiss her. Drag my hands up her hips to her breasts, cup them, and squeeze her nipples. She moans, the sound so sweet, so right.

I bring my hands down to her thighs, pull them wide apart. She swings her legs up and around my waist. *Fuck.* I grit my teeth; I need to slow down. Sweat beads my forehead. My heartbeat thunders in my ears. What's happening to me? This was meant to be some kind of hate fuck. A last try to overcome whatever hold she has on me. I'd sweetened her up with words—well, it was all truth, really— then tried to break her. *Instead, it's me who's broken.*

I squeeze the base of my dick, position myself at the entrance to her weeping pussy. Then tip my head up to stare into her eyes.

"I'm going to fuck you now."

She nods.

"You can say 'No.' "

"Yes."

"Last chance to walk away." *Am I warning her or myself?*

"Oh, for heaven's sake." She grabs my dick, lines me up with her slit, then slides forward.

She impales herself on my shaft. My cock slips all the way home. I can't stop the growl that rips out of me. Holding her gaze, I grip her hips, withdraw until I'm poised at the opening of her pussy. Pause a beat. Another. Then I thrust into her so hard that the entire desk shakes.

She links her arms around my neck and holds on.

"Good girl."

I proceed to fuck her with an intensity I've never felt before. A complete carnal possession that overrides any other intention I may have ever held.

Remember what I said about fucking thoughts of any other men from her mind? I lied. Again. *Turns out, I am the one who's never going to be able to think straight. Ever again.*

I thrust into her, again and again.

Fix my fingers on her nape, with my thumb pressed to the front of her neck, where I can sense every single vibration of her voice that emerges in small hoarse cries.

Sweat beads my shoulders. I don't stop. I withdraw then pound into her again and again.

Her lips part; a flush covers her breasts, her face. Her entire body trembles. She throws her head back, her gorgeous hair a halo tumbling down her shoulders. "Come," I growl. And she shatters. Beautifully.

Her eyes roll back in her head and she shudders.

I pull out of her, my balls draw up, and white streams of my cum splatter across her chest. I squeeze my dick from base to tip, empty every last drop of myself on her.

Reaching between us, I rub my seed into the skin exposed by the gaping front of her dress.

She slumps and I scoop her up in my arms. Walking around the desk, I sink into the chair. She curls into my chest and her breathing deepens.

I hold her close, tilt my chair back, turn it toward the window, and watch the raindrops drip down the windowpane.

44

"I didn't know how to love him. I only knew how to fuck,"
— *Lie With Me,* Director: Clement Virgo

Summer

I come awake to find that I am curled up in the center of the massive bed — his bed, in his house on Primrose Hill.

I sit up and the sheet slides down to pool at my waist. When I swing my legs over, I wince. My thighs ache; there is a soreness in my center. I straighten, glance down, and the breath leaves me. The skin on my thighs is chafed and abraded. I take a step forward and my arse hurts... Yeah, also that part of me where he had proceeded to butter me up, before driving into me from behind. A slow burn starts somewhere below. *No. I didn't enjoy it, I didn't. Who am I kidding?* He'd... surprised me again.

He'd brought to life one of the most notorious scenes from film history and ah! Liquid heat pools between my legs. It had been the singular most degrading experience of my life... and the most turned on I've ever been.

I squeeze my fingers at my sides.

Then he'd turned me around... and... kissed me. He'd made love to me.

"I'm more than halfway in love with you."

Did he mean it? Sinclair Sterling does not say anything lightly and definitely not the emotions associated with that particular sentiment. Perhaps my imagination is leading me down a path of wishful thinking?

What do I have to do to clear my head? Rid my body of the imprints of his palm that I can feel on my butt, on the curve of my waist, the thickness of his fingers... inside me, bringing me to orgasm, the cold slick of the butter as he'd lubricated me before he'd taken me, with absolute confidence.

He'd known that I wouldn't refuse him. I'd wanted to. *No… I'd wanted him.* When I am in his vicinity, I can't think of anything else but him… *Liar.* Even when I am not in the same room, I see him in my mind and yeah, my pussy has a way of homing in on how it will be to have him buried balls deep inside of me.

Jesus, get a grip, here. Stop with the pornographic scenes playing on repeat. Not that I've seen porn… If you don't count *9 1/2 weeks,* which had explored BDSM long before *Fifty Shades of Grey,* or *9 Songs.* Wait… What is it with the 9 anyway? I shake my head. Or any of the myriad other arthouse flicks that I'd snuck in to watch, whenever they came to play at the Prince Charles Theatre—one of the few existing arthouse cinemas near Leicester Square.

My entire life is beginning to resemble a badly-produced indie flick, for that matter… For he hadn't stopped there. After I'd fallen asleep on his chest… Yeah, it's large, hard, and surprisingly comfortable, and despite all of the ways he's fucked me over—literally— seems something in me innately trusts Mr. Big Bad.

I'd woken up to find he was carrying me up to the roof top. He'd ordered a helicopter because… Well yeah, he could.

He'd said he wanted to get inside me again and didn't want to wait. Of course, not. I swallow, lurch toward the bathroom.

He'd carried me inside the house to the kitchen. Fed me strawberries and cream. He'd insisted I eat it and drink every drop of the glass of orange juice he'd poured for me.

Then he'd shagged me.

Over the kitchen table, on the steps, against the wall of his bedroom, on the bed… He'd broken off to bring me some cheese and biscuits at dinner time. No alcohol because… he wanted all of my faculties about me.

I'd lost count somewhere after orgasm number thirteen, or was that twenty? I bite the inside of my cheek. I'd fallen asleep with him inside of me again. My pussy clenches. How can I miss him already?

I shove open the bathroom door and cross the floor to the sink on the left; the one with an array of feminine cosmetics, none of which I'd brought. The brand is absolutely top of the range. Individually, they'd account for what I'd probably get paid in a week working at FOK. *Fuck.*

I drag my fingers through my hair. I'd never gotten a chance to mention the reason I'd barged in on him. Because I'd had an idea for the marketing strategy. Something I need to bring up to him right away.

I glance at the mirror and notice the note tucked into a corner of the glass frame. Reach for it, pull it out. The gold SS on the cream paper confirms who it was from.

"The cosmetics are for you—don't refuse them."

Asshole. His cursive is as dominating as his presence.

"Breakfast is waiting for you in the kitchen."

Huh? You don't say.

"Because I'm feeling charitable, you may work from home today. You're welcome."

What? Am I supposed to be grateful or something? I purse my lips. Bring the note to my nose and sniff. Bergamot and leather… and a whiff of something intangible I label as testosterone. I chafe my thighs together. Place the note aside. Brush my teeth, shower in record time. When I return to the bedroom, I spot the dress he's laid out for me.

I slip it on, survey myself in the mirror. It has a long flowing skirt and the blouse fits me so closely, I have to wonder. Did he have it tailored to my specifications? Does he know my measurements that well?

He knows my body more intimately than anyone else ever has. I fondle the soft material. The skirt is a dark red. How did he guess that it's the color that sets off my coloring best? My pink hair flows around my shoulders, the blonde highlights in it seem lustrous, and my skin is a pearly effervescence against the fabric.

Once again, he's unerringly figured out what is right for me. Does he always know what is best? Am I beginning to harbor some kind of secret crush on him, where I am beginning to acquiesce to his every single demand? No. I drag the brush through my hair, drop it on the table. I won't wear any make up. After all, I'm not dressing for anyone. Besides, I don't want to use any of the cosmetics he bought for me. The dress? Well, that is different. I have to wear something—though left to the alphahole, I bet he'd prefer me to go naked.

Don't second guess me, Bird.

I scrutinize the room. The mussed-up bed where we'd spent the night, the table and chair at the far end, the comfortable-looking settee on one side of the fireplace. The furnishings are luxurious, but otherwise there is a sparseness to it that hints at... what?

Something more complex about the man than I've been giving him credit for?

Nothing to think about here. Nothing to unearth. He is a greedy, narcissistic, pompous prick, who thinks about one thing—himself. And how to amass more money. See? Puzzle resolved.

I slide on the ballet flats—made of the softest leather I've ever worn—then pivot and walk down the stairs. Walk into the kitchen and find a covered tray, with a note.

"Eat it all."

I stiffen. I should ignore the food, turn away, leave, right now, before this entire farce of a relationship backfires on me and I begin to harbor feelings for him. Too late. I feel something... already. Hate, yeah, that's all it is.

I uncover the tray to find a massive sandwich. A plate of fruit, crisps. There's another note stuck to the side of the plate.

"It's gluten free. You're welcome."

How did he know I am allergic to gluten? I've never mentioned it to him, and managed to ignore any food that could have traces of it so far.

Of course, he had to go and spoil it all with that know-it-all tone.

I crumple the note, fling it away,

The kettle clicks on. *What the—?* I hear the water boil. Did he set it on a timer? Some kind of sensing device that picks up when I'm in the room? I blow out a breath.

I walk to the kettle as it switches off. Make myself a cup of tea, and seat myself at the table. I've just finished the sandwich when the doorbell rings.

My heart begins to thud. Is he back? Did he decide he is going to work from home today? Better still, does he want to spend it with me? I am halfway across the floor, before I slow down. By the time I reach the front hallway, there's a banging on the door. I fling it open.

Familiar features peer down at me.

"You?"

"Hello, Summer."

I glare at the man who is my father.

The bastard who'd abandoned me and my sister when we'd needed him the most. He'd never looked back, until he'd sensed the first whiff of a possible business gain, and then he'd come running. The asshole would sacrifice his family for money—oh, wait, he already had.

There's a light roll of thunder in the distance—as if it is asking for permission. That's British weather for you, just like our vocabulary. Apparently, we use the word 'sorry' more than any other country—up to 8 times a day. Yeah, sorry—not sorry. I frown, "I don't want you here."

"Can I come in?"

It begins to drizzle outside, some of the drops blowing in to bead on his shoulder.

"Do I have a choice?" I jut out my chin.

"That's my girl. Still got a spine, huh?"

"No thanks to you, and don't call me your girl."

"You're my daughter."

"Really?" I stare. "You lost the right to that when you decided to leave me and Karma to the vagaries of our fate."

"Don't exaggerate." He frowns. "Look at you now. It doesn't look like you suffered too much."

If you don't count the fact that we'd gone from having an abundance of every luxury to having two meals a day, and a school where we were the laughingstock because of how different we were. So, we weren't abused physically. Mentally and emotionally, though, it was another story. I wrap a strand of my hair around my fingers. "You could have taken us with you—or better still, you could have told us what was going on, found a way to face up to the mess you'd created."

"And what? Gone to jail?" He rocks back on his feet, "Where would that have left you?"

"Exactly where you left us anyway. Fighting to make something of ourselves. Trying to undo the hurt of our childhood years, and betrayal. And yeah, issues with trust, let's not forget that."

"Your husband has money; he can afford the best mental health professionals."

"Are you listening to yourself?"

He draws in a breath, "I didn't come here to fight."

"Too bad." I wrap my arms around my waist, "I've been waiting for the chance to tell you how much of a shitty parent you were… No, strike that. That I disown you, for how you abandoned us." I attempt to close the door. He grabs the handle, "Sunshine, please."

I freeze. Only my father called me that. I'd been his ray of sunshine once, or so he'd told me. Those mornings when he'd cook me breakfast, before anyone else was up. Our time together. Then he'd drive me to school. Karma had been a baby then, and dependent on our mother. He'd been proud of me once. And I had looked up to him.

"Five minutes. That's all I'm asking." Oh, he knows how to push the point when he has an advantage, huh?

I step back, walk inside, then head toward the living room that overlooks the garden. He follows me.

I stop at the massive French doors, and he pauses behind me.

"I can explain, Summer."

"Save it. I don't want to listen to your sorry excuses."

He draws in a breath. "Everything I did was so I could ensure that you and your sister had a future."

"You expect me to believe that?"

"I was mixed up with the wrong people. After your mother died, I wasn't thinking straight. I made many wrong business decisions. Ended up falling into debt."

I don't want to hear it. I don't.

He swallows, the sound audible in the silence, interrupted by the patter of the rain outside.

"I ended up owing a lot of money to the Mafia. I had to leave before they took everything I held dear to me."

"So you dumped us?"

"The only way was to start afresh, for all of us." He moves away. "I put you in the care system, then faked my own death. I moved to the US, changed my identity, wiped all traces of our past."

"You did it very effectively too." I stare straight ahead. "Guess you were good at something."

He winces. "Everything I did was to throw the Mafia off of your tracks. It was for your good."

"So parents say. They have no idea how much they screw us kids up. So we have to spend the rest of our lives unlearning everything we were subjected to in our growing up years."

The breath whooshes out of him. "I'm sorry, Summer. I did what I thought was best for all of us..."

"Yeah, I'm sorry too." I turn on him. "You've assuaged your conscience, said your piece... Why don't you leave now, huh?"

"There is." He shuffles his weight from foot to foot. "One thing."

I knew it. "Money? You think because of this..." I wave my arms around, "that I have some claim to his wealth and his power? Then you are wrong."

"You're the wife of a rich and powerful man. It has to count for something."

"It means nothing."

"Not from where I am." He lowers his chin, "And it's not about the money."

"Don't lie." A headache begins to pound at my temples.

"I admit, it might have been one of the main reasons that I accepted Sinclair's offer, but when I saw you and your sister after all these years." His throat moves as he swallows, "I realized it wasn't about that at all."

I don't believe him. I don't. Something hot unfurls in my chest, "What then?"

"Are you happy?"

I blink.

"Excuse me?"

"Does he make you happy?"

"What's that got to do with anything?"

"You're my daughter"

"You lost all right to call me that."

He holds up a hand. "I get it. You're unhappy with the cards life dealt you, so far. It's normal. It's time you put it behind you as you start your new life."

"Is that why you're here? To give me advice?"

"When Sinclair asked me over, I agreed to come, on one condition. I had to be satisfied that he was the right man for you. Someone who could take care of you, protect you—"

"The way you never could."

His lips twist. "You grew up fine, with all your wits about you."

"No thanks to you."

"Tell me you are content, and I can seal the deal with him."

"Deal?"

"He didn't tell you?" Adam frowns.

"We haven't had the time to speak." Heat sears my cheeks. I hadn't meant it to come out that way.

My father doesn't seem to notice.

"It's understandable. Sinclair is a busy man. He bought me amnesty from the government, gave me a chance to return home to attend my daughter's wedding." Adam shuffles his feet. "Still, considering what he wants…"

My pulse begins to race. The hairs on the nape of my neck rise. I wipe my suddenly damp palms on the skirt. Something thrums at the edges of my conscious mind and I push it away. "What does he want?"

"What do you think?" A familiar voice cuts through the space.

I whip my head around to find my husband leaning against the door frame.

He trains his gaze on my father, "I want to ruin you, of course."

45

Sin

My wife stiffens.

Ahead of her, the man who was responsible for destroying my childhood stares past her at me. He looks confused.

"The deal was you'd keep me and my family safe and share enough business interests for me to redeem myself on my home turf."

I tilt my head.

"You didn't invite me to attend the wedding because my daughter wanted me here?"

I make a twirling motion with my fingers. "Go on."

"You want something more from me?"

I bare my teeth.

He swallows, "Either way, you don't intend to stick to your word?"

I walk toward them. "Now what makes you say that, hmm?" I pause next to my wife.

Adam looks at her, then back at me, "She's innocent." Sweat beads his forehead.

"That's what I told the men who kidnapped me."

"Kidnapped?" Summer angles her body to face me. "What are you talking about?"

"Ask your father."

She steps away, putting distance between herself and the both of us. Anger slices my gut.

Of course, she is wary of me.

She has the right to be, given how I had taken her in my office yesterday, and then I couldn't keep my hands off her body. She is singlehandedly, the biggest distraction in my life right now, and I would do well to be done with her and this sham of a marriage.

I'd hoped for time with her, hadn't reckoned things would come to a head so soon.

What-fucking-ever. I can work with the cards I've been dealt. So what if I told him I'd protect them? I don't owe him, or her, anything.

"Dad?"

Adam glances down at his daughter. "I haven't heard you call me that since—"

"Since you abandoned us."

He winces. "I've already explained to you, Summer—"

"Stop." She cuts the air with her hand. "I don't want to hear your excuses." She jerks her chin toward me without looking at me, "Tell me what he's referring to, will you?"

"I... I'm not sure." Adam looks between us.

"Bull-fucking-shit." I explode. Adam's shoulders hunch. My wife winces, but doesn't take her gaze off of his face.

"Tell her." I gesture toward the older man.

He blinks rapidly, then peruses my features. "Who... who are you... really?"

"Haven't you guessed yet?"

"It can't be," he whispers. His face blanches.

"Tell her what you did to me... you fucking piece of shit."

Adam takes a deep breath. "It's a long story."

I twist my lips, "Trust me, nothing as extended as the time I spent with the rest of the Seven locked up in a windowless cellar."

"You were locked up?" She whips her head around, and I feel every millimeter of that green gaze. Waves of confusion emanate from her. *Fuck that.* I don't need her sympathy; I don't need anyone feeling sorry for me. I want revenge. Anger coils my gut. A hot feeling stabs in my chest. I click the clasp on my watch. *Control it. You gotta rein in your temper. Stay focused.* I click the clasp again.

The cold metal soothes me; some of the noise in my head recedes. So close. I am so close to my goal, I can practically taste the ending. Revenge: his utter destruction, tracking down the men responsible, and putting this whole ugly segment of my life behind me.

A pressure builds behind my rib cage.

"Tell her right now, or I swear I'll kill you with my bare hands. Right now."

Summer inhales sharply. *Go on Bird, go to his defense, tell me off.* Show me how the blood of my enemy runs through your veins.

Her gaze is fixed on her father, "Spit it out, whatever you did to him." She firms her lips.

Huh?

Adam makes a choking sound. He pulls out a handkerchief and mops his forehead. "Can you get me some water?"

"No." My wife's features are pale. The hollows beneath her cheeks are pronounced. She grabs a strand of that glorious pink hair and chews on it, a giveaway that she is stressed. I take a step forward, then stop myself. *What am I doing?*

Why do I want to go to her, pull her close and ask her to lean on me? Tell her that she doesn't have to worry about anything as long as I am around. I'll take care of her forever. *Fuck.* These motherfucking emo thoughts? Where are they coming from? Just because I fucked her— *You made love to her, asshole.* Last night had been as close to a declaration of intention as you can get.

You worshipped her body with your own. You kissed her, took her arse, wrecked her pussy as if it were yours. For she is yours. She is. Only it's too late. I've come too far, planned too much. I owe it to the Seven to see this through.

She? She is collateral damage. A drumming intensifies behind my eyes. I drag my fingers through my hair.

"No point delaying the inevitable." I glare at the man.

He makes a choking sound.

"Don't faint on me now." I lean forward on the balls of my feet. "You're not getting any sympathy from me."

"I don't need it." He draws himself upright. Then turns to my wife. "You remember what I told you about owing money to the mob?"

She nods.

"I was in their control. I had to do what they asked. They threatened to kill you and Karma. Or worse."

"The fuck?" A growl rips up my chest.

Both of them turn in my direction.

"They threatened her life?" I flex my fingers at my sides,

Summer's gaze narrows, "What's your problem?"

I shoot her a glare; she juts out her chin. She takes a deep breath and opens her mouth. I shake my head. She purses her lips and I am sure she's going to speak or say something; instead, she wraps her arms around her waist and glowers back.

Later, Bird. You and me are going to have this out, and I promise, you won't be able to speak at all by the end.

Her cheeks redden. Perhaps she read the intention in my gaze, hmm?

I turn on Adam, sorry excuse of a human that he is. "And you call yourself a father? You left them in danger and ran away?"

"I faked my death, severed ties with them. I released them into the system because, let's face it, the government would have had more success in miring their trail in paper-work so that it would be difficult for anyone to find them."

"You did a brilliant job too. In fact, I'd almost forgotten about your existence." Summer's voice is harsh; there's an edge to it I've never heard before. She holds her body so tightly that her shoulders seem to vibrate.

"Too bad you couldn't do the same for yourself."

Adam loosens the tie about his neck, "What do you mean?"

"My husband tracked you down, didn't he? So you weren't as efficient in covering your tracks as you thought."

Adam turns to me, his eyes wide, "How did you find me, when the Mafia tried and failed for all these years?"

"Clearly, they aren't as resourceful as I am. Funny how almost dying can light a fire under you, and ensure that you never give up until you track down your quarry."

Summer angles her body toward me."Wha... what do you mean? Who almost died?"

I slice my hand through the air, "Doesn't matter."

I glare at her. Now is when she explodes, and tells me off, pulls off a snarky comment at my expense. My pulse rate picks up; my blood thrums in my veins. *Come on, little Bird, give me a taste of that sass and fire hidden below the surface.* I scan her features, wait... wait. She peruses my features with a searching look in her eyes, then shakes her head.

"Cora." Adam's chin quivers.

Summer stiffens, "You lost the right to call me that."

"When you were born, your face was a perfect heart shape. I wanted to name you Cora. Your mother insisted on Summer. We compromised, as was often the case." His lips twitch. "And Cora became your middle name." His features soften. "You were so beautiful. The tiniest little child with the sweetest disposition ever."

He sways; rubs his chest.

"I'll never forget how you lit up my life, my child. The time we spent together is among the most precious memories of my life."

She firms her lips, raises her chin, "I am pleased to say I don't remember much of my growing years."

He winces, "I deserve it."

I take a step forward, "Tell her what you did to us."

"You mean there's more?" Summer tucks her elbows into her sides, her entire body stiff. Her chest rises and falls. She's imagining — I can't begin to fathom what it is she's thinking, but the reality is far worse.

"I…" Adam licks his lips, "Please, can you get me some water first?"

I turn to do that.

"No."

I pause, glance toward my wife.

"The complete story first." Summer sets her jaw, "Enough with your delay tactics."

A small smile turns up his lips, "You remind me of your mother."

"You don't get to do that." Her chin trembles. "Spit it out already." She spits out his name, "Adam."

He squeezes his eyes shut and when he reopens them, they glitter with unshed tears. "Fine." He weaves on his feet, puts out his hand, and grabs onto the nearest chair. "They coerced me… I had to obey them." He looks from me to her, "I kidnapped your husband."

She scowls, "What do you mean?"

"Your father aligned with the Mob in furthering their business interests." My voice emerges as if it belongs to someone else.

I glare at Adam, "Tell her how you kidnapped me on the way home from school when I was twelve."

His gaze flicks to his daughter, "It's not how it sounds."

"Oh?" The blood thunders at my temple. "Are you denying what you did."

He tips his chin up, drags his fingers through his hair. His fingers tremble. "It's true that I delivered you to the Mafia."

I fold my fingers into fists, "As you did the rest of the Seven?"

He furrows his brow. "I wasn't responsible for any other children. The Mafia must have put others up to that." He raises his hands. "I swear. After taking you, I knew I couldn't do that again. That's when I faked my death."

Anger explodes behind my eyes; my vision tunnels.

"Why me?" I growl. "I was the sole scholarship kid in that school. My parents had no money, let alone the kind of old wealth that the rest of the Seven did."

"It was a mistake. Last-minute change of plans. The child they had set their eyes on didn't come to school that day. You walked out instead." He raises his shoulders. "I was desperate; you fit the bill."

"Wrong place, wrong time, huh?"

His lips twist. "You could say that."

There's a sharp inhalation from my wife.

"You were unlucky, Sinclair." He waves a hand at his surroundings, "But look what it did to you."

"The fuck you mean?" The blood drums at my temples with such intensity that the edges of my vision go dark.

"Clearly, it gave you the motivation you needed to lift yourself to the very top."

"Are you actually trying to take credit for my success? It drove my parents to an early grave, you dumb fuck. My entire life changed in an instant." A trembling stumbles up my spine. I grip my fingers at my sides. Take one step forward, then another.

"Sinclair." My wife's voice follows me

I reach him, grab his collar.

"Sin." She grips my collar, "Don't."

"Do it." Adam smiles, then his lips pull down. "I deserve all of it."

I pull back my hand in a fist; my wife screams.

Adam crumples to the ground.

46

Summer

The rhythmic whoosh-thump of the respirator thuds against my chest, mirroring the whump-whump-whump of my heart. I stare at the man who was... is my father.

I hadn't seen him in fifteen years and when he'd shown up at my wedding I had ignored him. I had insulted him when he'd turned up on my doorstep— Okay, *my husband's* doorstep. I had refused my father water. He'd asked for it twice and I had ignored him.

I curl my fingers into fists.

I had been too intent on revenge; on cutting into him with my words; wanting him to feel as broken as I had been in the years after he'd left me. When I'd found out he hadn't actually died, I'd wished him dead so many times... And here he is, on death's door. His ribs visible through the hospital gown, his face so pale it blends in with the sheets. When had his dark hair gone so grey? I hadn't noticed it earlier.

In the blurry images I carried in my head, he'd been tall, larger than life, a wide smile, a full head of dark hair. He'd been some kind of hero... a vision I'd wanted to cling to in my weaker moments. Someone who would one day come back for me and tell me that he was sorry, that he still loved me.

And he had returned. And I hadn't wanted to acknowledge that he still existed. He is the cause of every bad memory from my childhood come to life, and he claimed that he'd done it all for my own good. Typical. Why do parents always think that their children need to be shielded? That they can't bear what their parents are going through?

All he'd had to do was take us with him—love us, hate us, we'd have been together, and that's all that would have mattered.

But he hadn't.

And here we are in a hospital room. My father had crumpled and Sinclair had caught him before he could hit the floor. My husband had called for his helicopter, then phoned ahead for his private doctors to be on standby. For once I didn't begrudge him his wealth.

We'd arrived at the hospital, and Dad had been rushed in. A cardiac attack. They'd operated on him right away, put in a stent to widen his blocked arteries. Now all I have to do is wait. For what? What am I going to say when he comes around? What will I tell him? What is going to happen to him? To us?

Karma and Victoria were in to see him already, and now they are in the waiting room outside.

I'd put it off, until... until Karma had urged me to go in. She'd told me that if something were to happen to him, I'd regret it if I didn't at least see him. But Dad is in his fifties; nothing is going to happen to him, right?

People survive multiple bypasses and go on to live full lives. Surely, my father will be no different. He'll pull through. He has to. I press my knuckles into my eyes.

The door whispers open behind me, and a shiver runs down my back.

It's him. He's in the room.

Sinclair draws abreast; the scent of bergamot and leather cleaves through the cloud of antiseptic. I draw it into my lungs, hold it, savor it. How many times will I be able to do this?

"How are you?"

These are the first words he's spoken to me in the last many hours. He'd ensured I didn't have to deal with the paperwork, the formalities, talking to the doctors. He'd taken care of all of it, leaving me to grieve... What? How things could have been, had my father not abandoned us? How I could have handled things differently with him? Could I have told him everything I carried around in my mind? My father... Sin... Why are my emotions always such a tangled web?

"Bird."

"Summer." My voice is too loud in the room, "My name is Summer."

"You should take a break, go home—"

"No." I glance away, "And it's not *my* home."

"Call it mine then." He widens his stance. "Go, eat, take a bath."

"What if he dies while I am gone?"

"He won't."

"Oh?" I stop the chuckle that bubbles up. Hysteria? No way am I giving into that. Not in front of him. "You think you can stop death?"

"I know it."

I stiffen, "What do you mean?"

"I almost died as a child."

"What?" I swing around. He's staring at the opposite wall. A pulse flares to life at his jawline. "The Mafia kidnapped us and kept us captive."

"For how long?"

"Too long." He fiddles with the clasp of his watch. "It was close to a month." His jaw tenses.

I don't dare speak, don't want to break this line of thought. He's thinking of... something... caught in the throes of his nightmares. I am not the only one running from my past, eh?

"We were bound to our beds, kept drugged." He clicks open the clasp of his watch, then shuts it with a harder click. "I floated in and out of consciousness." The tendons of his throat flex. "In my lucid moments, I tried to communicate with the other boys in the room. There were —"

"Seven of you."

He nods. "That's how we met. From different homes, families, different realities; and our lives were changed irrevocably in that time."

"A powerful bond."

"One that unites you and haunts you for the rest of your life."

"What did they want?"

"They blackmailed our families for money. Until they realized mine didn't have any."

The clicking of his watch grows louder.

He pulls himself up to his full height, "After about 3 weeks in that hell hole, one of us managed to break free. He was caught and brought back. That day they decided to make an example of me. I was the expandable one, after all." His smile grows fierce. "They beat me so hard that I lost consciousness."

I gasp. "The scar over your eyebrow...?"

He nods.

"The other families paid up. The kidnappers took the money, revealed the location where they were holding us. I was rescued with the other boys." He clicks the clasp of his watch. "When I arrived at the hospital I wasn't breathing. They resuscitated me." The clicking grows louder.

"They brought you back." The breath rushes out of me.

"I chose to live."

"Is that why... uh! You're so intense?"

One side of his mouth kicks up, "Now you're being diplomatic."

Yeah, but when a man decides to reveal something of his deepest self, you don't exactly kick him for it, eh?

He straightens, rubs the back of his neck, "I almost died... The rest of the Seven didn't escape unscathed either."

"What do you mean?"

"That is their story to tell."

He turns to me.

His shirt is unbuttoned, his hair mussed as if he's been running his hands through the thick strands. It gives him a veneer of vulnerability. An act. Surely, it's an act?

He'd wanted me to draw my father into the open. He'd wanted to destroy him.... Guess he got his wish, huh? So, what's left? "Why share all of this with me... now?"

He holds out his hand. "Take a break."

I stare at his hand. "Is everything a negotiation?"

"Yes." He draws in a breath. "It's the most important lesson I learned during the time I was locked up there. You had to think on your feet, hold back. As long as you had something that your opponent wanted, you had a chance."

"Am I your opponent?" I tip my head back, peruse his features for the first time since he'd come into the room. Dark shadows circle his eyes, and his stubble seems wilder somehow.

It enhances his potency.

Those dark, brooding, smoldering good looks just kicked up a notch. Combined with that hint of defenselessness that laces his features, it's intoxicating. An addiction. A low burn simmers in my belly. My body is too conditioned to react to him. I don't stand a chance.

I reach for his hand, his fingers brush mine and he pulls me up. I straighten and our knees bump.

He tucks an errant strand of hair behind my ears and I shiver.

His gaze deepens as he surveys my face. He sighs, "Bird, I'm…"

A cough sounds from the bed. I blink. Sinclair withdraws. I swivel, walk toward the bed, "Daddy?"

My father's eyes blink open. "Summer?"

"I'm here."

His fingers twitch. I grasp his palm. His hand is bigger than mine, yet his bones seem hollow.

"I'm sorry, for everything."

"You need to rest and recover.'

"It's time for me to leave.

"Don't say that." My heart begins to race; a weakness hollows my knees. I grab the edge of the bed.

"You need to get better and…" My voice falters. I am not sure what to say. Come home with me? Do we have anything in common anymore? Our worlds are too different; so much time has passed. "We can… make a fresh start."

"You do that for me." He glances up at the man towering above us. "Take care of her."

Sinclair moves closer, until his warmth envelops me. "I will." His voice seems to be coming from far away.

"I can take care of myself."

"I know." My father's face lights up in a smile. "But life is a long walk; there are ups and downs, and the time goes faster when you have company."

My father's face waves in and out in front of my eyes. Only then do I realize that I am crying.

I swipe at the tears on my face. "Is that how it was between you and my mother?"

"I was never the same after she died." His chin trembles. "But it won't be long before I see her."

My blood pounds behind my eyes, "Don't talk like that," I sniffle. "You are going to be fine."

He gasps, glances up at Sinclair, "There's something you should know." He swallows; his chest heaves.

The beeping from the monitor next to him increases in pace. "Daddy, please don't talk. Please, you need to conserve your energy."

"I must." He draws in a breath, "I'm afraid he's tracked me down."

"Who?" Sinclair moves closer, "Tell me, Adam."

"Stop." I shove at Sin, "Back off, asshole, let him recover first."

"Mob. Underworld boss." My father coughs; all color leaches from his face. "He called me and threatened me. He's going to hurt my girls."

"Don't talk Dad. Please." I wring my fingers. He doesn't look well at all. "I'm going to get the doctor."

"No." My father wheezes. "Stay with me, Summer." He holds out his arm. I step forward, grasp his palm, twine my fingers with his.

He trains his gaze on Sinclair, "The same faction that was behind the kidnapping of you and your friends." His chest heaves.

The beeping in the room intensifies further.

My pulse begins to race. "Dad, don't exert yourself, please."

Sinclair comes closer. "Who is it? Tell me."

My father's eyelashes flutter, his lips move, but nothing emerges. *Shit. This is not good. Not good.* My throat closes. My stomach twists.

"Don't crowd him. Can't you see he needs to regain his health first." I yell, "Get away from him!"

Sinclair's feature harden. A nerve throbs at his temple. "Tell me who's responsible." He brushes past me and leans over Dad. "If I need to keep her safe, I need to know who I am after."

My father's mouth opens and closes. Sinclair places his ear next to his lips, "Say it."

His lips move. "Byron... Capo..."

The beeping monitor next to the bed flatlines.

"No." I scramble up, squeezing my father's fingers. "You can't do this." The door slams open and footsteps sound. A doctor, followed by two nurses, comes rushing in.

The doc checks out his heart with a stethoscope, nods to the nurse, who turns to me, "You need to wait outside."

"No." I hold onto my father's hand. It's warm. He can't have left me. I didn't get to tell him how much I care for him. That I forgive him. "Daddy."

"Ma'am, please." The nurse turns to the man by my side.

Sinclair pulls me close, "Bird."

I shake my head, tears pouring down my cheeks.

"Come with me." He tugs me back; my father's hand slips from my grasp. A second doctor, additional nurses flood the space. Cut the sight of the figure on the bed from my line of sight.

He urges me to turn; I follow him outside. He leads me down the corridor, through a door, into a waiting room. Faces... familiar faces turn to us.

"How is he?" Saint asks, from where he's waiting not far from Victoria.

I glance away.

Karma rushes to me; I open my arms and hug my sister.

Victoria stands with her fingers clasped in front of her. She's wearing a dark blue, almost black in color, dress that falls to below her knees. Her make up is perfect, her lips a red slash. She stares at the door, her features blank. Did she love my father? Maybe I should comfort her?

I try to move toward her, but Karma tightens her hold on me.

Or maybe not.

The doors open behind me.

No, I will not turn. Will not.

There's a soft murmur of voices. Then footsteps approach me. The doctor clears his throat. "Mrs. Sterling."

"It's Ms. West" I turn, with Karma holding onto me.

His face says everything.

"No." I swallow.

"I'm sorry, Mrs. Ah, Ms. West. His body rejected the stent. It's extremely rare but..." His voice fades.

Victoria approaches us. I meet her blank gaze. She draws Karma away from me. My sister shoves at Victoria half-heartedly, then folds her arm round the other woman's slim shoulders.

I brush past the doctor, walking toward Sinclair who watches me approach.

His lips move... I don't register the words. I stare at the broad chest, in that crisp white shirt… The color pristine, the tendrils of black hair that pepper his tanned skin. Up to that strong chin, the square jaw.

"You okay?" He dips his face, peers into my eyes. Cerulean, blue and black. Everything I hate.

"You killed him." A coldness grips my chest. "He wasn't old enough to die; he could have lived to be ninety."

Sinclair's jaw tics. "I'm sorry for your loss, Summer."

"No, you're not. This is what you wanted. You wanted to ruin him and you made me help you. Well, guess what? You've ruined all of us." My knees wobble. I clench my fingers at my sides. I thought I had done my share of grieving when my mother had died… the first time I thought my father had died… but this… Everything feels too sharp, too real. Is it because I am older now? Because I can separate each individual shred of emotion that pierces my gut? I press my fingers together in front of my chest.

"I didn't intend for this to happen." His jaw tics.

"Bullshit." My chest hurts and pressure builds behind my eyes. "You made him come; you subjected him to this farce. You threatened him, told him you were going to ruin him. You must have known this was a possible outcome."

The skin at the corners of his eyes creases. He firms his lips. "I didn't want him to die. I wanted Adam to be alive to witness his destruction."

"How big of you."

A vein pops to life at his temple.

"If it weren't for you," I stab a finger at him, "My father would be alive."

"And you'd still think he was dead."

I wince.

He drags his fingers through his hair, "Fuck, I'm sorry Summer."

I lean forward on the balls of my feet, "I hate you."

"You don't."

That hard certainty in his tone whips through the jumble of thoughts in my head. "You know nothing."

I throw myself at him.

Raise my fist until it connects with that beautiful jaw. Punch his neck, his chest, any part of him that I can reach.

"I loathe you. I never want to see you again. I want you to leave, I can't stand you. Go. Away." I raise my arm and he catches it.

"Do you mean it?"

I tilt my chin up. *Don't say it. Don't.* "Get away from me, you monster."

47

Sin

I'd turned and stalked toward the door of that hospital waiting room... and paused. I'd turned and caught a glimpse of Karma and Summer holding each other, Victoria, slightly to the side.

At least Summer would have company. My wife wouldn't be alone in her grief.

That had reassured me; enough that I'd walked away.

I had set her free, just as I'd intended to do all along. Arranged the funeral for her father; had told myself I wouldn't go. Then had contented myself with watching her from a distance.

Fuck, when had I started second-guessing my moves, huh?

Why is it that I can recall the shape of her black dress as it had hugged her curves, ending below her knees? Her pink hair had shone in the afternoon sun.

Yeah, unlike in the movies, in real life, the fucking sunshine bathes a funeral scene in golden light, even in rain-drenched London.

My wife had held onto her sister, flanked by her stepmother on the other side.

Saint had represented the Seven.

He'd stood at the other end of the crowd, his attention focused on Victoria. Again.

Summer had glanced up and spotted me.

Our gazes had connected. I'd held hers, willed her to come to me. She'd stiffened, then deliberately turned away, and I'd forced myself to leave.

That was exactly seven days ago. I'd focused on 7A and FOK media, had buried myself in my work.

She'd told me to get away from her, and I had.

For the first time in my life, I had gone against my every instinct, which had screamed at me to gather her close, comfort her, take care of her. She hadn't wanted it. And I had listened to her wishes. *Fuck me. Fuck her. Fuck this thing between us that seems to grow bigger with every second.*

I raise the bottle of whiskey and chug it down. The liquid hits my stomach like a fire-ball. I stare out through the open window of my office.

"Planning on alcohol poisoning yourself, huh?" Saint walks up to stand next to me.

I don't reply, stare into the distance, where London spreads her skirts out, waiting for the next big bastard who will fuck her in the cunt. Oh, wait. That's me. I am the one who's turned every innocent thing that's come my way into sordidness; who's made my millions doing whatever it took, for as everyone knows, you can't reach the top without stepping on some bodies.

That's all she'd been. Collateral damage. *So why am I standing here brooding when my plan had worked spectacularly?* I had destroyed Adam, and in the process, my wife. I hadn't thought she'd take me down with her. Without trying. Without raising a finger. She'd bared herself to me and I had crushed her.

"It wasn't your fault."

"Oh?" I raise the bottle to my lips, take another healthy swig.

"He could dish it out, too bad his heart couldn't take it."

Whatever.

He holds out his hand and I hand the bottle to him.

"How long are you going to sulk?"

"Do I look like I am sulking?"

"Abso-fucking-lutely."

I thrust out my hand and he holds out the bottle. It's empty. Typical.

"Why did you come here, Saint?"

"No reason."

"You always have a reason."

"Making sure you're alive, old chap."

"I am. You can bugger off now."

"You're in a pisser of a mood."

"Get off my balls, you knob."

"Have you spoken to her yet?"

I'd tried, once. She'd hung up on me. No one hangs up on me. No one. I'd almost walked out of there and to her house… And then what? What would I have done? Apologized? Told her I'd become a new man? This is what I am. And it is true that her father played a big role in that. Perhaps the old man had been right; I had forged my identity from that incident. I wouldn't be here if I hadn't forced myself forward. Aimed so high that no one could touch me. So I could have the perfect revenge until… It had gone all pear-shaped on me.

"I'm divorcing her."

Saint stiffens.

"I'll ensure that she's set up for life. Give her enough money so she won't have to work ever again."

"Is that what she wants?"

"It's what she gets." I place the bottle on the table nearby. "That should be enough compensation for what I put her through, right?"

"Well, then." He turns, walks to the bar. I hear the ice clink. He returns with two glasses of whiskey.

"A toast then." He raises his glass.

I toss the alcohol down my throat.

"You're such a *chutiya*."

"That's me." Always ready to bring out the worst in people.

"Maybe you should try to placate her?"

"Not my style."

"Not that you should change your approach or anything... not unless you want her."

"I don't—"

"If you love her—"

I scoff, "I don't."

Jace walks in. "The man doth protest too much."

"Thought you'd left the country." I glower.

"I returned last night. Sienna and I are buying the house up the street."

"What?" I frown, "Why?"

"Let it not be said that you didn't welcome me with open arms." He laughs. "It wasn't my call. She wants our child to grow up in the UK. Don't ask me why." He shakes his head. "Besides, she fell in love with Primrose Hill when she attended your wedding." Jace's face lights up, as it always does when he speaks about Sienna. All of this emo shit, fuck, it's too early for that. "She figured this way she could get to know your wife better as well."

"You missed the memo." I grind my teeth so hard, pain flicks up my jaw. "I'm getting divorced."

He shakes his head, "Don't be such a..." He turns to Saint, "What was the very eloquent word you used?"

"*Chutiya.*"

"Yep, that."

My left eyelid twitches, "And you're the master of relationships because?"

"I am the one who's married to a woman who lights up my days and my nights."

"What-fucking-ever. That flowery-ass bullshit may suit you, but it's not for me."

"Hmm." Jace approaches me. "Close your eyes."

"What?"

Saint snickers, "If I were you, I'd be careful. Whatever Jace is on, it's clearly infectious. I, for one, intend to savor my single status." He steps away, giving us both a wide berth.

Jace grimaces, "You going to be swayed by this sorry excuse of a douche, or you going to, for once in your sorry life, listen to your fucking heart?"

"Newsflash." Saint stretches out on the couch, "He doesn't have one."

Jace jerks his chin at me, "Didn't take you for a pussy."

Fuck this. I shut my eyes. "Now what?"

"What's the first image that flashes behind your eyes?"

Her.

"What's the first voice you hear?

Hers.

"The first scent?"

Her arousal.

"Color?"

The pink strands of her hair.

"The first touch you recall?"

How her lips had parted under mine. How she'd moaned, opened up for me. Welcomed me into her body, her life, her soul.

My eyes flash open.

"You doubt what you feel for her?"

A hot burn stabs at my chest.

"What are you going to do about it?"

Saint punches a cushion behind his neck, "Shag her out of your system, that's what you should do. Get it all out, man."

I turn in his direction.

"Then," he rubs his hands together, "divorce her."

I prowl toward him.

"After," He links his hands behind his neck, "making her sign a watertight contract that she gives up all rights to your name, your firm, every goddam thing that she's come in contact with."

I squint down at him. "You're right."

"I am?"

"Good thing I am not you, eh?"

48

"It was Beauty killed the Beast."
—*King Kong*. Directed by Merian C. Cooper and Ernest B. Schoedsack

Summer

"He didn't." I crumple the paper and fling it aside.

Karma looks up from her laptop, "Let me guess." She pretends to think, "It's the alphahole, otherwise known as, your husband?"

"My soon to be ex." A situation I can't wait for. Something hot stabs at my chest; my heart begins to race. I can't wait to be rid of him, to put all of this sordid mess behind me.

"Hmm." She resumes working.

"What are you doing?" I growl.

At least my own sister could be sympathetic to my cause, huh? She's been curiously controlled in her reactions the last few days. Every time I try to talk to her about Mr. Sterling. Yeah, it's back to that. Best to think of him in formal terms. Newsflash: tell that to my subconscious which has a one-track mind where Sin is concerned — Yeah, see what I did there?

"Karma." I march up to her, slap the laptop's face down, a second after she yanks her hand out of the way.

"Oy, you were never this violent before."

"Shit happens." I scowl at her. "What are you hiding from me?"

"Moi?" She fluffs up her hair, "Nothing. Honest." She widens her gaze, looking not innocent at all. "After all there's no crying in baseball."

"That's from *A League of Their Own*." I shoot back. "And, you can't distract me."

She huffs out a breath. "I tried."

"What?"

"You are overanalyzing this."

"Me?" A slow simmer starts somewhere inside. "I'm overanalyzing?"

I spot the piece of crumpled paper, scoop it up, and walking back, I thrust it under her nose. "Read it."

She accepts it, reluctance written in every angle of her body. She opens it, peers up at me.

"Go on."

She sighs, opens it up, and begins to read.

"Aloud."

"Dear Ms. West,

This is to inform you that you are appointed Head of FOK quizzes a new division of FOK Media. Please report for work, 9 am tomorrow, and present your long-overdue ideas in response to the earlier marketing brief—I take it you have the details?

PS. You're welcome."

"Aargh! That man."

She continues reading.

"Yours sincerely,
    Sinclair Sterling
    MD, FOK Media
    Chairman, 7A Investments"

"Yeah, yeah, I know all that." I grab the sheet from her, then thrust the other piece of paper at her.

She reads it and her eyebrows shoot up.

"Divorce proceedings?"

"Yeah." My shoulders slump.

"That's what you wanted, right?"

"Hmm? Yes."

"Then?"

"Don't you see the problem?" I scowl.

"That you'd be working with him?"

I glare at her, "You're taking the piss, right?"

"Why should it bother you?"

"Only that he'd be my ex, not to mention the history between us."

"He's giving you a chance to accomplish all of your dreams. You've always wanted your own quizzing company, and you'd be the CEO of it, so to speak."

"As a part of his company."

"So?"

"So, I want complete autonomy."

"Maybe that's what he's calling you to discuss?"

"Why is he doing this? It's favoritism, nepotism."

"It won't be if he's divorcing you."

"I'd be his ex."

"Gives more credibility to the fact that he's recognizing your potential."

"But I don't—" I bite my lips.

"You don't want to be separated from him?" She tilts her head.

"I didn't say that."

"You almost did." She continues, "You're making too much of all this."

"It's only my life."

"And he returned it to you."

"Huh?"

She waves her hand around. "Gave you back this shitty apartment, reinstated all your outstanding bills, transferred the £4.5M to your bank account."

Y-e-p.

You read that figure right. When I saw it, I almost fell over. Like, how many zeroes were there in that figure, huh? Well, ask me, I know. I counted and re-counted it quite a few times in my online bank balance.

"He hasn't backtracked on the money and he hasn't sneakily tried to pay off our debts." Karma steeples her fingers together. "He hasn't shown you favoritism... Hasn't bullied you into doing anything you don't want."

"Yeah, yeah." I huff. "What are you? The alphahole's personal PR flunkie?"

"No, that's your official role." She chortles.

I throw my hands up. "I walked into that one."

"No, seriously Summer. He's trying. He made sure I have access to Dr. Weston...if I choose to pursue the treatment with him."

"Which you are."

"It's something we need to discuss."

"What do you mean? He's the best heart specialist there is in the city."

"I..." She tips up her chin, "I'm not sure I want to see him."

"There." I stab a finger at her, "That's the problem. You're afraid of getting the right diagnosis, because then you'd have to do something about your condition. You'd have to stop pretending there's nothing wrong with you."

She jumps up to her feet, "So not true, and you should speak."

"What do you mean?"

"You're the one denying you have feelings for Mr. Gazillionaire."

"Not." I grind my teeth.

"You do. And now when he's doing everything as you wanted, you are livid."

She's right, though no way am I going to admit that.

"You were hoping for a chance to find fault with him, which you can't. In fact, I'd go so far as to say that you're missing him."

"You're deluded."

"Oh?"

"I can't be bought with good intentions."

"You should be telling him that."

I stiffen.

"Unless you are too chicken about keeping that appointment and telling him that to his face?"

Umm. I begin to pace. "I don't trust him."

"You mean you don't trust yourself?"

I swing around. "What?"

"You have to admit there are serious sparks between the two of you. Maybe that's why you don't want to keep the appointment?"

"I don't have to. I could sign the divorce papers, mail them to him. Then go tell him to stuff the job offer where the sun don't shine."

"You could." She relaxes into the sofa, places the computer on the side. "Or you could tell him to his face."

I grab a strand of my hair, bring it to my lips. "Imagine the look on his face, huh?"

She nods. "Bet he wouldn't be able to deal with the fact that someone could actually turn him down."

That's true.

She places her fingers together in front of her, "You'd have the last word. You'd enjoy that."

That would be cool. I raise my shoulders, and let them drop, "Well, nobody's perfect."

She snorts. "You're a long way from that, girlfriend."

"Gotcha." I clap my hands.

"Wait. What?" She sits up. "I'm confused."

"That last line of mine?" I chuckle, "It's from *Some Like It Hot.*"

"Not fair, Summer." She scowls.

"I got a point on you." I pump my fists in the air, then fling out my arms and do a shimmy. "Woohoo." It's childish of me, but gosh does it feel good to let off some steam.

"I'm not as obsessed with movie trivia." She tosses her head, "So I keep missing things. Not that I'm competing or anything."

"Such a sore loser." I grin.

"Now it's you changing the topic." She waggles a finger at me.

"Yeah." I sober, straighten my shoulders, "What should I wear tomorrow?"

49

"I thought about what you would look like having an orgasm."
— *Sex, Lies & Videotape.* Director: Stephen Soderbergh

Sin

I drag my finger around my collar of my shirt. Is it hot in this room or what?

I stalk to the desk in my office, grab the glass of water and chug it down. My stomach churns. I swallow down the bile that rises up, slap the glass back on the surface.

Why am I nervous? I don't need to be nervous. This is me at my A game. I am the CEO of this company, the fourth richest man in the country, a billionaire... Blah-bloody-blah.

I squeeze the bridge of my nose.

The last three days had been buggered to hell. I'd tried to bury myself in work, but every turn I took, every new investment I'd tried to consider was held up by the fact that FOK media isn't up and running yet. Yeah, I had delayed its launch. I snort.

Me. CEO, shark of an investor, a businessman at the top of his game, had been met with closed doors... of my own making. I'd sent her that letter with the divorce notice... The hardest fucking thing I've ever done. For once, I had parked my ego in a corner.

I know when I have to pretend to retreat so I can move in for the kill. Lure the prey into my lair, and then — I draw in a breath — I'll pounce. No... I'll seduce her into my web, ensure she understands what I need from her. I'll lay the fucking world at her feet if she'll allow me. As if.

I smirk.

The adamant pink-haired goddess won't allow me to treat her as special. She wants to be my equal. Entreated me to give up the thing I cherish most — my control. I'd opened my blasted world to her, revealed my regrets, told her things I hadn't shared with anyone else; I'd ripped out the darkness for her... Given her an insight into what made me what I am. But had it been enough? I rock back on the balls of my feet. Hell, no.

She wanted more.

She wanted every last thing that I had hidden away and tried to forget.

She needs me to show, not tell. Bloody fucking hell. That... is the hardest thing ever. And I am trying. Goddamn her sweet mouth, and her beautiful cunt that I remember every second of my waking moments, her gorgeous lips and her sun-kissed limbs, her husky voice and her alluring scent that clings to my pores and drives me insane until I can't sleep for fear that I'll recollect every single glance, moment, touch, kiss, regret... *Fuck!* I rub my chest.

She crawled under my skin, sank into my soul, and I hate it. And love it. She made me unrecognizable to myself, and damn, if that isn't the biggest welcome surprise ever. Is that why I am rooted in front of my desk, mumbling to myself? Definitely turning into a pussywhipped loser. The last I checked, I have my balls, thank fuck.

A whine sounds at my feet. Max nudges his head against my thigh. I glance down and rub his sleek head. "You miss her too, huh?"

He huffs, arches his neck. I lean down and rub under his ears. "You've been a good boy, always exiting the room whenever she was around. I swear, sometimes I think you are human... No, better than them. You had a sixth sense when it came to giving me my privacy with her. That ends now."

He stiffens, muscles quivering in that alert way whippets have. Where they are relaxed and tensed at the same time. Kind of like how I feel now, huh.

"You're going to meet the woman... I... want. The one who is something special to me, Max. The one who's going to change the future... for both of us."

He slumps on his behind, whines again. "Exactly. I'll do everything but beg... No, maybe even that. Okay, maybe... if it comes to it... Fuck." I roll my shoulders, "I sound insane, huh? Talking to myself, like I am a kid again."

I'd had to do it in that room, blindfolded. It was what had kept me sane. Hearing my voice in my head, hearing the others, communicating through claps and thumps. It had been the only way to communicate, since we'd been gagged. But I am not that boy anymore. I've come a long way. I've taken revenge. My shoulders slump. Only it hadn't been half as satisfying as I'd hoped.

My landline buzzes. Adrenaline laces my blood. I scoop up the receiver, "Send her in."

There's a pause. "You okay, Sinclair?" Meredith's voice is soothing.

"I won't be if you don't send her in, in the next second—"

"She's on her way."

I draw in a breath. *Stay calm, no need to panic now.* She's only a girl... standing in front of me, asking me to bare my emotions for her. No pressure. And now I sound like one of the movie trivia questions she loves to show round. It's fucking catching. She's catching. Onto me. My failures. My pretensions. "Sorry, M."

"You better not let her go this time."

"Yeah." I chuckle. "Thanks for the vote of confidence."

"I'm counting on it, boy, and when you get married this time around, for real, I—"

There's a knock on the door, "Gotta go, M."

I drop the receiver so fast that it crashes and bounces onto the desk. I grab it, balance it properly in its cradle. I can do this. I've stared down bigger negotiators, more lethal ones, none of whom had large green eyes, breasts that were an exact fit for my palms, and her lips, those lips. That crease at the bottom that is sure to drive me insane, if I let it. *You've got this, Sinner.*

I swivel around, lean against the desk. Drum my fingers on the surface. No, that won't do. I prop my hands on my hips.

The knock sounds again.

"The door's fucking open. What do you expect, a red-carpet invitation?"

50

Summer

The alphahole's voice crashes through the barrier. I freeze. My knuckles stretch white. He's the one who invited me. He could sound a little more welcoming. A little less intimidating. To hell with that. I am going to teach him that he can't mess with me. I've got this. I twist the door handle, and the double doors swing open. I step inside and pause.

"Well? You going to keep me waiting all day, woman?"

Anger thrums at my temples. I raise my head, and those indigo eyes lock with mine. All of the breath leaves me. The force of his dominance spears me with the precision of a heat-seeking missile, pinning me in place. The scent of him... bergamot and leather and woodsmoke. It fills the space, crawls into my cells, and I am instantly wet.

He frowns; his glare sweeps me from toe to head. He licks his lips and a whine bubbles up my throat.

He tilts his head and his jawline cuts through the air.

The rough chafe of those whiskers between my thighs, across my sensitive, swollen, throbbing pussy... I gulp. The image is sharp, larger than life, so real that I squeeze my thighs together.

"Close your mouth or you'll catch a fly, and it's not a sexy look, I promise you that."

I snap my teeth together. *What a wanker!* I'd forgotten he has this ability to turn me on and the next second dump freezing cold water on all of my heated desires. I walk forward and the door snicks shut behind me. The sound shivers up my spine and my knees knock together. I pause, hold onto the straps of my bag. Dig my fingers into the leather.

"How dare you?" he growls.

"What?" I stiffen.

Not a second in his presence and he is issuing orders and declarations. It's as if no time has passed between us, no incidents... Nothing except the death of my father, and his subsequent actions trying to show... What? That he is trying to put things right between us? As if that would ever be possible. "What are you talking about?"

He struts forward. I take a step back, but he's already standing in front of me. He shoots out his hand, I cringe.

"Your hair." The muscles of his jaw flex. "You changed it."

"The color... Yeah."

"Why?"

"Why?" I shuffle my weight from foot to foot. "I needed a change, I guess." I jut out my chin. "It's what some of us do when everything else spirals out of control. Unlike alphaholes, who decide to go about destroying other people's lives."

The skin across his cheeks stretches; he pales. The look in his eyes is bleak, so stricken, that I blink. It clears. The cerulean and blue roars forth. Nah, I was mistaken. He couldn't have revealed himself so clearly there. No way.

"Going auburn suits you."

"It does?"

"Makes you ordinary enough that you can blend in with the rest."

Ouch. My shoulders stiffen. I thrust out my chin. "Nice to see you've been polishing up your manners."

"Nice to see that you've accepted my job offer."

"I haven't."

He blinks. His features pale yet more.

Gotcha.

He drops his hands to his sides. "So why are you here?"

I reach for my bag, pull out the papers. My fingers tremble so hard that they flutter to the ground. The hell? I stare at the rectangle of white on the ground between us.

So does he.

Neither of us says a word.

Then he clicks his tongue, "Max, get it."

I frown, watch him. He has his gaze trained on the paper. I wait a second, another. A bead of sweat rolls down his temple.

"Sinclair?"

His jaw tics.

"Sin?"

A vein throbs at his temple.

"What's wrong?"

"Max." He clears his throat, tracks his gaze across the floor toward me. "You like her, don't you, boy?"

I scan the room again, see nothing... except for the pet rug in the corner—which I'd spotted before—and next to it, a leash. My heart begins to thud. "Sin, you're beginning to scare me."

"I knew you liked her from the moment you saw her at the pub. How she leaned across the counter as if she owned the place, sucked down that pink concoction—"

"It's called a Daiquiri—frozen, not stirred."

"What-bloody-ever."

I stiffen. For a second there, I was sure I'd sensed something different. "I signed it, so that's it. It's over between us." I pivot, walk toward the door.

"Stop."

I hasten my steps.

"Bird."

My heart stutters. No, I will not give in to his stupid nicknames. He doesn't mean anything when he calls me that. It is how he manipulates my emotions, which, apparently, I have a shit ton of when it comes to him.

I reach the door, grab the handle.

"Max, go to her."

My spine stiffens.

"Go on, good boy, that's it, brush up against her ankles, grab the hem of her skirt, rub her back—"

"Stop." I pivot to face him, "Who's Max?"

"My imaginary dog."

51

Sin

"Surprised?" I thrust out my chest. I've done it. I've told her the one thing I had confessed to no one else.

Not the Seven, not M. Definitely not my parents in the time that they'd taken me home and tried to understand what had happened to my mind.

She stares at me, a furrow between her eyebrows. "I... don't understand."

I widen my stance. "It's a coping mechanism."

"So Max... isn't... he's not —"

"Real."

"Oh."

"After I was rescued from the kidnappers, I spent a month at the hospital recuperating. When I was released, my parents struggled to cope with my changed behavior. Not that I had been the easiest child before," which was putting it mildly; I grimace, "but I became more withdrawn. I was pissed off with the world, with them, with myself for being in a situation where I'd had no control."

"It wasn't your fault." Her tone is soft.

Wasn't it? I drag my fingers through my hair.

"My parents were busy trying to make ends meet, as it were. They didn't know how to deal with me. My mother tried, I suppose," A pulse throbs at my temple. "She tried to get me to see a therapist, but —"

"You refused."

"Yeah," I glower. "I can be a stubborn twat."

"I hadn't noticed." Her lips curve.

Say something more. Say what a freak I am. Off my nutter... Yeah, that would be a more accurate description. Why the fuck would she want to stay with me after everything I've told her?

I bare my teeth, "You think I'm crazy, huh?"

"No." She shakes her head. "Not more than usual."

Turn around. *Fly away, little Bird*. The cage door is open. The world awaits you. Sail forth. Conquer. Find new friends... A lover. Another husband. My thighs spasm. My shoulder muscles bunch.

If she glances at anyone else, takes someone else in my place... I'd kill the asshole... Fuck that, I won't allow it. I can't.

I'd brought her here, thinking I'd coerce her to stay; bribe her with more money, a job that fulfills her dreams, a hint of what she's missing. I'd hoped she'd feel the loss of what could have been between us. I'd been sure that she'd take one look at me, and what? Throw herself at me, ask me to take her back? *Fuck*. I roll my shoulders.

That had been exactly my line of thinking. Then she'd walked in, and I'd known, it wouldn't work. All of my arrogance had been stunted and forced to take a back seat. I had done the unthinkable.

I'd ripped open the one thing that would unravel my entire persona, my existence, the face I show the world.

I'd exposed myself to her. I was bare. Nothing to hide. Almost. "You should leave now," I growl.

"Okay."

She turns, heads to the door.

The fuck? She's going? Sure, I'd told her to... But when had she ever obeyed me before? Without question.

This time. The one time I'd wanted her to disobey me, fight me, hold her own, she'd... flummoxed me again. She is perfect. She is mine. And I've lost her again. I squeeze my eyes shut. The blood thuds at my temples. My ribcage tightens. I draw in a breath. My lungs burn. Images from the past overwhelm my mind. Darkness envelops me.

Voices reach me in the damp musty space. Muffles, thuds, scrapes. I hear the moans of the boys in that enclosed room—six of them—I know them by their grunts, stifled by the rags in their mouths.

The door opens, footsteps sound. Someone is coming. Nearer, nearer. *No, please, not me. Not this time*. I'll do anything you want. Is there a God? I've never prayed before. If I knew how to... I could. I can't. So all I can say is help me. Someone. Anyone.

I try to swallow, but my throat is too raw. Attempt to breathe, but my lungs spasm. My face hurts. My arms are numb. Can't feel my fingers. My toes. I am floating... floating... looking down on my hurt broken body. Myself. I am no more.

Click. More. I need more. *Click*. *Click*. My fingers fumble with the clasp of my watch. Cold. Metallic. *Click*. *Click*. *Click*. The sound pierces through the noise in my head.

Focus. Focus on it.

The shape of the *clasp*. Rectangle. The indentation in the center. Like her lips. The crease. Pink. Soft. Beautiful. *Click*. *Click*. *Click*. *Click*.

"Sinclair."

Her voice. Soft and husky. Her breath catches. She does that when she comes. In my arms. On my dick. On my fingers. All over my tongue. *Click*. *Click*. *Click*. *Click*. *Click*.

"Sin." Her warm fingers encircle my wrist. Her scent fills my senses. Focus on that. On how she leans into me, her breasts thrust up and into my chest. The nipples erect. The pink areolae twitching, yearning for my mouth. My groin hardens. My dick lengthens.

"Sin." She grips my crotch through my pants.

Heat shoots up my spine, the darkness recedes, and I snap open my eyes.

I am back in my office, in the present, with the only person in my life who matters. *Her.*

"You don't want to do this." I glare at her.

"But I do." A smile curves those beautiful lips.

"You don't understand."

"Your watch." She glances down.

I pull my fingers away from the steel clasp.

She leans closer, "That's why you wear this worn out watch, huh?"

I set my jaw, "If you've figured it out this far, you don't need my help for the rest."

"You play with its clasp as a means of grounding yourself, connecting yourself with the present, right?"

I smirk. "Anyone tell you that you should have been a psychologist instead? I'd use your services. Hell, we'd make full use of your couch. I bet we'd wear it out in a week, tops." I angle my head, "What do you say?"

"I say that you shouldn't change the topic."

"Hmm." I thrust my pelvis forward and into her palm.

She swallows. "Sin. Please." Her tone turns beseeching. It doesn't stop her from gripping the bulge that tents my pants. Good. I widen my stance.

"Love it when you plead with me."

"Can I speak what's on my mind?"

"As long as you keep your hand on my dick, everything is fine."

She scowls. "It's not though."

"Oh?"

"You have an imaginary dog for a companion, Sin, and you have been holding onto a watch from your boyhood days, as a means of connecting you to your sanity. You need to face what happened to you. You need help."

"Not happening." I set my jaw.

"You overcame your past, Sin. Look at you today, an incredibly handsome, gorgeous, self-made gazillionaire with a heart of gold hidden behind that asshole exterior."

Heat flushes my neck. I've been complimented by many but this... from the woman who's mine... nothing tops this. I want to say something flippant—because a douche-canoe never changes his stripes, eh? I open my mouth, but there's something blocking my throat. A pressure builds at my temples.

I peer into her eyes, and all I see is myself. *The fuck?*

"What you've been through would have broken a lesser man." She rubs my dick through my pants. "Not you, Sinclair Sterling. You survived. You are here, standing in front of me, proud—"

"And hard."

She purses her lips, "And still an alphahole."

"Who's ready for you."

She withdraws her hand, but I am faster. I grab her fingers, press them into my aching hardness.

"Need you, Bird."

She swallows.

I tighten my grip, thrust myself into our joined hands. "See what you do to me?"

Her pupils dilate; her breathing grows shallow. She shuffles backward, putting more distance between us and my heart begins to thud. My throat closes; my guts churn, "Don't leave me, Bird."

"That's not fair." Her lips turn down. "You're playing the emo card."

What me? Nah! Uh!... okay, m-a-y-b-e. I'm not beyond using sneaky ways to get her attention, and if it means I can bind her to me? Well then, all bets are off.

I press down, use her hand to massage myself. "You mean this?" A groan rips up my chest. "See how I react to you?"

Her fingers curve and my balls tighten.

Sweat beads my forehead. "So fucking hot, Bird. Admit it, that no one else can make you come the way I do."

"You know it's true."

I smirk.

"It's not only that." She bites on her lower lip, and of course, I feel the tug all the way to tip of my cock. *Fuck!*

I lean in close enough for my breath to raise the hair on her forehead, "So, you don't want to feel me hard and throbbing and pulsing inside of you, hmm?"

She shivers.

"You don't want me?"

"I didn't say that."

"Then?" I glare at her. "Enlighten me here, help me out, Bird."

"It's your trusting me enough to reveal how—"

"Broken, I am?"

"I was going to say resilient, but if you want to put yourself down." She raises her shoulders. "Be my guest." Her fingers squeeze and blood rushes to my groin.

"Fuck." I groan.

She slides her hands down, cups my balls.

A snarl rumbles up my chest.

Her green eyes gleam, "You undervalue yourself."

I frown, then chuckle. "Good joke. Your sense of humor has improved."

"You think your sharing your nightmares and how you managed to not let them overwhelm you is—"

"—A sign of weakness."

"Let me finish." She squeezes my balls.

My cock thickens; blood rushes to my groin. I glare at her.

She glares back.

"Just because you've fooled the world into believing that you are an obnoxious asshole—"

"I'm being myself, Babe."

She twists my balls, and I growl. "The fuck, Summer?"

"Let me complete my train of thought."

I pull my hand out of my pocket, fix my fingers around her nape. "You dare tell me what to do?"

"No." She shakes her head. "I dare to show you what you really are."

"Oh?" I tilt my head, yank her close enough for our lips to almost touch. Almost. "And what's that?"

"A man who needs a soft touch."

"I don't know, from where I am, I am quite hard—"

She lets go of my balls only to grasp my cock once more. She massages it and all thoughts empty from my mind. This woman? Fuck! She knows exactly how to please me.

I shove myself forward, thrusting into her grasp, fucking her hand. I pull my fingers off her palm, grab the desk for support.

"That's fucking hot. But I'd much prefer to fuck your mouth—"

"Listen to me, this once, you prick."

"*Your* prick." I allow a smirk to curl my lips, "And you have my attention."

"What I have, is your manhood in the palm of my hand." She pumps me through my pants, a long hard swipe from base to tip. Goosebumps flare on my skin.

"Jesus, woman, spit it out already."

"It makes you human, okay? What you told me; it wouldn't have been easy for anyone to admit. And for a full-of-himself asshole such as you, well, it must have taken hours of prepping."

"Days... Weeks… Since I met you, actually."

She frowns.

I firm my lips, nod toward her.

"I mean, it means a lot to me… That you trusted me enough to share your secrets."

I lower my eyebrows. I sense a but coming there... *Nah! She wouldn't dare, would she?*

"But it's too little too late."

My mouth falls open. I know I am gaping, but fuck that. "Don't you dare do it, Bird."

"What?" She unzips my pants, and my dick swings free. She grabs my swollen shaft at the base, swipes up to the tip, and I huff.

Tighten my hold on her nape.

"What were you saying?" She peers up at me from under her thick eyelashes, massages me again. The blood rushes to my groin; my cock jumps.

"Don't you dare leave—"

She squeezes me with enough pressure for my shaft to thicken. The pulse thuds at my temples, behind my eyeballs. My balls are so fucking hard that I am sure I am going to come right now.

My head spins; my knees tremble. And fuck, this isn't about the blow job. It's simply that the woman I love, is getting me off— *Hold on.*

Love. What? No. I did not think that.

I mean, I'd confessed to *almost* being in love… When had I crossed the line? Is that why I'd spilled all my secrets to her like she was my sounding board? Which she was… *She is… Mine.*

I am hers. Hers. I stare at her flushed features. Take in the dilated pupils, the color on her cheeks. Her parted lips. She, too, is aroused. Good.

I force my shoulders to unlock. Widen my stance. "Bird."

"Hmm?"

She drags her fingers to the base of my very excited cock.

"I love you."

52

Summer

His features contort. His hard chest shudders. His hard, veiny shaft jumps in my palm and hot bursts of cum sear my forearm, my chest; streak the blouse I'd teamed with my short skirt.

Sin in the throes of an orgasm? It's the hottest thing I've ever seen. A moan bleeds up my throat, I swallow it. Tilt my chin up.

"You're lying."

His features relax. His dick pulses in the aftermath of the orgasm. My fingers don't meet around the column of his hardness. Damn him. And he just came. The hell?

He smirks, "When you have a man's balls in your grasp, it's more potent than a dying declaration."

I frown. "You mean that a man will say anything to get his dick sucked?"

"Are you offering?" He scowls.

"No." I release him and his hold on my neck tightens.

"Then I will."

He flips me around, so I am the one leaning against the desk. He drops to his knees in front of me.

"What the—?"

"Let me." He peers up at me from under hooded eyelids.

"Sinclair, what are you doing?"

"Let me pleasure you, Darling."

I shake my head, grip the edge of the desk with my palms, mirroring his stance from earlier.

"Please." His features soften.

"Wow."

"Didn't think I knew how to say that word, huh?" He smirks.
A chuckle bubbles up. "Only you could turn a simple request into a—"
"Demand?"
"An asinine string of words."
"Love it when you talk filthy to me."
I set my lips together. "That wasn't talking filthy you ass—" He leans in and touches his lips to the center of my body. Pleasure zings up my spine. I throw my head back, huff.
"Love it more when you moan."
"That was... a—"
"A yes?"
"Stop putting words in my mouth."
"Then say it aloud, Bird."
"I can't think when you touch me."
"Okay."
"What?" I blink. Sin being this... agreeable? Wow! All of my senses go on alert.
I glance down to find he's indeed holding his hands up.
"See? I can comply with your wishes."
Hmm. "So why don't I trust you?"
"Give me a chance, Bird."
I chew on my lower lip.
"If I don't make you come in the next five minutes—"
"Three."
"What?" He glares at me.
I shiver, shuffle my weight from foot to foot. That rough tone, that harsh edge to his intention... Wetness slicks my core, as he's going to find out in the next few seconds...
"Two minutes."
"Summer." He growls.
I bite the inside of my lips, "You have one minute to make me come. If I were you—"
His hands swoop out, he drags my skirt up above my hips again.
"You didn't wear panties."
"Didn't want a panty line."
"Liar." He drops his head, licks my pussy from my back hole up to my clit.
I gasp. "Not. Lying."
"You came here with the intention of seducing me."
"Not."
He licks my swollen nub and a trembling starts up my toes. *No, no, no.* I can't let him win this. I arch back, away from him. He grips the backs of my thighs, "Spread for me, Baby Girl."
My legs part like the words of my favorite movie prose.
"So beautiful. So sweet. Your cunt is my home, Darling."
I swallow, thrust my pelvis forward, and he plunges his tongue inside my pussy.
"Sin."
"Shh." His hum rolls deep inside of me. A whine slips from me and his grip tightens. He dives into me, licking, sucking. I dig my fingers into his hair and tug. Raise one leg and hook it over his shoulder. He lowers his other and fits it under my other knee. I am riding his face, as he fucks me with his tongue. Thrusting, throbbing, stabbing at my center. I'm coming. "I'm coming." I arch my shoulders back, my spine curves, and the

climax rips through me. Sparks of blue and white…Stormy, swirling, big fat tears roll
down my cheeks.

He doesn't stop. He thrusts that wicked sinful tongue of his into me, hooks it across
the most delicate part of me. Another orgasm throbs at my center and shoots out, vibrates
out to my extremities. He rips his mouth from my lower lips. "Come for me, Bird."

And I do. Again. I shatter on his desk. Moisture drools out from between my thighs.
He bends his head, laps up all of my cum. Wipes me clean.

I slump onto the table. He swoops up, rolling my legs up and around his waist, then
scoops me up.

My head falls against his chest. Thud-thud-thud. His heart gallops under my ear. Or
is it mine?

He walks around and sinks into his chair, holding me.

"Sinclair."

"Hmm?"

"I love you too."

A chuckle rumbles up his chest. "I know, Bird."

"You're still a jerk."

53

"Swoon, I'll catch you."
— *The English Patient.* Director: Anthony Minghella

Sin

"Have a good day, Sir." Peter pulls up to the curb in front of my office. I lean across and open the door of the Aston Martin, as he comes around.

"I got this." I wave him back.

His gaze widens, then he nods and retreats.

Max bounds out of the car, straining at the leash. He pauses in front of the homeless man next to the entrance.

His sign today reads, *"Morn came and went — and came, and brought no day..."*

I pause in front of him, "Bloody fuck. Can't you write something a little less depressing?"

He stares up at me.

I pull out my wallet, "There's a job waiting for you" I nod toward the building. "If you need one. Not that I'm one to mock your lifestyle, but so you know, if you change your mind."

He tilts his head.

Right. So all of a sudden I am some kind of a do-gooder? Trying to change the world? Not. It's Bird who's affecting me. Maybe I am so happy that I want to share my good fortune with the rest of the world? What-fucking-ever. I pull out a few bills, drop them into the hat in front of the man.

Max races toward the entrance, pulling me in his wake.

"It's from Darkness."

"Huh?" I turn, blink.

"A poem by Byron." Homeless Man stares at me. The fuck is up with that vacant gaze of his? Is he high on something?

A prickle of unease grips me. "Byron? You mean the poet or the Capo of the Mafia?"

He picks up the bills and pockets them. Then gathers up the hat, slams it on his head, without losing a single coin or bill. He strides away, board tucked under his arm.

The fuck? "Hey, hold on." I stalk forward and Max whines. I pause glance back.

Max wags his tail, pivots toward the office building. He whines, then tugs at his leash. "Jesus, hold on, you mutt."

I turn around to find Homeless Guy has disappeared.

What the fuck just happened there?

I rub the back of my neck, then prowl toward the entrance. Max keeps pace.

I shove open the door and he bounds ahead, dragging me along into the building that I own. Fuck my life.

He, flops on the ground in front of the receptionist's desk.

She smiles at the puppy.

I scowl. All of that sweetness that the bugger leaves in his wake is seriously cloying. But Bird had insisted.

It had been her gift to me on the first anniversary—the first month of her moving in with me. She'd made me promise I'd take the little fucker to work, and me... Well, I couldn't have refused her.

Max snaps up on all fours, and bounds toward me. He circles me once, then drops down on his hind legs, right in my path.

I blow out a breath, lean, tap his head. He rolls onto his back. Yeah, okay, it's a second more. I drop down on one knee, tickle his stomach.

His jaws open; his tongue lolls out. He wriggles his little body around, his eyes rolling back in his head.

A shocked gasp reaches me from the direction of the reception table. I glance up and she instantly reddens. She looks down, shuffles the papers in front of her.

I straighten, walk toward her.

She pales.

"Alia, right?

She blinks, peers up at me. "You... you remember my name?"

Lucky guess.

I'd assured Bird I'd tone down the grumpiness. This is me keeping my word. Make a note. Yeah, and on that... I gave in to her and saw a shrink yesterday; I'll survive. Besides, she's promised me a whole lot more in return. I smirk.

"You bet, I do, Ste—I mean Alia." I brush away an imaginary speck from my collar. "I know all of my employees by name." Not. Though, I *had* asked for the employee list. Another step toward the softening of my profile to the world.

Apparently, internal PR is more important than external, and the fastest way to fix our reputation in the market is to begin on home ground, by turning our people into ambassadors who'll amplify that message blah-bloody-blah... a whole lotta soft arse corporate bullshit if you ask me, b-u-t—Summer had asked it of me, and I'd never turn down my wife.

Besides, I have a sneaky suspicion that it might build the market image of FOK, which will go a long way in driving up the capitalization of 7A. Which is what I need right now. The butterfly effect, huh?

Bird had pointed all of that out to me—when I had finally let her share her marketing ideas with me... i.e. when I had spared her mouth long enough for her to get a word in. I've been keeping her busy, all right.

She'd seconded Saint's idea of holding a quick press briefing where we'd play the role of happy couple—no strike that—where we'd be ourselves, and introduce FOK Media properly to the public. Get the positive coverage, blah-fucking-blah.

I'd hated the idea and told her so. But she'd insisted, and well, that was that.

Besides, my wife's bloody smart, and that's the goddam truth. Though sneaky woman that she is, I know when I'm being manipulated into getting to know my employees better. Still I want her to have this little victory; and no, I'm not softening. Not.

She'd hated the name FOK... wanted me to change it; but I wasn't giving it to that... yet.

I scowl and the receptionist swallows.

She backs away from the desk. Bloody hell. Who knew trying to tone down my assholeness would take so much effort, huh? Eyes on the prize. If this makes Bird happy, it's worth it. I'll be nice to my employees if it's the last thing I do.

I peel back my lips, flash my teeth. So it's more a grimace than a smile, but it's the best I can do.

"Uh... Ah... Mr. Sterling, are you okay?"

I keep the smile fixed on my face. "Of course, Alia." I tilt my head, "You're doing a good job." I knock my knuckles on the receptionist's console. "Keep up the good work."

Her jaw drops.

Guess I convinced her, huh? I deserve an Oscar for my performance. I push away from the platform, stalk toward the elevators.

Then pause, "Oh, and Alia?"

I turn to face her.

She's staring after me, her mouth half open. "When Mrs. Sterling—"

She smiles, "You mean Summer?"

My heart jumps. Summer. My Bird. My sunshine. The woman I'd do anything for... because I am a pussywhipped motherfucker. That's me, all right, and her happiness is paramount. I want her happy. And naked. And content, after she's come in my arms. Everything else takes second place, including my wants.

I straighten my spine.

"Exactly. When *my wife* comes in, please ask her to come directly to my office?"

"Of course, Mr. Sinclair."

I pivot. Did she call me Mr. *Sinclair?* I pause, then raise my shoulders. What-bloody-ever. They can call me motherfucker for all I care. As long as they do what I command.

I stalk across to the elevators, pause in front of mine as the doors slide open. Max bounds in, and I follow. Stab the button for my offices, then drop down to one knee and scratch behind his ears.

"You think she'll enjoy the surprise, little bugger?"

54

"Why are you trying so hard to fit in when you were born to stand out?"
-What a Girl Wants. Director: Dennie Gordon

Summer

"Thanks Peter."

I open the door of the Aston Martin and cross the sidewalk to the 7A office building.

I am already two minutes late.

It had been a surprise when Karma had called me last night and asked me to come over.

What was more shocking? Sinclair had allowed me to leave. It was unlike him, to let me out of his sight. He liked me by his side, in bed and out of it. And every second in between. Possessive Jerkface—and I use that term affectionately, I promise.

He'd told me I must go if Karma needed me. He'd insisted that Peter drive me, and I had accepted. I didn't want to put myself in a situation where the Mafia could get to me either.

It would only compromise Sinclair's standing to do so. Besides I had found my way back to him, no way was I going to lose him again.

Still, a little bit of distance is also healthy, right? One night away from him, to have space to myself, to recuperate from the impact of his physical closeness that I am reeling from... Surely, my sore pussy and my thighs that have been getting one hell of a workout this last month would appreciate it... You'd think? I hasten my steps.

I had the money to buy out the apartment we'd rented and gift it to my sister. It had taken a good chunk from the money that had hit my bank account. Yeah, London's a bloody expensive city.

I had almost not accepted the cash, but Karma had reminded me that I had earned it fair and square. It was part of my deal with Sinclair.

Besides, it means I have a base and Karma has a home — as Sinclair had not hesitated to remind me. This once, the alphahole had been right too. So, I had taken the money and used it. He'd also had a bodyguard assigned to Karma, for which I was grateful.

I had accepted a job with him... as the Director of Marketing for FOK Media and 7A Investments.

The quizzing division he'd mentioned earlier? That was off the table.

Instead, I was relaunching my marketing consultancy as a quizzing company, using the money that I had earned.

It would be separate from any of Sinclair's other business interests.

When I'd mentioned this to Sin, he'd been more than supportive. He'd suggested that I pitch it for a loan with FOK Media to fund international expansion, rather than dip into my personal funds. Hmm, it couldn't be because he wanted to watch out for me, huh? It did make business sense though, so I'd agreed.

I glance at the time on my phone.

Damn it, I'm five minutes late now. I'd wasted time at Karma's this morning, not wanting to say good-bye. I'd have taken the tube to save time, but Sin had insisted I wait until Peter arrived to pick me up. Sinclair Sterling, still an alphahole. But he was *my* alphahole. *Mine.*

My fingers tingle and my scalp tightens.

So close to seeing him again. His masculine scent, that hard voice, those beautiful lips that could tease me to orgasm, while his tongue stabbed in and out of me... in a simulation of how his cock would be buried inside of me... soon, very soon. Moisture teases my core. Damn. How, I've missed the man. Missed his dominance, the sense of security, his warmth, his closeness, his ability to look inside my soul, and read my fears. I am complete when he is in me. Corny much? I huff out a breath.

If this is love... Well, I don't want to know the alternative. It isn't all physical — okay, a lot of the attraction is, and my poor ravaged cunt appreciates that, honestly. It's more... It's the way he follows me with his gaze, the way he watches me when he thinks I am not aware, how he holds the door open for me, loans me his jacket without asking if I am cold. How he'd agreed to my keeping a separate room in his house, no questions asked, even as his lips had firmed at the suggestion. Surprised? So was I.

I had wanted an expression of my independence, a place I could retreat to, where I could think, read, stare into the distance. He has his study and this retreat is mine. It is a room that opens up off of his bedroom, that he had insisted on, and I had agreed. No use prodding the monster more than needed, right?

He'd invited the rest of the Seven home — at my suggestion — and we'd played... One guess. Yeah, movie trivia night. OMG. It was hilarious, and addictive, and there had been sparks flying between my friends and some of the Seven. Karma had been absent that night...

All the more reason that I had made sure to go when she had called yesterday. We'd spent the night talking, gossiping, and she'd waved goodbye to me this morning with a strange look in her eyes. My footsteps slow.

Maybe I should have stayed with her, found out what was bothering her? I am sure that she'd called me to discuss something... but every time I had tried to bring it up, she'd changed the topic. And I... I had been too consumed by my new obsession, my passion, my love for the man who Sinclair Sterling is turning out to be.

Sin. As sinful in deed as in name. As sexy as hell when he spanks me, torments me to the edge, then makes love to me with a tenderness that soothes away the pain.

I reach the entrance to the offices of 7A, then barrel through. My chunky wedges slip, then catch, and I career past the receptionist, who flashes me a smile, "He wants you to go up to his offices."

"Oh?"

"Can't get enough of you, huh?"

I laugh, "Me neither."

"I don't know what you're doing to him... I mean, other than... You know." She flushes. "Didn't mean it that way, Mrs. Sterling."

"Summer, I told you to call me Summer."

She beams. "Summer. He's different since you came into his life."

"You mean one notch less than horrendous?"

"Many notches less than horrible."

"Ha." I smirk, "Don't let his charm get to you."

Her forehead furrows. "You're not jealous that he spoke to me?"

I laugh. "If I got envious of every woman who glanced at my husband..." I shake my head. "He has that impact, huh?"

She sighs, "You're one heck of a lady, Summer."

I grin, "Be sure to tell him that."

"You bet I will."

I wave my goodbye then, race for the bank of elevators and take his private elevator up. Glance up at the camera in the far corner. Yes, there is one; he had it installed, and only *he* has access to the feed. So, he can track me as I approach his office, he said. I know, slightly creepy, but... it means I can do this: I raise the hem of my slim pink skirt, it's conservative except for the slit that goes up to mid-thigh. Flash him the long line of my thigh. Then laugh. Heat simmers off the surface of the security cam...

Hope you got that, Alphahole. Two can play this game. Haven't you learned that by now? I blow him a kiss as the elevator slows to a stop. The doors slide open and I race out on the executive floor. I'd insisted on my office being three floors down, with the rest of the team.

He'd looked as if he was about to lose it... Then, he'd agreed. Huh? The man is trying, though he ends up calling me up for meetings five times a day. Once he'd met me halfway... in the stairwell, and we'd... Ah! Made out. It had been hot, I confess. We'd been late to our next meeting and he didn't care.

Yep, he's definitely trying. Wonder what he'll ask for in return though, hmm?

I pass the desk where Meredith normally sits. It's empty. Huh? Pick up speed, reach his office, prise open the door, and there's no one there. What the—? My heart picks up speed.

I place my tote on his desk, then cross the floor to the door that opens into the adjoining conference room. Swing it open and see him. His back is to me.

He grips the window frames with his arms outstretched on either side. His biceps bulge, stretching the perfectly cut sleeves of his tailor-made suit. My breath catches. He's as fucking hot as... Sin. If ever a name appropriately fit a man, it is his.

His dark jacket clings to every hard plane of his back. His waist is so damn narrow and that tight butt. I gulp. I know how it feels to palm that ass. Those powerful thighs with a smattering of hair that chafes across my sensitive skin. The thick calves, the wide stance.

"Bird."

I jerk my chin up. I hadn't made a sound. I swear the man has eyes at the back of his head.

"I know you're there."

I huff.

"Come on in, I've been waiting..."

I step in and the door closes with a snick behind me.

"Come close, you know I don't bite..." He laughs softly, turns around. "Not always."

I gasp.

"You... you shaved."

He smirks. Without the hair that covered his chin, his lips are exposed in all their glory, and that square jaw—"You have a dimple in the center of your chin?"

He frowns.

"It's..."

"Don't say it."

"So sweet."

His cheeks redden. "You make me sound like a cupcake."

"I'd love to lick off your cream."

His gaze widens. "Come again?"

"I'll come as many times as you want, if you promise to keep that school-boy look."

He prowls forward, "Care to repeat that?"

"Ah!" I take a step back.

He ambles closer.

I move away, until my butt hits the door. I search for the handle behind me as his long strides eat up the distance between us.

"School boy, huh?" He leans forward on the balls of his feet.

The light haloes his perfect features. That indigo glare envelops me, the scent of testosterone saturates the air, and I swallow.

He raises his hand, tucks a strand of dark hair behind my ear.

I'd opted to keep my natural auburn locks, and he loves it. Loves me as I am. Maybe this is what it means to be into someone? *When you miss a person even when he's standing right in front of you, eating you up with his gaze, when you know he's as turned on as you are. And you can't wait for him to kiss you, own you, possess you,* write his name on every cell of my body, script his language on my pussy, drag his tongue across the underside of my foot as he sucks on my toes before he bends me over and—

"Shall we shag now, or shag later, Baby?" He waggles his eyebrows.

"Austin Powers." I throw my hands up, "Of all the movies to quote from, you had to choose *that* one?"

He raises his shoulders, "I'm a guy, what did you expect?"

"Flowers, hearts, chocolate?" I count them off on my fingers. Okay, so you've got two out of three there. "Maybe a ring?" I let my lips curve up. "Nah, just kidding on that one." *Not.* I slap at his shoulder. "Whatever it is you have planned, Sinclair, it won't buy you into my good graces—not after that completely pathetic attempt at trying to be romantic."

He slides his hand into his pants pocket and his brows draw down.

"Seriously, if you think Austin freakin' Powers is your role model to be amorous then—"

He yanks his hand out, pats his breast pocket.

"What are you doing?"

"Nothing."

"It's something."

"Jesus, woman, give me a break, I am trying—"

"What?" I frown. "You're acting all mysterious and I hate it."

My pulse rate ratchets up.

"Give me a second—"

"What? Why?—"

He drops to his knees.

"No." I step back, hit the door again. I angle my shoulders, and his forehead smooths. The breath rushes out of him.

"Summer Cora West, will you be mine?" He holds up his palm. The sunlight slants over his head and golden flames explode from the single perfect yellow sapphire set in the center of beaten gold.

I swallow, lift my gaze to his face, "Why?"

His eyebrows lower. "Why?"

I flatten my lips. "Why should I marry you... a second time?"

He glares up at me.

"You really want to do this now?"

"Now." I tip up my chin. "Convince me, Sinclair Sterling, what's in it for me?"

55

Sin

This woman. Every time I expect her to act in a certain fashion, she throws me for a bouncer. I'd proposed to her and thought... What? That she'd fall into my arms, with declarations of love and forever? That she'd be floored, perhaps be so swayed that she'd collapse and I'd catch her? Then ease her into my arms and kiss her senseless? Then we'd... live happily ever after? She is going to make me work for it, huh?

My thigh muscles twinge. I ignore it. *Man up, bastard. Tell her what you really feel.* It's now or never.

"What? No words?" she peers down at me. "Apparently, I've finally rendered you speechless, eh?" She pushes a finger against her cheek. "Should I be congratulating myself on that?"

I glare up at her. One side of her lips curves.

"The alphahole who'll sit across a table and negotiate until he gets his own way on everything, struck dumb." She swipes her hair from her face, "And all because I asked you to navigate a delicate matter of the heart?"

My shoulders bunch; my pulse begins to race. Sweat slides down my spine.

She glances at the ring in my palm, then at my face. Her lips turn down. "Guess that's it, huh?"

She turns to leave.

"Flowers."

She pauses.

"I know you love the violets among the wildflowers because they remind you of my eyes."

She stiffens, reaches for the door handle.

"You're allergic to gluten, yet you sneak your favorite brand of cake from Gregg's because it's not available anywhere else, then you swallow down half a bottle of Benadryl to compensate for the allergic reaction."

She flinches.

"A habit you have to stop, by the way."

She pushes down on the handle and the door whispers open.

"You hate stuck up snobs who have way too much money they don't know what to do with, yet you forgave the worst of them, because you realized he was broken enough to have to overcompensate for his insecurities."

Her shoulders shake.

"You love waking up at dawn sometimes and walking on the grass barefoot, while you lift up your head and sniff the delicate breeze that wafts down from the East."

Her entire body tenses.

"You hate the color pink."

She swings around.

"Who told you?"

"It's why you colored your hair and bought clothes in that color, because it was a way of training yourself to realize that you don't get what you want, so you have to embrace your flaws, and look beyond the surface to what really matters."

"What matters?" Her throat moves as she swallows.

"You."

My phone buzzes.

I glance at the device placed face down on the table; so does she.

I walk toward it, pick it up, then glance at her.

Her breath catches.

Holding her gaze, I pitch it toward the wastebasket. The buzzing cuts out.

She blinks. "Don't you need to check who that was?"

"You come first."

Her gaze widens.

"It could have been a potential merger or acquisition deal worth millions."

"Screw that," I growl.

She grabs a strand of her hair and tugs, "Wow, you sure can be intense, huh?"

"Better get used to it Bird." I chuckle. "You are all that matters to me. Your smiles. Your laughs. Your sighs. Your little moans when you come, the soft mumbles when you talk in your sleep, the little crease..." I touch my lower lip, "That drives me crazy. The deep lines..." I rub the center of my forehead, "That form when you are arguing with yourself. The heated fires in your eyes when you are angry. Your scent which deepens when you are aroused." I lick my lips, "The way you chew on the strands of your hair—"

She releases the tendril, purses her lips.

"It's gross, but hell, I love every single quirk about you. Especially this sexy, professional look with the fuck me pumps."

She giggles. "These are 1-inch wedges."

"It kind of went with the entire speech."

I smirk and she firms her lips.

"Especially that."

"What?"

I jerk my chin up. "The way you challenge me. You never give an inch, always push my buttons, and when you grab my dick and squeeze it..."

She reddens.

"...Hell, you are the only woman who has had me by the balls and all I could think of was, she can take the fucking lead in bed if that is what she wants."

"Anytime?" Her gaze widens.

"Sometimes." I growl.

"Next time?" She bites on her lower lip, and my dick twitches.

"On one condition."

"Oh, no, no, no." She backs away, arms raised. "You're not making this into a deal."

"You started it, Babe, better deal with the repercussions now."

"So?" She draws in a breath.

"So." I draw my shoulders back. "Summer, you're my fucking other half, so get your arse here, so I can put this damn ring on your finger, then bend you over my desk and spank you until you are on the verge of climax; then bury myself balls deep inside of you and claim you again and again and again until you want to come, and then I won't let you, not until I've fucked every damn orifice in that sexy little body, so you have no more thoughts filling that over-stimulated brain, and you've run out of anything to say, and then, if you are good, and perhaps if I feel like it... I might..." My groin hardens. "Let you come at the same time as me."

Her mouth opens and shuts.

I angle my head, "Is what I think I might have said."

"Huh?"

"When actually... No... In reality, what I want to say... I mean..." I draw in a breath. *Fuck, get a grip on your emotions man.*

"You... You okay, Sin?"

Nope.

I've never been better, never as good as now, when everything is so clear to me. I square my shoulders, "What I actually want to say is that I loved you when I hated you. I loved you when I didn't want anything to do with you. When I thought I wanted revenge for something that wasn't your fault, and now when I know I love you... I can't stop thinking about you... The truth is, I am crazy about you Summer. I can't live without you. Not for one second more. So, what do you say, Bird, will you be mine?"

Her eyes shine. Her chin wobbles.

Fuck. I went too far. That will teach me to try and restrain myself. All it did, was bottle up my goddam true emotions and then it all surged forward... into the worst, terrible, unintentional, proposal. I am done. So done.

I swallow. My heart hammers; my pulse pounds. Adrenaline laces my blood. If she turns me down... I'll... I'll... fucking let her go, that's what. Then I'll haunt her for the rest of her life, while I jerk off every night to the images of her gorgeous face.

Her lips tremble, her chin quivers, then tears stream down her face.

"Fuck, Summer. Don't cry."

"Cry?" she sniffles. "You think I'm upset?"

"Aren't you?"

"Nope." She swallows, "That... that was the most romantic thing anyone has ever said to me. You didn't hold back. For the first time, you said what was on your mind without thinking, with real feeling. You were there, present, for every single second of that proposal." She wipes her face. "The first part wa-a-s a little convoluted, and very obscene, by the way."

"Why you little tease." I growl

"I forgive you for it."

I blink, "You do?"

"Yep." She nods. "I know how it is, sometimes your mind is racing forward and then the words pour out. It's called, obeying your instinct."

"Eh?"

"It's okay, Sin." She pats my cheek, "I'll take it, both your proposals, and also..." She holds out her fingers.

I chuckle, slide the ring onto her left ring finger.

She glances at it and fresh tears pour down her cheeks. My heart stutters; something hot stabs my gut. "Bloody hell, Bird, don't cry. I can't deal with your tears."

"Sorry." She sniffles. "It's just... It's so..."

"Gorgeous?"

"It's—"

"Stupendous?" I smirk. "You love it, I know."

"Sinclair Sterling, shut up and kiss me already."

"With pleasure." I spring up, wrap my fingers around her nape, tug her to me and lower my lips to hers.

She moans, that little throaty whine, and my cock thickens.

I kiss her deeply, nibble on her lower lip until her mouth opens, then thrust my tongue inside her honeyed mouth and draw on her essence. She twists her fingers on my lapel, pulls herself closer, until she's folded into me, her breasts crushed against my chest. The blood rushes to my groin. Fuck. I need her. Want her. Now. I slide my other arm around her waist, down to her—

Paws patter on the wooden floor, the door pushes open the rest of the way and Max rushes, in barking wildly.

She lurches closer, and I steady her.

"What the—" I glance down to find Max, clawing at my wife's skirt. She drops down and scoops him up. He licks her cheek and she giggles.

I frown. So now I am jealous of a dog? I lean in close and whisper, "Be home before me and undressed, on the bed, legs wide apart, pussy showing, with your fingers in your—"

"Shh!" She presses her lips to mine. Soft, Sweet. My heart fucking melts. "I'll be there." She murmurs.

"Promise?"

"What do you think?"

I laugh.

Saint appears at the entrance to the conference room. "The fuck happened to you?"

56

Summer

My husband plants his body in front of me, blocking me from Saint's line of sight.

"What the — ?" I shove at Sin's immovable bulk.

He wraps his arm around my waist, holding me in place.

"Sinclair."

He twists his neck and shoots me a glare.

I glower back. "What are you doing?"

"I am possessive."

"You don't say?" I tip up my chin.

"I can't change this part of me."

"I don't want you to change that part of you." I dig my fingers into his biceps. His muscles flex and the power thrums through the material of his shirt and jacket. His gaze drops to the ring on my finger.

"I really do love the ring."

"I'm glad." His lips kick up at the sides, "I'm sorry I couldn't get you another bouquet of wildflowers."

I stiffen, peer up at him, "So it was *you* who gathered the flowers for me at our wedding?"

"Ah." He shuffles his feet.

I blink. Sinclair Sterling, with an uncomfortable look on his features. Wow.

"I didn't mean for it to come out that way." He squeezes the bridge of his nose.

"Are you apologizing?" I widen my gaze, "Why do I find that hard to believe?"

"When it comes to you, Bird, I've learned never to underestimate your responses." The skin around his eyes creases, "Or mine toward you, for that matter."

"Oh."

"Oh!" He chuckles. "Love it when I drive you speechless, you know that."

"I love you... Full stop."

There's a gagging sound from the direction of the doorway.

"Shut up Saint." My husband says without turning around. "So, where were we, hmm?" He straightens, pulls me forward and into his side.

I melt into him, twine my arms about his lean waist, rub my cheek against that hard chest.

"Like I said." Saint retreats into the office and drops into an armchair. "You look different, Sinner."

"The fuck I care about your opinion?"

"It's not the fresh-faced look, which takes years off, by the way."

I glower at him.

"It's that disgustingly self-satisfied glow all you hitched-up couples in love have where you can't wait to shackle all of your friends into the same institution."

"Do you find me saying or doing anything to that effect?"

Saint raises his eyes skyward, "Thank fuck for that."

His phone pings, and he pulls it out of his pocket, glances at the screen. "The fuck?"

Sin's shoulders bunch. "What is it?"

"Probably a crank message, except..."

"Except?"

"He or she knows their poetry."

Sin stiffens. He walks forward, his arm around my shoulders. I lengthen my steps, to keep pace with him. We halt by his desk, and he pulls me against his chest. "Let me see that."

"Don't get your knickers in a twist, Sinclair, probably an irate woman I fucked."

"Read it out." Sin's voice is hard.

Saint's shoulders stiffen, then he glances at the screen.

"*I had a dream, which was not all a dream.*
The bright sun was extinguish'd, and the stars.
Did wander darkling in the eternal space..."

"Byron." Sinclair and Saint say in the same instant.

"Speaking of." Sinclair stiffens. He lets go of me long enough to grab his phone from the wastepaper basket. He straightens, pulls me back into the 'V' between his legs, then checks his phone.

He stiffens.

"What?"

He shows me his phone.

"*The crowd was famish'd by degrees; but two*
Of an enormous city did survive,
And they were enemies..."

I read out.

"The fuck?" Sin growls from somewhere above me.

Saint's shoulders bunch, "Byron again."

There's a buzzing sound from my bag.

"Sin." I nudge him, "I need to get my phone."

"Fine." He lets go of me so I can grab my bag and pull it toward me.

He pulls me close, keeps an arm around my waist as I fish out my phone.

There's a missed call from Karma and a voicemail. I listen to it, then frown.

"Everything okay, Babe?"

"Yes... No... I don't know. It's a message from Karma, saying she's going to Sicily. Her friend had an extra ticket so she's going with him."

"Him?" His hold stiffens on my hip.

"That's what she said. She shouldn't be traveling in her condition."

"She's stable, right?" He begins to draw circles over the curve of my waist.

I shiver.

"She's fine for now, but she needs to protect against over-exposure, excitement."

I dial her number and it goes to voicemail. "Shit! She isn't answering her phone." My heart begins to race. "She didn't mention anything yesterday or this morning, when I left her house."

Saint glances at Sin, then stands up and stretches, "A few days in the sun, with a man..." He curls his lip, all casual like. "Maybe that's what she needs?"

"Don't treat me like I don't know what's happening." I turn to glower at Saint then at my husband. "You guys are worried, admit it. First my father mentions Byron, the Mafia boss guy, then you two get messages quoting Lord Byron and now..." I frown at my phone. "Karma suddenly takes off for Sicily?" I shake my head. "Something's not right."

There's a knock on the door.

Max springs up from his rug, races to the door and scrapes at it.

Another knock, then Meredith pops her head through, "There's a woman here to see you."

"I'm not expecting anyone." Sin frowns. "Besides" he wraps a strand of my hair around his thick finger, he rests his chin on my head, "we were leaving."

"Not you, him." Meredith angles her head at Saint.

"Oh! And congratulations Mr. and Mrs. Sterling." She beams at me.

I flush. Wow. Mrs. Sterling. It sounds... sounds so right. My heart flutters. "Thanks, Meredith."

"Always a pleasure, my dear." Her entire face lights up.

"Thanks, M," Saint straightens, "send her in."

Meredith nods and retreats.

Sin growls, "Make yourself right at home."

Saint lifts a middle finger at him, then turns to the door. It swings open.

Victoria stands there. Not a hair out of place. Perfect make up. Except, her lipstick is smeared. She glances at me, "Hope I am not intruding." She twists her fingers together.

"You are already here." Saint looks her up from head to toe. "May as well come all the way in."

Her dress falls to below her knees, and there's a tear at the hem.

I stiffen, "Victoria, are you okay?"

Max sniffs at her ankles, whines. She bends, pets him. He licks her fingers, then runs to his rug, settles there with his chew toy.

"Victoria?"

She looks up at me, "Everything will be fine now." Her tone is composed. She turns to Saint. "I've been looking for you."

Saint smirks, "About time."

She takes a step forward, then stumbles.

"Hey." Saint closes the distance between them.

Her legs seem to wobble and she crumples, but he's already there. He grips her shoulders, straightens her, "You okay?"

"Help me."

To find out what happens next get Saint and Victoria's story HERE
For Karma and Michael Byron's story click HERE
Want Jace and Sienna's story? Click HERE
Read an excerpt from Karma and Michael Byron's story...

Karma

"Morn came and went—and came, and brought no day..."
Tears prick the back of my eyes. Goddamn Byron. Crept up on me when I am at my
weakest. Not that I am a poetry addict, by any measure, but words are my jam.

The one consolation I have, that when everything else in the world is wrong, I can
turn to them, and they'll be there, friendly steady, waiting with open arms. And this
particular poem had laced my blood, crawled into my gut when I'd first read it. Darkness
had folded into me like an insidious snake that raises its head when I least expect it. Like
now. I'd managed to give my bodyguard the slip and veered off my usual running route to
reach *Waterlow Park*.

I look out on the still sleeping city of London, from the grassy slope of the expanse.
Somewhere out there the Mafia was hunting me, apparently.

I purse my lips, close my eyes. Silence. The rustle of the wind between the leaves, the
faint tinkle of the water from the nearby spring.

I could be the last person on this planet, alone, unsung, bound for the grave.

Ugh! Stop. Right there. I drag the back of my hand across my nose. Try it again, focus,
get the words out, one after the other, like the steps of my sorry life.

"Morn came and went—and came, and brought no day..." My voice breaks. "Bloody,
asinine, hell." I dig my fingers into the grass and grab a handful and fling it out. Again.
From the top. I open my eyes, focus on a spot in the distance.

"Morn came and went—and came, and...."

"...brought no day."

I whip my head around. His profile fills my line of sight. Dark hair combed back by a
ruthless hand that booked no measure.

My throat dries.

Hooked nose, thin upper lip, a fleshy lower lip, that hints at hidden desires. Heat.
Lust. The sensuous scrape of that whiskered jaw over my innermost places. Across my
inner thigh, reaching toward that core of me that throbs, clenches, melts to feel the stab of
his tongue, the thrust of his hardness as he impales me, takes me, makes me his.

"Of this their desolation; and all hearts
Were chill'd into a selfish prayer for light.."
Sweat beads my palm; the hairs on my nape rise. "Who are you?"

He stares ahead, his lips moving,
"Forests were set on fire—but hour by hour
They fell and faded—and the crackling trunks
Extinguish'd with a crash—and all was black."
I swallow, squeeze my thighs together. Moisture gathers in my core. How can I be
wet by the mere cadence of this stranger's voice?

I spring up to my feet.

"Sit down."

His voice is unhurried, lazy even, his spine erect. The cut of his black jacket stretches across the width of his massive shoulders. His hair... I was mistaken. There are strands of dark gold woven between the darkness that pours down to brush the nape of his neck. My fingers tingle. My scalp itches.

I take in a breath and my lungs burn.

This man, he's sucked all the oxygen in this open space, as if he owns it, the master of all he surveys. The master of me. My death. My life. A shiver ladders its way up my spine. *Get away, get away now, while you still can.*

I take a step back.

"I won't ask again."

Ask. Command. Force me to do as he wants. He'll have me on my back, bent over, on the side, over him, under him, he'll surround me, overwhelm me, pin me down with the force of his personality. His charisma, his larger-than-life essence that will crush everything else out of me and I... I'll love it.

"No."

"Yes."

A fact. A statement of intent, spoken aloud. So true. So real. Too real. Too much. Too fast. All of my nightmares... my dreams come to life. Everything I've wanted is here in front of me. I'll die a thousand deaths before he'll be done with me... and then, will I be reborn? For him. For me. For myself. I live first and foremost to be the woman I am... am meant to be.

"You want to run?"

No.

No.

I nod my head

He turns his head and all of the breath leaves my lungs. Blue eyes, cerulean, dark like the morning skies, deep like the nighttime, hidden corners, secrets that I don't dare uncover. He'll destroy me, have my heart, and break it so casually.

My throat burns. A boiling sensation squeezes my chest.

"Go then, my beauty, fly. You have until I count to five. If I catch you, you are mine."

"If you don't?"

"Then I'll come after you, stalk your every living moment, possess your nightmares, and steal you away in the dead of midnight, and then..."

I draw in a shuddering breath; liquid heat drips from between my legs. "Then?" I whisper.

"Then, I'll ensure you'll never belong to anyone else, you'll never see the light of day again, for your every breath, your every waking second, your thoughts, your actions... and all of your words, every single last one, will belong to me." He peels back his lips, and his teeth glint in the first rays of the morning light. "Only me." He straightens to his feet, and rises, and rises.

He is massive. A beast. A monster who always gets his way. My guts churn. My toes curl. Something prial inside me insists I hold my own. I cannot give in to him. Cannot let him win whatever this is. I need to stake my ground in some form. *Say something. Anything. Show him you're not afraid of him.*

"Why?" I tilt my head back, all the way back. "Why are you doing this?"

He tilts his head, his ears almost canine in the way they are silhouetted against his profile.

"Is it because you can? Is it a... a..." I blink, "a debt of some kind?"

He stills.

"My father. This is about how he betrayed the Mafia, right? You're one of them?"

All expression is wiped clean of his face, and I know then I am right. My past... Why does it always catch up with me? *You can run, but you can never hide.*

"Tick-tock, Beauty." He angles his body and his shoulders shut out the sight of the sun, the dawn skies, the horizon, the city in the distance, the whisper of the grass, the trees, the rustle of the leaves... All of it fades, and leaves me and him. Us. *Run.*

"Five." He jerks his chin. Straightens the cuffs of his sleeves.

My knees wobble.

"Four."

My heart hammers in my chest. I should go. Leave. But my feet are welded to this earth. This piece of land where we first met. What am I, but a speck in the larger scheme of things? To be hurt. To be forgotten. To be brought to the edge of climax and taken without an ounce of retribution. To be punished... by him.

"Three." He thrusts out his chest, widens his stance, every muscle in his body relaxed. "Two."

I swallow. The pulse beats at my temples. My blood thrums.

"One."

Michael

"Go."

She pivots and races down the slope. The fabric of her dress streams behind her, scarlet in the blue morning. Her scent, lushly feminine with silver moonflowers, clings to my nose, then recedes. I reach forward, thrust out my chin, sniff the air, but there's only the green scent of dawn. She stumbles and I jump forward. Pause when she straightens. *Wait. Wait. Give her a lead. Let her think she has almost escaped, that she's gotten the better of me... As if.* I clench my fists at my sides, force myself to relax. *Wait. Wait.* She reaches the bottom of the incline, turns. I surge forward. One foot in front of the other, my heels dig into the grassy surface as mud flies up, clinging to the edges of my £4000 Italian pants. Like I care? Plenty more where that came from. An entire walk-in closet full of tailor-made clothes, to suit every occasion, with every possible accessory needed by a man in my position to impress... everything, except the one thing that I have coveted from the first time I had laid eyes on her. Sitting there on the grassy slope, unshed tears in her eyes, and reciting... Byron? For hell's sake. Of all the poet's in the world, she had to choose the Lord of Darkness.

I huff. All a ploy. Clearly, she'd known I was sitting near her... No, not possible. I had walked toward her and she hadn't stirred, hadn't been aware. Yeah, I am that good. I've been known to slice a man from ear to ear while he was awake and fully aware. Alive one second, dead the next. That's how it is in my world. You want it, you take it. And I... I want her.

I increase my pace, eat up the distance between myself and the girl... that's all she is. A slip of a thing, a slim blur of motion. Beauty in hiding. A diamond in the rough, waiting for me to get my hands on her, polish her, show her what it means to be... dead. She is dead. That's why I am here.

Her skirts flash behind her, exposing a creamy length of thigh. My groin hardens; my legs wobble. I lurch over a bump in the ground. The hell? I right myself, leap forward, inching closer, closer. She reaches a curve in the path, disappears out of sight. My heart hammers in my chest. I will not lose her, will not. *Here, Beauty, come to Daddy.* The wind whistles past my ears. I pump my legs, lengthen my strides, turn the corner. There's no one there, huh?

My heart hammers, the blood pounds at my wrists and my temples, and adrenaline thrums through my veins. I slow down, come to a stop. Scan the clearing.

The hairs on my forearms prickle. She's here. Not far. Where? *Where is she?* I prowl across to the edge of the clearing, under the tree with its spreading branches. *When I get my hands on you, Beauty, I'll spread your legs like the pages of a poem. Dip into your honeyed sweetness, like a quill into an inkwell, drag my aching shaft across that melting weeping entrance.* My balls throb. My groin tightens. The crack of a branch above shivers across my stretched nerve endings. Instinctively, I swoop forward, hold out my arms. A blur of red, dark blonde hair, skirt swept up in a gust of breeze. She drops into my arms and I close my grasp around the trembling, squirming mass of precious humanity. I cradle her close to my chest, heart beating thud-thud-thud, overwhelming any other thought.

Mine. All mine. The hell is wrong with me? She wriggles her little body, and her curves slide across my forearms. My shoulders bunch, my fingers tingle. She kicks out with her legs and arches her back. Her breasts thrust up, the nipples outlined against the fabric of her jogging vest. *She'd dared come out dressed like that…? In that scrap of fabric that barely covered her luscious flesh?*

"Let me go." She whips her head toward me, her hair flowing around her shoulders, across her face. She blows it out of the way. "You monster, get away from me."

Anger drums at the backs of my eyes; desire tugs at my groin. The scent of her is sheer torture, something that I had dreamed of in the wee hours of twilight when dusk turned into night. She's not real. Not the woman I think she is. She is my downfall. My sweet poison. The bitter medicine I must imbibe to cure the ills that plague my company.

"Fine." I lower my arms and she tumbles to the floor, hits the ground butt first.

"How dare you?" She huffs out a breath, her hair messily arranged across her face.

I shove my hands into the pockets of my fitted pants, knees slightly bent, legs apart. Tip my chin down and watch her as she sprawls at my feet.

"You… dropped me?" She makes a sound deep in her throat.

So damn adorable.

"Your wish is my command." I quirk my lips.

"You don't mean it."

"You're right." I lean my weight forward on the balls of my feet and she flinches.

"What… what do you want?"

"You."

She pales. "You want to… rob me? I have nothing of value. I'm not carrying anything… except." She reaches for her pocket.

"Don't." I growl.

"It's only my phone."

"So you say, hmm?"

"You can…" She swallows, "you can trust me."

I chuckle.

"I mean, it's not like I can deck you with a phone or anything, right?"

I glare at her and she swallows. "Fine… you… you take it."

Interesting.

"Hands behind your neck."

She hesitates.

"Now."

She instantly folds her arms at the elbows, cradles the back of her head with her palms.

I lean down and every muscle in her body tenses. Good. She's wary. She should be. She should have been alert enough to have run as soon as she sensed my presence. But she hadn't. And I'd delayed what was meant to happen long enough.

I pull the gun from my pocket, hold it to her temple. "Goodbye Beauty."

TO FIND OUT WHAT HAPPENS NEXT READ KARMA AND MICHAEL BYRON'S STORY HERE

CLAIM YOUR FREE CONTEMPORARY ROMANCE BOOK. CLICK HERE
CLAIM YOUR FREE PARANORMAL ROMANCE BOOK HERE
MORE BOOKS BY L. STEELE
MORE BOOKS BY LAXMI

ABOUT THE AUTHOR

Hello 👋 I'm L. Steele. I love to take down alphaholes. I write romance stories with douche canoes who meet their match in sassy, curvy, spitfire women :) I also write dark sexy paranormal romance as NY Times bestseller Laxmi Hariharan.

Married to a man who cooks as well as he talks :) I live in London.
Claim your FREE book
Follow me on AMAZON
Follow me on BookBub
Follow on Goodreads
Follow my Pinterest boards
Follow me on FB
Follow me on Instagram
Join my secret Facebook Reader Group; I am dying to meet YOU!
Read my Books HERE

From Laxmi (L. Steele)

I LOVED writing this book. The movie quotes and the trivia... OMG, this is how my husband and I converse... I hadn't meant to use it, but the banter between Summer and Karma....appeared... and Sinclair of course demanded to make it his own; it took off and became a character of its own in the book. Don't you agree? Message me in my Reader Group and let me know!

The one quote I absolutely love and couldn't find an excuse to use... I wanted to leave you with it...

"...Stay here with me. We'll start a jazz band."
—*Lost in Translation*, Director: Sofia Coppola

FREE BOOK

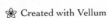 Created with Vellum